The
Mariah Delany
Lending Library
Disaster

SHEILA GREENWALD

Houghton Mifflin Company Boston

Library of Congress Cataloging-in-Publication Data

Greenwald, Sheila.
The Mariah Delany Lending Library disaster / Sheila Greenwald.
p. cm.
Summary: An eleven-year-old girl sets up her own
lending library in competition with the New York Public Library
and finds herself involved in more than she bargained for.
PAP ISBN 0-618-04929-0
[1. Libraries — Fiction. 2. Humorous stories.] I. Title.
PZ7.G852Mar   2000
[Fic] — dc21
99-054318

Manufactured in the United States of America
HAD 10 9 8 7 6 5 4 3 2 1

To my sister Lila

1

Mariah Delany," her mother said solemnly, "if you would only apply yourself to your school work and your books the way you do to all your enterprises and money-making schemes, you would be at the very top of your class."

Mariah stuck out her lower lip and cut a jelly doughnut in half. This was not the first or even the fiftieth time she had heard her mother offer this particular observation, and the doughnut was far more interesting to contemplate. They were sitting at the kitchen table only six months after the collapse of the Magic Mariah Method for the Harmonica. It was early November. The first report card had just come in and was being held at this moment in Mrs. Delany's hand. The messages from her teachers written on this card all seemed to agree that Mariah Delany "could do better," that Mariah Delany "did not apply herself," that she "somehow resisted books and whatever they had to say." Mrs. Delany and Mariah were going over the comments on this report with a fine-toothed comb. Even sweetening the sour words with sugary doughnuts was not much help.

"I guess you'll make a bigger effort now?" Mrs. Delany asked hopefully. "And try to apply yourself a little more, dear. Let up on all your enterprises and become a student for a change; that's what you should be doing at this time in your life.

After all, you're eleven years old, and not in need of supporting yourself."

Mariah pushed the shaggy no-colored hair behind her oversized ears. With her distant green eyes she observed her mother. She liked her mother, even though Mrs. Delany was hopeless about plans of any kind. A forgetful dreamy lady who wrote long boring articles on writers Mariah had never heard of, Mrs. Delany also taught English at a school on Long Island and seemed cut off from the world by the thickest pair of glasses anybody ever saw. Mariah knew that if anyone was more hopeless at plans and schemes than her mother, it was her father. He could hardly get through a toll booth without putting in too much money. He was a book publisher and he wrote articles that were about as boring as Mrs. Delany's, only they had to do with history. The Delanys' apartment was so crammed with books that you practically had to be a contortionist to walk around them. Mariah had learned not only to walk around them but to avoid them in every way. Right now she could tell her mother was warming up for a BOOK LECTURE. Mariah bit into the half doughnut so that the jelly spilled out all around her tongue, and confectioners' sugar powdered her upper lip and even tickled the inside of her nose. Her mother began to talk. Mariah began to not listen.

Mariah Delany at the age of eleven had a well-established reputation for being enterprising. Enterprising Mariah had introduced a sideline of comics at her lemonade stand the summer she turned ten, causing the three other stands on her street to fold. When two lemonade stands reopened, offering a sideline of comics, Mariah switched to used and broken toys plus a selection of Kool-Aid flavors. Then she took over the other stands as subsidiary branches.

When she was ten and a half, Mariah learned to play "Turkey in the Straw" on the harmonica. The day after she learned this she posted a sign in her school. The sign said that she would offer harmonica lessons on a group or individual basis and that she guaranteed the student would play "Turkey in the Straw" after the first half-hour lesson. Mariah's friend Lea Coopersmith stood in front of the sign playing "Turkey in the Straw" and assuring everyone that she had learned from the Magic Mariah Method for the Harmonica. Twenty-five people signed up for lessons, including the math teacher. Since fifteen of her students had no harmonicas, Mariah consulted a local musical instrument shop and learned that she could get a discount if she ordered fifteen harmonicas. Mariah collected the full price from her students, bought the harmonicas at a discount, and kept the difference.

Her very first student was a small boy

named Clark Bunce. He could not master "Turkey in the Straw" in the half-hour lesson and wanted his money back. Mariah was determined to teach him and make good on her guarantee. She worked with him for two and one-half hours. Finally, even determined, enterprising Mariah had had it. She threw the harmonica at Clark Bunce and hollered, "You idiot! You don't know how to make music; you only make noise." Then she slammed out of his house. As she walked home the thought came to her that she just might have twenty-five Clark Bunces on her hands. She decided very quickly to get out of the harmonica business.

But all these projects were small potatoes, or, as Mariah would say, "peanuts," compared to one that she could not even have imagined on that spring evening walking home from Clark Bunce's.

"Mariah dear, if you'd just get into the

habit of reading, I know you'd love it," Mrs. Delany was saying. The jelly doughnut was nearly gone. Mariah had successfully not listened to her mother for several minutes. "Every day pick up a book for just half an hour. Give it a chance. There are such wonderful things to read."

"Not in our house," Mariah said. "I don't like our books."

Mrs. Delany bit her lip trying to hold back vexation. "All right," she said, suddenly determined. "Finish your doughnut, put on your coat, and come with me."

"Where? "

"To the Public Library, my dear Mariah, where there has *got* to be something you will want to read."

Mariah frowned. There went the afternoon's plans. She had a date with her friend Levine to set up a plant store in the building's outer lobby. Levine's mother, a plant freak, would not mind their taking cuttings and clippings of this and that. Mariah figured that, by sticking them in paper cups, with very little investment they could rake in a possible five dollars. "I have a date."

"Break it," Mrs. Delany said. "You have entirely too many dates, too many schemes, and too many enterprises for an eleven-year-old with terrible grades."

Mariah called Levine on the house phone and told her that if she went ahead on the plant store idea without her, Mariah would never include her in another plan. Then she pulled on her jacket and marched off with her mother to the local branch of the New York Public Library.

2

The library was closed. A white cardboard sign hanging in the glass door announced that, due to cutbacks in the city budget, the library would not open at all on Thursday and would only be open half-days for the rest of the week.

"Why, this is outrageous," Mrs. Delany gasped. She squinted at the sign and registered true anguish. As she often told Mariah, she had spent her entire childhood in the library. It had been her sanctuary,

her refuge, her very favorite place. She went to it every day after school and read and read. Mariah thought that her mother must have been the most out-of-it little nitwit anybody ever knew. She would have probably been embarrassed to know her.

"I guess we'd better go home," Mariah said.

Mrs. Delany tore herself away from the

11

sign, but on the long walk home she didn't stop talking for a minute. "Do you realize what this means, Mariah? To be locked out of the library like this? What this means for all the children who *love* books and reading? Why, it's a terrible, terrible thing."

Mariah was thinking, "What luck." She could still call Levine and start clipping spider-plant shoots. But when they entered the lobby of their building, Mariah found that Levine had set up the plant business with a little jerk named Mona from the sixth floor, whose mother had contributed four African violets. Mariah was furious. "I warned you," she said.

"I couldn't help it," Levine insisted.

Mariah stormed upstairs, where she was left to roam around the book-crammed apartment. "No TV today," her mother had said.

Mrs. Delany sat at her desk, busily at work. Mariah prowled.

"Haven't you anything to do?" her mother said, slamming her pen down. "A book to read, homework, something?"

Books, books, books, books. Books had ruined the day.

"Okay," Mariah tripped on a stack of un-shelved volumes. She flopped on the sofa and picked up one of the tumbled books and looked around her at the piles and piles and shelves and shelves of them. She was surrounded. And then it hit her. The best idea she had ever had in her life. Immediately, Levine's plants withered in her mind. Plants were for anybody.

This new idea had everything. It filled a crying need, if her mother was right. It involved practically no investment. She had the market and she had the goods.

Mrs. Delany looked up. "Why, Mariah! You look positively radiant. Did you finally find a good book?"

"I found many good books," Mariah beamed. "And I *love* them all."

"How nice," Mrs. Delany said. Her eyes glowed like mellow candle flames behind the thick circles of tinted glass.

3

That night Mariah was in the first full fever of her enterprising plan-making. She would go to the library the very next day to check on a few things, observe the librarian in action, and take notes on what she saw. She wanted to be sure to do things right and not make an amateurish, sloppy hash out of such a potentially good scheme. She also had to decide whether to take in partners or to work alone. Levine was out; an untrustworthy type. However, on the second floor of her building there was a boy named Something-or-other Pollack, Joe maybe, who looked reliable. Coopersmith was a possibility though she didn't live in the building, and a building associate could come in handy for this enterprise. Finally, Mariah decided to settle the personnel problems later. At dinner she was so preoccupied, she could hardly eat. Aside from her parents, Mariah's family included her brother, Irwin, who was in high school. Irwin, a regular book-reading Delany, was their parents' pride and joy. Mariah had already concluded that when she grew up she would probably have to support Irwin. Every time he went out on the street Irwin either got lost or lost his money. No one even had to rip Irwin off; he managed to get separated from his money all by himself. However, he had the sort of grades that cause envy. He was at the top of every class and his scores had wings. He was Super Student, equally good at every subject, a

16

fact that seemed unbelievable to Mariah. The Delanys thought Irwin was just about perfect. They had no idea, however, what to make of Mariah, and sometimes seemed a little scared of her.

"And so what did my girl do today?" Mariah's father asked as the stew was being ladled out.

"We went to the library, me and Mom."

Henry Delany practically ignited, he glowed so. "The library! Why Mariah, how fine."

"It was closed, Henry," Mrs. Delany said in tragic tones. "Closed. I know we read about these awful budget cuts in the newspaper, but when you stand there in front of the closed door, it all becomes horribly real. Locked — a building full of wonderful books that should be available to children and adults, that *were* available to me and to you every day. Every day I ran to the library, my favorite place in all the world. The library was where I learned about books and the miracles of stories, fairy tales, and, later, novels. The library was where the seeds of all my work were planted. When I think of how children today are to be denied what I had, I cannot believe it."

"Terrible, terrible." Mr. Delany nodded. "Whom can we write to or call?"

"The mayor, the governor, the city councilmen," Mrs. Delany intoned.

"Jerks," Mariah thought. Didn't they know that all those letters went into a big trash can or got answered by a computer? She had sent just such a letter off last year to the mayor. It had to do with an idea she had for garbage collection. When she got a reply, she made sure to rub the mayor's signature with a wet finger. The ink didn't budge. A form letter from beginning to end. She pushed a piece of bread around her dish to sop up gravy.

"Mariah's first reports came today." Mrs. Delany switched the subject alarmingly.

"Mmm." Mr. Delany looked up. "How's it going?"

"The same."

Mr. Delany sighed. "Of course, we all know that when the day comes when Mariah decides to invest the kind of time and energy she uses up in her enterprises on her school work, she'll be an A-plus student."

"I don't want to be an A-plus student," Mariah said.

This remark drew Irwin's head out of his dish. "You don't?"

"No, I don't."

Irwin ducked back into his stew, and shook his head in disgust.

After the stew, Mariah could not wait to get into her room so that she could start some specific planning. She always loved this first phase of any brainstorm.

"Don't you want any dessert dear?" Mrs. Delany called as Mariah bolted from the table.

"Unh-unh. I have loads of work to do."

"Oh, Mariah, that's wonderful," and then, more softly, to her husband, "You know Henry, I really think something happened this afternoon that changed Mariah's entire point of view about books and learning. I saw her suddenly looking at our own collection, as if seeing it for the very first time. She was on fire. It was beautiful to see. She actually said she loved books. You know how she has never had any interest in them whatsoever. "Perhaps . . ." Mrs. Delany put her chin on her palm and stared thoughtfully into her coffee cup. "Perhaps it was that trip to the library, finding it closed and realizing what a gift books are and how not everyone is lucky enough to have them . . . perhaps that did it."

"Mmmmmm, maybe," Mr. Delany lit up his pipe.

Mariah closed her door and restrained herself from guffawing. "Okay," she said out loud. "First thing, I've got to set it up." She began to write on the back of her notebook. "I need pockets in each book for the cards, then I need cards." She chewed on her lower lip as she wrote, thinking of more and more things that were needed. Soon her list filled a page and a half . . . glue, Scotch tape, shoebox for card catalogue . . . masking tape, rubber stamp with date and ink pad, and, of course, that trip to the library to see exactly how they operated.

At ten-thirty Mrs. Delany poked her head into the room. "Still working, Mariah? Oh my."

"I had a lot to do," Mariah sat at her desk in her pajamas, bent over her notebook. "By the way, Mom, tomorrow I'll be a little late coming home. I'm going to the library direct from school."

Mrs. Delany nearly fell over. "You are? Oh, Mariah, how nice. How terrifically nice."

"It sure is," Mariah said.

"Good night." Mrs. Delany blew a kiss, and giggled to herself. "This is just unbelievable."

"Good night," Mariah said. When the door had closed she thought to herself, "Yes, unbelievable for now anyway." The Mariah Delany Lending Library was still but a dream in the mind of its creator.

4

The next day was Friday. Mariah bounded
out of bed and got dressed for school. The
school she attended was medium-sized and
eight blocks to the south of their building,
facing Central Park. This school had appeared to be very informal and casual, but
Mariah had soon learned not to trust ap-
pearances. In fact, it seemed to Mariah
that her teachers constantly demanded
perfect work, and if they didn't get it, they
never stopped breathing down your neck.

Mariah's neck had been breathed down, till it felt like a wind tunnel, by more teachers than she cared to remember. Surprisingly, this did not prevent Mariah from liking school. Many of her enterprises could never have gotten off the ground without school. She had run a juice concession in the fourth grade, but had been forced to close it down for sanitary reasons. In third grade she had set up a frame service for the art work of first- and second-graders. Using school masking tape (no investment), she got three cents a frame. Also she had sold old gum cards, mittens, and stickers through school connections. Mariah had enlisted many good associates at school. Aside from Coopersmith, there were Suzy Bellamy and Emma Pinkwater. As she brushed her teeth, Mariah was considering which, if any, of these should be included in her fantastic new enterprise.

"Good morning, Mariah dear," Mrs. Delany sang as Mariah flopped onto a kitchen chair. "How sweet you look this morning."

Mariah wondered if her mother could see her at all through those jam jars over her eyes.

"I know you're going to school this morning well prepared. Isn't it a nice feeling, dear?"

"Uh-huh."

"When you get used to that nice feeling of doing your work and being prepared, you'll never want to go back to the other way, Mariah."

"Uh-huh."

"I just have a feeling your reports will be very different from now on."

"Yup." Mariah bit into a bagel and chewed and chewed. It wasn't that she didn't love her mother. She loved her very much. However, she felt the same way about her as she felt about Irwin; both could hardly cross the street by themselves. Mariah knew that though Gertrude Delany had wonderful book knowledge and very high standards, neither she nor her husband had any business sense at all. Mariah had realized this several years before when she had taken the trouble to train several caterpillars she'd found in the country to answer to their names. She had carefully brought these caterpillars back to the city to sell as trained caterpillars. When the Delanys got wind of what she was doing, they made her return the money she had received, and lectured her on ethics. They told her that she knew full well that those caterpillars didn't know their names, and that what she was doing was dishonest. Mariah didn't argue with them on this issue, but she quietly continued to believe that if people wanted to think there was such a thing as a trained caterpiller and were willing to pay for it, they should be entitled to do so without any meddlesome bookworm Delany interfering.

So she chewed her bagel and "uh-huhed"

and "yupped" until her happy, misguided mother kissed her off to school with an extra tug on the muffler.

In school Mariah decided to tell Pinkwater, Coopersmith, and Bellamy that something big was in the works, but could not be talked about just yet. This news got the three girls very worked up.

"Why don't you tell?" Pinkwater wanted to know at lunch. "I mean, what's the secret for?" Emma Pinkwater was tremendously tall. She was already bigger than anyone in sixth grade — boy, girl, or teacher — and she was still growing. In spite of her size she was timid and given to awful spates of slouching, mumbling, and tearfulness.

"I always told you all *my* plans right away, Mariah," she mumbled sulkily.

"Yeah, and they weren't worth much."

"Pinkwater's right," Suzy Bellamy said. "I bet you don't have any plans."

"Teasing won't work," said Mariah.

"You'll just have to wait and see." She gathered up her paper bag, sandwich wrappings, and empty container and left the table with a confident lift of her chin. She kept the secret all day, and by leaving school immediately upon dismissal, managed to avoid walking with any of her friends, or being followed by them.

She did exactly what her mother had done as a girl. She ran to the library as soon as school was out. The seven blocks were traversed in fewer minutes, and Mariah appeared at the children's reading room in a breathless, excited state.

"My word," the librarian behind the desk remarked, "you were certainly in a rush to get here."

"Yes indeed," Mariah agreed. "Now, how do I get a card?"

The librarian seemed delighted by Mariah's interest and intensity; she looked as if she would die if she didn't get a card.

"First of all, catch your breath, and then

28

step this way." They walked to the other
end of the long desk. The librarian had a
nice face, with wide-set gray eyes and a
pleasant smiling mouth. "Have you ever
had a card?"

"Yes, but I lost it."

"Okay, then, fill out this card and I'll
give you a temporary one till the new card
comes in the mail. That way, you'll be able
to take out books today."

Mariah filled in the card.

"Very good," said the librarian, reading

over the card. "Now you just have a nice time looking around, Mariah, and if you need any help finding something, don't hesitate to ask."

Mariah walked a few paces from the desk, pulled out a low stool, sat down on it, and positioned herself so that she could observe how books were returned and withdrawn. She certainly didn't need the machine the library used to photograph the borrower's card and the book's card. A simple rubber stamp with the date on it would suit her library just as well. After she had satisfied herself on this point she strolled slowly up and down the aisles, occasionally jotting down a note to herself in her notebook. Then she opened a few books and inspected them thoroughly: the envelopes inside, the cards, the covers, the stamps. Then she examined paperbacks, magazines, picture books, and the card catalogue. When she had done all this and was satisfied, she wrapped the muffler around her neck, put on her mittens, and prepared to leave.

"Oh, Mariah," the librarian called after her just as she was going out the door, "didn't you find a single book you wanted?"

"Not really," Mariah said.

"Well, my goodness, you were so eager, I thought you'd walk out with half the collection. What were you looking for?"

"I was, uh, just looking to see how you operate."

"How we operate?" The librarian was amazed. "What do you mean? Do you want to be a librarian?"

"Sort of," said Mariah.

"My name is Lizzy Phipps and if I can be of any assistance, let me know." Lizzy Phipps put out her hand for shaking and looked very amused.

"Sure thing," Mariah said, wishing to be gone. She had masses of work to do. As she ran down the steps of the library she thought, "Watch out Lizzy Phipps; here comes the competition."

When Mariah got to the apartment, nobody was home. Mrs. Delany had a full day of teaching on Friday and then stayed late to meet with students. Mariah rejoiced in the empty apartment. First she poured out a large glass of milk, and while drinking it, rummaged around the breadbox, hoping to turn up a leftover cupcake or a box of cookies. Finding nothing in that category, she consoled herself with three slices of toast drenched with butter and sprinkled with cinnamon. Having finished this snack, she cleaned up carefully and washed her hands. One thing Mariah had noticed at the library was that it was a clean and orderly and tidy establishment.

She unpacked the fresh new file cards she had just purchased at the stationery store, and set them on her desk. Then she did a bit of searching in her mother's desk drawers for such items as paper clips, rubber bands, Scotch tape, pencils, and ink pads. She was quickly stocked to meet all her needs. When this was done and Mariah could look with satisfaction and pleasure at her supplies, she went into the living room, where the largest collection of the Delanys' books was kept.

Books, books, books, and books. They were crammed into every inch of space on every shelf. Bookshelves lined every bit of wall space. Books were heaped on the desk and table tops; piles of them rose from the floor, in the corners, and near the bottoms of the shelves, under the piano and on the radiator. Books and books. Mariah rubbed her very clean hands together and grinned.

She referred to the notes she had taken in the library. Categories: Biography, Fiction, Geography, Fairy Tales, Picture Books. She would begin with Biography, as that seemed the easiest to gather since

"Biography" was usually in the title of the book: *The Biography of Helen Keller* or *The Biography of Beethoven*. Using a small stepladder for the higher shelves, Mariah put together a decent Biography section in forty minutes. She carried the books into her room and stacked them on the floor. Then she returned to the living room to fill in the gaps on the shelves with books from the piles on the floor. She happily observed that no spaces could be detected.

After Biography, Mariah assembled her Fiction collection. This was a little more difficult because she didn't know which of all the novels she found would be suitable. She picked out books by authors she had heard of or knew about from school. She chose a set of Dickens because it was so beautifully bound in a rich leather. She also chose Tarkington, Poe, Conan Doyle, and Alcott. Fairy Tales came next and were easier. Like "Biography" the titles helped. For Geography she used some atlases.

By five o'clock she had her initial collection stacked on the floor under her bed. By six, when Irwin came in the door, Mariah had pasted the envelope pockets into half the books and had written, in black Magic Marker, PROPERTY OF THE MARIAH DELANY LENDING LIBRARY across the endpapers and title pages. By seven, when her parents came home, Mariah was beginning on the file card system (two cards for each book in the collection).

"Hello," Gertrude Delany called from the foyer. "We're hoooome."

Mariah came out of her room and closed the door quickly behind her.

"Where did you go this afternoon, Mariah?" Mrs. Delany asked a trifle too casually.

"I told you yesterday," Mariah replied. "To the library."

"Oh, Henry." Mrs. Delany beamed as if all her prayers had been answered. "You see she did, she did. At last our Mariah has found books."

"That's for sure," Mariah said.

5

Over the weekend Mariah stashed the collection in her closet and under the bed, which was unnecessary since Mrs. Delany never quite cleaned up her own room much less anybody else's. She rarely ventured into Irwin's and Mariah's rooms, assuming that Teresa, the weekly cleaning lady, did. Teresa really didn't do much more than tidy the kitchen, polish the silver, and change the linen.

At any rate, everything was going according to plan. Mariah had finished both

the cards and the card catalogue by Sunday
night. She really loved her card catalogue.
She loved the way she could flip the file
cards in the shoebox and look up books by
author and title. She had blank spaces for
the date of withdrawal and return. She
only needed to get a stamp with the date on
it and several nice new pencils and a flower
to put into a vase on her desk. (She had
noticed the nice flowers on Lizzy Phipps's
desk.) She would place this vase next to the

shoebox with the file cards and a cup full of pencils, and then she would be in business. The only other thing that remained to be done was the clearing out of her book-shelves and the arranging of the collection upon them, complete with labels marking the categories. She would do these things Monday afternoon. However, she had a great deal to do on Monday.

In art class Monday morning, Mariah made her first poster.

THE MARIAH DELANY LENDING LIBRARY

LOCKED OUT AT THE PUBLIC LIBRARY?

BUDGET CUTS GETTING YOU DOWN?

CAN'T FIND YOUR FAVORITE BOOK

WHEN YOU WANT IT?

DON'T DESPAIR

THE MARIAH DELANY LENDING LIBRARY

IS HERE FOR YOUR READING PLEASURE

OPEN WEEKDAY AFTERNOONS

FROM THREE-THIRTY TO FIVE

HOT COCOA SERVED FREE

ON OPENING DAY

Beneath this Mariah wrote her address and drew a small map of the surrounding blocks, marking the route to take from school. She hung up the poster on the bulletin board while Pinkwater and Bellamy looked on.

"So that's it," Pinkwater said. "For crying out loud. Why didn't you tell us?"

"Had my reasons," Mariah said. "If it's a success I'll need some help — more posters and an assistant, maybe."

Pinkwater shrugged, but Bellamy was definitely interested. "Is it a real library, Mariah?"

"Come have a look."

Mariah didn't know whether it was the cocoa or the books, but it seemed everyone came to "have a look." Opening day at the Mariah Delany Lending Library was a complete success. No enterprise of hers had ever gotten off to a stronger start. It surpassed her greatest expectations.

The entire sixth grade of her school arrived, with the exception of Coopersmith, who much to her disgust had an orthodontist appointment.

Teresa was the only one at home (aside from Mariah) when the crowds began to arrive.

"What's going on?" Teresa looked up from the stacks of cutlery she was polishing, as Mariah filled paper cups (left over from the lemonade business) with cocoa.

"Just some kids from school," Mariah said.

"Some kids from school? It looks like the whole entire place to me. You're some popular young lady." Teresa shook her head in wonder.

Mariah's room was packed. Kids on the floor, kids on her bed, kids on the windowsill, two in the closet, and four more in the bathroom. Mariah brought in the cocoa by the trayful. There were empty cups all over. "Does everybody understand how this works?" she asked loudly. "The books are free only if you return them within the two-week period. That's two weeks on the nose. If you go one day over two weeks, it starts costing you. It costs to the tune of two cents per day each day over the two weeks. Now two cents a day is cheaper than the Public Library of New York, and furthermore, I am open *every* weekday afternoon and am unaffected by budget cuts. I give personal attention and feature a homelike atmosphere." These last words reminded Mariah that she had better check the time. Very soon, she figured, Irwin would return to the "homelike atmosphere," not to mention her parents, who well might wonder what was up and ask a lot of questions.

"You've got five minutes to make your selections because the library will be closing."

It was amazing. Everybody chose at least one book. The collection was depleted by more than half. Mariah sat at her desk

with the shoebox in front of her and a vase
with a daisy in it just to the side. She wrote
out file cards and stamped the date on
them and made up duplicates and stamped
and filed and smiled at her customers. Soon
they were all milling around in the foyer,
putting on their jackets, preparing to
leave. Almost everyone had gone by the

time Mrs. Delany opened the front door and blinked at the last six borrowers, who were about to depart.

"Oh my. Well, hello. I'm Mrs. Delany. Mariah, is this a gathering of some sort?"

"Yes," Mariah said.

"How nice." Mrs. Delany looked a bit concerned. "A social gathering, Mariah? Not some new venture, I trust."

"We have a sort of book club," Mariah whispered.

"That's lovely." Mrs. Delany could hardly believe the good news. "How truly fine."

"So long, Mariah." Bellamy waved. "Are you sure you don't need an assistant yet?"

"A what?" Mrs. Delany asked and whipped out of the coat closet. The word "assistant" had alarmed her.

"Uh, no. Not necessary." Mariah shoved Bellamy out the door, along with the other stragglers.

"Mariah dear." Mrs. Delany waited till

the door was closed behind the last visitor. A worried wrinkle was on her brow. "I really hope you aren't in some sort of enterprise again. I mean, I hope you aren't, you know . . ."

"Wheeling and dealing," Mariah provided.

"Yes, wheeling and dealing. You do know how we feel about that and how we want to see all that wonderful energy channeled into . . . other things."

"That's just what I'm doing, Ma," Mariah said, knowing that "other things" was another way of saying "books." Then she grinned from oversized ear to oversized ear. "Honest."

"Oh, good." Mrs. Delany, smiling and reassured, went to restock her desk, which had so suddenly and mysteriously run out of paper clips, tape, and rubber bands.

6

As the days of the opening week passed, the amazing success of the Mariah Delany Lending Library not only continued but grew. Mariah had to replenish her collection from the living room, hall, study, bedroom, and even the kitchen (she started a Cookbook section). She began to worry that her parents would begin to notice what were now a few real gaping spaces on the shelves. She filled them in as best she could from the stacks on the floor. Once in a while she wondered if what she was doing was dishonest, since she did it in a secretive way, as far as her parents were concerned. However, she decided she was not dishonest because she was not taking anything, merely borrowing. She was simply utilizing a natural resource in the Delany apartment. She had also decided that when the money started to come in, she would give her parents a percentage, perhaps in the form of a gift. At the moment of presenting this gift she would very carefully tell them what she had been doing. In the meantime, even without cocoa, the library was a would-be gold mine. Every day borrowers came, not only from the sixth grade, but from the fifth and seventh and eighth. In order to satisfy the older group, Mariah dipped into her parents collection of sexy books and even made that a category: Sexy Books. In this, she included novels as well as works of anatomy, with a key to the good pages. She took Pinkwater on as an assistant because Pinkwater was a terrific reader and very good at finding specific chapters in books for interested borrowers. Bellamy helped out with the growing card system, and poor little Levine came up one day nearly crying to be let in on it, bearing half the profits from the plant business as a peace offering. Mariah told her she would think it over. Mariah was a very cool operator.

"Mariah," Mrs. Delany said at supper on the Thursday evening of the first brilliantly successful week. "Every day when I come home, there are six or seven children just leaving, and they are all so businesslike. I mean, it doesn't strike me as if you've been having a date or meeting or anything. It's as if . . ." She paused, looking upset. "It's as if you were back in business. What I mean to say, Mariah dear, is, I hope that you are truly trying at school as you said you would, and are not all distracted again. I have a conference next week with

Mrs. Demot, your teacher, but I have always said that I knew as much as I needed to know by observing closely on the home front."

At moments like this, Mariah had to respect her mother for what struck her as weird psychic powers. Mrs. Delany, for all her near-blindness and bookishness, had these flashes of intuition, which set Mariah back several paces and made her sweat. She felt somewhat guilty and had a strong impulse to sit down on her mother's lap and tell her everything. Having a success wasn't much fun if you couldn't share it. But she stopped herself from spilling the beans. This was not the right time, and to tell her parents at the wrong time would get her into nothing but trouble. It could also run the risk of closing down the most ingenious enterprise she'd ever dreamed up. A risk she could not take; not now. So she sucked in her cheeks and bit her tongue and sweated as Mr. Delany gave her a sharp look and exchanged a heavy glance with his wife.

"Mariah," he said slowly, "what's cooking?"

"Nothing." She felt a new pulse in her forehead and wondered if it would show. "Nothing."

"Are you suddenly wildly popular? Why are these groups of kids around every day?"

"It's a club."

"What sort of club?"

"Book."

The magic word. "Ahhhhh."

Both Delanys shelved their misgivings at the sound of that magic word. Dessert was served. Mr. Delany tasted his pudding.

"Gertrude, the pudding is strange."

"I had to put it together from memory, dear. That's why it's a little different."

"Really?"

"I went to look up my recipe in *Best Desserts of the World* and I couldn't find the book. I looked all over for it. It's one of my favorites, and I know I didn't lend it to anyone. I never even let it out of the kitchen."

"Odd."

"Odd isn't the word for it. Though odd would describe this pudding." Mrs. Delany pushed her own dessert away, uneaten. "I can't believe anyone would have pinched that book. This is the kind of thing that makes you believe in goblins."

Henry Delany gave up eating the pudding.

Mrs. Delany went on: "This is one of those things that can drive you right up the wall. My mind keeps dwelling on it. Where, oh where, is my book?"

Mariah had an image of her mother climbing the wall. She decided that cookbooks would have to be one-week deals. She would recall *Best Desserts of the World* immediately. The pudding was terrible. There were a few liabilities to this library business, but she'd straighten them out.

After dinner she had a million things to do: check lists of borrowed books, replenish stock, and so on.

She heard her mother in the kitchen. "Henry, my *Gourmet Tips* is gone. I *must* be going nuts if I misplaced that. This is terrible. I know I had it on the counter."

Mariah closed her door and chewed on a fingernail. She had not thought of the possibility of what was happening now. She figured she had to screw up her courage and tell them, even if she jeopardized everything. She cast a farewell look at her beloved shoebox full of cards, and opened the door.

"Henry, the *Puff Pastry Made Easy Cookbook* is gone, too. If I find out who's responsible for this, I'll . . . I'll murder him."

Mariah closed the door and fell on her bed. She could see now that success was sometimes a lonely and complicated thing.

7

By the end of the second week Mariah was less nervous. Soon the first batch of borrowed books would be coming in, and if not, the money profits would begin to flow. This promise of money cheered her up. How she loved the sound of change jingling in her pockets. How happy it made her to hear it there and to know that when she walked into a shop she could price things and really consider buying them. Her parents, when they had observed this delight she took in having money, were alarmed.

"Whom did she get it from, Gertrude?" her father had once asked. "We, who care so little for material things, who value the mind and the intellect, have produced a child who cares only for the purse, for money, and the things it can buy."

"She's a materialist; let's face it." Mrs. Delany had sighed dramatically. "Let's hope it's a phase and she'll outgrow it."

But Mariah did not think she was a materialist. She didn't compete with other girls over clothes and possessions. She just enjoyed the game of figuring out ways of making money. She enjoyed knowing that she could make money and have it if she liked. She considered herself to be a business person. When she was in the middle of an enterprise she experienced a pleasure and excitement that she got from nothing else. Once her grandfather had told her how he had gone to work at the age of twelve to support his widowed mother and four brothers. He had sold hankies on the street and then saved to rent a store. He told her the story so that she would know about his hard childhood. But Mariah had envied him. How she would love to go out and make the family's money. Then her parents would be grateful and would appreciate her enterprising talents. They would not complain about her. When she had told her grandfather how she felt, he had looked astonished and said, "Why, Mariah, you are a businesswoman." Which was exactly what she wanted to be.

The third week of the Lending Library began without a single book's being returned, including *Best Desserts of the World* and *Gourmet Tips*, which Mrs. Delany seemed to talk about and hunt for several times a day. At first Mariah was delighted because each day a book was overdue meant money. But as the days went by the collection dwindled. No books came in and more books were borrowed. Mariah became apprehensive. Finally she posted an announcement in school, saying that there could be no more borrowing by those who had not returned books.

That did it. No one came to borrow and no one came to return. The Mariah Delany Lending Library was dead as a doornail. Over one hundred and fifty books were gone and not a penny had come in. Mariah was frantic.

"Pinkwater." She cornered her tall friend in school. "Why don't you return your books?"

"Oh gosh, Mariah, I keep forgetting."

"Every day you forget costs you."

"I don't know how to tell you this, Mariah. I feel just terrible, but I don't know what happened to them. Last night I looked and looked. I think they're just lost."

"JUST LOST? What's that supposed to mean?" Mariah yelped.

"Well some person, I won't mention any name, was seen *gift* wrapping one of your precious books."

"Gift wrapping? You mean to give away?"

"Draw your own conclusions, but I think it's a lot worse than their just being lost."

Mariah's heart thudded and sank.

Later, in the lunch room, Pinkwater pretended not to see Mariah and sat down at a distant corner table.

On the lunch line, Mariah grabbed Bellamy. "You'd better return my books," she said.

"But I'm right in the middle."

"Then you have to pay."

"But I don't get an allowance. I can't pay."

"Then return the books right away, and you'll owe me."

"But Mariah, I'm your friend."

Mariah didn't answer her, and Bellamy joined Pinkwater at the corner table.

In the middle of the third week Henry Delany called from the living room to his wife, who was preparing dinner in the kitchen. "Gertrude, my Dickens collection is *gone*. I can't believe it. It was right here. It's always been right here. I just went to look up something in *Great Expectations* and it's gone. They're all gone."

"Along with my *Best Desserts*, and *Gourmet Tips* and *Puff Pastry*."

"This is incredible. I couldn't have misplaced the entire set, Gertrude. Those books are very valuable. They're a special limited edition, worth a small fortune."

"We really should be better organized about our books," Mrs. Delany said. "Perhaps this is a lesson to us. We must arrange them better and make lists of what we've got."

"But I was certain about the Dickens. It was right here." Henry Delany scratched his scalp and looked miserable.

Mariah's stomach turned right over.

This was the first time an enterprise of hers had resulted in such horrendous problems. How did a lending library get its books back? Obviously she did not have the proper technique and obviously she was involved up to the eyeballs. In fact, as she sat on the edge of her bed contemplating her library problems, as well as all the homework she had let slide due to business affairs, her entire throat began to lock off and something like tears could be felt to rise up, though she managed to hold them back. Mariah was no crier. However, she was fast getting into a really bad mess and she needed help. Whom could she turn to? Her mother? Murder had been mentioned. Her father would surely share her mother's point of view after he heard what had become of his priceless set of Dickens. Irwin wouldn't understand. Her grandfather was in Florida.

At dinner everything got worse. "That set of Dickens was probably worth more than anything we own, Gertrude. Though not actually a first edition it's damn close. You know, I wonder if it was stolen."

Mrs. Delany looked at her husband sympathetically. "I just can't imagine how that would have happened, dear. There's been no evidence of anyone's breaking in. My jewelry and the silver are untouched. Would anybody have gone to the trouble to sneak into our apartment and filch a set of Dickens?"

"You thought your cookbooks had been stolen," Henry Delany reminded her.

"So I did," Mrs. Delany admitted. "At the time I couldn't think of any other way they could have left my kitchen. They're so much a part of my life, those books. I reach for them without even thinking, to find out how many eggs or what to set the oven for. Not finding them in their proper place is like not finding a trusted part of myself."

"I know what you mean exactly." Henry Delany looked truly mournful. "A part of

oneself. You don't realize how important these things have become, and what they mean to you until you've lost them." He looked over at Mariah and smiled. "We've called Mariah a materialist, and here we are, hopelessly, helplessly attached to our books. Why, if I knew who took my Dickens, I'd wring his neck."

Mrs. Delany reached over and patted her husband's hand soothingly. Then she noticed Mariah's dish. "Mariah, aren't you hungry? You haven't touched your food."

"I don't feel good."

"Why don't you go and lie down? Perhaps it's all the work you've been doing lately." Mrs. Delany's tone was so sweet and understanding that Mariah could hardly stand it.

She went into her room and curled up on her bed. Inside herself she felt a great black space gathering. "Oooooo," Mariah whimpered. "I need help, somebody." Then she thought of Lizzy Phipps and began to feel a little better. Better enough, at least, to fall asleep.

8

Lizzy Phipps remembered Mariah. "There you are, the one who couldn't find a single book. How have you been?"

"Terrible." Mariah leaned over the desk. She had barely made it through the day. No one had returned a single book. Dave Peterson told her he had lost *Great Expectations*, but would gladly give her a paperback copy of it as a replacement.

"A paperback?" Mariah had gasped. She could just imagine what her father would think if he found a paperback in place of his beloved almost-first edition. "You're out of your mind," she said. "The copy you lost was very, very valuable."

"Aw, come off it," Dave said. "It was one of those fancy-looking jobs you can pick up at any secondhand place for a few bucks."

"That's not true," Mariah said. "It was the real thing."

"Who says?"

"My father."

"Your father doesn't know in his entire head what my mother knows in her pinkie about books."

Mariah was so exasperated she was temporarily speechless. Finally she told Dave that her father "lived, breathed, and practically ate" books. "He's a publisher of them, you idiot."

"And my mother . . ." Dave smiled like somebody with a handful of aces. ". . . is a dealer in old, rare, and valuable books."

"You showed her that book?" asked

Mariah. A dark suspicion had begun to grow in back of her mind. She watched Dave carefully.

His cheeks colored. "Uh, not really showed her. She saw it last week, before I lost it, and she said it was one of those cheap flashy jobs, imitation leather and gilt. So, anyway Mariah, I'll replace it with this neat Penguin version, which is probably worth more."

Mariah had run to the library all the way from school. She had hardly eaten since lunch the day before. That afternoon somewhere in the school her mother was having a parent-teacher conference with Mrs. Demot. The jig was definitely up.

Lizzie Phipps stopped smiling. She seemed to recognize that there was something truly awful going on in the depths of the soul of Mariah Delany. "What is it?" she said.

"What do you do in a library," Mariah

blurted, "if nobody brings back the books?"
To her surprise and mortification, the mere
act of unburdening herself to another person was going to make her start to cry. But
she could not stop talking. "If they borrow
and borrow and take all the books (gulp)
and say they'll bring them back and then
they aren't even my . . . the library's books
and it turns out that they're practically
priceless (gasp) and nobody brings them
back or even pays you and somebody saw
somebody *gift wrap* one of them and what
do you do?" Mariah was crying hard. She
let Lizzy Phipps escort her to a chair in the
(thank heavens) empty reading room and
she let her bring a glass of water and she
let her hold a Kleenex to her eyes.

"Mariah, have you gone and opened your
own library?"

Mariah nodded. "Lending library," she
corrected, and then in a feeble small voice
added, "the Mariah Delany Lending Library."

"And so you loaned lots of books?"

Mariah nodded again.

"And not one has been returned?"

More nodding.

"They are well past due and they aren't strictly speaking your books?"

Nod, nod, nod.

"Mariah, you have a problem. "

Mariah buried her face in her two hands.

"But we will figure something out. Did you keep records?"

"Yes."

"You know exactly who took what book?"

Nod.

"I won't ask where you got the books, Mariah, but I suggest that you toughen your collection techniques."

"I asked and asked. People won't even eat lunch with me anymore."

"I'm afraid that's the price you pay. It will get even worse, but you'll find out who your friends are."

"I found out. I don't have any friends."
Mariah began to sob again.

"Of course you do. Only it's a little embarrassing for them now. They'll shape up. You'll have to go to work on it. You can start by writing a firm letter explaining the whole thing."

"I'm not a good letter-writer," Mariah said.

"I'll help you with it, then. Come." She took Mariah to her desk, where she picked up paper and pencils. Then she settled her at one of the round library tables. There were books spread out on the table. One of them was *Great Expectations*. The sight of it made Mariah shudder. One of the priceless Dickens. She wondered what was so priceless about it and opened the book. She began to read. It seemed pretty good. Good enough for her to want to turn the page.

"You can read later," Mrs. Phipps said. "Now it's time to write tough letters." She

sat down beside Mariah and pushed the
pencil and paper in front of her. "Write
down what I say." Lizzy Phipps cleared her
throat and looked into space. "According to
our records your borrowed book has not
been returned to this library and is overdue. Will you kindly return the above as
soon as possible so that we do not need to
turn this problem over to our collecting
agent."

Mariah was writing furiously. "Who,"

she asked, looking up, "is our collecting agent?"

"We'll get to that when the time comes and let's hope that it won't come. Make copies of this letter and give them by hand to every person who has an overdue book. Then see what happens."

"Okay." Mariah folded up the letter and put it in her knapsack.

"Now go home and start writing."

Mariah got up wearily. She felt empty and weak and sick at heart. She looked down at the table. "Oh, can I take this with me?" She picked up the copy of *Great Expectations*.

On the walk home, she realized that she would never write the letters. The whole idea seemed pointless to her. People had come to her house and had taken books with an agreement to return them. They had broken that agreement and now she was going to write a letter? Ridiculous.

Baloney. Mariah's despair began to turn to rage, and as soon as that happened she got hungry. She stopped in and had a pizza, and as she ate she got madder. The madder she got, the more stupid the letter idea seemed. She was too mad to write. What was that about a collecting agent anyway? What collecting agent? She washed down the last bit of pizza crust with a grape soda. She had gotten into this thing and she'd get out of it. Mariah grabbed her book bag and stuffed *Great Expectations* into it. She picked herself up and struck off to Pink-water's.

Mariah Delany, Collecting Agent.

9

Oh," Pinkwater said when she opened the door to Mariah. "Hi."

"Hi." Mariah gave a half-wave. "I came to get the books back."

"I don't know how to tell you this, Mariah, but I lost them someplace."

"I don't know how to tell you this, Emma Pinkwater, but we're going to find them." Mariah pushed past her into the foyer.

"Listen, Mariah, they're only a week past due, for heaven's sake."

"Well, that's one week too much."

Emma Pinkwater followed Mariah back
to the room she shared with her sister.
"What are you going to do?" she squeaked.

Mariah was pulling out drawers and
heaving things out of them at random.
"Find my books."

"I told you I don't know where . . . Oh,
Mariah, stop. My sister will kill me. Wait a
minute. I think I put them someplace in

my desk." Pinkwater was running all around the room in a frenzy, her long legs climbing over the beds and onto a chair and down. "Oh, puh-lease stop making such a mess."

Mariah had just toppled a huge stack of comics from Emma's desk. They slithered all across the bed and floor, and there at the very bottom of the stack were the two borrowed library books.

"Oh, look, Mariah. I had no idea they were at the bottom of that pile of stuff. What luck."

Mariah grabbed the books. "Maybe one day I'll be able to call you a friend again, Emma Pinkwater, but at this moment you are definitely off my list."

"Oh Mariah." Emma fluttered and folded. "What can I do?"

"Nothing." Mariah stormed out of the room. "You're an untrustworthy person."

"I didn't intend to be. I thought I'd lost them, Mariah."

As she opened the door Mariah had an idea. She paused and turned on her heel. Pinkwater was slouched miserably a few paces behind her. "If you mean it about doing something, Emma, I will perhaps consider taking you on as my collecting agent."

"What's a collecting agent?" Emma looked suspicious.

"You'll go around doing what I just did, collecting the books for the Lending Library from other kids."

"Oh no," Emma wailed. "I couldn't."

"I'll think about it, but I make no promises," Mariah said, disregarding Emma's reaction. She opened the door and got out fast.

The walk home was invigorating. True, she had forgotten to collect a cent from Emma, but at least she'd gotten two books back, one of them a Dickens, and she had dreamed up a plan for Pinkwater to go to work for her. These things buoyed up her spirits right to the moment when she opened her own door.

As Mariah took off her jacket, Mrs. Delany approached from the living room. "Mariah, I had a conference with Mrs. Demot."

How could she have forgotten? She looked at her mother's face. BIG TROUBLE.

"Let's sit down, Mariah." Mrs. Delany had never sounded quite this somber. Her lectures were usually of the I'm-sure-you-understand-and-will-do-better variety. But now her long narrow face seemed pinched, and behind the glasses there was real distress in her eyes. "Mariah, Mrs. Demot says that your work has not improved one bit in the past two weeks. I felt such a fool. I started off telling her what a great change had taken place in you and how you are working in a steady and orderly way. She looked at me as if I were mad, Mariah. She said that if anything, your school work has fallen off and you seem preoccupied by some new project. She wasn't sure what."

Mariah rubbed her sweaty palms on her knees and stared at what seemed to her to be a gaping hole on the bookshelf where the Dickens collection had been.

"Oh, Mariah." Mrs. Delany raised hurt and unhappy eyes to her daughter's face. "Have you been deceiving us all along about your new-found love of books? Were you putting us on?"

"No," Mariah said. "It's true. I did have a new-found interest in books." When she said this she felt rotten. She vowed to herself that as soon as all the books were safely back on the shelves she would tell her parents everything, come what may. She just couldn't tell them now. They'd worry themselves sick that she'd never get the books back. She would spare them that worry and at the same time spare herself the horrendous job of telling them at this awful point.

"Can you please help me to understand what you have been doing, Mariah?" Mrs. Delany asked. "I want to know because I want to help. I can't help if I don't understand."

When confronted with questions like this, Mariah's usually active mind went completely numb. She chased frantically around her head for some suitable answer. "I just, uh. I can't seem . . . Well, I enjoy reading the books, but I get carried away and then I don't have time for my school work."

Mrs. Delany's face melted in a sympathetic smile.

Hooray. Mariah knew she had said the right thing.

"I understand so well what you are saying. I always had that very same problem. I'd read and forget everything. I could never put a book down once I started it. I would forget school work, dinner, everything. After lights were supposed to be out,

I'd turn on my flashlight and start reading." Mrs. Delany's face grew soft and pink
at the recollection. Mariah was touched by
the depth and intensity of her mother's
feelings. Mrs. Delany clasped and un-
clasped her hands and smiled and twin-
kled, remembering those precious nights of
reading. Her enthusiasm about books was
almost catching, as was the delight she
radiated when talking about them.
Mariah, who had just gone to the Public

Library for a bit of peace and comfort herself, did not see her mother as a "jerk," right now.

"Why, Mariah, if I'd known how you felt, I could have explained to Mrs. Demot."

"Yeah, but I should learn to manage my reading and my school work better," Mariah said virtuously.

"You're very mature to understand that, Mariah. Our talk has made me confident that you will begin to put all these things together from now on. You are a very special person."

Home free. Mariah sighed. Everything was okay, at least for the time being.

Mrs. Delany got up. "I'd best start dinner. I'll explain to Daddy about Mrs. Demot's report." She paused and looked back shyly at her daughter. "Mariah, I think we had such a good talk." She gave Mariah a small hug and went off happily to the kitchen.

Mariah had to restrain herself from running after her mother and telling her everything. She experienced a new low in feeling rotten. She improved her spirits a little when she returned Emma Pinkwater's books to the shelf and even more when she dialed Pinkwater's number to inform her that she had decided to appoint her the Official Collecting Agent for the Mariah Delany Lending Library. Emma, who was usually delighted to be appointed anything by Mariah, was not delighted.

"I don't want everybody to hate me," she muttered.

"You are the very first person I asked," Mariah said, trying to make the job sound like an honor. "I asked you because I trust you and I think you can do a good job. Anyway, did you hate me when I collected your books?"

"No," said Pinkwater.

"Okay, so what are you worried about?"

The conversation went on for a while, with Mariah exerting more and more pressure and Pinkwater finally agreeing, though not exactly thanking Mariah for the "honor."

By the time she hung up the phone, it was time to set the table and wash up for dinner. Henry Delany had come home. He was sitting in the living room, sipping sherry and reading something. He called to Mariah as she arranged plates and napkins in the dining room. "Mother told me about the good talk you two had, Mariah. You may end up as one of the Delany Bookworms after all." He chuckled delightedly at this thought.

Mariah had returned to the kitchen to fetch the plates when she heard her father call out, "Gertrude, for heaven's sake! One of the missing Dickens books is back on the shelf, exactly where it has always been. I'd swear it wasn't here yesterday."

"Maybe Teresa dusted it and put it down someplace and forgot and then put it back," Mrs. Delany called from the kitchen.

Mariah went to the kitchen door, from where she could see her father standing by the living room shelf holding the returned book lovingly in his hands. Suddenly, just as he opened the volume, she remembered with a sinking feeling that she had forgotten to remove the pocket and card.

There was a terribly long long moment when everything in the apartment seemed to stop, and then Henry Delany roared, "What the hell is the Mariah Delany Lending Library?"

Gertrude Delany looked up from the pot of rice she was fluffing with a fork. She blinked. Then her magnified soft brown eyes fell upon Mariah with immediate understanding.

"Oh Mariah." She sighed, a deep and disappointed sigh.

Harmonicas had been a fizzle. This Lending Library was a Disaster.

10

It was a very rough time Mariah had that night. In fact, once again she found she was too upset to eat her dinner. She really loved her parents and she felt that she had betrayed them. What made it worse was that they didn't say much about it. Henry Delany sat with an expression of real pain in his eyes. He asked Mariah if she had lent many books and if the rest of the Dickens collection was out.

Mariah told him it was, and then

brought in her card catalogue and the
shoebox so that her parents could see
exactly how many books were involved and
where they had gone. Even though they
were miserable, they were impressed by
her organization and enterprise. She did
not inform them that the books were all
overdue and that nobody had made a move
to return them. In fact, she went out of her
way to reassure them that soon all the
books would be back on the Delany shelves,
safe and sound. Her parents were not reassured. They looked sad and upset and,

worst of all, not angry. This lack of anger bothered Mariah more than anything. She wished they would yell and scream, even punish her, but they were too distressed to bother.

Mariah went to bed, but certainly not to sleep. She lay awake thinking for the first time about where being "enterprising" had gotten her. She even made a solemn vow. She promised that if she got back all the books she would really knuckle down and devote her time to her school work and not engage in enterprising ventures of any sort until her grades were up and everybody was pleased with her. This vow gave her some comfort and provided her troubled mind with enough peace so that she could go to sleep.

The next afternoon, walking home from school, Mariah saw Dave Peterson and his mother just half a block in front of her. She began to run, determined to nab him and

make a heavy pitch for her book in front of
his book-dealer mother.

"Dave," she called out. She knew he
heard her because he began to speed up as
if he were trying to get away, but his

mother nudged him and turned around.

"David dear, someone is calling you."

"Oh, hi." Dave shrugged. "Hi, Mariah, uh, we're going to get me a pair of shoes."

"I just wondered if my *Great Expectations* showed up."

"Why David!" Mrs. Peterson blinked. "Don't you introduce me to your friends?"

"Oh, meet Mariah Delany," Dave said unenthusiastically.

"We're in kind of a rush, Mariah dear," Mrs. Peterson said. "Saturday we are celebrating our anniversary with a big party and I did so want David to have a new pair of shoes. Today is the only day we can shop."

Dave seemed to be drowning in a sea of mortification.

"But I need to talk to Dave about my book."

"Your book?" Mrs. Peterson looked confused.

"The copy of *Great Expectations* you told him wasn't worth much."

"*I* told him wasn't worth much?" Mrs. Peterson had become a parrot. "My dear, I must confess I don't know what you're talking about but it's been nice meeting a classmate of David's." She was backing away almost as fast as her son.

"I have got to talk to you about my books," Mariah called to the two figures who were by this time running across the street.

For the three days after this incident Mariah tried to collect in earnest. She realized that Pinkwater was doing a terrible job. Nobody took her seriously. If there was to be any collecting, she would have to do it herself. But when she started to collect she found she was received with embarrassment, excuses, and delay. Sometimes there was even ill will. One thing there wasn't was a single returned book. Most of her schoolmates tried to avoid her. When she pinned them down, they fumbled in their book bags, grabbed at their foreheads, and said, "Oh Lord, I forgot, but I'll *definitely* remember tomorrow." Somebody named Jenny Popkin snidely referred to Mariah as "The Collecting Agent," and got a laugh out of a small group in the lunch room.

Mariah cornered Bellamy. "Who did you see gift wrapping one of my books?"

"I didn't see him myself."

"Who is it?"

"I really couldn't say." Bellamy looked at a faraway place over Mariah's shoulder.

Mariah's heart sank. This was the first time she had been avoided by her schoolmates. Even her gang — Pinkwater, Coopersmith, and Bellamy — looked the other way when they saw her coming. After school on Friday she decided it was time for a consultation with Lizzy Phipps.

She dug her hands deep into her pockets and hunched her chin down into her collar and passed a group of classmates on the corner. Some turned away and some stared back until she crossed the street.

"How's it going, Mariah?" Lizzy Phipps asked.

"Lousy," Mariah said. "My folks know. They're in shock. The kids at school won't return the books. They hate me."

"I wish I had the time to talk to you right now, Mariah," said Lizzy Phipps, "but as you can see I've got twenty zillion things to do." She was pushing a cart of unshelved books around the reading room, returning them to their proper places. She lurched to a halt and clapped a hand to her forehead. Idea! "Hey, Mariah, I just thought of something. You could help me out. These budget cuts are murder and I'm always short-handed. How about your joining the system for a while and giving me a hand in *my* library?"

"What do you mean?" Mariah was actually sick to death of the very word "library."

"I mean shelve these books for me. At this point, with your own experience you know all about categories and alphabetizing. Tell me when you're finished."

"Well, I . . ." Mariah was looking around for a way out, but Lizzy Phipps had more or less pushed the cart at her and run back to her desk.

Mariah shelved the books carefully, even taking pleasure in completing the job quickly. The work took her mind off her problems. Just as she replaced the last book, Lizzy Phipps ran up to her with one of the *Curious George* books in her hand. "Would you please read this story to that group of children, Mariah, before they wreck the place?"

Mariah settled herself on a low stool in the Picture Book section, with *Curious George* on her knee. A circle of small children formed around her. They listened to every word, and when she finished they pleaded for more. She read them *Madeline* next. She held up the book so that they could see the pictures. They crowded around her and leaned against her and put their hands on her shoulders. They were completely still when she read, still and listening. After the reading she told them that her voice was tired and it was time to read her own book to herself. She selected a

copy of *Great Expectations* and opened it to
the chapter where she had left off. Before
long, Mariah was as lost in her book as the
children had been in theirs. When she
looked up at the clock, she couldn't believe
how the time had flown. She had surely
found peace and pleasure in this quiet
place. After the hurly-burly of her life at
home and at school, it was nothing short of
miraculous.

"Library's closing," Mrs. Phipps called.
Mariah put on her jacket. Mrs. Phipps
came over to her. "Thanks for being such a

help, Mariah. You really saved my life today. I hope you'll come whenever you can and give me a hand. You're very good at it. Maybe tomorrow we can have a talk."

Walking home, Mariah realized that no talk would help. There were tough times ahead. She began to wonder about how she had gotten herself into such a lot of trouble. She had done it all by herself. She couldn't blame anybody; that was for sure. No one had pushed her into making a lending library. It was completely her own idea. It had seemed such a great idea, too. She could never in a million years have predicted that all these troubles would grow out of it. The fact that they had, shook Mariah to her toes. Her confidence was shot. She had gone too far and she hadn't known it till it was too late. The people she had taken for granted most, her parents, were miserable, and the people she thought she could trust, her classmates, were not dependable. She had miscalculated. It was very unlike Mariah to think and think about things she had done. Usually she just went ahead and did something new. But this Lending Library was different, or maybe she was changing. She couldn't think of doing something new. She was in too much trouble and she would have to keep facing up to it until it was over. Somehow the library had helped her. It was a good place to get in touch with your thoughts and get some distance from outside problems and pressures. But those problems still existed, and they had to be dealt with.

Irwin was the only Delany at home. He was working on his second bunch of bananas with his face only inches out of a large book in Latin.

"Hi," Mariah said.

"Pinkwater called; said to call her right back." He didn't look up for a minute.

On the telephone Pinkwater sounded teary. "Listen, Mariah, nobody pays any attention when I tell them to bring back their books. They laugh at me, and they're beginning to detest you. Some people say, 'If she wants them let her come and get them.'"

"Okay then, that's what I'll have to do."

"Good," Pinkwater said and sighed with relief.

"And I want you to come with me."

"Oh Mariah, I can't do that."

"You can and you will and we start at Dave Peterson's tomorrow morning."

"Oh, but Dave gift wrapped his . . . uh."

"So he's the one," Mariah said triumphantly. "Thank you very much."

"Oh dear," Emma wailed.

Mariah slammed down the telephone. Finks and traitors surrounded her. Her path was set, even though her course would be rough. She had gotten into this thing and somehow she'd get out of it. No matter what.

11

The next morning, which was Saturday, Mariah Delany, short, round, and pale, stood beside Emma Pinkwater, tall, skinny, and stooped, outside the door of Dave Peterson's apartment, number 14D. Mariah was ringing the bell. Her green eyes fixed on the penciled name card stuck to the door just below its peephole.

TAMARA PETERSON

DEALER IN RARE AND ANTIQUE BOOKS

Beneath this namecard was a large colorful poster decorated with flowers, curlicues, and balloons. It said, "Welcome to the Petersons' Glorious Fifteenth Anniversary Bash."

It took forever till Dave opened the door, and when he saw Mariah he began to close it, but she slipped herself into the foyer and Pinkwater followed. The foyer was festooned with crèpe paper, which was looped from wall to chandelier, creating a tent ceiling. A metal clothes rack was pushed to one side. Through the archway Mariah could see into the living room where party preparations were going on. Folding chairs

lay stacked on the floor, card tables leaned against the wall, and on a long wooden shelf was a pile of gaily wrapped gifts with anniversary cards opened for display behind them. Mrs. Peterson was going back and forth from the living room to the kitchen, just behind it, setting up a table for drinks.

"What do you want?" Dave scratched his ear and looked nervously into the living room.

"You know what I want and I'm not leaving till I get it."

"Then I guess you've come to live with us."

"What's that supposed to mean?"

"It means . . . Look, Mariah," Dave suddenly changed his mood from annoyance to humble distress. "I told you I'd replace the book with a brand-new paperback because the one I borrowed from you is lost."

"Where?"

"If I knew, it wouldn't be . . ."

"Okay, let me help you find it." She started past him but he hopped backward and blocked her way.

"It's not here and this isn't the way libraries work," he informed her. "If you lose a book from the Public Library, they let you replace it with another copy."

"My library doesn't work that way," Mariah said. "Anyway how do you know it's not here? You told me it was lost."

Dave looked into the living room nervously. "I lost it someplace else."

At that moment Mariah was certain that the book was on the gift-laden shelf in the living room, gift-wrapped and awaiting presentation to Mr. and Mrs. Peterson. She guessed it was Dave's dumb way of giving his folks an impressive anniversary present for practically nothing. She had to think up some way to examine the stack of gift-wrapped packages.

"David," Mrs. Peterson called from the living room. "We need you to come in and help."

"Okay." He stood uncomfortably on one foot, not wanting to leave the foyer.

"Go ahead," said Mariah. "We'll just wait for you right here."

"Uh, I'd rather you didn't," Dave said.

"David." Mrs. Peterson appeared in the archway. "Why hello, girls. I didn't realize you were here. I'd ask you in, but as you can see we're setting up for the big bash." She giggled. "Oh well, I suppose the girls could join you in the kitchen for a fast soda, David."

"No, Ma." Dave waved awkwardly. "It's not that kind of visit."

"Oh, uh-huh." Mrs. Peterson's mind was now on something else. "Then finish up and you can come help us open the chairs and tables."

"We'd be happy to help out," Mariah said. "Me and Pinkwater we'd love to help."

She forged after Mrs. Peterson, dragging Pinkwater behind her.

"Aren't you sweet."

"Aw, please don't," Dave followed, protesting weakly. But it was too late. Mariah had begun to unfold the rented chairs that were piled on the floor.

"Come on, Emma. Grab a chair."

In no time the entire bunch of chairs were unfolded and arranged around the sides of the long living room.

"You're very kind." Mrs. Peterson smiled. "I don't know what your business with David was, but you've certainly helped me out."

"My business with Dave," Mariah said, "is, he borrowed a book from my Lending Library and never returned it."

"Oh, I *am* sorry," said Mrs. Peterson.

"I told her I'd replace it," Dave said.

"Good boy," said his mother proudly.

"But that won't do," said Mariah. "The original is very valuable."

Dave had begun to walk them back to the foyer.

"Valuable?" Mrs. Peterson looked amused. "You know, dear, valuable books are my business and there aren't all that many of them. What did it look like, this valuable book?"

"It was covered in leather," said Mariah, her eyes sweeping the pile of gifts on the shelf in the living room. "Dark, rich-looking leather."

"Mmmm-hmm." Mrs. Peterson nodded.

Mariah knew as certainly as she had ever known anything in her life that the book was there on that heap in the living room, probably the sloppy-looking package with the dirty wool bow, a real Dave Peterson job if she ever saw one. The question was how to get her hands on it. "It had dark brown leather corners and the spine was brown too," Mariah went on describing and stalling for time, struggling for an inspiration. "Actually, Dave told me you had seen it and said it wasn't worth much."

"I said that?" Mrs. Peterson looked confused. "Well, so many things happen around here, I just don't remember. Now I must go back inside, I have so much to do. Good-by, dears, you've been sweet to help." She waved and returned to the kitchen.

What to do now? Mariah gripped her hands together behind her back. It seemed they would have to leave. Dave had opened the door for them. His mother had said good-by. Mariah couldn't think of a solitary reason to prolong the visit, when Pinkwater, starting her nervous, gawky trek across the foyer, and not noticing a chair stacked with boxes of crèpe paper, stumbled over it, sprawling on the floor between the overturned box and the upset chair.

Trust Pinkwater. The idea came to Mariah in a flash. "Emma," she cried. "It's happening to you."

"Huh?" Pinkwater started to get up, but Mariah pushed her back down.

"Stay there, you know your doctor told you not to move when it starts."

"What starts?" Dave whinnied.

"Her fits. She has fits. Oh Lord." Mariah appealed to the ceiling.

Pinkwater was struggling to get up, but Mariah sat on her chest.

"Hey, Mariah," Pinkwater howled. "Get off of me."

"See, she's losing control. She goes crazy, doesn't remember anything."

"What thing?" Pinkwater screamed.

"Fits, you lunatic," Mariah bellowed into her face. Oh, why couldn't she be working with Coopersmith? Coopersmith would have understood immediately.

"Fits?" Pinkwater asked.

"Get your mother in here, Dave. Please. She'll know what to do. Hurry. I can't restrain Pinkwater all day. She gets violent and is very strong."

Dave ran out of the foyer, through the living room and into the kitchen. He was gone just long enough for Mariah to inform Pinkwater of her fits. By the time Dave rushed in with Mrs. Peterson behind him, Pinkwater was doing a first-class fit. Flailing the air with her long arms and legs, she let her head roll crazily from side to side. She also made weird noises.

"I can't stand it." Mariah wept and pulled back just as it seemed Pinkwater would strike her.

Mrs. Peterson looked at the girl on the floor. It seemed as if any minute she might join her in a fit of her own. "Oh, my God," she said over and over.

"I'll get her some water," Mariah said. She ran out of the foyer, made a bee line to the gift table, seized the sloppily-wrapped package, and tore it open. Victory. *Great Expectations*.

In the foyer, Mrs. Peterson and Dave were attempting to approach Pinkwater by grabbing at her wheeling limbs.

"Fit's over," Mariah cried, holding the book up in the air.

Mrs. Peterson stood up, Pinkwater stood up. "I beg your pardon, my dear," Mrs. Peterson said cooly. "You are making an outrageous accusation and I demand that you return my book. That is a present from Dave and his sister, an anniversary present. It does not belong to you." She reached out and snatched the book from Mariah's grasp.

Mariah tugged back, but Mrs. Peterson had the book clasped firmly against her chest.

"David and his sister have chosen a beautiful gift for me. I won't let you spoil it."

"It's mine and and my father's," said Mariah.

"It's mine and a beauty." Mrs. Peterson smiled at Dave and opened the book. "A truly wonderful editionnnnn." She gazed at the first page. Mariah watched her eyes grow frighteningly large. Written across the page in black Magic Marker was PROPERTY OF THE MARIAH DELANY LENDING LIBRARY.

"DAVID!" Mrs. Peterson gasped.

Mariah took this opportunity to grab the book from her limp hand, shove her limp son out of the way, and beat it. Pinkwater moved speedily behind her. As they ran down the corridor toward the elevator, they heard "David, I *am* disappointed," followed by, "I didn't think it was so serious. I said I'd replace it."

"The dope didn't even have the brains to tear out the title page," Mariah hooted once they were out on the sidewalk and laughing so they could hardly breathe.

Mariah stopped laughing. She remembered that she hadn't had the brains to tear out the title page either before returning

the book to her father's shelf. She remembered that she too had somehow taken
books that didn't really belong to her and
then she actually felt a wave of sympathy
for David Peterson of apartment 14D.

12

The story of the return of *Great Expectations* spread through school the following Monday with embellishments, exaggerations, and twists until it acquired some of the proportions of a folk tale. Mariah and Emma were heroines of the tale, and no one gave either of them any trouble that day. Mariah was treated with a kind of awed respect that was new to her. Pinkwater was proud to be known as the first Collecting Agent. Several people came up to

Mariah to ask if the Lending Library
would be open for returns later that day.

After school Mariah went home to wait.
It wasn't long before the doorbell started to
ring and books began to pile up on her
desk. When the last book was turned in, its
borrower, little Enid Lucton, peered over
the top of Mariah's desk and said, "Oh,
Miss Librarian, where do I go to take out a
new book?"

Mariah leaned forward and took Enid's round face in her two hands. "The Mariah Delany Lending Library is officially closed," she said slowly and with emphasis. "Forever."

"Oh." Enid sighed. "I liked the cocoa."

Mariah made her some in celebration. Then she checked each and every card against the books and replaced every book lovingly upon its proper shelf or stack. She put *Best Desserts in the World* back in the kitchen and washed her hands. Its cover was sticky.

When Gertrude and Henry Delany returned from work late in the afternoon, Mariah wordlessly produced the shoebox full of cards, each one marked RETURNED.

"Does this mean that they're all back, Mariah?" asked her mother.

"Yes," Mariah said. "You can check them."

"We don't have to," Henry Delany said. "We have always trusted your abilities as

116

far as your enterprises are concerned, Mariah. When you told us that the books would come back, we knew they would. You'd find a way if anyone could."

The Delanys sat down to dinner. Mariah was very proud of herself in a subdued sort of way. After dinner her mother noticed a far-off look in her daughter's green eyes.

"Oh, Mariah, you have that look. I think you're planning a new venture."

"No," Mariah said.

"Mariah dear, I know you," was all Mrs. Delany said, but those few words were all that were needed. Mariah knew by heart the rest of the words and the feelings behind them. In spite of this and in spite of everything she had just been through, she knew her mother's fears were justified. Mariah was hatching a new plan.

"Mariah, please remember," Mrs. Delany pleaded softly, over her bowl of pudding.

"I do, I do," Mariah said. But even as she

said it the new plan was at work within her. After dinner Mariah went to her room. She remembered her vow and gratefully did every last bit of homework before she read a few chapters in *Great Expectations*.

The next day Mariah's teachers were delighted by the carefully completed homework she turned in. It was a good day. By the end of her last class Mariah was in a fever of impatience to begin her new enterprise. She grabbed her books, ran down the steps, and raced toward the corner. Pinkwater and Coopersmith followed at her heels. They were running, and calling breathlessly, "Hey, wait up, Delany."

She stood impatiently. Couldn't they tell she was in a big hurry and didn't have all day?

"Delany." Pinkwater gasped, clutching her sides. "We just wondered, what's your new business? We want to be included."

"I can't include you."

"Oh Mariah, puh-lease . . ." Coopersmith
wailed. "Don't keep us out."

"Sorry." She started to cross the street.

"You couldn't have done the Lending Library without me," Pinkwater reminded
her.

"I know, and thanks."

"Harmonicas wouldn't have gotten off

the ground if I hadn't helped," Cooper-smith piped up. They were walking three abreast, and fast.

"C'mon, Mariah, include us."

"No."

"Well tell us where you're going, or we'll follow you."

Mariah stopped right in the middle of the sidewalk. Pinkwater and Coopersmith lurched to a halt. "I said no more enter-prises. I'm through. I got into too much trouble with the last one. I don't need that kind of trouble."

"But the way you're hurrying, you look like you're on to something."

"I am."

"Well?" they chorused triumphantly. "Where are you going?"

"I'm going to the Public Library."

"Oh yeah." Disappointment.

There was a moment of silence and then Coopersmith said to Pinkwater, "Do you want to come to my place for TV?"

"Okay." Pinkwater eyed Mariah. "You coming too?"

"I told you, I'm going to the library."

Unable to contain herself for another minute, Pinkwater blurted, "Mariah Delany, whatever for?"

"Because it's got everything," Mariah said.

Pinkwater was suspicious, but Coopersmith shrugged. They said good-by.

Mariah began to skip and then, whistling tunelessly, she ran down the remaining streets and up the block and then the stairs. She thought of all the things she had to do. She had to shelve at least two carts of books, read out loud to a bunch of kids, and help arrange a display case. Then, if she was lucky, there would be time to read a few more chapters of *Great Expectations*.

The Public Library was the best enterprise she had ever thought up. It *did* have
everything. It was a friendly place, the
people were nice, there were interesting
jobs to do that really desperately needed
doing. Mariah's work was terribly important. Of course, there wasn't any money in
the library, but then she didn't have to
make an investment, or hoodwink anybody, or make enemies, or get into awful
hot water; and after her last experience all
this seemed very good. And of course there

were all those books to browse among. Yes, it was a great relief, Mariah decided, to be part of the system, the public library system.

EXPLORATIONS

WILLIAM BUTLER YEATS
From a painting by Augustus John, O.M., R.A.

W. B. Yeats
EXPLORATIONS

SELECTED BY MRS. W. B. YEATS

Collier Books
New York

Macmillan Publishing Co., Inc.
866 Third Avenue, New York, N.Y. 10022

Explorations was originally published in a hardcover
edition by The Macmillan Company.

Library of Congress Catalog Card Number: 63-9338

First Collier Books Edition 1973

Printed in the United States of America

PUBLISHERS' NOTE

THE longest item in this varied collection of Yeats's prose papers is *The Irish Dramatic Movement, 1901–1919*, which previously formed a part of *Plays and Controversies*, no longer in print. Here Yeats explains and defends the principles that inspired him and his collaborators in their work for what he thought of as an Irish 'People's Theatre', and records many of the actual productions at the Abbey.

There are also uncollected forewords to books Yeats greatly admired: Lady Gregory's retelling of Irish heroic legends in *Cuchulain of Muirthemne* (1902) and *Gods and Fighting Men* (1904); and Percy Arland Ussher's translation from the Gaelic of *The Midnight Court*, by Brian Merriman. Other important material has previously been obtainable only in editions issued by the Cuala Press: 'If I were Four and Twenty' (1919) from the book of that title, which also contained 'Swedenborg, Mediums, and the Desolate Places' (1914); *Pages from a Diary written in 1930;* and a miscellany, *On the Boiler* (1939), which includes some later reflections on the Irish theatre. In addition there are the Introductions—excluded from the *Collected Plays* for reasons of space—to the plays from *Wheels and Butterflies* (1934), now out of print: 'The Words upon the Window-pane', 'Fighting the Waves' (with text), 'The Resurrection', and 'The Cat and the Moon'. The order is chronological.

CONTENTS

I

EXPLORATIONS I

II

THE IRISH DRAMATIC MOVEMENT: 1901-1919

vii

Contents

FRONTISPIECE

W. B. YEATS, by *Augustus John, O.M., R.A.*
By courtesy of the Kelvingrove Art Gallery, Glasgow

I
EXPLORATIONS I

CUCHULAIN OF MUIRTHEMNE[1]

I

I THINK this book is the best that has come out of Ireland in my time. Perhaps I should say that it is the best book that has ever come out of Ireland; for the stories which it tells are a chief part of Ireland's gift to the imagination of the world—and it tells them perfectly for the first time. Translators from the Irish have hitherto retold one story or the other from some one version, and not often with any fine understanding of English, of those changes of rhythm for instance that are changes of the sense. They have translated the best and fullest manuscripts they knew, as accurately as they could, and that is all we have the right to expect from the first translators of a difficult and old literature. But few of the stories really begin to exist as great works of imagination until somebody has taken the best bits out of many manuscripts. Sometimes, as in Lady Gregory's version of *Deirdre*, a dozen manuscripts have to give their best before the beads are ready for the necklace. It has been as necessary also to leave out as to add, for generations of copyists, who had often but little sympathy with the stories they copied, have mixed versions together in a clumsy fashion, often repeating one incident several times, and every century has ornamented what was once a simple story with its own often extravagant ornament. We do not perhaps exaggerate

[1] *Cuchulain of Muirthemne.* The story of the men of the Red Branch of Ulster, arranged and put into English by Lady Gregory.

when we say that no story has come down to us in
the form it had when the story-teller told it in the
winter evenings. Lady Gregory has done her work of
compression and selection at once so firmly and so
reverently that I cannot believe that anybody, except
now and then for a scientific purpose, will need another
text than this, or than the version of it the Gaelic
League is about to publish in Modern Irish. When she
has added her translations from other cycles, she will
have given Ireland its *Mabinogion*, its *Morte d'Arthur*,
its *Nibelungenlied*. She has already put a great mass of
stories, in which the ancient heart of Ireland still lives,
into a shape at once harmonious and characteristic;
and without writing more than a very few sentences
of her own to link together incidents or thoughts taken
from different manuscripts, without adding more indeed than the story-teller must often have added to
amend the hesitation of a moment. Perhaps more than
all she had discovered a fitting dialect to tell them in.
Some years ago I wrote some stories of mediaeval
Irish life, and as I wrote I was sometimes made wretched
by the thought that I knew of no kind of English that
fitted them as the language of Morris's prose stories—
the most beautiful language I had ever read—fitted his
journeys to woods and wells beyond the world. I
knew of no language to write about Ireland in but raw
modern English; but now Lady Gregory has discovered a speech as beautiful as that of Morris, and a
living speech into the bargain. As she moved about
among her people she learned to love the beautiful
speech of those who think in Irish, and to understand

that it is as true a dialect of English as the dialect that Burns wrote in. It is some hundreds of years old, and age gives a language authority. We find in it the vocabulary of the translators of the Bible, joined to an idiom which makes it tender, compassionate, and complaisant, like the Irish language itself. It is certainly well suited to clothe a literature which never ceased to be folk-lore even when it was recited in the Courts of Kings.

II

Lady Gregory could with less trouble have made a book that would have better pleased the hasty reader. She could have plucked away details, smoothed out characteristics till she had left nothing but the bare stories; but a book of that kind would never have called up the past, or stirred the imagination of a painter or a poet, and would be as little thought of in a few years as if it had been a popular novel.

The abundance of what may seem at first irrelevant invention in a story like the death of Conaire, is essential if we are to recall a time when people were in love with a story, and gave themselves up to imagination as if to a lover. We may think there are too many lyrical outbursts, or too many enigmatical symbols here and there in some other story, but delight will always overtake us in the end. We come to accept without reserve an art that is half epical, half lyrical, like that of the historical parts of the Bible, the art of a time when perhaps men passed more readily than they do now from one mood to another, and found it harder

than we do to keep to the mood in which we tot up
figures or banter a friend.

The Church, when it was most powerful, taught
learned and unlearned to climb, as it were, to the great
moral realities through hierarchies of Cherubim and
Seraphim, through clouds of Saints and Angels who
had all their precise duties and privileges. The story-
tellers of Ireland, perhaps of every primitive country,
created as fine a fellowship, only it was aesthetic
realities that they would have us tell for kin and
fellow. They created, for learned and unlearned alike,
a communion of heroes, a cloud of stalwart witnesses;
but because they were as much excited as a monk over
his prayers, they did not think sufficiently about the
shape of the poem and the story. We have to get a
little weary or a little distrustful of our subject, perhaps,
before we can lie awake thinking how to make the
most of it. They were more anxious to describe
energetic characters, and to invent beautiful stories,
than to express themselves with perfect dramatic logic
or in perfectly ordered words. They shared their
characters and their stories, their very images, with
one another, and handed them down from generation
to generation; for nobody, even when he had added
some new trait, or some new incident, thought of
claiming for himself what so obviously lived its own
merry or mournful life. The image-maker or worker
in mosaic who first put Christ upon the Cross would

6

have as soon claimed as his own a thought which was perhaps put into his mind by Christ himself. The Irish poets had also, it may be, what seemed a supernatural sanction, for a chief poet had to understand not only innumerable kinds of poetry, but how to keep himself for nine days in a trance. Surely they believed or half-believed in the historical reality of their wildest imaginations. And as soon as Christianity made their hearers desire a chronology that would run side by side with that of the Bible, they delighted in arranging their Kings and Queens, the shadows of forgotten mythologies, in long lines that ascended to Adam and his Garden. Those who listened to them must have felt as if the living were like rabbits digging their burrows under walls that had been built by Gods and Giants, or like swallows building their nests in the stone mouths of immense images, carved by nobody knows who. It is no wonder that we sometimes hear about men who saw in a vision ivy-leaves that were greater than shields, and blackbirds whose thighs were like the thighs of oxen. The fruit of all those stories, unless indeed the finest activities of the mind are but a pastime, is the quick intelligence, the abundant imagination, the courtly manners of the Irish country people.

IV

William Morris came to Dublin when I was a boy, and I had some talk with him about these old stories. He had intended to lecture upon them, but 'the ladies and gentlemen'—he put a Communistic fervour of hatred into the phrase—knew nothing about them. He spoke of the Irish account of the battle of Clontarf, and of the Norse account, and said that we saw the Norse and Irish tempers in the two accounts. The Norseman was interested in the way things are done, but the Irishman turned aside, evidently well pleased to be out of so dull a business, to describe beautiful supernatural events. He was thinking, I suppose, of the young man who came from Aoibhell of the Grey Rock, giving up immortal love and youth, that he might fight and die by Murrugh's side. He said that the Norseman had the dramatic temper, and the Irishman had the lyrical. I think I should have said, like Professor Ker, epical and romantic rather than dramatic and lyrical, but his words, which have so great authority, mark the distinction very well, and not only between Irish and Norse, but between Irish and other un-Celtic literatures. The Irish story-teller could not interest himself with an unbroken interest in the way men like himself burned a house, or won wives no more wonderful than themselves. His mind constantly escaped out of daily circumstance, as a bough that has been held down by a weak hand suddenly straightens itself out. His imagination was always running off to Tir nà nOg, to the Land of Promise, which is as near to the country-people of to-day as it was to Cuchulain and his companions. His belief in its nearness cherished in its turn the lyrical temper, which is always athirst for an emotion, a beauty which cannot be found in its perfection upon earth, or only for a moment. His imagination, which

had not been able to believe in Cuchulain's greatness, until it had brought the Great Queen, the red-
eyebrowed goddess, to woo him upon the battlefield,
could not be satisfied with a friendship less romantic
and lyrical than that of Cuchulain and Ferdiad, who
kissed one another after the day's fighting, or with a
love less romantic and lyrical than that of Baile and
Aillinn, who died at the report of one another's deaths,
and married in Tir nà nOg. His art, too, is often at
its greatest when it is most extravagant, for he only
feels himself among solid things, among things with
fixed laws and satisfying purposes, when he has re-
shaped the world according to his heart's desire. He
understands as well as Blake that the ruins of time
build mansions in eternity, and he never allows anything that we can see and handle to remain long unchanged. The characters must remain the same, but
the strength of Fergus may change so greatly that he,
who a moment before was merely a strong man among
many, becomes the master of Three Blows that would
destroy an army, did they not cut off the heads of three
little hills instead, and his sword, which a fool had
been able to steal out of its sheath, has of a sudden
the likeness of a rainbow. A wandering lyric moon
must knead and kindle perpetually that moving world
of cloaks made out of the fleeces of Manannan; of
armed men who change themselves into sea-birds; of
goddesses who become crows; of trees that bear fruit
and flower at the same time. The great emotions of
love, terror, and friendship must alone remain untroubled by the moon in that world, which is still the

9

world of the Irish country-people, who do not open
their eyes very wide at the most miraculous change, at
the most sudden enchantment. Its events, and things,
and people are wild, and are like unbroken horses,
that are so much more beautiful than horses that have
learned to run between shafts. We think of actual life,
when we read those Norse stories, which were already
in decadence, so necessary were the proportions of
actual life to their efforts, when a dying man remembered his heroism enough to look down at his
wound and say, 'Those broad spears are coming into
fashion'; but the Irish stories make us understand why
the Greeks call myths the activities of the daemons.
The great virtues, the great joys, the great privations
come in the myths, and, as it were, take mankind
between their naked arms, and without putting off
their divinity. Poets have taken their themes more
often from stories that are all, or half, mythological,
than from history or stories that give one the sensation
of history, understanding, as I think, that the imagination which remembers the proportions of life is but a
long wooing, and that it has to forget them before it
becomes the torch and the marriage-bed.

v

We find, as we expect, in the work of men who
were not troubled about any probabilities or necessities
but those of emotion itself, an immense variety of
incident and character and of ways of expressing emotion. Cuchulain fights man after man during the quest

of the Brown Bull, and not one of those fights is like
another, and not one is lacking in emotion or strangeness; and when we think imagination can do no more,
the story of the Two Bulls, emblematic of all contests,
suddenly lifts romance into prophecy. The characters
too have a distinctness we do not find among the
people of the *Mabinogion*, perhaps not even among
the people of the *Morte d'Arthur*. We know we shall
be long forgetting Cuchulain, whose life is vehement
and full of pleasure, as though he always remembered
that it was to be soon over; or the dreamy Fergus
who betrays the sons of Usnach for a feast, without
ceasing to be noble; or Conall who is fierce and friendly
and trustworthy, but has not the sap of divinity that
makes Cuchulain mysterious to men, and beloved of
women. Women indeed, with their lamentations for
lovers and husbands and sons, and for fallen rooftrees
and lost wealth, give the stories their most beautiful
sentences; and, after Cuchulain, we think most of
certain great queens—of angry, amorous Maeve, with
her long pale face; of Findabair, her daughter, who
dies of shame and of pity; of Deirdre who might be
some mild modern housewife but for her prophetic
wisdom. If we do not set Deirdre's lamentations among
the greatest lyric poems of the world, I think we may be
certain that the wine-press of the poets has been
trodden for us in vain; and yet I think it may be proud
Emer, Cuchulain's fitting wife, who will linger longest
in the memory. What a pure flame burns in her always,
whether she is the newly married wife fighting for pre-
cedence, fierce as some beautiful bird, or the confident

housewife, who would awaken her husband from his magic sleep with mocking words; or the great queen who would get him out of the tightening net of his doom, by sending him into the Valley of the Dead, with Niamh, his mistress, because he will be more obedient to her; or the woman whom sorrow has sent with Helen and Iseult and Brunnhilda, and Deirdre, to share their immortality in the rosary of the poets.

' "And oh! my love!" she said, "we were often in one another's company, and it was happy for us; for if the world had been searched from the rising of the sun to sunset, the like would never have been found in one place, of the Black Sainglain and the Grey of Macha, and Laeg the chariot-driver, and myself and Cuchulain."

'And after that Emer bade Conall to make a wide, very deep grave for Cuchulain; and she laid herself down beside her gentle comrade, and she put her mouth to his mouth, and she said: "Love of my life, my friend, my sweetheart, my one choice of the men of the earth, many is the women, wed or unwed, envied me until to-day; and now I will not stay living after you". '

VI

We Irish should keep these personages much in our hearts, for they lived in the places where we ride and go marketing, and sometimes they have met one another on the hills that cast their shadows upon our doors at evening. If we will but tell these stories to our children the Land will begin again to be a Holy Land,

as it was before men gave their hearts to Greece and
Rome and Judea. When I was a child I had only to
climb the hill behind the house to see long, blue, ragged
hills flowing along the southern horizon. What beauty
was lost to me, what depth of emotion is still perhaps
lacking in me, because nobody told me, not even
the merchant captains who knew everything, that
Cruachan of the Enchantments lay behind those long,
blue, ragged hills!

March 1902

GODS AND FIGHTING MEN[1]

I

A FEW months ago I was on the bare Hill of Allen, 'wide Almhuin of Leinster', where Finn and the Fianna lived, according to the stories, although there are no earthen mounds there like those that mark the sites of old buildings on so many hills. A hot sun beat down upon flowering gorse and flowerless heather; and on every side except the east, where there were green trees and distant hills, one saw a level horizon and brown boglands with a few green places and here and there the glitter of water. One could imagine that had it been twilight and not early afternoon, and had there been vapours drifting and frothing where there were now but shadows of clouds, it would have set stirring in one, as few places even in Ireland can, a thought that is peculiar to Celtic romance, as I think, a thought of a mystery coming not as with Gothic nations out of the pressure of darkness, but out of great spaces and windy light. The hill of Teamhair, or Tara, as it is now called, with its green mounds and its partly wooded sides, and its more gradual slope set among fat grazing lands, with great trees in the hedgerows, had brought before one imaginations, not of heroes who were in their youth for hundreds of years, or of women who came to them in the likeness of hunted fawns, but of kings that lived brief and politic

[1] *Gods and Fighting Men*: the story of the Tuatha de Danaan arranged and put into English by Lady Gregory.

14

lives, and of the five white roads that carried their armies to the lesser kingdoms of Ireland, or brought to the great fair that had given Teamhair its sovereignty, all that sought justice or pleasure or had goods to barter.

II

It is certain that we must not confuse these kings, as did the mediaeval chroniclers, with those half-divine kings of Almhuin. The chroniclers, perhaps because they loved tradition too well to cast out utterly much that they dreaded as Christians, and perhaps because popular imagination had begun the mixture, have mixed one with another ingeniously, making Finn the head of a kind of Militia under Cormac MacArt, who is supposed to have reigned at Teamhair in the second century, and making Grania, who travels to enchanted houses under the cloak of Aengus, god of Love, and keeps her troubling beauty longer than did Helen hers, Cormac's daughter, and giving the stories of the Fianna, although the impossible has thrust its proud finger into them all, a curious air of precise history. It is only when we separate the stories from that mediaeval pedantry, as in this book, that we recognise one of the oldest worlds that man has imagined, an older world certainly than we find in the stories of Cuchulain, who lived, according to the chroniclers, about the time of the birth of Christ. They are far better known, and we may be certain of the antiquity of incidents that are known in one form or another to every Gaelic-speaking countryman in Ireland or in the Highlands of Scotland. Sometimes a labourer digging near to a cromlech, or Bed of Diarmuid and Grania as it is called, will tell us a tradition that seems older and more barbaric than any description of their adventures or of themselves in written text or story that has taken form in the mouths of professed story-tellers. Finn and the Fianna found welcome among the Court poets later than did Cuchulain; and one finds memories of Danish invasions and standing armies mixed with the imaginations of hunters and solitary fighters among great woods. We never hear of Cuchulain delighting in the hunt or in woodland things; and we imagine that the story-teller would have thought it unworthy in so great a man, who lived a well-ordered, elaborate life, and could delight in his chariot and his chariot-driver and his barley-fed horses. If he is in the woods before dawn we are not told that he cannot know the leaves of the hazel from the leaves of the oak; and when Emer laments him no wild creature comes into her thoughts but the cuckoo that cries over cultivated fields. His story must have come out of a time when the wild wood was giving way to pasture and tillage, and men had no longer a reason to consider every cry of the birds or change of the night. Finn, who was always in the woods, whose battles were but hours amid years of hunting, delighted in the 'cackling of ducks from the Lake of the Three Narrows; the scolding talk of the blackbird of Doire an Cairn; the bellowing of the ox from the Valley of the Berries; the whistle of the eagle from the Valley of Victories or from the rough branches of the Ridge of the Stream; the grouse of the heather of Cruachan; the call of the otter of Druim de Coir'. When sorrow comes upon the queens of the stories, they have sympathy for the wild birds and beasts that are like themselves: 'Credhe wife of Cael came with the others and went looking through the bodies for her comely comrade, and crying as she went. And as she was searching she saw a crane of the meadows and her two nestlings, and the cunning beast the fox watching the nestlings; and when the crane covered one of the birds to save it, he would make a rush at the other bird, the way she had to stretch herself out over the birds; and she would sooner have got her own death by the fox than the nestlings to be killed by him. And Credhe was looking at that, and she said: "It is no wonder I to have such love for my comely sweetheart, and the bird in that distress about her nestlings".'

III

We often hear of a horse that shivers with terror, or of a dog that howls at something a man's eyes cannot see, and men who live primitive lives where instinct does the work of reason are fully conscious of many things that we cannot perceive at all. As life becomes more orderly, more deliberate, the super-natural world sinks further away. Although the gods come to Cuchulain, and although he is the son of one of the greatest of them, their country and his are far apart, and they come to him as god to mortal; but Finn is their equal. He is continually in their houses; he meets with Bodb Dearg, and Aengus, and Manannan, now as friend with friend, now as with an enemy he overcomes in battle; and when he has need of their help his messenger can say: 'There is not a king's son or a prince, or a leader of the Fianna of Ireland, without having a wife or a mother or a foster-mother or a sweetheart of the Tuatha de Danaan.' When the Fianna are broken up at last, after hundreds of years of hunting, it is doubtful that he dies at all, and certain that he comes again in some other shape, and Oisin, his son, is made king over a divine country. The birds and beasts that cross his path in the woods have been fighting men or great enchanters or fair women, and in a moment can take some beautiful or terrible shape. We think of him and of his people as great-bodied men with large movements, that seem, as it were, flowing out of some deep below the narrow stream of personal impulse, men that have broad brows and quiet eyes full of confidence in a good luck that proves every day afresh that they are a portion of the strength of things. They are hardly so much individual men as portions of universal nature, like the clouds that shape themselves and reshape themselves momentarily, or like a bird between two boughs, or like the gods that have given the apples and the nuts; and yet this but brings them the nearer to us, for we can remake them in our image when we will, and the woods are the more beautiful for the thought. Do we not always fancy hunters to be something like this, and is not that why we think them poetical when we meet them of a sudden, as in these lines in *Pauline*:

Gods and Fighting Men

An old hunter
Talking with gods; or a high-crested chief
Sailing with troops of friends to Tenedos?

IV

We must not expect in these stories the epic lineaments, the many incidents, woven into one great event,
of, let us say, the story of the War for the Brown Bull
of Cuailgne, or that of the last gathering at Muirthemne. Even *Diarmuid and Grania*, which is a long
story, has nothing of the clear outlines of *Deirdre*, and
is indeed but a succession of detached episodes. The
men who imagined the Fianna had the imagination of
children, and as soon as they had invented one wonder,
heaped another on top of it. Children—or, at any rate,
it is so I remember my own childhood—do not understand large design, and they delight in little shut-in
places where they can play at houses more than in
great expanses where a country-side takes, as it were,
the impression of a thought. The wild creatures and
the green things are more to them than to us, for they
creep towards our light by little holes and crevices.
When they imagine a country for themselves, it is
always a country where you can wander without aim,
and where you can never know from one place what
another will be like, or know from the one day's
adventure what may meet you with to-morrow's sun.

Explorations I

V

Children play at being great and wonderful people, at the ambitions they will put away for one reason or another before they grow into ordinary men and women. Mankind as a whole had a like dream once; everybody and nobody built up the dream bit by bit, and the ancient story-tellers are there to make us remember what mankind would have been like, had not fear and the failing will and the laws of nature tripped up its heels. The Fianna and their like are themselves so full of power, and they are set in a world so fluctuating and dream-like, that nothing can hold them from being all that the heart desires.

I have read in a fabulous book that Adam had but to imagine a bird, and it was born into life, and that he created all things out of himself by nothing more important than an unflagging fancy; and heroes who can make a ship out of a shaving have but little less of the divine prerogatives. They have no speculative thoughts to wander through eternity and waste heroic blood; but how could that be otherwise, for it is at all times the proud angels who sit thinking upon the hill-side and not the people of Eden. One morning we meet them hunting a stag that is 'as joyful as the leaves of a tree in summer-time'; and whatever they do, whether they listen to the harp or follow an enchanter over-sea, they do for the sake of joy, their joy in one another, or their joy in pride and movement; and even their battles are fought more because of their delight in a good fighter than because of any gain that is in victory. They live always as if they were playing a game; and so far as they have any deliberate purpose at all, it is that they may become great gentlemen and be worthy of the songs of poets. It has been said, and I think the Japanese were the first to say it, that the four essential virtues are to be generous among the weak, and truthful among one's friends, and brave among one's enemies, and courteous at all times; and if we understand by courtesy not merely the gentleness the story-tellers have celebrated, but a delight in courtly things, in beautiful clothing and in beautiful verse, we understand that it was no formal succession of trials that bound the Fianna to one another. Only the Table Round, that is indeed, as it seems, a rivulet from the same river, is bound in a like fellowship, and there the four heroic virtues are troubled by the abstract virtues of the cloister. Every now and then some noble knight builds himself a cell upon the hill-side, or leaves kind women and joyful knights to seek the vision of the Grail in lonely adventures. But when Oisin or some kingly forerunner—Bran, son of Febal, or the like— rides or sails in an enchanted ship to some divine country, he but looks for a more delighted companion-ship, or to be in love with faces that will never fade. No thought of any life greater than that of love, and the companionship of those that have drawn their swords upon the darkness of the world, ever troubles their delight in one another as it troubles Iseult amid her love, or Arthur amid his battles. It is an ailment of our speculation that thought, when it is not the plan-ning of something, or the doing of something, or some memory of a plain circumstance, separates us from one another because it makes us always more unlike, and because no thought passes through another's ear unchanged. Companionship can only be perfect when it is founded on things, for things are always the same under the hand, and at last one comes to hear with envy the voices of boys lighting a lantern to ensnare moths, or of the maids chattering in the kitchen about the fox that carried off a turkey before breakfast. Lady Gregory's book of tales is full of fellowship untroubled like theirs, and made noble by a courtesy that has gone perhaps out of the world. I do not know in literature better friends and lovers. When one of the Fianna finds Osgar dying the proud death of a young man, and asks is it well with him, he is answered, 'I am as you would have me be'. The very heroism of the Fianna is indeed but their pride and joy in one another, their good-fellowship. Goll, old and savage, and letting himself die of hunger in a cave because he is angry and sorry, can speak lovely words to the wife whose help he refuses. '"It is best as it is," he said, "and I never took the advice of a woman east or west, and I never will take it. And oh, sweet-voiced queen," he said, "what ails you to be fretting after me? and remember now your silver and your gold, and your silks . . . and do not be crying tears after me, queen with the white hands," he said, "but remember your constant lover Aodh, son of the best woman of the world, that came from Spain asking for you, and that I fought on Corcar-an-Dearg; and go to him now," he said, "for it is bad when a woman is without a good man."'

VI

They have no asceticism, but they are more visionary than any ascetic, and their invisible life is but the life about them made more perfect and more lasting, and the invisible people are their own images in the water. Their gods may have been much besides this, for we know them from fragments of mythology picked out with trouble from a fantastic history running backward to Adam and Eve, and many things that may have seemed wicked to the monks who imagined that history, may have been altered or left out; but this they must have been essentially, for the old stories are confirmed by apparitions among the country-people to-day. The Men of Dea fought against the mis-shapen Fomor, as Finn fights against the Cat-Heads and the Dog-Heads; and when they are overcome at last by men, they make themselves houses in the hearts of hills that are like the houses of men. When they call men to their houses and to their country Under-Wave they promise them all that they have upon earth, only in greater abundance. The god Midhir sings to Queen Etain in one of the most beautiful of the stories: 'The young never grow old; the fields and the flowers are as pleasant to be looking at as the blackbird's eggs; warm streams of mead and wine flow through that country; there is no care or no sorrow on any person; we see others, but we ourselves are not seen'. These gods are indeed more wise and beautiful than men; but men, when they are great men, are stronger than they are, for men are, as it were, the foaming tide-line of their sea. We remember the Druid who answered, when someone asked him who made the world, 'The Druids made it'. All was indeed but one life flowing everywhere, and taking one quality here, another there. It sometimes seems as if there is a kind of day and night of religion, and that a period when the influences are those that shape the world is followed by a period when the greater power is in influences that would lure the soul out of the world, out of the body. When Oisin is speaking with Saint Patrick of the friends and the life he has outlived, he can but cry out constantly against a religion that has no meaning for him. He laments, and the country-people have remembered his words for centuries: 'I will cry my fill, but not for God, but because Finn and the Fianna are not living'.

VII

Old writers had an admirable symbolism that attributed certain energies to the influence of the sun, and certain others to the lunar influence. To lunar influence belong all thoughts and emotions that were created by the community, by the common people, by nobody knows who, and to the sun all that came from the high disciplined or individual kingly mind. I myself imagine a marriage of the sun and moon in the arts I take most pleasure in; and now bride and bridegroom but exchange, as it were, full cups of gold and silver, and now they are one in a mystical embrace. From the moon come the folk-songs imagined by reapers and spinners out of the common impulse of their labour, and made

not by putting words together, but by mixing verses
and phrases, and the folk-tales made by the capricious
mixing of incidents known to everybody in new ways,
as we deal out cards, never getting the same hand twice
over. When we hear some fine story, we never know
whether it has not been hazard that put the last touch
of adventure. Such poetry, as it seems to me, desires an
infinity of wonder or emotion, for where there is no
individual mind there is no measurer-out, no marker-
in of limits. The poor fisher has no possession of the
world and no responsibility for it; and if he dreams of
a love-gift better than the brown shawl that seems too
common for poetry, why should he not dream of a
glove made from the skin of a bird, or shoes made
from the skin of a fish, or a coat made from the glitter-
ing garment of the salmon? Was it not Aeschylus who
said he but served up dishes from the banquet of
Homer?—but Homer himself found the great banquet
on an earthen floor and under a broken roof. We do
not know who at the foundation of the world made
the banquet for the first time, or who put the pack of
cards into rough hands; but we do know that, unless
those that have made many inventions are about to
change the nature of poetry, we may have to go where
Homer went if we are to sing a new song. Is it because
all that is under the moon thirsts to escape out of
bounds, to lose itself in some unbounded tidal stream,
that the songs of the folk are mournful, and that the
story of the Fianna, whenever the queens lament for
their lovers, reminds us of songs that are still sung in
country places? Their grief, even when it is to be brief

like Grania's, goes up into the waste places of the sky. But in supreme art or in supreme life there is the influence of the sun too, and the sun brings with it, as old writers tell us, not merely discipline but joy; for its discipline is not of the kind the multitudes impose upon us by their weight and pressure, but the expression of the individual soul turning itself into a pure fire and imposing its own pattern, its own music, upon the heaviness and the dumbness that is in others and in itself. When we have drunk the cold cup of the moon's intoxication, we thirst for something beyond ourselves, and the mind flows outward to a natural immensity; but if we have drunk from the hot cup of the sun, our own fullness awakens, we desire little, for wherever we go our heart goes too; and if any ask what music is the sweetest, we can but answer, as Finn answered, 'what happens'. And yet the songs and stories that have come from either influence are a part, neither less than the other, of the pleasure that is the bride-bed of poetry.

VIII

Gaelic-speaking Ireland, because its art has been made, not by the artist choosing his material from wherever he has a mind to, but by adding a little to something which it has taken generations to invent, has always had a popular literature. We cannot say how much that literature has done for the vigour of the race, for we cannot count the hands its praise of kings and high-hearted queens made hot upon the sword-hilt, or the amorous eyes it made lustful for strength and beauty. We remember indeed that when the farming people and the labourers of the towns made their last attempt to cast out England by force of arms they named themselves after the companions of Finn. Even when Gaelic has gone, and the poetry with it, something of the habit of mind remains in ways of speech and thought and 'come-all-ye's' and poetical sayings; nor is it only among the poor that the old thought has been for strength or weakness. Surely these old stories, whether of Finn or Cuchulain, helped to sing the old Irish and the old Norman-Irish aristocracy to their end. They heard their hereditary poets and story-tellers, and they took to horse and died fighting against Elizabeth or against Cromwell; and when an English-speaking aristocracy had their place, it listened to no poetry indeed, but it felt about it in the popular mind an exacting and ancient tribunal, and began a play that had for spectators men and women that loved the high wasteful virtues. I do not think that their own mixed blood or the habit of their time need take all, or nearly all, credit or discredit for the impulse that made our modern gentlemen fight duels over pocket-handkerchiefs, and set out to play ball against the gates of Jerusalem for a wager, and scatter money before the public eye; and at last, after an epoch of such eloquence the world has hardly seen its like, lose their public spirit and their high heart and grow querulous and selfish as men do who have played life out not heartily but with noise and tumult. Had they understood the people and the game a little better, they might have created an aristocracy in an age that has lost the meaning of the word. When we read of the Fianna, or of Cuchulain, or of some great hero, we remember that the fine life is always a part played finely before fine spectators. There also we notice the hot cup and the cold cup of intoxication; and when the fine spectators have ended, surely the fine players grow weary, and aristocratic life is ended. When O'Connell covered with a dark glove the hand that had killed a man in the duelling field, he played his part; and when Alexander stayed his army marching to the conquest of the world that he might contemplate the beauty of a plane-tree, he played his part. When Osgar complained, as he lay dying, of the keening of the women and the old fighting men, he too played his part: 'No man ever knew any heart in me,' he said, 'but a heart of twisted horn, and it covered with iron; but the howling of the dogs beside me,' he said, 'and the keening of the old fighting men and the crying of the women one after another, those are the things that are vexing me'. If we would create a great community—and what other game is so worth the labour?—we must recreate the old foundations of life, not as they existed in that splendid misunderstanding of the eighteenth century, but as they must always exist when the finest minds and Ned the beggar and Seàn the fool think about the same thing, although they may not think the same thought about it.

IX

When I asked the little boy who had shown me the pathway up the Hill of Allen if he knew stories of Finn

and Oisin, he said he did not, but that he had often
heard his grandfather telling them to his mother in
Irish. He did not know Irish, but he was learning it at
school, and all the little boys he knew were learning
it. In a little while he will know enough stories of Finn
and Oisin to tell them to his children some day. It is
the owners of the land whose children might never
have known what would give them so much happiness.
But now they can read Lady Gregory's book to their
children, and it will make Slieve-na-man, Allen, and
Ben Bulben, the great mountain that showed itself
before me every day through all my childhood and
was yet unpeopled, and half the country-sides of south
and west, as populous with memories as her *Cuchulain
of Muirthemne* will have made Dundealgan and Emain
Macha and Muirthemne; and after a while somebody
may even take them to some famous place and say,
'This land where your fathers lived proudly and finely
should be dear and dear and again dear'; and perhaps
when many names have grown musical to their ears, a
more imaginative love will have taught them a better
service.

x

I praise but in brief words the noble writing of these
books, for words that praise a book wherein something
is done supremely well, will remain in the ears of a
later generation, like the foolish sound of church bells
from the tower of a church when every pew is full.

1904

Explorations I

SWEDENBORG, MEDIUMS, AND THE DESOLATE PLACES

I

Sᴏᴍᴇ fifteen years ago I was in bad health and could not work, and Lady Gregory brought me from cottage to cottage while she began to collect stories, and presently when I was at work again she went on with her collection alone till it grew to be, so far as I know, the most considerable of its kind. Except that I had heard some story of 'The Battle of the Friends' at Aran and had divined that it might be the legendary common accompaniment of death, she was not guided by any theory of mine, but recorded what came, writing it out at each day's end and in the country dialect. It was at this time mainly she got the knowledge of words that makes her little comedies of country life so beautiful and so amusing. As that ancient system of belief unfolded before us, with unforeseen probabilities and plausibilities, it was as though we had begun to live in a dream, and one day Lady Gregory said to me when we had passed an old man in the wood: 'That old man may know the secret of the ages'.

I had noticed many analogies in modern spiritism and began a more careful comparison, going a good deal to séances for the first time and reading all writers of any reputation I could find in English or French. I found much that was moving, when I had climbed to the top storey of some house in Soho or Holloway, and, having paid my shilling, awaited, among servant girls, the wisdom of some fat old medium. That is an absorbing drama, though if my readers begin to seek it they will spoil it, for its gravity and simplicity depend on all, or all but all, believing that their dead are near.

I did not go there for evidence of the kind the Society for Psychical Research would value, any more than I would seek it in Galway or in Aran. I was comparing one form of belief with another, and, like Paracelsus who claimed to have collected his knowledge from midwife and hangman, I was discovering a philosophy. Certain things had happened to me when alone in my own room which had convinced me that there are spiritual intelligences which can warn us and advise us, and, as Anatole France has said, if one believes that the Devil can walk the streets of Lisbon, it is not difficult to believe that he can reach his arm over the river and light Don Juan's cigarette. And yet I do not think I have been easily convinced, for I know we make a false beauty by a denial of ugliness and that if we deny the causes of doubt we make a false faith, and that we must excite the whole being into activity if we would offer to God what is, it may be, the one thing germane to the matter, a consenting of all our faculties. Not but that I doubt at times, with the animal doubt of the Middle Ages that I have found even in pious countrywomen when they have seen some life come to an end like the stopping of a clock, or that all the perceptions of the soul, or the weightiest intellectual deductions, are not at whiles but a feather in the daily show.

I pieced together stray thoughts written out after

questioning the familiar of a trance medium or auto-
matic writer, by Allen Cardec, or by some American,
or by myself, and arranged the fragments into some
pattern, till I believed myself the discoverer of a vast
generalisation. I lived in excitement, amused to make
Holloway interpret Aran, and constantly comparing
my discoveries with what I have learned of mediaeval
tradition among fellow students, with the reveries of a
Neo-platonist, of a seventeenth-century Platonist, of
Paracelsus or a Japanese poet. Then one day I opened
the *Spiritual Diary* of Swedenborg which I had not
taken down for twenty years, and found all there, even
certain thoughts I had not set on paper because they
had seemed fantastic from the lack of some traditional
foundation. It was strange I should have forgotten so
completely a writer I had read with some care before
the fascination of Blake and Boehme had led me away.

II

It was indeed Swedenborg who affirmed for the
modern world, as against the abstract reasoning of
the learned, the doctrine and practice of the desolate
places, of shepherds and of midwives, and discovered a
world of spirits where there was a scenery like that of
earth, human forms, grotesque or beautiful, senses that
knew pleasure and pain, marriage and war, all that
could be painted upon canvas, or put into stories to
make one's hair stand up. He had mastered the science
of his time, he had written innumerable scientific works
in Latin, had been the first to formulate the nebular

hypothesis and wrote a cold abstract style, the result, it may be, of preoccupation with stones and metals, for he had been assessor of mines to the Swedish Government, and of continual composition in a dead language.

In his fifty-eighth year he was sitting in an inn in London, where he had gone about the publication of a book, when a spirit appeared before him who was, he believed, Christ himself, and told him that henceforth he could commune with spirits and angels. From that moment he was a mysterious man, describing distant events as if they were before his eyes, and knowing dead men's secrets, if we are to accept testimony that seemed convincing to Immanuel Kant. The sailors who carried him upon his many voyages spoke of the charming of the waves and of favouring winds that brought them sooner than ever before to their journey's end, and an ambassador described how a queen, he himself looking on, fainted when Swedenborg whispered in her ear some secret known only to her and to her dead brother. All this happened to a man without egotism, without drama, without a sense of the picturesque, and who wrote a dry language lacking fire and emotion, and who to William Blake seemed but an arranger and putter-away of the old Church, a Samson shorn by the Churches, an author not of a book, but of an index. He considered heaven and hell and God, the angels, the whole destiny of man, as if he were sitting before a large table in a Government office putting little pieces of mineral ore into small square boxes for an assistant to pack away in drawers.

Explorations I

All angels were once men, he says, and it is therefore men who have entered into what he calls the Celestial State and become angels, who attend us immediately after death, and communicate to us their thoughts, not by speaking, but by looking us in the face as they sit beside the head of our body. When they find their thoughts are communicated they know the time has come to separate the spiritual from the physical body. If a man begins to feel that he can endure them no longer, as he doubtless will, for in their presence he can think and feel but sees nothing, lesser angels who belong to truth more than to love take their place and he is in the light again, but in all likelihood these angels also will be too high and he will slip from state to state until he finds himself after a few days 'with those who are in accord with his life in the world; with them he finds his life, and, wonderful to relate, he then leads a life similar to that he led in the world'. This first state of shifting and readjustment seems to correspond with a state of sleep more modern seers discover to follow upon death. It is characteristic of his whole religious system, the slow drifting of like to like. Then follows a period which may last but a short time or many years, while the soul lives a life so like that of the world that it may not even believe that it has died, for 'when what is spiritual touches and sees what is spiritual the effect is the same as when what is natural touches what is natural'. It is the other world of the early races, of those whose dead are in the rath or the faery hill, of all who see no place of reward and punishment but a continuance of this life, with cattle and sheep markets and war. He describes what he has seen, and only partly explains it, for, unlike science which is founded upon past experience, his work, by the very nature of his gift, looks for the clearing-away of obscurities to unrecorded experience. He is revealing something and that which is revealed, so long as it remains modest and simple, has the same right with the child in the cradle to put off to the future the testimony of its worth. This earth-resembling life is the creation of the image-making power of the mind, plucked naked from the body, and mainly of the images in the memory. All our work has gone with us, the books we have written can be opened and read or put away for later use, even though their print and paper have been sold to the buttermen; and reading his description one notices, a discovery one had thought peculiar to the last generation, that the 'most minute particulars which enter the memory remain there and are never obliterated', and there as here we do not always know all that is in our memory, but at need angelic spirits who act upon us there as here, widening and deepening the consciousness at will, can draw forth all the past, and make us live again all our transgressions and see our victims 'as if they were present, together with the place, words, and motives'; and that suddenly, as when a scene bursts upon the 'sight' and yet continues 'for hours together', and like the transgressions, all the pleasures and pains of sensible life awaken again and again, all our passionate events rush up about us and not as seeming imagination, for imagination is now the world. And yet another impulse comes and goes, flitting through all, a preparation for the spiritual abyss, for out of the celestial world, immediately beyond the world of form, fall certain seeds as it were that exfoliate through us into forms, elaborate scenes, buildings, alterations of form that are related by 'correspondence' or 'signature' to celestial incomprehensible realities. Meanwhile those who have loved or fought see one another in the unfolding of a dream, believing, it may be, that they wound one another or kill one another, severing arms or hands, or that their lips are joined in a kiss, and the countryman has need but of Swedenborg's keen ears and eagle sight to hear a noise of swords in the empty valley, or to meet the old master hunting with all his hounds upon the stroke of midnight among the moonlit fields. But gradually we begin to change and possess only those memories we have related to our emotion or our thought; all that was accidental or habitual dies away and we begin an active present life, for apart from that calling-up of the past we are not punished or rewarded for our actions when in the world but only for what we do when out of it. Up till now we have disguised our real selves, and those who have lived well for fear or favour have walked with holy men and women, and the wise man and the dunce have been associated in common learning, but now the ruling love has begun to remake circumstance and our body.

Swedenborg had spoken with shades that had been learned Latinists, or notable Hebrew scholars, and found, because they had done everything from the memory and nothing from thought and emotion, they had become but simple men. We have already met our friends, but if we were to meet them now for the first time we should not recognise them, for all has been kneaded up anew, arrayed in order and made one piece. 'Every man has many loves, but still they all have reference to his ruling love and make one with it or together compose it', and our surrender to that love, as to supreme good, is no new thought, for Villiers de l'Isle-Adam quotes Thomas Aquinas as having said, 'Eternity is the possession of one's self, as in a single moment'. During the fusing and rending man flits, as it were, from one flock of the dead to another, seeking always those who are like himself, for as he puts off disguise he becomes unable to endure what is unrelated to his love, even becoming insane among things that are too fine for him.

So heaven and hell are built always anew and in hell or heaven all do what they please and all are surrounded by scenes and circumstances which are the expression of their natures and the creation of their thought. Swedenborg, because he belongs to an eighteenth century not yet touched by the romantic revival, feels horror amid rocky uninhabited places, and so believes that the evil are in such places while the good are amid smooth grass and garden walks and the clear sunlight of Claude Lorraine. He describes all in matter-of-fact words, his meeting with this or that dead man, and the place where he found him, and yet we are not to understand him literally, for space as we know it has come to an end and a difference of state has begun to take its place, and wherever a spirit's thought is, the spirit cannot help but be. Nor should we think of spirit as divided from spirit, as men are from each other, for they share each other's thoughts and life, and those whom he has called celestial angels, while themselves mediums to those above, commune with men and lower spirits, through orders of mediatorial spirits, not by a conveyance of messages, but as though a hand were thrust within a hundred gloves,[1] one glove outside another, and so there is a continual influx from God to man. It flows to us through the evil angels as through the good, for the dark fire is the perversion of God's life and the evil angels have their office in the equilibrium that is our freedom, in the building of that fabulous bridge made out of the edge of a sword.

To the eyes of those that are in the high heaven 'all things laugh, sport and live', and not merely because they are beautiful things but because they arouse by a minute correspondence of form and emotion the heart's activity, and being founded, as it were, in this changing heart, all things continually change and shimmer. The garments of all befit minutely their affections, those that have most wisdom and most love being the most nobly garmented, in ascending order from shimmering white, through garments of many colours and garments that are like flame, to the angels of the highest heaven that are naked.

In the west of Ireland the country people say that

[1] The Japanese Noh play 'Awoi no Uye' has for its theme the exorcism of a ghost which is itself obsessed by an evil spirit. This evil spirit, drawn forth by the exorcism, is represented by a dancer wearing a 'terrible mask with golden eyes'.

after death every man grows upward or downward to the likeness of thirty years, perhaps because at that age Christ began His ministry, and stays always in that likeness; and these angels move always towards 'the springtime of their life' and grow more and more beautiful, 'the more thousand years they live', and women who have died infirm with age, and yet lived in faith and charity, and true love towards husband or lover, come 'after a succession of years' to an adolescence that was not in Helen's mirror, 'for to grow old in heaven is to grow young'.

There went on about Swedenborg an intermittent 'Battle of the Friends' and on certain occasions had not the good fought upon his side, the evil troop, by some carriage accident or the like, would have caused his death, for all associations of good spirits have an answering mob, whose members grow more hateful to look on through the centuries. 'Their faces in general are horrible, and empty of life like corpses, those of some are black, of some fiery like torches, of some hideous with pimples, boils, and ulcers; with many no face appears, but in its place a something hairy or bony, and in some one can but see the teeth.' And yet among themselves they are seeming men and but show their right appearance when the light of heaven, which of all things they most dread, beats upon them; and seem to live in a malignant gaiety, and they burn always in a fire that is God's love and wisdom, changed into their own hunger and misbelief.

III

In Lady Gregory's stories there is a man who heard the newly dropped lambs of Faery crying in November, and much evidence to show a topsy-turvydom of seasons, our spring being their autumn, our winter their summer, and Mary Battle, my uncle George Pollexfen's old servant, was accustomed to say that no dream had a true meaning after the rise of the sap; and Lady Gregory learned somewhere on Slieve Ochte that if one told one's dreams to the trees fasting the trees would wither. Swedenborg saw some like opposition of the worlds, for what hides the spirits from our sight and touch, as he explains, is that their light and heat are darkness and cold to us and our light and heat darkness and cold to them, but they can see the world through our eyes and so make our light their light. He seems, however, to warn us against a movement whose philosophy he announced or created, when he tells us to seek no conscious intercourse with any that fall short of the celestial rank. At ordinary times they do not see us or know that we are near, but when we speak to them we are in danger of their deceits. 'They have a passion for inventing', and do not always know that they invent. 'It has been shown me many times that the spirits speaking with me did not know but that they were the men and women I was thinking of; neither did other spirits know the contrary. Thus yesterday and to-day one known of me in life was personated. The personation was so like him in all respects, so far as known to me, that nothing could be more like. For there are genera and species of spirits of similar faculty (as the dead whom we seek), and when like things are called up in the memory of men and so are represented to them they think they are the same persons. At other times they enter into the fantasy of other spirits and think that they are them, and sometimes they will even believe themselves to be the Holy Spirit', and as they identify themselves with a man's affection or enthusiasm they may drive him to ruin, and even an angel will join himself so completely to a man that he scarcely knows 'that he does not know of himself what the man knows', and when they speak with a man they can but speak in that man's mother tongue, and this they can do without taking thought, for 'it is almost as when a man is speaking and thinks nothing about his words'. Yet when they leave the man 'they are in their own angelical or spiritual language and know nothing of the language of man', they are not even permitted to talk to a man from their own memory, for did they do so the man would not know 'but that the things he would then think were his when yet they would belong to the spirit', and it is these sudden memories occurring sometimes by accident, and without God's permission, that gave the Greeks the idea they had lived before. They have bodies as plastic as their minds that flow so readily into the mould of ours and Swedenborg remembers having seen the face of a spirit change continually and yet keep always a certain generic likeness. It had but run through the features of the individual ghosts of the fleet it belonged to, of those bound into the one mediatorial communion.

He speaks too, again and again, of seeing palaces and mountain ranges and all manner of scenery built up in a moment, and even believes in imponderable troops of magicians that build the like out of some deceit or in malicious sport.

IV

There is in Swedenborg's manner of expression a seeming superficiality. We follow an easy narrative, sometimes incredulous, but always, as we think, understanding, for his moral conceptions are simple, his technical terms continually repeated, and for the most part we need but turn for his 'correspondence', his symbolism as we would say, to the index of his *Arcana Celestia*. Presently, however, we discover that he treads upon this surface by an achievement of power almost as full of astonishment as if he should walk upon water charmed to stillness by some halcyon; while his disciple and antagonist Blake is like a man swimming in tumbling sea, surface giving way to surface and deep showing under broken deep. A later mystic has said of Swedenborg that he but half felt, half saw, half tasted the kingdom of heaven, and his abstraction, his dryness, his habit of seeing but one element in everything, his lack of moral speculation have made him the founder of a Church, while William Blake, who grows always more exciting with every year of his life, grows also more obscure. An impulse towards what is definite and sensuous, and an indifference towards the abstract and the general, are the lineaments, as I understand the word, of all that comes not from the learned, but out of common antiquity, out of the 'folk' as we say, and in certain languages, Irish for instance—and these languages are all poetry—it is not possible to speak an abstract thought. This impulse went out of Swedenborg when he turned from vision. It was inseparable from this primitive faculty, but was not a part of his daily bread, whereas Blake carried it to a passion and made it the foundation of his thought. Blake was put into a rage by all painting where detail is generalised away, and complained that Englishmen after the French Revolution became as like one another as the dots and lozenges in the mechanical engraving of his time, and he hated histories that gave us reasoning and deduction in place of the events, and Saint Paul's Cathedral because it came from a mathematical mind, and told Crabb Robinson that he preferred to any others a happy, thoughtless person. Unlike Swedenborg he believed that the antiquities of all peoples were as sacred as those of the Jews, and so rejecting authority and claiming that the same law for the lion and the ox was oppression, he could believe 'all that lives is holy', and say that a man if he but cultivated the power of vision would see the truth in a way suited 'to his imaginative energy', and with only so much resemblance to the way it showed in for other men as there is between different human forms. Born when Swedenborg was a new excitement, growing up with a

Swedenborgian brother, who annoyed him 'with bread and cheese advice', and having, it may be, for nearest friend the Swedenborgian Flaxman with whom he would presently quarrel, he answered the just-translated *Heaven and Hell* with the paradoxical violence of *The Marriage of Heaven and Hell*. Swedenborg was but 'the linen clothes folded up' or the angel sitting by the tomb, after Christ, the human imagination, had arisen. His own memory being full of images from painting and from poetry, he discovered more profound 'correspondences', yet always in his boys and girls walking or dancing on smooth grass and in golden light, as in pastoral scenes cut upon wood or copper by his disciples Palmer and Calvert, one notices the peaceful Swedenborgian heaven. We come there, however, by no obedience but by the energy that 'is eternal delight', for 'the treasures of heaven are not negations of passion but realities of intellect from which the passions emanate uncurbed in their eternal glory'. He would have us talk no more of 'the good man and the bad', but only of 'the wise man and the foolish', and he cries, 'Go put off holiness and put on intellect'.

Higher than all souls that seem to theology to have found a final state, above good and evil, neither accused, nor yet accusing, live those who have come to freedom, their senses sharpened by eternity, piping or dancing or 'like the gay fishes on the wave when the moon sucks up the dew'. Merlin, who in the verses of Chrétien de Troyes was laid in the one tomb with dead lovers, is very near and the saints are far away. Believing too that crucifixion and resurrection were the soul's diary and no mere historical events, which had been transacted in vain should a man come again from the womb and forget his salvation, he could cleave to the heroic doctrine the angel in the crystal made Sir Thomas Kelly renounce and have a 'vague memory' of having been 'with Christ and Socrates'; and stirred as deeply by hill and tree as by human beauty, he saw all Merlin's people, spirits 'of vegetable nature' and faeries whom we 'call accident and chance'. He made possible a religious life to those who had seen the painters and poets of the romantic movement succeed to theology, but the shepherd and the midwife had they known him would have celebrated him in stories, and turned away from his thought, understanding that he was upon an errand to their masters. Like Swedenborg he believed that heaven came from 'an improvement of sensual enjoyment', for sight and hearing, taste and touch grow with the angelic years, but unlike him he could convey to others 'enlarged and numerous senses' and the mass of men know instinctively they are safer with an abstract and an index.

v

It was, I believe, the Frenchman Allen Cardec and an American shoemaker's clerk called Jackson Davies, who first adapted to the séance-room the philosophy of Swedenborg. I find Davies, whose style is vague, voluble, and pretentious, almost unreadable, and yet his books have gone to many editions and are full of stories that had been charming or exciting had he lived in Connacht or any place else where the general mass of the people has an imaginative tongue. His mother was learned in country superstition, and had called in a knowledgeable man when he believed a neighbour had bewitched a cow, but it was not till his fifteenth year that he discovered his faculty, when his native village, Poughkeepsie, was visited by a travelling mesmerist. He was fascinated by the new marvel, and, mesmerised by a neighbour, he became clairvoyant, describing the diseases of those present and reading watches he could not see with his eyes. One night the neighbour failed to awake him completely from the trance and he stumbled out into the street and went to his bed ill and stupefied. In the middle of the night he heard a voice telling him to get up and dress himself and follow. He wandered for miles, now wondering at what seemed the unusual brightness of the stars and once passing a visionary shepherd and his flock of sheep, and then again stumbling in cold and darkness. He crossed the frozen Hudson and became unconscious. He awoke in a mountain valley to see once more the visionary shepherd and his flock, and a very little, handsome, old man who showed him a scroll and told him to write his name upon it.

A little later he passed, as he believed, from this mesmeric condition and found that he was among the Catskill Mountains and more than forty miles from home. Having crossed the Hudson again he felt the trance coming upon him and began to run. He ran, as he thought, many miles and as he ran became unconscious. When he awoke he was sitting upon a gravestone in a graveyard surrounded by a wood and a high wall. Many of the gravestones were old and broken. After much conversation with two stately phantoms, he went stumbling on his way. Presently he found himself at home again. It was evening and the mesmerist was questioning him as to where he had been since they lost him the night before. He was very hungry and had a vague memory of his return, of country roads passing before his eyes in brief moments of wakefulness. He now seemed to know that one of the phantoms with whom he had spoken in the graveyard was the physician Galen, and the other, Swedenborg.

From that hour the two phantoms came to him again and again, the one advising him in the diagnosis of disease, and the other in philosophy. He quoted a passage from Swedenborg, and it seemed impossible that any copy of the newly translated book that contained it could have come into his hands, for a Swedenborgian minister in New York traced every copy which had reached America.

Swedenborg himself had gone upon more than one somnambulistic journey, and they occur a number of times in Lady Gregory's stories, one woman saying that when she was among the faeries she was often glad to eat the food from the pigs' troughs.

Once in childhood, Davies, while hurrying home through a wood, heard footsteps behind him and began to run, but the footsteps, though they did not seem to come more quickly and were still the regular pace of a man walking, came nearer. Presently he saw an old, white-haired man beside him who said: 'You cannot run away from life', and asked him where he was going. 'I am going home', he said, and the phantom answered, 'I also am going home', and then vanished. Twice in later childhood, and a third time when he had grown to be a young man, he was overtaken by the same phantom and the same words were spoken, but the last time he asked why it had vanished so suddenly. It said that it had not, but that he had supposed that 'changes of state' in himself were 'appearance and disappearance'. It then touched him with one finger upon the side of his head, and the place where he was touched remained ever after without feeling, like those places always searched for at the witches' trials. One remembers 'the touch' and 'the stroke' in the Irish stories.

VI

Allen Cardec, whose books are much more readable than those of Davies, had himself no mediumistic gifts. He gathered the opinions, as he believed, of spirits speaking through a great number of automatist and trance speakers, and all the essential thought of Swedenborg remains, but like Davies, these spirits do not believe in an eternal Hell, and like Blake they describe unhuman races, powers of the elements, and declare that the soul is no creature of the womb having lived many lives upon the earth. The sorrow of death, they tell us again and again, is not so bitter as the sorrow of birth, and had our ears the subtlety we could listen amid the joy of lovers and the pleasure that comes with sleep to the wailing of the spirit betrayed into a cradle. Who was it that wrote: 'O Pythagoras, so good, so wise, so eloquent, upon my last voyage, I taught thee, a soft lad, to splice a rope'? This belief, common among the continental spiritists, is denied by those of England and America, and if one question the voices at a séance they take sides according to the medium's nationality. I have even heard what professed to be the shade of an old English naval officer denying it with a fine phrase: 'I did not leave my oars crossed; I left them side by side'.

VII

Much as a hashish eater will discover in the folds of a curtain a figure beautifully drawn and full of delicate detail all built up out of shadows that show to other eyes, or later to his own, a different form or none, Swedenborg discovered in the Bible the personal symbolism of his vision. If the Bible was upon his side, as it seemed, he had no need of other evidence, but had he lived when modern criticism had lessened its authority, even had he been compelled to say that the primitive beliefs of all peoples were as sacred, he could but have run to his own gift for evidence. He might even have held of some importance his powers of discovering the personal secrets of the dead and set up as medium. Yet it is more likely he had refused, for the medium has his gift from no heightening of all the emotions and intellectual faculties till they seem as it were to take fire, but commonly because they are altogether or in part extinguished while another mind controls his body. He is greatly subject to trance and awakes to remember nothing, whereas the mystic and the saint plead unbroken consciousness. Indeed the author of *Sidonia the Sorceress*, a really learned authority, considered this lack of memory a certain sign of possession by the Devil, though this is too absolute. Only yesterday, while walking in a field, I made up a good sentence with an emotion of triumph, and half a minute after could not even remember what it was about, and several minutes had gone by before I as suddenly found it. For the most part, though not always, it is this unconscious condition of mediumship, a dangerous condition it may be, that seems to make possible 'psychical phenomena' and that overshadowing of the memory by some spirit memory, which Swedenborg thought an accident and unlawful.

In describing and explaining this mediumship and so making intelligible the stories of Aran and Galway I shall say very seldom, 'it is said', or 'Mr. So-and-So reports', or 'it is claimed by the best authors'. I shall write as if what I describe were everywhere established, everywhere accepted, and I had only to remind my reader of what he already knows. Even if incredulous he will give me his fancy for certain minutes, for at the worst I can show him a gorgon or chimera that has never lacked gazers, alleging nothing (and I do not write out of a little knowledge) that is not among the sober beliefs of many men, or obvious inference from those beliefs, and if he wants more—well, he will find it in the best authors.[1]

VIII

All spirits for some time after death, and the 'earth-bound', as they are called, the larvae, as Beaumont, the seventeenth-century Platonist, preferred to call them, those who cannot become disentangled from old habits and desires, for many years, it may be for centuries, keep the shape of their earthly bodies and carry on their old activities, wooing or quarrelling, or totting figures on a table, in a round of dull duties or passionate events. To-day while the great battle in Northern France is still undecided, should I climb to the top of that old house in Soho where a medium is sitting among servant girls, some one would, it may be, ask for news of Gordon Highlander or Munster Fusilier, and the fat old woman would tell in Cockney language how the dead do not yet know they are dead, but stumble on amid visionary smoke and noise, and how angelic spirits seek to awaken them but still in vain.

[1] Besides the well-known books of Aksakof, Myers, Lodge, Flammarion, Flournoy, Maxwell, Albert de Rochas, Lombroso, Madame Bisson, Delanne, etc., I have made considerable use of the researches of Ochorowicz published during the last ten or twelve years in *Annales des Sciences Psychiques* and in the English *Annals of Psychical Science*, and of those of Professor Hyslop published during the last four years in the *Journal* and *Transactions* of the American Society for Psychical Research. I have myself been a somewhat active investigator.

Explorations I

Those who have attained to nobler form, when they appear in the séance-room, create temporary bodies, commonly like to those they wore when living, through some unconscious constraint of memory, or deliberately, that they may be recognised. Davies, in his literal way, said the first sixty feet of the atmosphere was a reflector and that in almost every case it was mere images we spoke with in the séance-room, the spirit itself being far away. The images are made of a substance drawn from the medium, who loses weight, and in a less degree from all present, and for this light must be extinguished or dimmed or shaded with red as in a photographer's room. The image will begin outside the medium's body as a luminous cloud, or in a sort of luminous mud forced from the body, out of the mouth it may be, from the side or from the lower parts of the body.[1] One may see a vague cloud condense and diminish into a head or arm or a whole figure of a man, or to some animal shape.

I remember a story told me by a friend's steward in Galway of the faeries playing at hurley in a field and going in and out of the bodies of two men who stood at either goal. Out of the medium will come perhaps a cripple or a man bent with years and sometimes the apparition will explain that, but for some family

---

[1] Henry More considered that 'the animal spirits' were 'the immediate instruments of the soul in all vital and animal functions' and quotes Harpocrates, who was contemporary with Plato, as saying 'that the mind of man is . . . not nourished from meats and drinks from the belly but by a clear and luminous substance that redounds by separation from the blood'. Ochorowicz thought that certain small oval lights were perhaps the root of personality itself.

portrait, or for what it lit on while rummaging in our memories, it had not remembered its customary clothes or features, or cough or limp or crutch. Sometimes, indeed, there is a strange regularity of feature and we suspect the presence of an image that may never have lived, an artificial beauty that may have shown itself in the Greek mysteries. Has some cast in the Vatican or at Bloomsbury been the model? Or there may float before our eyes a mask as strange and powerful as the lineaments of Servian's *Frowning Man* or of Rodin's *Man with the Broken Nose*. And once a rumour ran among the séance-rooms to the bewilderment of simple believers, that a heavy middle-aged man who took snuff, and wore the costume of a past time, had appeared while a French medium was in his trance, and somebody had recognised the Tartuffe of the Comédie Française. There will be few complete forms, for the dead are economical, and a head, or just enough of the body for recognition, may show itself above hanging folds of drapery that do not seem to cover solid limbs, or a hand or foot is lacking, or it may be that some *revenant* has seized the half-made image of another, and a young girl's arm will be thrust from the withered body of an old man. Nor is every form a breathing and pulsing thing, for some may have a distribution of light and shade not that of the séance-room, flat pictures whose eyes gleam and move; and sometimes material objects are thrown together (drifted in from some neighbour's wardrobe, it may be, and drifted thither again) and an appearance kneaded up out of these, and that luminous mud or vapour almost as

vivid as are those pictures of Antonio Mancini which
have fragments of his paint-tubes embedded for the
high lights into the heavy masses of the paint. Sometimes there are animals, bears frequently for some unknown reason, but most often birds and dogs. If an
image speak it will seldom seem very able or alert, for
they come for recognition only, and their minds are
strained and fragmentary; and should the dogs bark, a
man who knows the language of our dogs may not be
able to say if they are hungry or afraid or glad to meet
their master again. All may seem histrionic or a hollow
show. We are the spectators of a phantasmagoria that
affects the photographic plate or leaves its moulded
image in a preparation of paraffin. We have come to
understand why the Platonists of the sixteenth and
seventeenth centuries, and visionaries like Boehme and
Paracelsus confused imagination with magic, and why
Boehme will have it that it 'creates and substantiates as
it goes'.

Most commonly, however, especially of recent
years, no form will show itself, or but vaguely and
faintly and in no way ponderable, and instead there
will be voices flitting here and there in darkness, or
in the half-light, or it will be the medium himself fallen
into trance who will speak, or without a trance write
from a knowledge and intelligence not his own. Glanvil, the seventeenth-century Platonist, said that the
higher spirits were those least capable of showing
material effects, and it seems plain from certain Polish
experiments that the intelligence of the communicators
increases with their economy of substance and energy.

Swedenborg, Mediums, Desolate Places

Often now among these faint effects one will seem to speak with the very dead. They will speak or write some tongue that the medium does not know and give correctly their forgotten names, or describe events one only verifies after weeks of labour. Here and there amongst them one discovers a wise and benevolent mind that knows a little of the future and can give good advice. They have made, one imagines, from some finer substance than a phosphorescent mud, or cobweb vapour that we can see or handle, images not wholly different from themselves, figures in a galanty show not too strained or too extravagant to speak their very thought.

Yet we never long escape the phantasmagoria nor can long forget that we are among the shape-changers. Sometimes our own minds shape that mysterious substance, which may be life itself, according to desire or constrained by memory, and the dead no longer remembering their own names become the characters in the drama we ourselves have invented. John King, who has delighted melodramatic minds for hundreds of séances with his career on earth as Henry Morgan the Buccaneer, will tell more scientific visitors that he is merely a force, while some phantom long accustomed to a decent name, questioned by some pious Catholic, will admit very cheerfully that he is the Devil. Nor is it only present minds that perplex the shades with phantasy, for friends of Count Albert de Rochas once wrote out names and incidents but to discover that though the surname of the shade that spoke had been historical, Christian name and incidents were from a romance running at the time in some clerical newspaper no one there had ever opened.

All these shadows have drunk from the pool of blood and become delirious. Sometimes they will use the very word and say that we force delirium upon them because we do not still our minds, or that minds not stupefied with the body force them more subtly, for now and again one will withdraw what he has said, saying that he was constrained by the neighbourhood of some more powerful shade.

When I was a boy at Sligo, a stable boy met his late master going round the yard, and having told him to go and haunt the lighthouse, was dismissed by his mistress for sending her husband to haunt so inclement a spot. Ghosts, I was told, must go where they are bid, and all those threatenings by the old *grimoires* to drown some disobedient spirit at the bottom of the Red Sea, and indeed all exorcism and conjuration, affirm that our imagination is king. *Revenants* are, to use the modern term, 'suggestible', and may be studied in the 'trance personalities' of hypnosis and in our dreams which are but hypnosis turned inside out, a modeller's clay for our suggestions, or, if we follow the *Spiritual Diary*, for those of invisible beings. Swedenborg has written that we are each in the midst of a group of associated spirits who sleep when we sleep and become the *dramatis personae* of our dreams, and are always the other will that wrestles with our thought, shaping it to our despite.

We speak, it may be, of the Proteus of antiquity which has to be held or it will refuse its prophecy, and there are many warnings in our ears. 'Stoop not down', says the Chaldean Oracle, 'to the darkly splendid world wherein continually lieth a faithless depth and Hades wrapped in cloud, delighting in unintelligible images', and amid that caprice, among those clouds, there is always legerdemain; we juggle, or lose our money, with the same pack of cards that may reveal the future. The magicians who astonished the Middle Ages with power as incalculable as the fall of a meteor were not so numerous as the more amusing jugglers who could do their marvels at will; and in our day the juggler Houdini, sent to Morocco by the French Government, was able to break the prestige of the dervishes whose fragile wonders were but worked by fasting and prayer.

Sometimes, indeed, a man would be magician, jester, and juggler. In an Irish story a stranger lays three rushes upon the flat of his hand and promises to blow away the inner and leave the others unmoved, and thereupon puts two fingers of his other hand upon the outer ones and blows. However, he will do a more wonderful trick. There are many who can wag both ears, but he can wag one and not the other, and thereafter, when he has everybody's attention, he takes one ear between finger and thumb. But now that the audience are friendly and laughing the moment of miracle has come. He takes out of a bag a skein of silk thread and throws it into the air, until it seems as though one end were made fast to a cloud. Then he takes out of his bag first a hare and then a dog and then a young man and then 'a beautiful, well-dressed young woman' and sends them all running up the thread. Nor, the old writers tell us, does the association of juggler and magician cease after death, which only gives to legerdemain greater power and subtlety. Those who would live again in us, becoming a part of our thoughts and passions, have, it seems, their sport to keep us in good humour, and a young girl who has astonished herself and her friends in some dark séance may, when we have persuaded her to become entranced in a lighted room, tell us that some shade is touching her face, while we can see her touching it with her own hand, or we may discover her, while her eyes are still closed, in some jugglery that implies an incredible mastery of muscular movement. Perhaps too in the fragmentary middle world there are souls that remain always upon the brink, always children. Dr. Ochorowicz finds his experiments upset by a naked girl, one foot one inch high, who is constantly visible to his medium and who claims never to have lived upon the earth. He has photographed her by leaving a camera in an empty room where she had promised to show herself, but is so doubtful of her honesty that he is not sure she did not hold up a print from an illustrated paper in front of the camera. In one of Lady Gregory's stories a countryman is given by a stranger he meets upon the road what seems wholesome and pleasant food, but a little later his stomach turns and

he finds that he has eaten chopped grass, and one remembers Robin Goodfellow and his joint-stool, and
witches' gold that is but dried cow-dung. It is only,
one does not doubt, because of our preoccupation with
a single problem, our survival of the body, and with
the affection that binds us to the dead, that all the
gnomes and nymphs of antiquity have not begun their
tricks again.

x

Plutarch, in his essay on the daimon, describes how
the souls of enlightened men return to be the schoolmasters of the living, whom they influence unseen;
and the mediums, should we ask how they escape the
illusions of that world, claim the protection of their
guides. One will tell you that when she was a little girl
she was minding geese upon some American farm and
an old man came towards her with a queer coat upon
him, and how at first she took him for a living man.
He had come again and again, and now that she has
to earn her living by her gift, he warns her against
deceiving spirits, or if she is working too hard, but
sometimes she will not listen and gets into trouble.
The old witch doctor of Lady Gregory's story learned
his curse from his dead sister whom he met from time
to time, but especially at Hallowe'en, at the end of the
garden, but he had other helpers harsher than she, and
once he was beaten for disobedience.

Reginald Scot gives a fine plan for picking a guide.
You promise some dying man to pray for the repose
of his soul if he will but come to you after death and

give what help you need, while stories of mothers who come at night to be among their orphan children are as common among spiritists as in Galway or in Mayo. A French servant girl once said to a friend of mine who helped her in some love affair: 'You have your studies, we have only our affections'; and this I think is why the walls are broken less often among us than among the poor. Yet according to the doctrine of Soho and Holloway and in Plutarch, those studies that have lessened in us the sap of the world may bring to us good, learned, masterful men who return to see their own or some like work carried to a finish. 'I do think', wrote Sir Thomas Browne, 'that many mysteries ascribed to our own invention have been the courteous revelations of spirits; for those noble essences in heaven bear a friendly regard unto their fellow creatures on earth.'

XI

Much that Lady Gregory has gathered seems but the broken bread of old philosophers, or else of the one sort with the dough they made into their loaves. Were I not ignorant, my Greek gone and my meagre Latin all but gone, I do not doubt that I could find much to the point in Greek, perhaps in old writers on medicine, much in Renaissance or Mediaeval Latin. As it is, I must be content with what has been translated or with the seventeenth-century Platonists who are the handier for my purpose because they found in the affidavits and confessions of the witch trials, descriptions like those in our Connacht stories. I have Henry

Swedenborg, *Mediums*, *Desolate Places*

More in his verse and in his prose and I have Henry More's two friends, Joseph Glanvil, and Cudworth in his *Intellectual System of the Universe*, three volumes violently annotated by an opposed theologian; and two essays by Mr. G. R. S. Mead clipped out of his magazine, *The Quest*. These writers quote much from Plotinus and Porphyry and Plato and from later writers, especially Synesius and John Philoponus in whom the School of Plato came to an end in the seventh century.

We should not suppose that our souls began at birth, for as Henry More has said, a man might as well think 'from souls new souls' to bring as 'to press the sunbeams in his fist' or 'wring the rainbow till it dye his hands'. We have within us an 'airy body' or 'spirit body' which was our only body before our birth as it will be again when we are dead and its 'plastic power' has shaped our terrestrial body as some day it may shape apparition and ghost. Porphyry is quoted by Mr. Mead as saying that 'Souls who love the body attach a moist spirit to them and condense it like a cloud', and so become visible, and so are all apparitions of the dead made visible; though necromancers, according to Henry More, can ease and quicken this condensation 'with reek of oil, meal, milk, and such like gear, wine, water, honey'. One remembers that Dr. Ochorowicz's naked imp once described how she filled out an appearance of herself by putting a piece of blotting paper where her stomach should have been and that the blotting paper became damp because, as she said, a materialisation, until it is completed, is a damp vapour. This airy body which so compresses vapour, Philoponus says, 'takes the shape of the physical body as water takes the shape of the vessel that it has been frozen in', but it is capable of endless transformations, for 'in itself it has no especial form', but Henry More believes that it has an especial form, for its 'plastic power' cannot but find the human form most 'natural', though 'vehemency of desire to alter the figure into another representation may make the appearance to resemble some other creature; but no forced thing can last long'. 'The better genii' therefore prefer to show 'in a human shape yet not it may be with all the lineaments' but with such as are 'fit for this separate state' (separate from the body, that is) or are 'requisite to perfect the visible features of a person', desire and imagination adding clothes and ornament. The materialisation, as we would say, has but enough likeness for recognition. It may be that More but copies Philoponus who thought the shade's habitual form, the image that it was, as it were, frozen in for a time, could be again 'coloured and shaped by fantasy', and that 'it is probable that when the soul desires to manifest it shapes itself, setting its own imagination in movement, or even that it is probable with the help of daemonic co-operation that it appears and again becomes invisible, becoming condensed and rarefied'. Porphyry, Philoponus adds, gives Homer as his authority for the belief that souls after death live among images of their experience upon earth, phantasms impressed upon the spirit body. While Synesius, who lived at the end of the fourth century and had Hypatia among his friends, also describes the spirit body as capable of taking any form and so of enabling us after death to work out our purgation; and says that for this reason the oracles have likened the state after death to the images of a dream. The seventeenth-century English translation of Cornelius Agrippa's *De Occulta Philosophia* was once so famous that it found its way into the hands of Irish farmers and wandering Irish tinkers, and it may be that Agrippa influenced the common thought when he wrote that the evil dead see represented 'in the fantastic reason' those shapes of life that are 'the more turbulent and furious . . . sometimes of the heavens falling on their heads, sometimes of their being consumed with the violence of flames, sometimes of being drowned in a gulf, sometimes of being swallowed up in the earth, sometimes of being changed into divers kinds of beasts . . . and sometimes of being taken and tormented by demons . . . as if they were in a dream'. The ancients, he writes, have called these souls 'hobgoblins', and Orpheus has called them 'the people of dreams', saying 'the gates of Pluto cannot be unlocked; within is a people of dreams'. They are a dream indeed that has place and weight and measure, and seeing that their bodies are of an actual air, they cannot, it was held, but travel in wind and set the straws and the dust twirling; though being of the wind's weight they need not, Dr. Henry More considers, so much as feel its ruffling, or if they should do so, they can shelter in a house or behind a wall, or gather into themselves as it were, out of the gross wind and vapour. But there are good dreams among the airy people, though we cannot properly name that a dream which is but analogical of the deep unimaginable virtues and has, therefore, stability and a common measure. Henry More stays himself in the midst of the dry learned and abstract writing of his treatise *The Immortality of the Soul* to praise 'their comely carriage . . . their graceful dancing, their melodious singing and playing with an accent so sweet and soft as if we should imagine air itself to compose lessons and send forth musical sounds without the help of any terrestrial instrument', and imagines them at their revels in the thin upper air where the earth can but seem 'a fleecy and milky light' as the moon to us, and he cries out that they 'sing and play and dance together, reaping the lawful pleasures of the very animal life, in a far higher degree than we are capable of in this world, for everything here does, as it were, taste of the cask and has some measure of foulness on it'.

There is, however, another birth or death when we pass from the airy to the shining or ethereal body, and 'in the airy the soul may inhabit for many ages and in the ethereal for ever', and indeed it is the ethereal body which is the root 'of all that natural warmth in all generations' though in us it can no longer shine. It lives while in its true condition an unimaginable life and is sometimes described as of 'a round or oval figure' and as always circling among gods and among the stars, and sometimes as having more dimensions than our penury can comprehend.

Last winter Mr. Ezra Pound was editing the late Professor Fenollosa's translations of the Noh Drama of Japan, and read me a great deal of what he was doing. Nearly all that my fat old woman in Soho learns from her familiars is there in an unsurpassed lyric poetry and in strange and poignant fables once danced or sung in the houses of nobles. In one a priest asks his way of some girls who are gathering herbs. He asks if it is a long road to town; and the girls begin to lament over their hard lot gathering cress in a cold wet bog where they sink up to their knees and to compare themselves with ladies in the big town who only pull the cress in sport, and need not when the cold wind is flapping their sleeves. He asks what village he has come to and if a road near by leads to the village of Ono. A girl replies that nobody can know that name without knowing the road, and another says: 'Who would not know that name, written on so many pictures, and know the pine trees they are always drawing?' Presently the cold drives away all the girls but one and she tells the priest she is a spirit and has taken solid form that she may speak with him and ask his help. It is her tomb that has made Ono so famous. Conscience-struck at having allowed two young men to fall in love with her she refused to choose between them. Her father said he would give her to the best archer. At the match to settle it both sent their arrows through the same wing of a mallard and were declared equal. She being ashamed and miserable because she had caused so much trouble and for the death of the mallard, took her own life. That, she thought, would end the trouble, but her lovers killed themselves beside her tomb, and now she suffered all manner of horrible punishments. She had but to lay her hand upon a pillar to make it burst into flame; she was perpetually burning. The priest tells her that if she can but cease to believe in her punishments they will cease to exist. She listens in gratitude but she cannot cease to believe, and while she is speaking they come upon her and she rushes away enfolded in flames. Her imagination has created all those terrors out of a scruple, and one remembers how Lake Harris, who led Laurence Oliphant such a dance, once said to a shade, 'How did you know you were damned?' and that it answered, 'I saw my own thoughts going past me like blazing ships'.

In a play still more rich in lyric poetry a priest is wandering in a certain ancient village. He describes the journey and the scene, and from time to time the chorus sitting at the side of the stage sings its comment. He meets with two ghosts, the one holding a red stick, the other a piece of coarse cloth, and both dressed in the fashion of a past age, but as he is a stranger he supposes them villagers wearing the village fashion. They sing as if muttering, 'We are entangled up—whose fault was it, dear? Tangled up as the grass patterns are tangled up in this coarse cloth, or that insect which lives and chirrups in dried seaweed. We do not know where are to-day our tears in the undergrowth of this eternal wilderness. We neither wake nor sleep and passing our nights in sorrow, which is in the end a vision, what are these scenes of spring to us? This thinking in sleep for someone who has no thought for you, is it more than a dream? And yet surely it is the natural way of love. In our hearts there is much, and in our bodies nothing, and we do nothing at all, and only the waters of the river of tears flow quickly.' To the priest they seem two married people, but he cannot understand why they carry the red stick and the coarse cloth. They ask him to listen to a story. The two young people had lived in that village long ago and night after night for three years the young man had offered a charmed red stick, the token of love, at the young girl's window, but she pretended not to see and went on weaving. So the young man died and was buried in a cave with his charmed red sticks and presently the girl died too, and now because they were never married in life they were unmarried in their death. The priest, who does not yet understand that it is their own tale, asks to be shown the cave, and says it will be a fine tale to tell when he goes home. The chorus describes the journey to the cave. The lovers go in front, the priest follows. They are all day pushing through long grasses that hide the narrow paths. They ask the way of a farmer who is mowing. Then night falls and it is cold and frosty. It is stormy and the leaves are falling and their feet sink into the muddy places made by the autumn showers; there is a long shadow on the slope of the mountain, and an owl in the ivy of the pine tree. They have found the cave and it is dyed with the red sticks of love to the colour of 'the orchids and chrysanthemums which hide the mouth of a fox's hole'; and now the two lovers have 'slipped into the shadow of the cave'. Left alone and too cold to sleep the priest decides to spend the night in prayer. He prays that the lovers may at last be one.

Explorations I

Presently he sees to his wonder that the cave is lighted up 'where people are talking and setting up looms for spinning and painted red sticks'. The ghosts creep out and thank him for his prayer and say that through his pity 'the love promises of long past incarnations' find fulfilment in a dream. Then he sees the love story unfolded in a vision and the chorus compares the sound of weaving to the clicking of crickets. A little later he is shown the bridal room and the lovers drinking from the bridal cup. The dawn is coming. It is reflected in the bridal cup and now singers, cloth, and stick break and dissolve like a dream, and there is nothing but 'a deserted grave on a hill where morning winds are blowing through the pine'.

I remember that Aran story of the lovers who came after death to the priest for marriage. It is not uncommon for a ghost, 'a control' as we say, to come to a medium to discover some old earthly link to fit into a new chain. It wishes to meet a ghostly enemy to win pardon or to renew an old friendship. Our service to the dead is now narrowed to our prayers, but may be as wide as our imagination. I have known a control to warn a medium to unsay her promise to an old man, to whom, that she might be rid of him, she had promised herself after death. What is promised here in our loves or in a witch's bond may be fulfilled in a life which is a dream. If our terrestrial condition is, as it seems, the territory of choice and of cause, the one ground for all seed-sowing, it is plain why our imagination has command over the dead and why they must keep from sight and earshot. At the British Museum at the end of the Egyptian Room and near the stairs are two statues, one an august decoration, one a most accurate-looking naturalistic portrait. The august decoration was for a public site, the other, like all the naturalistic art of the epoch, for burial beside a mummy. So buried it was believed, the Egyptologists tell us, to be of service to the dead. I have no doubt it helped a dead man to build out of his spirit-body a recognisable apparition, and that all boats or horses or weapons or their models buried in ancient tombs were helps for a flagging memory or a too weak fancy to imagine and so substantiate the old surroundings. A shepherd at Doneraile told me some years ago of an aunt of his who showed herself after death stark naked and bid her relatives to make clothes and give them to a beggar, and while remembering her.[1] Presently she appeared again wearing the clothes and thanked them.

XII

Certainly in most writings before our time the body of an apparition was held for a brief, artificial, dreamy, half-living thing. One is always meeting such phrases as Sir Thomas Browne's 'they steal or contrive a body'. A passage in the *Paradiso* comes to mind describing Dante in conversation with the blessed among their spheres, although they are but in appearance there,

[1] Herodotus has an equivalent tale. Periander, because the ghost of his wife complained that it was 'cold and naked', got the women of Corinth together in their best clothes and had them stripped and their clothes burned.

being in truth in the petals of the yellow rose; and another in the *Odyssey* where Odysseus speaks not with 'the mighty Heracles', but with his phantom, for he himself 'hath joy at the banquet among the deathless gods and had to wife Hebe of the fair ankles, child of Zeus and Hera of the golden sandals', while all about the phantom 'there was a clamour of the dead, as it were fowls flying everywhere in fear, and he, like black night with bow uncased, and shaft upon the string, fiercely glancing around like one in the act to shoot'.

1914

II
THE IRISH DRAMATIC MOVEMENT
1901-1919

NOTE

The Irish Dramatic Movement is part of the contents of
Samhain, Beltaine, The Arrow, occasional publications
connected with the Irish Theatre. A very active iras-
cible friend of mine once wrote that these publications
'made a man of W. B. Yeats', meaning, I suppose,
that they had rescued me from such thoughts as occupy
the rest of this volume [*Plays and Controversies*]. I do
not agree with him; I doubt the value of the embittered
controversy that was to fill my life for years, but
certainly they rang down the curtain so far as I was
concerned on what was called 'The Celtic Movement'.
An 'Irish Movement' took its place.—(1931).

SAMHAIN: 1901

WHEN Lady Gregory, Mr. Edward Martyn, and myself planned the Irish Literary Theatre, we decided that it should be carried on in the form we had projected for three years. We thought that three years would show whether the country desired to take up the project, and make it a part of the national life, and that we, at any rate, could return to our proper work, in which we did not include theatrical management, at the end of that time. A little later, Mr. George Moore[1] joined us; and, looking back now upon our work, I doubt if it could have been done at all without his knowledge of the stage; and certainly if the performances of this present year bring our adventure to a successful close, a chief part of the credit will be his. Many, however, have helped us in various degrees, for in Ireland just now one has only to discover an idea that seems of service to the country for friends and helpers to start up on every hand. While we needed guarantors we had them in plenty, and though Mr. Edward Martyn's public spirit made it unnecessary to call upon them, we thank them none the less.

Whether the Irish Literary Theatre has a successor made on its own model or not, we can claim that a dramatic movement which will not die has been started. When we began our work, we tried in vain to get a play

[1] Both Mr. Moore and Mr. Martyn dropped out of the movement after the third performance at the Irish Literary Theatre in 1901.—1908.

in Gaelic. We could not even get a condensed version of the dialogue of Oisin and Patrick. We wrote to Gaelic enthusiasts in vain, for their imagination had not yet turned towards the stage, and now there are excellent Gaelic plays by Dr. Douglas Hyde, by Father O'Leary, by Father Dineen, and by Mr. MacGinlay; and the Gaelic League has had a competition for a one-act play in Gaelic, with what results I do not know. There have been successful performances of plays in Gaelic at Dublin and at Macroom, and at Letterkenny, and I think at other places; and Mr. Fay has got together an excellent little company which plays both in Gaelic and in English. I may say, for I am perhaps writing an epitaph, and epitaphs should be written in a genial spirit, that we have turned a great deal of Irish imagination towards the stage. We could not have done this if our movement had not opened a way of expression for an impulse that was in the people themselves. The truth is that the Irish people are at that precise stage of their history when imagination, shaped by many stirring events, desires dramatic expression. One has only to listen to a recitation of Raftery's *Argument with Death* at some country Feis to understand this. When Death makes a good point, or Raftery a good point, the audience applaud delightedly, and applaud, not, as a London audience would, some verbal dexterity, some piece of smartness, but the movements of a simple and fundamental comedy. One sees it too in the reciters themselves, whose acting is at times all but perfect in its vivid simplicity. I heard a little Claddagh girl tell a folk-story at Galway Feis with a restraint and a delightful energy that could hardly have been bettered by the most careful training.

The organisation of this movement is of immediate importance. Some of our friends propose that somebody begin at once to get a small stock company together, and that he invite, let us say, Mr. Benson, to find us certain well-trained actors, Irish if possible, but well trained of a certainty, who will train our actors, and take the more difficult parts at the beginning. These friends contend that it is necessary to import our experts at the beginning, for our company must be able to compete with travelling English companies, but that a few years will be enough to make many competent Irish actors. The Corporation of Dublin should be asked, they say, to give a small annual sum of money, such as they give to the Academy of Music; and the Corporations of Cork and Limerick and Waterford, and other provincial towns, to give small endowments in the shape of a hall and attendants and lighting for a week or two out of every year; and the Technical Board to give a small annual sum of money to a school of acting which would teach fencing and declamation, and gesture and the like. The stock company would perform in Dublin perhaps three weeks in spring, and three weeks in autumn, and go on tour the rest of the time through Ireland, and through the English towns where there is a large Irish population. It would perform plays in Irish and English, and also, it is proposed, the masterpieces of the world, making a point of performing Spanish, and Scandinavian, and French, and perhaps Greek masterpieces rather more than Shakespeare, for Shakespeare is seen, not well done indeed, but not unendurably ill done, in the theatre of commerce. It would do its best to give Ireland a hardy and shapely national character by opening the doors to the four winds of the world, instead of leaving the door that is towards the east wind open alone. Certainly, the national character, which is so essentially different from the English that Spanish and French influences may well be most healthy, is at present like one of those miserable thorn-bushes by the sea that are all twisted to one side by some prevailing wind.

It is contended that there is no reason why the company should not be as successful as similar companies in Germany and Scandinavia, and that it would be even of commercial advantage to Dublin by making it a pleasanter place to live in, besides doing incalculable good to the whole intellect of the country. One, at any rate, of those who press the project on us has much practical knowledge of the stage and of theatrical management, and knows what is possible and what is not possible.

Others among our friends, and among these are some who have had more than their share of the hard work which has built up the intellectual movement in Ireland, argue that a theatre of this kind would require too much money to be free, that it could not touch on politics, the most vital passion and vital interest of the country, as they say, and that the attitude of continual compromise between conviction and interest, which it would necessitate, would become demoralising to everybody concerned, especially at moments of political excitement. They tell us that the war between an Irish Ireland and an English Ireland is about to become much fiercer, to divide families and friends, it may be, and that the organisations that will lead in the war must be able to say everything the people are thinking. They would have Irishmen give their plays to a company like Mr. Fay's, when they are within its power, and if not, to Mr. Benson or to any other travelling company which will play them in Ireland without committees, where everybody compromises a little. In this way, they contend, we would soon build up an Irish theatre from the ground, escaping to some extent the conventions of the ordinary theatre, and those English voices which give a foreign air to our words. And though we might have to wait some years, we would get even the masterpieces of the world in good time. Let us, they think, be poor enough to whistle at the thief who would take away some of our thoughts, and after Mr. Fay has taken his company, as he plans, through the villages and the country towns, he will get the little endowment that is necessary, or if he does not, some other will.

I do not know what Lady Gregory or Mr. Moore thinks of these projects. I am not going to say what I think. I have spent much of my time and more of my thought these last ten years on Irish organisation, and now that the Irish Literary Theatre has completed the plan I had in my head ten years ago, I want to go down again to primary ideas. I want to put old stories into verse, and if I put them into dramatic verse it will matter less to me henceforward who plays them than what they play, and how they play. I hope to get our Heroic Age into verse, and to solve some problems of the speaking of verse to musical notes.

There is only one question which is raised by the two projects I have described on which I will give an opinion. It is of the first importance that those among us who want to write for the stage should study the dramatic masterpieces of the world. If they can get them on the stage, so much the better, but study them they must if Irish drama is to mean anything to Irish intellect. At the present moment, Shakespeare being the only great dramatist known to Irish writers has made them cast their work too much on the English model. Miss Milligan's *Red Hugh*, which was successfully acted in Dublin the other day, had no business to be in two scenes; and Father O'Leary's *Tadg Saor*, despite its most vivid and picturesque, though far too rambling dialogue, shows in its half-dozen changes of scene the influence of the same English convention, which arose when there was no scene-painting, and is often a difficulty where there is, and is always an absurdity in a farce of thirty minutes, breaking up the emotion and sending our thoughts here and there. Mr. MacGinlay's *Elis agus an bhean deirce* has not this defect, and though I had not Irish enough to follow it when I saw it played, and excellently played, by Mr. Fay's company, I could see from the continual laughter of the audience that it held them with an unbroken emotion. The best Gaelic play after Dr. Hyde's is, I think, Father Dineen's *Creadeamh agus Gorta*, and though it changes the scene a little oftener than is desirable under modern conditions, it does not remind me of an English model. It reminds me of Calderón by its treatment of a religious subject, and by something in Father Dineen's sympathy with the people that is like his. But I think if Father Dineen had studied that great Catholic dramatist he would not have failed, as he has done once or twice, to remember some necessary detail of a situation. In the first scene he makes a servant ask his fellow-servants about things he must have known as well as they; and he loses a dramatic moment in his third scene by forgetting that Seagan Gorm has a pocketful of money which he would certainly, being the man he was, have offered to the woman he was urging into temptation. The play towards the end changes from prose to verse, and the reverence and simplicity of the verse makes one think of a mediaeval miracle play. The subject has been so much a part of Irish life that it was bound to be used by an Irish dramatist, though certainly I shall always prefer plays which attack a more eternal devil than the proselytiser. He has been defeated, and the arts are at their best when they are busy with battles that can never be won. It is possible, however, that we may have to deal with passing issues until we have re-created the imaginative tradition of Ireland, and filled the popular imagination again with saints and heroes. These short plays (though they would be better if their writers knew the masters of their craft) are very dramatic as they are, but there is no chance of our writers of Gaelic, or our writers of English, doing good plays of any length if they do not study the masters. If Irish dramatists had studied the romantic plays of Ibsen, the one great master the modern stage has produced, they would not have sent the Irish Literary Theatre imitations of Boucicault, who had no relation to literature, and Father O'Leary would have put his gift for dialogue, a gift certainly greater than, let us say, Mr. Jones's or Mr. Grundy's, to better use than the writing of that long, rambling dramatisation of the *Tain bo Cuailgne*, in which I hear in the midst of the exuberant Gaelic dialogue the worn-out conventions of English poetic drama. The moment we leave even a little the folk-tradition of the peasant, as we must in drama, if we do not know the best that has been said and written in the world, we do not even know ourselves. It is no great labour to know the best dramatic literature, for there is very little of it. We Irish must know it all, for we have, I think, far greater need of the severe discipline of French and Scandinavian drama than of Shakespeare's luxuriance.

If the *Diarmuid and Grania* and the *Casadh an t-Sugain* are not well constructed, it is not because Mr. Moore and Dr. Hyde and myself do not understand the importance of construction, and Mr. Martyn has shown by the triumphant construction of *The Heather Field* how much thought he has given to the matter; but for the most part our Irish plays read as if they were made without a plan, without a 'scenario', as it is called. European drama began so, but the European drama had centuries for its growth, while our art must grow to perfection in a generation or two if it is not to be smothered before it is well above the earth by what is merely commercial in the art of England.

Let us learn construction from the masters, and dialogue from ourselves. A relation of mine has just written me a letter, in which he says: 'It is natural to an Irishman to write plays; he has an inborn love of dialogue and sound about him, of a dialogue as lively, gallant, and passionate as in the times of great Eliza. In these days an Englishman's dialogue is that of an amateur—that is to say, it is never spontaneous. I mean in *real life*. Compare it with an Irishman's, above all a poor Irishman's, reckless abandonment and naturalness, or compare it with the only fragment that has come down to us of Shakespeare's own conversation.' (He is remembering a passage in, I think, Ben Jonson's *Underwoods*). 'Petty commerce and puritanism have brought to the front the wrong type of Englishman; the lively, joyous, yet tenacious man has transferred himself to Ireland. We have him and we will keep him unless the combined nonsense of . . . and . . . and . . . succeed in suffocating him.'

In Dublin the other day I saw a poster advertising a play by a Miss . . . under the patronage of certain titled people. I had little hope of finding any reality in it, but I sat out two acts. Its dialogue was above the average, though the characters were the old rattle-traps of the stage, the wild Irish girl, and the Irish servant, and the bowing Frenchman, and the situations had all been squeezed dry generations ago. One saw everywhere the shadowy mind of a woman of the Irish upper classes as they have become to-day, but under it all there was a kind of life, though it was but the life of a string and a wire. I do not know who Miss . . . is, but I know that she is young, for I saw her portrait in a weekly paper, and I think that she is clever enough to make her work of some importance. If she goes on doing bad work she will make money, perhaps a great deal of money, but she will do a little harm to her country. If, on the other hand, she gets into an original relation with life, she will, perhaps, make no money, and she will certainly have her class against her.

The Irish upper classes put everything into a money measure. When any one among them begins to write or paint they ask him, 'How much money have you made?' 'Will it pay?' Or they say, 'If you do this or that you will make more money'. The poor Irish clerk or shopboy,[1] who writes verses or articles in his brief leisure, writes for the glory of God and of his country; and because his motive is high, there is not one vulgar thought in the countless little ballad books that have been written from Callanan's day to this. They are often clumsily written, for they are in English, and if you have not read a great deal, it is difficult to write well in

[1] The mood has gone, with Fenianism and its wild hopes. The National movement has been commercialised in the last few years. How much real ideality is but hidden for a time one cannot say.—March 1908.

a language which has been long separated from the 'folk-speech'; but they have not a thought a proud and simple man would not have written. The writers were poor men, but they left that money measure to the Irish upper classes. <u>All Irish writers have to choose whether they will write as the upper classes have done, not to express but to exploit this country; or join the intellectual movement which has raised the cry that was heard in Russia in the 'seventies, the cry, 'To the people'.</u>

Moses was little good to his people until he had killed an Egyptian; and for the most part a writer or public man of the upper classes is useless to this country till he has done something that separates him from his class. We wish to grow peaceful crops, but we must dig our furrows with the sword.

Our plays this year will be produced by Mr. Benson at the Gaiety Theatre on October the 21st, and on some of the succeeding days. They are Dr. Douglas Hyde's *Casadh an t-Sugain*, which is founded on a well-known Irish story of a wandering poet; and *Diarmuid and Grania*, a play in three acts and in prose by Mr. George Moore and myself, which is founded on the most famous of all Irish stories, the story of the lovers whose beds were the cromlechs. The first act of *Diarmuid and Grania* is in the great banqueting-hall of Tara, and the second and third are on the slopes of Ben Bulben in Sligo. We do not think there is anything in either play to offend anybody, but we make no promises. We thought our plays inoffensive last year and the year before, but we were accused the one year of sedition, and the other of heresy.

I have called this little collection of writings *Samhain*, the old name for the beginning of winter, because our plays this year are in October, and because our Theatre is coming to an end in its present shape.

Samhain : 1902

SAMHAIN: 1902

THE Irish Literary Theatre wound up its three years of experiment last October with *Diarmuid and Grania*, which was played by Mr. Benson's company, Mr. Benson himself playing Diarmuid with poetry and fervour, and *Casadh an t-Sugain*, played by Dr. Hyde and some members of the Gaelic League. *Diarmuid and Grania* drew large audiences, but its version of the legend was a good deal blamed by critics, who knew only the modern text of the story. There are two versions, and the play was fully justified by Irish and Scottish folk-lore, and by certain early Irish texts, which do not see Grania through very friendly eyes. Any critic who is interested in so dead a controversy can look at the folk-tales quoted by Campbell in, I think, *West Highland Superstitions*, and at the fragments translated by Kuno Meyer, at page 458 of vol. i. of the *Zeitschrift für Keltische Philologie*. Dr. Hyde's play, on the other hand, pleased everybody, and has been played a good many times in a good many places since. It was the first play in Irish played in a theatre, and did much towards making plays a necessary part of Irish propaganda.

The Irish Literary Theatre has given place to a company of Irish actors. Its committee saw them take up the work all the more gladly because it had not formed them or influenced them. A dramatic society with guarantors and patrons can never have more than a passing use, because it can never be quite free; and it is not successful until it is able to say it is no longer wanted. Amateur actors will perform for *Cumann na n-Gaedheal* plays chosen by themselves, and written by A. E., by Mr. Cousins, by Mr. Ryan, by Mr. MacGinlay, and by myself. These plays will be given at the Antient Concert Rooms at the end of October, but the National Theatrical Company will repeat their successes with new work in a very little hall they have hired in Camden Street. If they could afford it they would have hired some bigger house, but, after all, M. Antoine founded his *Théâtre Libre* with a company of amateurs in a hall that only held three hundred people.

The first work of theirs to get much attention was their performance, last spring, at the invitation of *Inghinidhe na h-Eireann*, of A. E.'s *Deirdre*, and my *Cathleen ni Houlihan*. They had Miss Maud Gonne's help, and it was a fine thing for so beautiful a woman to consent to play my poor old Cathleen, and she played with nobility and tragic power. She showed herself as good in tragedy as Dr. Hyde is in comedy, and stirred a large audience very greatly. The whole company played well, too, but it was in *Deirdre* that they interested me most. They showed plenty of inexperience, especially in the minor characters, but it was the first performance I had seen since I understood these things in which the actors kept still enough to give poetical writing its full effect upon the stage. I had imagined such acting, though I had not seen it, and had once asked a dramatic company to let me rehearse them in barrels that they might forget gesture and have their minds free to think of speech for a while. The barrels, I thought, might be on castors, so that I could shove them about with a pole when the action required it. The other day I saw Sarah Bernhardt and De Max in *Phèdre*, and understood where Mr. Fay, who stage-manages the National Theatrical Company, had gone for his model.[1] For long periods the performers would merely stand and pose, and I once counted twenty-seven quite slowly before anybody on a fairly well-filled stage moved, as it seemed, so much as an eyelash. The periods of stillness were generally shorter, but I frequently counted seventeen, eighteen, or twenty before there was a movement. I noticed, too, that the gestures had a rhythmic progression. Sarah Bernhardt would keep her hands clasped over, let us say, her right breast for some time, and then move them to the other side, perhaps, lowering her chin till it touched her hands, and then, after another long stillness, she would unclasp them and hold one out, and so on, not lowering them till she had exhausted all the gestures of uplifted hands. Through one long scene De Max, who was quite as fine, never lifted his hand above his elbow, and it was only when the emotion came to its climax that he raised it to his breast. Beyond them stood a crowd of white-robed men who never moved at all, and the whole scene had the nobility of Greek sculpture, and an extraordinary reality and intensity. It was the most beautiful thing I had ever seen upon the stage, and made me understand, in a new

---

[1] An illusion, as he himself explained to me. He had never seen *Phèdre*. The players were quiet and natural, because they did not know what else to do. They had not learned to go wrong.—March 1908.

way, that saying of Goethe's which is understood everywhere but in England, 'Art is art because it is not nature'. Of course, our amateurs were poor and crude beside those great actors, perhaps the greatest in Europe, but they followed them as well as they could, and got an audience of artisans, for the most part, to admire them for doing it. I heard somebody who sat behind me say, 'They have got rid of all the nonsense'.

I thought the costumes and scenery, which were designed by A. E. himself, good, too, though I did not think them simple enough. They were more simple than ordinary stage costumes and scenery, but I would like to see poetical drama, which tries to keep at a distance from daily life that it may keep its emotion untroubled, staged with but two or three colours. The background, especially in small theatres, where its form is broken up and lost when the stage is at all crowded, should, I think, be thought out as one thinks out the background of a portrait. One often needs nothing more than a single colour, with perhaps a few shadowy forms to suggest wood or mountain. Even on a large stage one should leave the description of the poet free to call up the martlet's procreant cradle or what he will. But I have written enough about decorative scenery elsewhere, and will probably lecture on that and like matters before we begin the winter's work.

The performances of *Deirdre* and *Cathleen ni Houlihan*, which will be repeated in the Antient Concert Rooms, drew so many to hear them that great numbers

were turned away from the doors of Saint Theresa's
Hall. Like the plays of the Irish Literary Theatre, they
started unexpected discussion. Mr. Standish O'Grady,
who had done more than any other to make us know
the old legends, wrote in his *All Ireland Review* that old
legends could not be staged without danger of 'banish-
ing the soul of the land'. The old Irish had many wives,
for instance, and we had best leave their histories to the
vagueness of legend. How could uneducated people
understand heroes who lived amid such different circumstances? And so we were to 'leave heroic cycles
alone, and not to bring them down to the crowd'. A. E.
replied in *The United Irishman* with an impassioned
letter. 'The old, forgotten music' he writes about in his
letter is, I think, that regulated music of speech at which
both he and I have been working, though on somewhat
different principles. I have been working with Miss Farr
and Mr. Arnold Dolmetsch, who has made a psaltery
for the purpose, to perfect a music of speech which can
be recorded in something like ordinary musical notes;
while A. E. has got a musician to record little chants
with intervals much smaller than those of modern
music.

After the production of these plays the most important Irish dramatic event was, no doubt, the acting of
Dr. Hyde's *An Posadh*, in Galway. Through an accident it had been very badly rehearsed, but his own acting made amends. One could hardly have had a play
that grew more out of the life of the people who saw it.
There may have been old men in that audience who
remembered its hero the poet Raftery, and there was

nobody there who had not come from hearing his poems repeated at the Galway Feis. I think from its effect upon the audience that this play, in which the chief Gaelic poet of our time celebrates his forerunner in simplicity, will be better liked in Connacht at any rate than even *Casadh an t-Sugain*. His *Tincear agus Sidheog*, acted in Mr. Moore's garden, at the time of the Oireachtas, is a very good play, but is, I think, the least interesting of his plays as literature. His imagination, which is essentially the folk-imagination, needs a looser construction, and probably a more crowded stage. A play that gets its effect by keeping close to one idea reminds us, when it comes from the hands of a folk-poet, of Blake's saying, that 'Improvement makes straight roads, but the crooked roads are the roads of genius'. The idea loses the richness of its own life, while it destroys the wayward life of his mind by bringing it under too stern a law. Nor could charming verses make amends for that second kiss in which there was profanation, and for that abounding black bottle. Did not M. Tribulat Bonhomet discover that one spot of ink would kill a swan?

Among the other plays in Irish acted during the year, Father Dineen's *Tobar Draoidheachta* is probably the best. He has given up the many scenes of his *Creadeamh agus Gorta*, and has written a play in one scene, which, as it can be staged without much trouble, has already been played in several places. One admires its *naïveté* as much as anything else. Father Dineen, who, no doubt, remembers how Finn mac Cumhal when a child was put in a field to catch hares and keep him out of mischief, has sent the rival lovers of his play, when he wanted them off the scene for a moment, to catch a hare that has crossed the stage. When they return the good lover is carrying it by the heels, and modestly compares it to a lame jackass. One rather likes this bit of nonsense when one comes to it, for in that world of folk-imagination one thing seems as possible as another. On the other hand, there is a moment of beautiful dramatic tact. The lover gets a letter telling of the death of a relative in America, for whom he has no particular affection, and who has left him a fortune. He cannot lament, for that would be insincere, and his first words must not be rejoicing. Father Dineen has found for him the one beautiful thing he could say: 'It's a lonesome thing death is'. With, perhaps, less beauty than there is in the closing scene of *Creadeamh agus Gorta*, the play has more fancy and a more sustained energy.

Father Peter O'Leary has written a play in his usual number of scenes which has not been published, but has been acted amid much Munster enthusiasm. But neither that nor *La an Amadan*, which has also been acted, is likely to have any long life on our country stages. A short play, with many changes of scene, is a nuisance in any theatre, and often an impossibility on our poor little stages. Some kind of play, in English, by Mr. Standish O'Grady, has been acted in the open air in Kilkenny. I have not seen it, and I cannot understand anything by the accounts of it, except that there were magic-lantern slides and actors on horseback, and Mr. Standish O'Grady as an Elizabethan night-watchman, speaking prologues, and a contented audience of two or three thousand people.

As we do not think that a play can be worth acting and not worth reading, all our plays will be published in time. Some have been printed in *The United Irishman* and *The All Ireland Review*. I have put my *Cathleen ni Houlihan* and a little play by Dr. Hyde into this *Samhain*. Once already this year I have had what somebody has called the noble pleasure of praising, and I can praise this *Lost Saint* with as good a conscience as I had when I wrote of *Cuchulain of Muirthemne*. I would always admire it, but just now, when I have been thinking that literature should return to its old habit of describing desirable things, I am in the mood to be stirred by that old man gathering up food for fowl with his heart full of love, and by those children who are so full of the light-hearted curiosity of childhood, and by that schoolmaster who has mixed prayer with his gentle punishments. It seems natural that so beautiful a prayer as that of the old saint should have come out of a life so full of innocence and peace. One could hardly have thought out the play in English, for those phrases of a traditional simplicity and of a too deliberate prettiness which become part of an old language would have arisen between the mind and the story. We might even have made something as unreal as the sentimental schoolmaster of the Scottish novelist, and how many children who are but literary images would we have had to hunt out of our minds before meeting with those little children? Even if one could have thought it out in English one could not have written it in English, unless perhaps

in that dialect which Dr. Hyde had already used in
the prose narrative that flows about his *Love Songs of
Connacht.*

Dr. Hyde has written a little play about the birth of
Christ which has the same beauty and simplicity. These
plays remind me of my first reading of the *Love Songs
of Connacht.* The prose parts of that book were to me,
as they were to many others, the coming of a new power
into literature. I find myself now, as I found myself then, grudging to propaganda, to scholarship, to
oratory, however necessary, a genius which might in
modern Irish or in that idiom of the English-speaking
countrypeople discover a new region for the mind to
wander in. In Ireland, where we have so much to prove
and to disprove, we are ready to forget that the creation
of an emotion of beauty is the only kind of literature
that justifies itself. Books of literary propaganda and
literary history are merely preparations for the creation
or understanding of such an emotion. It is necessary to
put so much in order, to clear away so much, to explain
so much, that somebody may be moved by a thought
or an image that is inexplicable as a wild creature.

I cannot judge the language of his Irish poetry, but
it is so rich in poetical thought, when at its best, that it
seems to me that if he were to write more he might
become to modern Irish what Mistral was to modern
Provençal. I wish, too, that he could put away from
himself some of the interruptions of that ceaseless propaganda, and find time for the making of translations,
loving and leisurely, like those in *Beside the Fire* and the

The Irish Dramatic Movement

Love Songs of Connacht. He has begun to get a little careless lately. Above all I would have him keep to that English idiom of the Irish-thinking people of the West which he has begun to use less often. It is the only good English spoken by any large number of Irish people to-day, and we must found good literature on a living speech. English men of letters found themselves upon the English Bible, where religious thought gets its living speech. Blake, if I remember rightly, copied it out twice, and I remember once finding a few illuminated pages of a new decorated copy that he began in his old age. Byron read it for the sake of style, though I think it did him little good; and Ruskin founded himself in great part upon it. Indeed, we find everywhere signs of a book which is the chief influence in the lives of English children. The translation used in Ireland has not the same literary beauty, and if we are to find anything to take its place we must find it in that idiom of the poor, which mingles so much of the same vocabulary with turns of phrase that have come out of Gaelic. Even Irish writers of considerable powers of thought seem to have no better standard of English than a schoolmaster's ideal of correctness. If their grammar is correct they will write in all the lightness of their hearts about 'keeping in touch', and 'object-lessons', and 'shining examples', and 'running in grooves', and 'flagrant violations' of various things. Yet, as Sainte-Beuve has said, there is nothing immortal except style. One can write well in that country idiom without much thought about one's words; the emotion will bring the right word itself, for there everything is old and everything alive

94

and nothing common or threadbare. I recommend to the Intermediate Board—a body that seems to benefit by advice—a better plan than any they know for teaching children to write good English. Let every child in Ireland be set to turn a leading article or a piece of what is called excellent English, written perhaps by some distinguished member of the Board, into the idiom of his own countryside. He will find at once the difference between dead and living words, between words that meant something years ago and words that have the only thing that gives literary quality—personality, the breath of men's mouths. Zola, who is sometimes an admirable critic, has said that some of the greatest pages in French literature are not even right in their grammar: 'They are great because they have personality'.

The habit of writing for the stage, even when it is not countrypeople who are the speakers, and of considering what good dialogue is, will help to increase our feeling for style. Let us get back in everything to the spoken word, even though we have to speak our lyrics to the psaltery or the harp, for, as A. E. says, we have begun to forget that literature is but recorded speech, and even when we write with care we have begun 'to write with elaboration what could never be spoken'. But when we go back to speech let us see that it is the idiom either of those who have rejected, or of those who have never learned, the base idioms of the newspapers.

Mr. Martyn argued in *The United Irishman* some months ago that our actors should try to train themselves for the modern drama of society. The acting of plays of heroic life or plays like *Cathleen ni Houlihan*, with its speech of the countrypeople, did not seem to him a preparation. It is not; but that is as it should be. Our movement is a return to the people, like the Russian movement of the early 'seventies, and the drama of society would but magnify a condition of life which the countryman and the artisan could but copy to their hurt. The play that is to give them a quite natural pleasure should tell them either of their own life, or of that life of poetry where every man can see his own image, because there alone does human nature escape from arbitrary conditions. Plays about drawing-rooms are written for the middle classes of great cities, for the classes who live in drawing-rooms; but if you would ennoble the man of the roads you must write about the roads, or about the people of romance, or about great historical people. We should, of course, play every kind of good play about Ireland that we can get, but romantic and historical plays, and plays about the life of artisans and countrypeople, are the best worth getting. In time, I think, we can make the poetical play a living dramatic form again, and the training our actors will get from plays of country life, with its unchanging outline, its abundant speech, its extravagance of thought, will help to establish a school of imaginative acting. The play of society, on the other hand, could but train up realistic actors who would do badly, for the most part, what English actors do well, and would, when at all good, drift away to wealthy English theatres. If, on the other hand, we busy ourselves with poetry and the countryman, two things which have always mixed with one another in life as on the stage, we may recover, in the course of years, a lost art which, being an imitation of nothing English, may bring our actors a secure fame and a sufficient livelihood.

The Irish Dramatic Movement

I CANNOT describe the various dramatic adventures of
the year with as much detail as I did last year, mainly
because the movement has got beyond me. The most
important event of the Gaelic Theatre has been the two
series of plays produced in the Round Room of the
Rotunda by the Gaelic League. Father Dineen's *Tobar
Draoidheachta*, and Dr. Hyde's *An Posadh*, and a
chronicle play about Hugh O'Neill, and, I think, some
other plays, were seen by immense audiences. I was not
in Ireland for these plays, but a friend tells me that he
could only get standing-room one night, and the Round
Room must hold about 3000 people. A performance of
Tobar Draoidheachta I saw there some months before was
bad, but I believe there was great improvement, and that
the players who came up from somewhere in County
Cork to play it at this second series of plays were admirable. The players, too, that brought Dr. Hyde's *An
Posadh* from Ballaghadereen, in County Mayo, where
they had been showing it to their neighbours, were also,
I am told, careful and natural. The play-writing, always good in dialogue, is still very poor in construction, and I still hear of plays in many scenes, with no
scene lasting longer than four or six minutes, and few
intervals shorter than nine or ten minutes, which have
to be filled up with songs. The Rotunda chronicle play
seems to have been rather of this sort, and I suspect
that when I get Father Peter O'Leary's *Meadhbh*, a
play in five acts produced at Cork, I shall find the

masterful old man, in spite of his hatred of English thought, sticking to the Elizabethan form. I wish I could have seen it played last week, for the spread of the Gaelic Theatre in the country is more important than its spread in Dublin, and of all the performances of Gaelic plays in the country during the year I have seen but one—Dr. Hyde's new play, *Cleamhnas*, at Galway Feis. I got there a day late for a play by the Master of Galway Workhouse, but heard that it was well played, and that his dialogue was as good as his construction was bad. There is no question, however, about the performance of *Cleamhnas* being the worst I ever saw. I do not blame the acting, which was pleasant and natural, in spite of insufficient rehearsal, but the stage-management. The subject of the play was a match-making. The terms were in debate between two old men in an inner room. An old woman, according to the stage directions, should have listened at the door and reported what she heard to her daughter's suitor, who is outside the window, and to her daughter. There was no window on the stage, and the young man stood close enough to the door to have listened for himself. The door, where she listened, opened now on the inner room, and now on the street, according to the necessities of the play, and the young men who acted the fathers of grown-up children, when they came through the door, were seen to have done nothing to disguise their twenty-five or twenty-six birthdays. There had been only two rehearsals, and the little boy who should have come in laughing at the end came in shouting, 'Ho ho, ha ha', evidently believing that these were Gaelic words he had never heard before.

The only Gaelic performances I have seen during the year have been ill done, but I have seen them sufficiently well done in other years to believe my friends when they tell me that there have been good performances. *Inghinidhe na h-Eireann* is always thorough, and one cannot doubt that the performance of Dr. Hyde's *An Naom ar Iarriad*, by the children from its classes, was at least careful. A powerful little play in English against enlisting, by Mr. Colum, was played with it, and afterwards revived, and played with a play about the Royal Visit, also in English. I have no doubt that we shall see a good many of these political plays during the next two or three years, and it may be even the rise of a more or less permanent company of political players, for the revolutionary clubs will begin to think plays as necessary as the Gaelic League is already thinking them. Nobody can find the same patriotic songs and recitations sung and spoken by the same people, year in year out, anything but mouldy bread. It is possible that the players who are to produce plays in October for the Samhain festival of *Cumann na n-Gaedheal* may grow into such a company.

Though one welcomes every kind of vigorous life, I am, myself, most interested in 'The Irish National Theatre Society', which has no propaganda but that of good art. The little Camden Street Hall it had taken has been useful for rehearsal alone, for it proved to be too far away, and too lacking in dressing-rooms for our short plays, which involve so many changes. Successful performances were given, however, at Rathmines, and in one or two country places.

Deirdre, by A. E., *The Racing Lug*, by Mr. Cousins, *The Foundations*, by Mr. Ryan, and my *Pot of Broth* and *Cathleen ni Houlihan* were repeated, but no new plays were produced until March 14, when Lady Gregory's *Twenty-five* and my *Hour-Glass* drew a good audience. On May 2 *The Hour-Glass*, *Twenty-five*, *Cathleen ni Houlihan*, *The Pot of Broth*, and *Foundations* were performed before the Irish Literary Society in London, at the Queen's Gate Hall, and plays and players were generously commended by the Press—very eloquently by the critic of *The Times*. It is natural that we should be pleased with this praise, and that we should wish others to know of it, for is it not a chief pleasure of the artist to be commended in subtle and eloquent words? The critic of *The Times* has seen many theatres and he is, perhaps, a little weary of them, but here in Ireland there are one or two critics who are so much in love, or pretend to be so much in love, with the theatre as it is, that they complain when we perform on a stage two feet wider than Molière's that it is scarce possible to be interested in anything that is played on so little a stage. We are to them foolish sectaries who have revolted against that orthodoxy of the commercial theatre which is so much less pliant than the orthodoxy of the Church, for there is nothing so passionate as a vested interest disguised as an intellectual conviction. If you inquire into its truth it becomes as angry as a begging-letter writer when you find some hole in that beautiful story about the five children and the broken mangle. In Ireland, wherever the enthusiasts are shaping life, the critic who does the will of the commercial theatre can but stand against his lonely pillar defending his articles of belief among a wild people, and thinking mournfully of distant cities, where nobody puts a raw potato into his pocket when he is going to hear a musical comedy.

The Irish Literary Society of New York, which has been founded this year, produced *The Land of Heart's Desire*, *The Pot of Broth*, and *Cathleen ni Houlihan*, on June 3 and 4, very successfully, and propose to give Dr. Hyde's Nativity Play, *Drama Breithe Chriosta*, and his *Casadh an t-Sugain*, *An Posadh*, and *An Naom ar Iarriad* next year, at the same time of year, playing them both in Irish and English. I heard too that his Nativity Play will be performed in New York, but I know no particulars except that it will be done in connection with some religious societies. The National Theatre Society will, I hope, produce some new plays of his this winter, as well as new plays by Mr. Synge, Mr. Colum, Lady Gregory, myself, and others. They have taken the Molesworth Hall for three days in every month, beginning with the 8th, 9th, and 10th of October, when they will perform Mr. Synge's *Shadow of the Glen*, a little country comedy, full of a humour that is at once harsh and beautiful, *Cathleen ni Houlihan*, and a longish one-act play in verse of my own, called *The King's Threshold*. This play is founded on the old story of Seanchan the poet, and King Guaire of Gort, but I have seen the story from the poet's point of view, and not,

Samhain : 1903

like the old story-tellers, from the king's. Our repertory of plays is increasing steadily, and when the winter's work is finished, a play Mr. Bernard Shaw has
promised us[1] may be ready to open the summer session.
His play will, I imagine, unlike the plays we write for
ourselves, be long enough to fill an evening, and it will,
I know, deal with Irish public life and character.
Mr. Shaw, more than anybody else, has the love of
mischief that is so near the core of Irish intellect,
and should have an immense popularity among us. I
have seen a crowd of many thousands in possession
of his spirit, and keeping the possession to the small
hours.

This movement should be important even to those
who are not especially interested in the Theatre, for it
may be a morning cockcrow to that impartial meditation about character and destiny we call the artistic life in
a country where everybody, if we leave out the peasant
who has his folk-songs and his music, has thought
the arts useless unless they have helped some kind of
political action, and has, therefore, lacked the pure joy
that only comes out of things that have never been
indentured to any cause. The play which is mere propaganda shows its leanness more obviously than a propagandist poem or essay, for dramatic writing is so full
of the stuff of daily life that a little falsehood, put in that

[1] This play was *John Bull's Other Island.* When it came out in
the spring of 1905 we felt ourselves unable to cast it without wrong-
ing Mr. Shaw. We had no 'Broadbent' or money to get one.—
March 1908.

the moral may come right in the end, contradicts our experience. If Father Dineen or Dr. Hyde were asked why they write their plays, they would say they write them to help their propaganda; and yet when they begin to write the form constrains them, and they become artists—one of them a very considerable artist, indeed. Dr. Hyde's early poems have even in translation a *naïveté* and wildness that sets them, as I think, among the finest poetry of our time; but he had ceased to write any verses but those Oireachtas odes that are but ingenious rhetoric. It is hard to write without the sympathy of one's friends, and though the country-people sang his verses the readers of Irish read them but little, partly, it may be, because he had broken with that elaborate structure of later Irish poetry which seemed a necessary part of their propaganda. They read plenty of pamphlets and grammars, but they disliked—as do other people in Ireland—serious reading, reading that is an end and not a means, that gives us nothing but a beauty indifferent to our profuse purposes. But now Dr. Hyde with his cursing Hanrahan, his old saint at his prayers, is a poet again; and the Leaguers go to his plays in thousands—and applaud in the right places, too—and the League puts many sixpences into its pocket.

We who write in English have a more difficult work, for English has been the language in which the Irish cause has been debated; and we have to struggle with traditional phrases and traditional points of view. Many would give us limitless freedom as to the choice of subject, understanding that it is precisely those subjects on which people feel most passionately, and, therefore, most dramatically, we would be forbidden to handle if we made any compromise with powers. But fewer know that we must encourage every writer to see life afresh, even though he sees it with strange eyes. Our National Theatre must be so tolerant, and, if this is not too wild a hope, find an audience so tolerant, that the half-dozen minds who are likely to be the dramatic imagination of Ireland for this generation may put their own thoughts and their own characters into their work; and for that reason no one who loves the arts, whether among Unionists or among the Patriotic Societies, should take offence if we refuse all but every kind of patronage. I do not say every kind, for if a mad king, a king so mad that he loved the arts and their freedom, should offer us unconditioned millions, I, at any rate, would give my voice for accepting them.

We will be able to find conscientious playwrights and players, for our young men have a power of work —when they are interested in their work—one does not look for outside a Latin nation, and if we are certain of being granted this freedom we would be certain that the work would grow to great importance. It is a supreme moment in the life of a nation when it is able to turn now and again from its preoccupations, to delight in the capricious power of the artist as one delights in the movement of some wild creature, but nobody can tell with certainty when that moment is at hand.

The Irish Dramatic Movement

The two plays in this year's *Samhain* represent the two sides of the movement very well, and are both written out of a deep knowledge of the life of the people. It should be unnecessary to praise Dr. Hyde's comedy,[1] that comes up out of the foundation of human life, but Mr. Synge is a new writer and a creation of our movement. He has gone every summer for some years past to the Aran Islands, and lived there in the houses of the fishers, speaking their language and living their lives, and his play[2] seems to me the finest piece of tragic work done in Ireland of late years. One finds in it, from first to last, the presence of the sea, and a sorrow that has majesty as in the work of some ancient poet.

[1] *The Poor-House*, written in Irish by Dr. Hyde on a scenario by Lady Gregory.

[2] *Riders to the Sea*. This play made its way very slowly with our audiences, but is now very popular.—March 1908.

Samhain : 1903

SAMHAIN: 1903

THE REFORM OF THE THEATRE

I THINK the theatre must be reformed in its plays, its speaking, its acting, and its scenery. That is to say, I think there is nothing good about it at present.

First. We have to write or find plays that will make the theatre a place of intellectual excitement—a place where the mind goes to be liberated as it was liberated by the theatres of Greece and England and France at certain great moments of their history, and as it is liberated in Scandinavia to-day. If we are to do this we must learn that beauty and truth are always justified of themselves, and that their creation is a greater service to our country than writing that compromises either in the seeming service of a cause. We will, doubtless, come more easily to truth and beauty because we love some cause with all but all our heart; but we must remember when truth and beauty open their mouths to speak, that all other mouths should be as silent as Finn bade the son of Lugaidh be in the houses of the great. Truth and beauty judge and are above judgment. They justify and have no need of justification.

Such plays will require, both in writers and audiences, a stronger feeling for beautiful and appropriate language than one finds in the ordinary theatre. Sainte-Beuve has said that there is nothing immortal in literature except style, and it is precisely this sense of style, once common among us, that is hardest for us to recover. I do not mean by style words with an air of literature about them, what is ordinarily called eloquent writing. The speeches of Falstaff are as perfect in their style as the soliloquies of Hamlet. One must be able to make a king of Faery or an old countryman or a modern lover speak that language which is his and nobody else's, and speak it with so much of emotional subtlety that the hearer may find it hard to know whether it is the thought or the word that has moved him, or whether these could be separated at all.

If we do not know how to construct, if we cannot arrange much complicated life into a single action, our work will not hold the attention or linger in the memory, but if we are not in love with words it will lack the delicate movement of living speech that is the chief garment of life; and because of this lack the great realists seem to the lovers of beautiful art to be wise in this generation, and for the next generation, perhaps, but not for all generations that are to come.

Second. But if we are to restore words to their sovereignty we must make speech even more important than gesture upon the stage.

I have been told that I desire a monotonous chant, but that is not true, for though a monotonous chant may be a safer beginning for an actor than the broken and prosaic speech of ordinary recitation, it puts me to sleep none the less. The sing-song in which a child says a verse is a right beginning, though the child grows out of it. An actor should understand how so to discriminate cadence from cadence, and so to cherish the musical lineaments of verse or prose that he delights the ear with a continually varied music. Certain passages of lyrical feeling, or where one wishes, as in the Angel's part in *The Hour-Glass*, to make a voice sound like the voice of an Immortal, may be spoken upon pure notes which are carefully recorded and learned as if they were the notes of a song. Whatever method one adopts, one must always be certain that the work of art, as a whole, is masculine and intellectual, in its sound as in its form.

Hulme

Third. We must simplify acting, especially in poetical drama, and in prose drama that is remote from real life like my *Hour-Glass*. We must get rid of everything that is restless, everything that draws the attention away from the sound of the voice, or from the few moments of intense expression, whether that expression is through the voice or through the hands; we must from time to time substitute for the movements that the eye sees the nobler movements that the heart sees, the rhythmical movements that seem to flow up into the imagination from some deeper life than that of the individual soul.

Fourth. Just as it is necessary to simplify gesture that it may accompany speech without being its rival, it is necessary to simplify both the form and colour of scenery and costume. As a rule the background should be but a single colour, so that the persons in the play, wherever they stand, may harmonise with it and pre-occupy our attention. In other words, it should be thought out not as one thinks out a landscape, but as if it were the background of a portrait, and this is especially necessary on a small stage where the moment the stage is filled, the painted forms of the background are broken up and lost. Even when one has to represent trees or hills they should be treated in most cases decoratively, they should be little more than an unobtrusive pattern. There must be nothing unnecessary, nothing that will distract the attention from speech and movement. An art is always at its greatest when it is most human. Greek acting was great because it did all but everything with the voice, and modern acting may be great when it does everything with voice and movement. But an art which smothers these things with bad painting, with innumerable garish colours, with continual restless mimicries of the surface of life, is an art of fading humanity, a decaying art.

Samhain : 1903

SAMHAIN: 1903

MORAL AND IMMORAL PLAYS

A WRITER in *The Leader* has said that I told my audience after the performance of *The Hour-Glass* that I did not care whether a play was moral or immoral. He said this without discourtesy, and as I have noticed that people are generally discourteous when they write about morals, I think that I owe him upon my part the courtesy of an explanation. I did not say that I did not care whether a play was moral or immoral, for I have always been of Verhaeren's opinion that a masterpiece is a portion of the conscience of mankind. My objection was to the rough-and-ready conscience of the newspaper and the pulpit in a matter so delicate and so difficult as literature. Every generation of men of letters has been called immoral by the pulpit or the newspaper, and it has been precisely when that generation has been illuminating some obscure corner of the conscience that the cry against it has been more confident.

The plays of Shakespeare had to be performed on the south side of the Thames because the Corporation of London considered all plays immoral. Goethe was thought dangerous to faith and morals for two or three generations. Every educated man knows how great a portion of the conscience of mankind is in Flaubert and Balzac, and yet their books have been proscribed in the courts of law, and I found some time ago that our own National Library, though it had two books on the

genius of Flaubert, had refused on moral grounds to
have any books written by him. With these stupidities
in one's memory, how can one, as many would have
us, arouse the mob, and in this matter the pulpit and
the newspaper are but voices of the mob, against the
English theatre in Ireland upon moral grounds? If that
theatre became conscientious as men of letters understand the conscience, many that now cry against it
would think it even less moral, for it would be more
daring, more logical, more free-spoken. The English
theatre is demoralising, not because it delights in the
husband, the wife, and the lover, a subject which has
inspired great literature in most ages of the world, but
because the illogical thinking and insincere feeling we
call bad writing make the mind timid and the heart
effeminate. I saw an English play in Dublin a few
months ago called *Mice and Men*. It had run for five
hundred nights in London, and been called by all the
newspapers 'a pure and innocent play', 'a welcome
relief', and so on. In it occurred this incident: The
typical scapegrace hero of the stage, a young soldier,
who is in love with the wife of another, goes away for
a couple of years, and when he returns finds that he is
in love with a marriageable girl. His mistress, who has
awaited his return with what is represented as faithful
love, sends him a letter of welcome, and because he has
grown virtuous of a sudden he returns it unopened,
and with so careless a scorn that the husband intercepts
it; and the dramatist approves this manner of crying off
with an old love, and rings down the curtain on his
marriage bells. Men who would turn out of their club

a man who could so treat a letter from his mistress bring their wives and daughters to admire him upon the stage, so demoralising is a drama that has no intellectual tradition behind it. I could not endure it, and went out into the street and waited there until the end of the play, when I came in again to find the friends I had brought to hear it, but had I been accustomed to the commercial theatre I would not even have known that anything strange had happened upon the stage. If a man of intellect had written of such an incident he would have made his audience feel for the mistress that sympathy one feels for all that have suffered insult, and for that young man an ironical emotion that might have marred the marriage bells, and who knows what the curate and the journalist would have said of the man of intellect? Even Ireland would have cried out: Catholic Ireland that should remember the gracious tolerance of the Church when all nations were its children, and how Wolfram of Eschenbach sang from castle to castle of the courtesy of Parzival, the good husband, and of Gawain, the light lover, in that very Thuringia where a generation later the lap of Saint Elizabeth was full of roses. A Connacht Bishop told his people a while since that they 'should never read stories about the degrading passion of love', and one can only suppose that, being ignorant of a chief glory of his Church, he has never understood that his new puritanism is but an English cuckoo.

The Irish Dramatic Movement

AN IRISH NATIONAL THEATRE

[The performance of Mr. Synge's *Shadow of the Glen* started a quarrel with the extreme National party, and the following paragraphs are from letters written in the play's defence. The organ of the party was at the time *The United Irishman*, but the first serious attack began in *The Independent*. *The United Irishman*, however, took up the quarrel, and from that on has attacked almost every play produced at our theatre, and the suspicion it managed to arouse among the political clubs against Mr. Synge especially led a few years later to the organised attempt to drive *The Playboy of the Western World* from the stage.—1908.]

WHEN we were all fighting about the selection of books for the New Irish Library some ten years ago, we had to discuss the question, What is National Poetry? In those days a patriotic young man would have thought but poorly of himself if he did not believe that *The Spirit of the Nation* was great lyric poetry, and a much finer kind of poetry than Shelley's *Ode to the West Wind*, or Keats's *Ode on a Grecian Urn*. When two or three of us denied this, we were told that we had effeminate tastes or that we were putting Ireland in a bad light before her enemies. If one said that *The Spirit of the Nation* was but salutary rhetoric, England might overhear us and take up the cry. We said it, and who will say that Irish literature has not a greater name in the world to-day than it had ten years ago?

To-day there is another question that we must make

up our minds about, and an even more pressing one, What is a National Theatre? A man may write a book of lyrics if he have but a friend or two that will care for them, but he cannot write a good play if there are not audiences to listen to it. If we think that a national play must be as near as possible a page out of *The Spirit of the Nation* put into dramatic form, and mean to go on thinking it to the end, then we may be sure that this generation will not see the rise in Ireland of a theatre that will reflect the life of Ireland as the Scandinavian theatre reflects the Scandinavian life. The brazen head has an unexpected way of falling to pieces. We have a company of admirable and disinterested players, and the next few months will, in all likelihood, decide whether a great work for this country is to be accomplished. The poetry of Young Ireland, when it was an attempt to change or strengthen opinion, was rhetoric; but it became poetry when patriotism was transformed into a personal emotion by the events of life, as in that lamentation written by Doheny ' on his keeping' among the hills. Literature is always personal, always one man's vision of the world, one man's experience, and it can only be popular when men are ready to welcome the visions of others. A community that is opinion-ridden, even when those opinions are in themselves noble, is likely to put its creative minds into some sort of a prison. If creative minds preoccupy themselves with incidents from the political history of Ireland, so much the better, but we must not enforce them to select those incidents. If, in the sincere working-out of their plot, they alight on a moral that is obviously and directly serviceable to the National cause, so much the better, but we must not force that moral upon them. I am a Nationalist, and certain of my intimate friends have made Irish politics the business of their lives, and this made certain thoughts habitual with me, and an accident made these thoughts take fire in such a way that I could give them dramatic expression. I had a very vivid dream one night, and I made *Cathleen ni Houlihan* out of this dream. But if some external necessity had forced me to write nothing but drama with an obviously patriotic intention, instead of letting my work shape itself under the casual impulses of dreams and daily thoughts, I would have lost, in a short time, the power to write movingly upon any theme. I could have aroused opinion; but I could not have touched the heart, for I would have been busy at the oakum-picking that is not the less mere journalism for being in dramatic form. Above all, we must not say that certain incidents which have been a part of literature in all other lands are forbidden to us. It may be our duty, as it has been the duty of many dramatic movements, to bring new kinds of subjects into the theatre, but it cannot be our duty to make the bounds of drama narrower. For instance, we are told that the English theatre is immoral, because it is preoccupied with the husband, the wife, and the lover. It is, perhaps, too exclusively preoccupied with that subject, and it is certain it has not shed any new light upon it for a considerable time, but a subject that inspired Homer and about half the great literature of the world will, one doubts not, be a necessity to our National Theatre also. Literature is, to my mind, the great teaching power of the world, the ultimate creator of all values, and it is this, not only in the sacred books whose power everybody acknowledges, but by every movement of imagination in song or story or drama that height of intensity and sincerity has made literature at all. Literature must take the responsibility of its power, and keep all its freedom: it must be like the spirit and like the wind that blows where it listeth; it must claim its right to pierce through every crevice of human nature, and to describe the relation of the soul and the heart to the facts of life and of law, and to describe that relation as it is, not as we would have it be; and in so far as it fails to do this it fails to give us that foundation of understanding and charity for whose lack our moral sense can be but cruelty. It must be as incapable of telling a lie as Nature, and it must sometimes say before all the virtues, 'The greatest of these is charity'. Sometimes the patriot will have to falter and the wife to desert her home, and neither be followed by divine vengeance or man's judgment. At other moments it must be content to judge without remorse, compelled by nothing but its own capricious spirit that has yet its message from the foundation of the world. Aristophanes held up the people of Athens to ridicule, and even prouder of that spirit than of themselves, they invited the foreign ambassadors to the spectacle.

I would sooner our theatre failed through the indifference or hostility of our audiences than gained an immense popularity by any loss of freedom. I ask nothing that my masters have not asked for, but I ask all that they were given. I ask no help that would limit our freedom from either official or patriotic hands, though I am glad of the help of any who love the arts so dearly that they would not bring them into even honourable captivity. A good Nationalist is, I suppose, one who is ready to give up a great deal that he may preserve to his country whatever part of her possessions he is best fitted to guard, and that theatre where the capricious spirit that bloweth as it listeth has for a moment found a dwelling-place, has good right to call itself a National Theatre.

Samhain : 1903

SAMHAIN: 1903

THE THEATRE, THE PULPIT, AND
THE NEWSPAPERS

I WAS very well content when I read an unmeasured attack in *The Independent* on the Irish National Theatre. There had, as yet, been no performance, but the attack was confident, and it was evident that the writer's ears were full of rumours and whisperings. One knew that some such attack was inevitable, for every dramatic movement that brought any new power into literature arose among precisely these misunderstandings and animosities. Drama, the most immediately powerful form of literature, the most vivid image of life, finds itself opposed, as no other form of literature does, to those enemies of life, the chimeras of the Pulpit and the Press. When a country has not begun to care for literature, or has forgotten the taste for it, and most modern countries seem to pass through this stage, these chimeras are hatched in every basket. Certain generalisations are everywhere substituted for life. Instead of individual men and women and living virtues differing as one star differeth from another in glory, the public imagination is full of personified averages, partisan fictions, rules of life that would drill everybody into the one posture, habits that are like the pinafores of charity-school children. The priest, trained to keep his mind on the strength of his Church and the weakness of his congregation, would have all mankind painted with a halo or with horns. Literature is nothing to him, he has to remember that Seaghan the Fool might take to drinking again if he knew of pleasant Falstaff, and that Paudeen might run after Red Sarah again if some strange chance put Plutarch's tale of Antony or Shakespeare's play into his hands, and he is in a hurry to shut out of the schools that Pandora's box, *The Golden Treasury*. The newspaper he reads of a morning has not only the haloes and horns of the vestry, but it has crowns and fools' caps of its own. Life, which in its essence is always surprising, always taking some new shape, always individualising, is nothing to it, it has to move men in squads, to keep them in uniform, with their faces to the right enemy, and enough hate in their hearts to make the muskets go off. It may know its business well, but its business is building and ours is shattering. We cannot linger very long in this great dim temple where the wooden images sit all round upon thrones, and where the worshippers kneel, not knowing whether they tremble because their gods are dead or because they fear they may be alive. In the idol-house every god, every demon, every virtue, every vice, has been given its permanent form, its hundred hands, its elephant trunk, its monkey head. The man of letters looks at those kneeling worshippers who have given up life for a posture, whose nerves have dried up in the contemplation of lifeless wood. He swings his silver hammer and the keepers of the temple cry out, prophesying evil, but he must not mind their cries and their prophecies, but break the wooden necks in two and throw down the wooden bodies. Life will put living bodies in their place till new image-brokers have set up their benches.

Whenever literature becomes powerful, the priest, whose forerunner imagined Saint Patrick driving his chariot-wheels over his own erring sister, has to acknowledge, or to see others acknowledge, that there is no evil that men and women may not be driven into by their virtues all but as readily as by their vices, and the politician, that it is not always clean hands that serve a country or foul hands that ruin it. He may even have to say at last, as an old man who had spent many years in prison to serve a good cause said to me, 'There never was a cause so evil that it has not been served by good men for what seemed to them sufficient reasons'. And if the priest or the politician should say to the man of letters, 'Into how dangerous a state of mind are you not bringing us?' the man of letters can but answer, 'It is dangerous, indeed', and say, like my Seanchan, 'When did we promise safety?'

Thought takes the same form age after age, and the things that people have said to me about this intellectual movement of ours have, I doubt not, been said in every country to every writer who was a disturber of the old life. When *The Countess Cathleen* was produced, the very girls in the shops complained to us that to describe an Irishwoman as selling her soul to the Devil was to slander the country. The silver hammer had threatened, as it seems, one of those personifications of an average. Someone said to me a couple of weeks ago, 'If you put on the stage any play about marriage that does not point its moral clearly, you will make it difficult for us to go on attacking the English theatre for its immorality'. Again, we were disordering the squads, the muskets might not all point in the same direction.

Now that these opinions have found a leader and a voice in *The Independent*, it is easy at any rate to explain how much one differs from them. I had spoken of the capricious power of the artist and compared it to the capricious movements of a wild creature, and *The Independent*, speaking quite logically from its point of view, tells me that these movements were only interesting when 'under restraint'. The writers of the Anglo-Irish movement, it says, 'will never consent to serve except on terms that never could or should be conceded'. I had spoken of the production of foreign masterpieces, but it considers that foreign masterpieces would be very dangerous. I had asked in *Samhain* for audiences sufficiently tolerant to enable the half-dozen minds who are likely to be the dramatic imagination of Ireland for this generation to put their own thought and their own characters into their work. That is to say, I had asked for the amount of freedom which every nation has given to its dramatic writers. But the newspaper hopes and believes that no 'such tolerance will be extended to Mr. Yeats and his friends'.

I have written these lines to explain our thoughts and intentions to many personal friends, who live too deep in the labour of politics to give the thought to these things that we have given, and because not only in our theatre, but in all matters of national life, we have need of a new discovery of life—of more precise thought, of a more perfect sincerity. I would see, in every branch

Samhain : 1903

of our National propaganda, young men who would
have the sincerity and the precision of those Russian
revolutionists that Kropotkin and Stepniak tell us of,
men who would never use an argument to convince
others which would not convince themselves, who
would not make a mob drunk with a passion they could
not share, and who would above all seek for fine things
for their own sake, and for precise knowledge for its
own sake, and not for its momentary use. One can
serve one's country alone out of the abundance of one's
own heart, and it is labour enough to be certain one is
in the right, without having to be certain that one's
thought is expedient also.

The Irish Dramatic Movement

THE DRAMATIC MOVEMENT

THE National Theatre Society has had great difficulties because of the lack of any suitable playhouse. It has been forced to perform in halls without proper lighting for the stage, and almost without dressing-rooms, and with level floors in the auditorium that prevented all but the people in the front row from seeing properly. These halls are expensive too, and the players of poetical drama in an age of musical comedy have light pockets. But now a generous English friend, Miss Horniman, has rearranged and in part rebuilt, at very considerable expense, the old Mechanics' Institute Theatre, now the Abbey Theatre, and given us the use of it without any charge, and I need not say that she has gained our gratitude, as she will gain the gratitude of our audience. The work of decoration and alteration has been done by Irishmen, and everything, with the exception of some few things that are not made here, or not of a good enough quality, has been manufactured in Ireland. The stained glass in the entrance hall is the work of Miss Sarah Purser and her apprentices, the large copper mirror-frames are from the new metal works at Youghal, and the pictures of some of our players are by an Irish artist. These details and some details of form and colour in the building, as a whole, have been arranged by Miss Horniman herself.

Having been given the free use of this theatre, we

may look upon ourselves as the first endowed theatre in any English-speaking country, the English-speaking countries and Venezuela being the only countries which have never endowed their theatres; but the correspondents who write for parts in our plays or posts in the Theatre at a salary are in error. We are, and must be for some time to come, contented to find our work its own reward, the player giving[1] his work, and the playwright his, for nothing; and though this cannot go on always, we start our winter very cheerfully with a capital of some forty pounds. We playwrights can only thank these players, who have given us the delight of seeing our work so well performed, working with so much enthusiasm, with so much patience, that they have found for themselves a lasting place among the artists, the only aristocracy that has never been sold in the market or seen the people rise up against it.

It is a necessary part of our plan to find out how to perform plays for little money, for it is certain that every increase in expenditure has lowered the quality of dramatic art itself, by robbing the dramatist of freedom in experiment, and by withdrawing attention from his words and from the work of the players. Sometimes one friend or another has helped us with costumes or scenery, but the expense has never been very great, ten or twenty pounds being enough in most cases for quite a long play. These friends have all accepted the

[1] The players, though not the playwrights, are now all paid.—March 1908. The playwrights have, for a good many years now, drawn the usual royalties.—1923.

principles I have explained from time to time in *Samhain*, but they have interpreted them in various ways according to their temperament.

Miss Horniman staged *The King's Threshold* at her own expense, and she both designed and made the costumes. The costumes for the coming performances of *On Baile's Strand* are also her work and her gift and her design. She made and paid for the costumes in *The Shadowy Waters*, but in this case followed a colour-scheme of mine. The colour-scheme in *The Hour-Glass*, our first experiment, was worked out by Mr. Robert Gregory and myself, and the costumes were made by Miss Lavelle, a member of the company; while Mr. Robert Gregory has designed the costumes and scenery for *Kincora*. As we gradually accumulate costumes in all the main colours and shades, we will be able to get new effects by combining them in different ways without buying new ones. Small dramatic societies, and our example is beginning to create a number, not having so many friends as we have, might adopt a simpler plan, suggested to us by a very famous decorative artist. Let them have one suit of clothes for a king, another for a queen, another for a fighting-man, another for a messenger, and so on, and if these clothes are loose enough to fit different people, they can perform any romantic play that comes without new cost. The audience would soon get used to this way of symbolising, as it were, the different ranks and classes of men, and as the king would wear, no matter what the play might be, the same crown and robe, they could have them very fine in the end. Now one wealthy theatre-goer and now another might add a pearl to the queen's necklace, or a jewel to her crown, and be the more regular in attendance at the theatre because that gift shone out there like a good deed.

We can hardly do all we hope unless there are many more of these little societies to be centres of dramatic art and of the allied arts. But a very few actors went from town to town in ancient Greece, finding everywhere more or less well-trained singers among the principal townsmen to sing the chorus that had otherwise been the chief expense. In the days of the stock companies two or three well-known actors would go from town to town, finding actors for all the minor parts in the local companies. If we are to push our work into the small towns and villages, local dramatic clubs must take the place of the old stock companies. A good-sized town should be able to give us a large enough audience for our whole, or nearly our whole, company to go there; but the need for us is greater in those small towns where the poorest kinds of farce and melodrama have gone and Shakespearian drama has not gone, and it is here that we will find it hardest to get intelligent audiences. If a dramatic club existed in one of the larger towns near, they could supply us not only with actors, should we need them, in their own town, but with actors when we went to the small towns and to the villages where the novelty of any kind of drama would make success certain. These clubs would play in Gaelic far better than we can hope to, for they would have native Gaelic speakers, and should we succeed in stirring the imagination of the people enough to keep the rivalry between plays in English and Irish to a rivalry in quality, the certain development of two schools with distinct though very kindred ideals would increase the energy and compass of our art.

At a time when drama was more vital than at present, unpaid actors, and actors with very little training, have influenced it deeply. The Mystery Plays and the Miracle Plays got their players at no great distance from the church door, and the classic drama of France had for a forerunner performances of Greek and Latin classics, given by students and people of quality, and even at its height Racine wrote two of his most famous tragedies to be played by young girls at school. This was before acting had got so far away from our natural instincts of expression. When the play is in verse, or in rhythmical prose, it does not gain by the change, and a company of amateurs, if they love literature, and are not self-conscious, and really do desire to do well, can often make a better hand of it than the ordinary professional company.

The greater number of their plays will, in all likelihood, be comedies of Irish country life, and here they need not fear competition, for they will know an Irish countryman as no professional can know him; but whatever they play, they will have one advantage the English amateur has not: there is in their blood a natural capacity for acting, and they have never, like him, become the mimics of well-known actors. The arts have

always lost something of their sap when they have been
cut off from the people as a whole; and when the
theatre is perfectly alive, the audience, as at the Gaelic
drama to-day in Gaelic-speaking districts, feels itself to
be almost a part of the play. I have never felt that the
dignity of art was imperilled when the audience at Dr.
Hyde's *An Posadh* cheered the bag of flour or the ham
lent by some local shopkeepers to increase the bridal
gifts. It was not merely because of its position in the
play that the Greek chorus represented the people, and
the old ballad-singers waited at the end of every verse
till their audience had taken up the chorus; while Ritual,
the most powerful form of drama, differs from the
ordinary form, because everyone who hears it is also a
player. Our modern theatre, with the seats always growing more expensive, and its dramatic art drifting always
from the living impulse of life, and becoming more and
more what Rossetti would have called 'soulless self-
reflections of man's skill', no longer gives pleasure to
any imaginative mind. It is easy for us to hate England
in this country, and we give that hatred something of
nobility if we turn it now and again into hatred of the
vulgarity of commercial syndicates, of all that commercial finish and pseudo-art she has done so much to
cherish. Mr. Standish O'Grady has quoted somebody
as saying, 'The passions must be held in reverence, they
must not, they cannot be excited at will', and the noble
using of that old hatred will win for us sympathy and
attention from all artists and people of good taste, and
from those of England more than anywhere, for there
is the need greatest.

The Irish Dramatic Movement

Before this part of our work can be begun, it will be necessary to create a household of living art in Dublin, with principles that have become habits, and a public that has learnt to care for a play because it is a play, and not because it is serviceable to some cause. Our patent is not so wide[1] as we had hoped for, for we had hoped to have a patent as little restricted as that of the Gaiety or the Theatre Royal. We were, however, vigorously opposed by these theatres and by the Queen's Theatre, and the Solicitor-General, to meet them half-way, has restricted our patent to plays written by Irishmen or on Irish subjects or to foreign masterpieces, provided these masterpieces are not English. This has been done to make our competition against the existing theatres as unimportant as possible. It does not directly interfere with the work of our society to any serious extent, but it would have indirectly helped our work had such bodies as the Elizabethan Stage Society, which brought *Everyman* to Dublin some years ago, been able to hire the theatre from Miss Horniman, when it is not wanted by us, and to perform there without the limitations imposed by a special licence.

Everything that creates a theatrical audience is an advantage to us, and the small number of seats in our theatre would have kept away that kind of drama, in whatever language, which spoils an audience for good work.

The enquiry itself was not a little surprising, for the legal representatives of the theatres, being the representatives of Musical Comedy, were very anxious for

[1] Our patent has been widened since.—1923.

the morals of the town. I had spoken of the Independent Theatre, and a lawyer wanted to know if a play of mine which attacked the institution of marriage had not been performed by it recently. I had spoken of M. Maeterlinck and of his indebtedness to a theatre somewhat similar to our own, and one of our witnesses, who knew no more about it than the questioner, was asked if a play by M. Maeterlinck called *L'Intruse* had not been so immoral that it was received with a cry of horror in London. I have written no play about marriage, and the Independent Theatre died some twelve years ago, and *L'Intruse* might be played in a nursery with no worse effects than a little depression of spirits. Our opponents, having thus protested against our morals, went home with the fees of Musical Comedy in their pockets.

For all this, we are better off so far as the law is concerned than we would be in England. The theatrical law of Ireland was made by the Irish Parliament, and though the patent system, the usual method of the time, has outlived its use and come to an end everywhere but in Ireland, we must be grateful to that ruling caste of free spirits, that being free themselves they left the theatre in freedom. In England there is a Censor, who forbids you to take a subject from the Bible or from politics, or to picture public characters, or certain moral situations which are the foundation of some of the greatest plays of the world. When I was at the great American Catholic University of Notre-Dame I heard that the students had given a performance of *Oedipus the King*, and *Oedipus the King* is forbidden in London. A censorship created in the eighteenth century by Walpole, because somebody had written against election bribery, has been distorted by a puritanism which is not the less an English invention for being a pretended hatred of vice and a real hatred of intellect. Nothing has ever suffered so many persecutions as the intellect, though it is never persecuted under its own name. It is but according to old usage when a law that cherishes Musical Comedy and permits to every second melodrama the central situation of *The Sign of the Cross*, attempted rape, becomes one of the secondary causes of the separation of the English theatre from life. It does not interfere with anything that makes money, and Musical Comedy, with its hints and innuendoes, and its consistently low view of life, makes a great deal, for money is always respectable; but would a group of artists and students see once again the masterpieces of the world, they would have to hide from the law as if they had been a school of thieves; or were we to take with us to London that beautiful Nativity Play of Dr. Hyde's, which was performed in Sligo Convent a few months ago, that holy vision of the central story of the world, as it is seen through the minds and the traditions of the poor, the constables might upset the cradle. And yet it is precisely these stories of the Bible that have all to themselves—in the imagination of English people, especially of the English poor—the place they share in this country with the stories of Finn and of Oisin and of Patrick.

Milton set the story of Samson into the form of a

Greek play, because he knew that Samson was, in the
English imagination, what Herakles was in the imagination of Greece; and I have never been able to see any
other subjects for an English dramatist who looked for
some common ground between his own mind and
simpler minds. An English poet of genius once told
me that he would have tried his hand in plays for the
people, if they knew any story the Censor would pass,
except Jack and the Beanstalk.

The Gaelic League has its great dramatic opportunity because of the abundance of stories known in Irish-
speaking districts, and because of the freedom of choice
and of treatment the leaders of a popular movement
can have if they have a mind for it. The Gaelic plays
acted and published during the year selected their subjects from the popular mind, but the treatment is dis-
appointing. Dr. Hyde, dragged from gathering to
gathering by the necessities of the movement, has
written no new play; and Father Peter O'Leary has
thrown his dramatic power, which is remarkable, into
an imaginative novel. Father Dineen has published a
little play that has some lifelike dialogue, but the action
is sometimes irrelevant, and the motives of the principal
character are vague and confused, as if it were written
in a hurry. Father Dineen seems to know that he has
not done his best, for he describes it as an attempt
to provide more vivid dialogue for beginners than
is to be found in the reading-books rather than a
drama. An anonymous writer has written a play called
The Money of the Narrow Cross, which tells a very

simple tale, like that of a child's book, simply and adequately. It is very slight, in low relief as it were, but if its writer is a young man it has considerable promise.

A play called *Seaghan na Scuab* was described in *The United Irishman* as the best play ever written in Irish; but though the subject of it is a dramatic old folk-tale, which has shown its vigour by rooting itself in many countries, the treatment is confused and conventional and there is a flatness of dialogue unusual in these plays. There is, however, an occasional sense of comic situation which may come to something if its writer will work seriously at his craft. One is afraid of quenching the smoking flax, but this play was selected for performance at the Oireachtas before a vast audience in the Rotunda. It was accompanied by *The Doctor* in English and Irish, written by Mr. O'Beirne, and performed by the Tawin players, who brought it from their seaside village in Galway. Mr. O'Beirne deserves the greatest praise for getting this company together, as well as for all he has done to give the Tawin people a new pleasure in their language; but I think a day will come when he will not be grateful to the Oireachtas Committee for bringing this first crude work of his into the midst of so many thousand people. It would be very hard for a much more experienced dramatist to make anything out of the ugly violence, the threadbare, second-hand imaginations that flow in upon a man out of the newspapers, when he has founded his work on proselytising zeal, instead of his experience of life and his curiosity about it. These two were the only plays, out of a number that have been played in Irish, that I have seen this year. I went to Galway Feis, like many others, to see Dr. Hyde's *Lost Saint*, for I had missed every performance of it hitherto though I had read it to many audiences in America, and I awaited the evening with some little excitement. Although the *Lost Saint* was on the programme, an Anti-Emigration play was put in its place. I did not wait for this, but, whatever its merits, it is not likely to have contained anything so beautiful as the old man's prayer in the other: 'O Lord, O God, take pity on this little soft child. Put wisdom in his head, cleanse his heart, scatter the mist from his mind and let him learn his lessons like the other boys. O Lord, Thou wert Thyself young one time; take pity on youth. O Lord, Thou Thyself didst shed tears; dry the tears of this little lad. Listen, O Lord, to the prayer of Thy servant, and do not keep from him this little thing he is asking of Thee. O Lord, bitter are the tears of a child, sweeten them: deep are the thoughts of a child, quiet them: sharp is the grief of a child, take it from him: soft is the heart of a child, do not harden it.'

A certain number of propagandist plays are unavoidable in a popular movement like the Gaelic revival, but they may drive out everything else. The plays, while Father Peter O'Leary and Father Dineen and Dr. Hyde were the most popular writers and the chief influence, were full of the traditional folk-feeling that is the mastering influence in all old Irish literature.

Father O'Leary chose for his subjects a traditional
story of a trick played upon a simple villager, a sheep-
stealer frightened by what seemed to him a ghost, the
quarrels between Maeve and Ailell of Cruachan; Father
Dineen chose for his a religious crisis, alive as with the
very soul of tragedy, or a well sacred to the faeries;
while Dr. Hyde celebrated old story-tellers and poets,
and old saints, and the Mother of God with the coun-
tenance she wears in Irish eyes. Hundreds of men
scattered through the world, angry at the spectacle of
modern vulgarity, rejoiced in this movement, for it
seemed impossible for anything begun in so high a
spirit, so inspired by whatever is ancient, or simple, or
noble, to sink into the common base level of our
thought. This year one has heard little of the fine work,
and a great deal about plays that get an easy cheer,
because they make no discoveries in human nature, but
repeat the opinions of the audience, or the satire of its
favourite newspapers. I am only speaking of the plays
of a year, and that is but a short period in what one
hopes may be a great movement, but it is not wise to
say, as do many Gaelic Leaguers, who know the weak-
nesses of their movement, that if the present thinks but
of grammar and propaganda the future will do all the
rest. A movement will often in its first fire of enthusiasm create more works of genius than whole easy-going
centuries that come after it.

Nearly everything that is greatest as English prose
was written in a generation or two after the first beautiful use of prose in England: and Mistral has made the
poems of modern Provence, as well as reviving and all

but inventing the language: for genius is more often of the spring than of the middle green of the year. We cannot settle times and seasons, flowering-time and harvest-time are not in our hands, but we are to blame if genius comes and we do not gather in the fruit or the blossom. Very often we can do no more for the man of genius than to distract him as little as may be with the common business of the day. His own work is more laborious than any other, for not only is thought harder than action, as Goethe said, but he must brood over his work so long and so unbrokenly that he find there all his patriotism, all his passion, his religion even—it is not only those that sweep a floor that are obedient to Heaven—until at last he can cry with Paracelsus, 'In this crust of bread I have found all the stars and all the heavens'.

The following new plays were produced by the National Theatre Society during the last twelve months: *The Shadow of the Glen* and *Riders to the Sea*, by Mr. J. M. Synge; *Broken Soil*, by Mr. Colum; *The Townland of Tamney*, by Mr. Seumas MacManus; *The Shadowy Waters* and *The King's Threshold*, by myself. The following plays were revived: *Deirdre*, by A. E.; *Twenty-five*, by Lady Gregory; *Cathleen ni Houlihan*, *The Pot of Broth*, and *The Hour-Glass*, by myself. We could have given more plays, but difficulties about the place of performance, the shifting of scenery from where we rehearsed to where we acted, and so on, always brought a great deal of labour upon the Society. The Society went to London in March and gave two performances at the Royalty to full houses. They played there Mr. Synge's two plays, Mr. Colum's play, and my *King's Threshold* and *Pot of Broth*. We were commended by the critics with generous sympathy, and had an enthusiastic and distinguished audience.

We have many plays awaiting performance during the coming winter. Mr. Synge has written us a play in three acts called *The Well of the Saints*, full, as few works of our time are, of temperament, and of a true and yet bizarre beauty. Lady Gregory has written us an historical tragedy in three acts about King Brian, and a very merry comedy of country life. Mr. Bernard Shaw has written us a play[1] in four acts, his first experiment in Irish satire; Mr. Tarpey, an Irishman whose comedy *Windmills* was successfully produced by the Stage Society some years ago, a little play which I have not yet seen; and Mr. Boyle, a village comedy in three acts; and I hear of other plays by competent hands that are coming to us. My own *On Baile's Strand* is in rehearsal, and I hope to have ready for the spring a play on the subject of *Deirdre*, with choruses somewhat in the Greek manner. We are, of course, offered from all parts of the world great quantities of plays which are impossible for literary or dramatic reasons. Some of them have a look of having been written for the commercial theatre and of having been sent to us on rejection. It will save trouble if I point out that a play which seems to its writer to promise an ordinary London or New York success is very unlikely to please us, or succeed

[1] *John Bull's Other Island.*

with our audience if it did. Writers who have a better ambition should get some mastery of their art in little plays before spending many months of what is almost sure to be wasted labour on several acts.

We were invited to play in the St. Louis Exhibition, but thought that our work should be in Ireland for the present, and had other reasons for refusing.

A company which has been formed in America by Miss Wycherley, who played in *Everyman* during a part of its tour in America, to take some of our plays on tour, has begun with three one-act plays of mine, *Cathleen ni Houlihan*, *The Hour-Glass*, and *The Land of Heart's Desire*. It announces on its circulars that it is following the methods of our Theatre.

Though the commercial theatre of America is as unashamedly commercial as the English, there is a far larger audience interested in fine drama than here. When I was lecturing in, I think, Philadelphia—one town mixes with another in my memory at times— some one told me that he had seen *The Duchess of Malfi* played there by one of the old stock companies in his boyhood; and *Everyman* has been far more of a success in America than anywhere else. They have numberless University towns each with its own character and with an academic life animated by a zeal and by an imagination unknown in these countries. There is nearly everywhere that leaven of highly cultivated men and women so much more necessary to a good theatrical audience to-day than were ever Raleigh and Sidney, when the groundling could remember the folk-songs and the imaginative folk-life. The more an age is busy with temporary things, the more must it look for leadership in matters of art to men and women whose business or whose leisure has made the great writers of the world their habitual company. Literature is not journalism because it can turn the imagination to whatever is essential and unchanging in life.

SAMHAIN: 1904

FIRST PRINCIPLES

Two Irish writers had a controversy a month ago, and they accused one another of being unable to think, with entire sincerity, though it was obvious to uncommitted minds that neither had any lack of vigorous thought. But they had a different meaning when they spoke of thought, for the one, though in actual life he is the most practical man I know, meant thought as Pascal, as Montaigne, as Shakespeare, or as, let us say, Emerson, understood it—a reverie about the adventures of the soul, or of the personality, or some obstinate questioning of the riddle. Many who have to work hard always make time for this reverie, but it comes more easily to the leisured, and in this it is like a broken heart, which is, a Dublin newspaper assured us lately, impossible to a busy man. The other writer had in mind, when he spoke of thought, the shaping energy that keeps us busy, and the obstinate questionings he had most respect for were, how to change the method of government, how to change the language, how to revive our manufactures, and whether it is the Protestant or the Catholic that scowls at the other with the darker scowl. Ireland is so poor, so misgoverned, that a great portion of the imagination of the land must give itself to a very passionate consideration of questions like these, and yet it is precisely these loud questions that drive away the reveries that incline the imagination to the lasting work of literature and give, together with religion, sweetness, and nobility, and dignity to life. We should desire no more from these propagandist thinkers than that they carry out their work, as far as possible, without making it more difficult for those fitted by nature or by circumstance for another kind of thought to do their work also; and certainly it is not well that Martha chide at Mary, for they have the one Master over them.

When one all but despairs, as one does at times, of Ireland welcoming a National literature in this generation, it is because we do not leave ourselves enough of time, or of quiet, to be interested in men and women. A writer in *The Leader*, who is unknown to me, elaborates this argument in an article full of beauty and dignity. He is speaking of our injustice to one another, and he says that we are driven into injustice 'not wantonly but inevitably, and at call of the exacting qualities of the great things. Until this latter dawning, the genius of Ireland has been too preoccupied really to concern itself about men and women; in its drama they play a subordinate part, born tragic comedians though all the sons and daughters of the land are. A nation is the heroic theme we follow, a mourning, wasted land its moving spirit; the impersonal assumes personality for us.' When I wrote my *Countess Cathleen*, I thought, of course, chiefly of the actual picture that was forming before me, but there was a secondary meaning that came into my mind continually. 'It is the soul of one that loves Ireland', I thought, 'plunging into unrest, seeming to lose itself, to bargain itself away to the very wickedness of the world, and to surrender what is eternal for what is temporary', and I know that this meaning seemed natural to others, for that great orator, J. F. Taylor, who was not likely to have searched very deeply into any work of mine, for he cared little for mine, or, indeed, any modern work, turned the play into such a parable in one of his speeches.

There is no use being angry with necessary conditions, or failing to see that a man who is busy with some reform that can only be carried out in a flame of energetic feeling, will not only be indifferent to what seems to us the finer kind of thinking, but will support himself by generalisations that seem untrue to the man of letters. A little play, *The Rising of the Moon*, which is in the present number of *Samhain*, and is among those we are to produce during the winter, has, for instance, roused the suspicions of a very resolute leader of the people, who has a keen eye for rats behind the arras. A Fenian ballad-singer partly converts a policeman, and is it not unwise under any circumstances to show a policeman in so favourable a light? It is well known that many of the younger policemen were Fenians: but it is necessary that the Dublin crowds should be kept of so high a heart that they will fight the police at any moment. Are not morals greater than literature? Others have objected to Mr. Synge's *Shadow of the Glen* because Irish women, being more chaste than those of England and Scotland, are a valuable part of our National argument. Mr. Synge should not, it is said by some, have chosen an exception for the subject of his play, for who knows but the English may misunderstand him? Some even deny that such a thing could happen at all, while others that know the country better, or remember the statistics, say that it could, but should never, have been staged. All these arguments, by their methods, even more than by what they have tried to prove, misunderstand how literature does its work. Men of letters have sometimes said that the characters of a romance or of a play must be typical. They mean that the character must be typical of something which exists in all men because the writer has found it in his own mind. It is one of the most inexplicable things about human nature that a writer, with a strange temperament, an Edgar Allan Poe, let us say, made what he is by conditions that never existed before, can create personages and lyric emotions which startle us by being at once bizarre and an image of our own secret thoughts. Are we not face to face with the microcosm, mirroring everything in universal Nature? It is no more necessary for the characters created by a romance-writer, or a dramatist, to have existed before, than for his own personality to have done so; characters and personality alike, as is perhaps true in the instance of Poe, may draw half their life not from the solid earth but from some dreamy drug. This is true even of historical drama, for it was Goethe, the founder of the historical drama of Germany, who said, 'We do the people of history the honour of naming after them the creations of our own minds'. All that a dramatic writer need do is to persuade us, during the two hours' traffic of the stage, that the events of his play did really happen. He must know enough of the life of his country, or of history, to create this illusion, but no matter how much he knows, he will fail if his audience is not ready to give up something of the dead letter. If his mind is full of energy he will not be satisfied with little knowledge, but he will be far more likely to alter incidents and characters, wilfully even as it may seem, than to become a literal historian. It was one of the complaints against Shakespeare, in his own day, that he made Sir John Falstaff out of a praiseworthy old Lollard preacher. One day, as he sat over Holinshed's *History of England,* he persuaded himself that Richard II, with his French culture, 'his too great friendliness to his friends', his beauty of mind, and his fall before dry, repelling Bolingbroke, would be a good image for an accustomed mood of fanciful, impracticable lyricism in his own mind. The historical Richard has passed away for ever and the Richard of the play lives more intensely, it seems, than did ever living man. Yet Richard II, as Shakespeare made him, could never have been born before the Renaissance, before the Italian influence, or even one hour before the innumerable streams that flowed in upon Shakespeare's mind, the innumerable experiences we can never know, brought Shakespeare to the making of him. He is typical not because he ever existed, but because he has made us know of something in our own minds we had never known of had he never been imagined.

Our propagandists have twisted this theory of the men of letters into its direct contrary, and when they say that a writer should make typical characters they mean personifications of averages, of statistics, or even personified opinions, or men and women so faintly imagined that there is nothing about them to separate them from the crowd, as it appears to our hasty eyes. We must feel that we could engage a hundred others to wear the same livery as easily as we could engage a coachman. We must never forget that we are engaging them to be the ideal young peasant, or the true patriot, or the happy Irish wife, or the policeman of our prejudices, or to express some other of those invaluable generalisations without which our practical movements would lose their energy. Who is there that likes a coachman to be too full of human nature, when he has his livery on? No one man is like another, but one coachman should be as like another as possible, though he may assert himself a little when he meets the gardener. The patriots would impose on us heroes and heroines, like those young couples in the Gaelic plays, who might all change brides or bridegrooms in the dance and never find out the difference. The personifications need not be true even, if they are about our enemy, for it might be more difficult to fight out our necessary fight if we remembered his virtue at wrong moments; and might not Teigue and Bocach, that are light in the head, go over to his party?

Ireland is indeed poor, is indeed hunted by misfortune, and has indeed to give up much that makes life desirable and lovely, but is she so very poor that she can afford no better literature than this? Perhaps so, but if it is a Spirit from beyond the world that decides when a nation shall awake into imaginative energy, and no philosopher has ever found what brings the moment, it cannot be for us to judge. It may be coming upon us now, for it is certain that we have more writers who are thinking, as men of letters understand thought, than we have had for a century, and he who wilfully makes their work harder may be setting himself against the purpose of that Spirit.

I would not be trying to form an Irish National Theatre if I did not believe that there existed in Ireland, whether in the minds of a few people or of a great number I do not know, an energy of thought about life itself, a vivid sensitiveness as to the reality of things, powerful enough to overcome all those phantoms of the night. Everything calls up its contrary, unreality calls up reality, and, besides, life here has been sufficiently perilous to make men think. I do not think it a national prejudice that makes me believe we are harder, a more masterful race than the comfortable English of our time, and that this comes from an essential nearness to reality of those few scattered people who have the right to call themselves the Irish race. It is only in the exceptions, in the few minds where the flame has burnt, as it were, pure, that one can see the permanent character of a race. If one remembers the men who have dominated Ireland for the last hundred and fifty years, one understands that it is strength of personality, the individualising quality in a man, that stirs Irish imagination most deeply in the end. There is scarcely a man who has led the Irish people, at any time, who may not give some day to a great writer precisely that symbol he may require for the expression of himself. The critical mind of Ireland is far more subjugated than the critical mind of England by the phantoms and misapprehensions of politics and social necessity, but the life of Ireland has rejected them more resolutely. Indeed, it is in life itself in England that one finds the dominion of what is not human life.

We have no longer in any country a literature as great as the literature of the old world, and that is because the newspapers, all kinds of second-rate books, the preoccupation of men with all kinds of practical changes, have driven the living imagination out of the world. I have read hardly any books this summer but Cervantes and Boccaccio and some Greek plays. I have felt that these men, divided from one another by so many hundreds of years, had the same mind. It is we who are different; and then the thought would come to me, that has come to me so often before, that they lived in times when the imagination turned to life itself for excitement. The world was not changing quickly about them. There was nothing to draw their imagination from the ripening of the fields, from the birth and death of their children, from the destiny of their souls, from all that is the unchanging substance of literature. They had not to deal with the world in such great masses that it could only be represented to their minds by figures and by abstract generalisations. Everything that their minds ran on came on them vivid with the colour of the senses, and when they wrote it was out of their own rich experience, and they found their symbols of expression in things that they had known all their life long. Their very words were more vigorous than ours, for their phrases came from a common mint, from the market, or the tavern, or from the great poets of a still older time. It is the change that followed the Renaissance, and was completed by newspaper government and the scientific movement, that has brought upon us all these phrases and generalisations, made by minds that would grasp what they have never seen. Yesterday I went out to see the reddening apples in the garden, and they faded from my imagination sooner than they would have from the imagination of that old poet who made the songs of the seasons for the Fianna, or out of Chaucer's, that celebrated so many trees. Theories, opinions, these opinions among the rest, flowed in upon me and blotted them away. Even our greatest poets see the world with preoccupied minds. Great as Shelley is, those theories about the coming changes of the world, which he has built up with so much elaborate passion, hurry him from life continually. There is a phrase in some old Cabbalistic writer about man falling into his own circumference, and every generation we get further away from life itself, and come more and more under the influence which Blake had in his mind when he said, 'Kings and Parliament seem to me something other than human life'. We lose our freedom more and more as we get away from ourselves, and not merely because our minds are overthrown by abstract phrases and generalisations, reflections in a mirror that seem living, but because we have turned the table of values upside-down, and believe that the root of reality is not in the centre but somewhere in that whirling circumference. How can we create like the ancients, while innumerable considerations of external probability or social utility destroy the seeming irresponsible creative power that is life itself? Who to-day could set Richmond's and Richard's tents side by side on the battlefield, or make Don Quixote, mad as he was, mistake a windmill for a giant in broad daylight? And when I think of free-spoken Falstaff I know of no audience but the tinkers of the roadside that could encourage the artist to an equal comedy. The old writers were content if their inventions had but an emotional and moral consistency, and created out of themselves a fantastic, energetic, extravagant art. A civilisation is very like a man or a woman, for it comes in but a few years into its beauty, and its strength, and then, while many years go by, it gathers and makes order about it, the strength and beauty going out of it the while, until in the end it lies there with its limbs straightened out and a clean linen cloth folded upon it. That may well be, and yet we need not follow among the mourners, for, it may be, before they are at the tomb, a messenger will run out of the hills and touch the pale lips with a red ember, and wake the limbs to the disorder and the tumult that is life. Though he does not come, even so we will keep from among the mourners and hold some cheerful conversation among ourselves; for has not Virgil, a knowledgeable man and a wizard, foretold that other Argonauts shall row between cliff and cliff, and other fair-haired Achaeans sack another Troy?

Samhain : 1904

Every argument carries us backwards to some religious conception, and in the end the creative energy of men depends upon their believing that they have, within themselves, something immortal and imperishable, and that all else is but as an image in a looking-glass. So long as that belief is not a formal thing, a man will create out of a joyful energy, seeking little for any external test of an impulse that may be sacred, and looking for no foundation outside life itself. If Ireland could escape from those phantoms of hers she might create, as did the old writers; for she has a faith that is as theirs, and keeps alive in the Gaelic traditions—and this has always seemed to me the chief intellectual value of Gaelic—a portion of the old imaginative life. When Dr. Hyde or Father Peter O'Leary is the writer, one's imagination goes straight to the century of Cervantes, and, having gone so far, one thinks at every moment that they will discover his energy. It is precisely because of this reason that one is indignant with those who would substitute for the ideas of the folk-life the rhetoric of the newspapers, who would muddy what had begun to seem a fountain of life with the feet of the mob. Is it impossible to revive Irish and yet to leave the finer intellects a sufficient mastery over the more gross, to prevent it from becoming, it may be, the language of a nation, and yet losing all that has made it worthy of a revival, all that has made it a new energy in the mind?

Before the modern movement, and while it was but new, the ordinary man, whether he could read and write or not, was ready to welcome great literature. When Ariosto found himself among the brigands, they repeated to him his own verses, and the audience in the Elizabethan theatres must have been all but as clever as an Athenian audience. But to-day we come to understand great literature by a long preparation, or by some accident of nature, for we only begin to understand life when our minds have been purified of temporary interests by study.

But if literature has no external test, how are we to know that it is indeed literature? The only test that Nature gives, to show when we obey her, is that she gives us happiness, and when we are no longer obedient she brings us to pain sooner or later. Is it not the same with the artist? The sign that she makes to him is that happiness we call delight in beauty. He can only convey this in its highest form after he has purified his mind with the great writers of the world; but their example can never be more than a preparation. If his art does not seem, when it comes, to be the creation of a new personality, in a few years it will not seem to be alive at all. If he is a dramatist his characters must have a like newness. If they could have existed before his day, or have been imagined before his day, we may be certain that the spirit of life is not in them in its fullness. This is because art, in its highest moments, is not a deliberate creation, but the creation of intense feeling, of pure life; and every feeling is the child of all past ages and would be different if even a moment had been left out. Indeed, is it not that delight in beauty which tells the artist that he has imagined what may never die, itself but a delight in the permanent yet ever-changing form of life, in her very limbs and lineaments? When life has given it, has she given anything but herself? Has she any other reward, even for the saints? If one flies to the wilderness, is not that clear light that falls about the soul when all irrelevant things have been taken away, but life that has been about one always, enjoyed in all its fullness at length? It is as though she had put her arms about one, crying, 'My beloved, you have given up everything for me'. If a man spend all his days in good works till there is no emotion in his heart that is not full of virtue, is not the reward he prays for eternal life? The artist, too, has prayers and a cloister, and if he do not turn away from temporary things, from the zeal of the reformer and the passion of revolution, that jealous mistress will give him but a scornful glance.

What attracts me to drama is that it is, in the most obvious way, what all the arts are upon a last analysis. A farce and a tragedy are alike in this, that they are a moment of intense life. An action is taken out of all other actions; it is reduced to its simplest form, or at any rate to as simple a form as it can be brought to without our losing the sense of its place in the world. The characters that are involved in it are freed from everything that is not a part of that action; and whether it is, as in the less important kinds of drama, a mere bodily activity, a hairbreadth escape or the like, or as it is in the more important kinds, an activity of the souls of the characters, it is an energy, an eddy of life purified from everything but itself. The dramatist must picture life in action, with an unpreoccupied mind, as the musician pictures it in sound and the sculptor in form.

But if this be true, has art nothing to do with moral judgments? Surely it has, and its judgments are those from which there is no appeal. The character whose fortune we have been called in to see, or the personality of the writer, must keep our sympathy, and whether it be farce or tragedy, we must laugh and weep with him and call down blessings on his head. This character who delights us may commit murder like Macbeth, or fly the battle for his sweetheart as did Antony, or betray his country like Coriolanus, and yet we will rejoice in every happiness that comes to him and sorrow at his death as if it were our own. It is no use telling us that the murderer and the betrayer do not deserve our sympathy. We thought so yesterday, and we still know what crime is, but everything has been changed of a sudden; we are caught up into another code, we are in the presence of a higher court. Complain of us if you will, but it will be useless, for before the curtain falls, a thousand ages, grown conscious in our sympathies, will have cried *Absolvo te*. Blame if you will the codes, the philosophies, the experiences of all past ages that have made us what we are, as the soil under our feet has been made out of unknown vegetations: quarrel with the acorns of Eden if you will, but what has that to do with us? We understand the verdict and not the law; and yet there is some law, some code, some judgment. If the poet's hand had slipped, if Antony had railed at Cleopatra in the monument, if Coriolanus had abated that high pride of his in the presence of death, we might have gone away muttering the Ten Commandments. Yet maybe we are wrong to speak of judgment, for we have but contemplated life, and what more is there to say when she that is all virtue, the gift and the giver, the fountain whither all flows again, has given all herself? If the subject of drama or any other art were a man himself, an eddy of momentary breath, we might desire the contemplation of perfect characters; but the subject of all art is passion, and a passion can only be contemplated when separated by itself, purified of all but itself, and aroused into a perfect intensity by opposition with some other passion, or it may be with the law, that is the expression of the whole whether of Church or Nation or external nature. Had Coriolanus not been a law-breaker, neither he nor we had ever discovered, it may be, that noble pride of his, and if we had not seen Cleopatra through the eyes of so many lovers, would we have known that soul of hers to be all flame, and wept at the quenching of it? If we were not certain of law we would not feel the struggle, the drama, but the subject of art is not law, which is a kind of death, but the praise of life, and it has no commandments that are not positive.

But if literature does not draw its substance from history, or anything about us in the world, what is a National literature? Our friends have already told us,

writers for the Theatre in Abbey Street, that we have
no right to the name, some because we do not write in
Irish, and others because we do not plead the National
cause in our plays, as if we were writers for the newspapers. I have not asked my fellow-workers what they
mean by the words National literature, but though I
have no great love for definitions, I would define it in
some such way as this: It is the work of writers who
are moulded by influences that are moulding their
country, and who write out of so deep a life that they
are accepted there in the end. It leaves a good deal
unsettled—was Rossetti an Englishman, or Swift an
Irishman?—but it covers more kinds of National
literature than any other I can think of. If you say a
National literature must be in the language of the
country, there are many difficulties. Should it be
written in the language that your country does speak
or the language that it ought to speak? Was Milton an
Englishman when he wrote in Latin or Italian, and
had we no part in Columbanus when he wrote in Latin
the beautiful sermon comparing life to a highway and
to a smoke? And then there is Beckford, who is in
every history of English literature, and yet his one
memorable book, a story of Persia, was written in
French.

Our theatre is of no great size, for though we know
that if we write well we shall find acceptance among
our countrymen in the end, we would think our
emotions were on the surface if we found a ready
welcome. Edgar Allan Poe and Walt Whitman are

National writers of America, although the one had his first true acceptance in France and the other in England and Ireland. When I was a boy, six persons, who, alone out of the whole world, it may be, believed Walt Whitman a great writer, sent him a message of admiration, and of those names four were English and two Irish, my father's and Prof. Dowden's. It is only in our own day that America has begun to prefer him to Lowell, who is not a poet at all.

I mean by deep life that men must put into their writing the emotions and experiences that have been most important to themselves. If they say, 'I will write of Irish countrypeople and make them charming and picturesque like those dear peasants my great-grandmother used to put in the foreground of her watercolour paintings', then they had better be satisfied with the word 'provincial'. If one condescends to one's material, if it is only what a popular novelist would call local colour, it is certain that one's real soul is somewhere else. Mr. Synge, upon the other hand, who is able to express his own finest emotions in those curious ironical plays of his, where, for all that, by the illusion of admirable art, every one seems to be thinking and feeling as only countrymen could think and feel, is truly a National writer, as Burns was when he wrote finely and as Burns was not when he wrote *Highland Mary* and *The Cotter's Saturday Night*.

A writer is not less National because he shows the influence of other countries and of the great writers of the world. No nation, since the beginning of history, has ever drawn all its life out of itself. Even The Well of English Undefiled, the Father of English Poetry himself, borrowed his metres, and much of his way of looking at the world, from French writers, and it is possible that the influence of Italy was more powerful among the Elizabethan poets than any literary influence out of England herself. Many years ago, when I was contending with Sir Charles Gavan Duffy over what seemed to me a too narrow definition of Irish interests, Professor York Powell either said or wrote to me that the creative power of England was always at its greatest when her receptive power was greatest. If Ireland is about to produce a literature that is important to her, it must be the result of the influences that flow in upon the mind of an educated Irishman to-day, and, in a greater degree, of what came into the world with himself. Gaelic can hardly fail to do a portion of the work, but one cannot say whether it may not be some French or German writer who will do most to make him an articulate man. If he really achieve the miracle, if he really make all that he has seen and felt and known a portion of his own intense nature, if he puts it all into the fire of his energy, he need not fear being a stranger among his own people in the end. There never have been men more unlike an Englishman's idea of himself than Keats and Shelley, while Campbell, whose emotion came out of a shallow well, was very like that idea. We call certain minds creative because they are among the moulders of their nation and are not made upon its mould, and they resemble one another in this only—they have never been foreknown or fulfilled an expectation.

It is sometimes necessary to follow in practical matters some definition which one knows to have but a passing use. We, for instance, have always confined ourselves to plays upon Irish subjects, as if no others could be National literature. Our Theatre inherits this limitation from previous movements, which found it necessary and fruitful. Goldsmith and Sheridan and Burke had become so much a part of English life, were so greatly moulded by the movements that were moulding England, that, despite certain Irish elements that clung about them, we could not think of them as more important to us than any English writer of equal rank. Men told us that we should keep our hold of them, as it were, for they were a part of our glory; but we did not consider our glory very important. We had no desire to turn braggarts, and we did suspect the motives of our advisers. Perhaps they had reasons, which were not altogether literary, for thinking it might be well if Irish men of letters, in our day also, would turn their faces to England. But what moved me always the most, and I had something to do with forcing this limitation upon our organisations, is that a new language of expression would help to awaken a new attitude in writers themselves, and that if our organisations were satisfied to interpret a writer to his own countrymen merely because he was of Irish birth, the organisations would become a kind of trade union for the helping of Irishmen to catch the ear of London publishers and managers, and for upholding writers who had been beaten by abler Englishmen. Let a man turn his face to us, accepting the commercial disadvantages that would bring upon him, and talk of what is near to our hearts, Irish Kings and Irish Legends and Irish Countrymen, and we would find it a joy to interpret him. Our one philosophical critic, Mr. John Eglinton, thinks we were very arbitrary, and yet I would not have us enlarge our practice. England and France, almost alone among nations, have great works of literature which have taken their subjects from foreign lands, and even in France and England this is more true in appearance than reality. Shakespeare observed his Roman crowds in London, and saw, one doubts not, somewhere in his own Stratford, the old man that gave Cleopatra the asp. Somebody I have been reading lately finds the Court of Louis XIV in *Phèdre* and *Andromaque*. Even in France and England almost the whole prose fiction professes to describe the life of the country, often of the districts where its writers have lived, for, unlike a poem, a novel requires so much minute observation of the surface of life that a novelist who cares for the illusion of reality will keep to familiar things. A writer will indeed take what is most creative out of himself, not from observation, but experience, yet he must master a definite language, a definite symbolism of incident and scene. Flaubert explains the comparative failure of his Salammbô by saying, 'One cannot frequent her'. He could create her soul, as it were, but he could not tell with certainty how it would express itself before Carthage fell to ruins. In the small nations which have

to struggle for their national life, one finds that almost
every creator, whether poet or novelist, sets all his
stories in his own country. I do not recollect that
Björnson ever wrote of any land but Norway, and
Ibsen, though he lived in exile for many years, driven
out by his countrymen, as he believed, carried the little
seaboard towns of Norway everywhere in his imagination. So far as we can be certain of anything, we may
be certain that Ireland with her long National struggle,
her old literature, her unbounded folk-imagination,
will, in so far as her literature is National at all, be
more like Norway than England or France.

If literature is but praise of life, if our writers are
not to plead the National cause, nor insist upon the
Ten Commandments, nor upon the glory of their
country, what part remains for it, in the common life of
the country? It will influence the life of the country
immeasurably more, though seemingly less, than have
our propagandist poems and stories. It will leave to
others the defence of all that can be codified for ready
understanding, of whatever is the especial business of
sermons, and of leading articles; but it will bring all the
ways of men before that ancient tribunal of our sympathies. It will measure all things by the measure not
of things visible but of things invisible. In a country
like Ireland, where personifications have taken the
place of life, men have more hate than love, for the
unhuman is nearly the same as the inhuman, but literature, which is a part of that charity that is the forgive-
ness of sins, will make us understand men no matter

how little they conform to our expectations. We will be more interested in heroic men than in heroic actions, and will have a little distrust for everything that can be called good or bad in itself with a very confident heart. Could we understand it so well, we will say, if it were not something other than human life? We will have a scale of virtues, and value most highly those that approach the indefinable. Men will be born among us of whom it is possible to say, not 'What a philanthropist', 'What a patriot', 'How practical a man', but, as we say of the men of the Renaissance, 'What a nature', 'How much abundant life'. Even at the beginning we will value qualities more than actions, for these may be habit or accident; and should we say to a friend, 'You have advertised for an English cook', or 'I hear that you have no clerks who are not of your own faith', or 'You have voted an address to the King', we will add to our complaint, 'You have been unpatriotic and I am ashamed of you, but if you cease from doing any of these things because you have been terrorised out of them, you will cease to be my friend'. We will not forget how to be stern, but we will remember always that the highest life unites, as in one fire, the greatest passion and the greatest courtesy.

A feeling for the form of life, for the graciousness of life, for the dignity of life, for the moving limbs of life, for the nobleness of life, for all that cannot be written in codes, has always been greatest among the gifts of literature to mankind. Indeed, the Muses being women, all literature is but their love-cries to the manhood of the world. It is now one and now another that cries,

Samhain : 1904

but the words are the same: 'Love of my heart, what matter to me that you have been quarrelsome in your cups, and have slain many, and have given your love here and there? It was because of the whiteness of your flesh and the mastery in your hands that I gave you my love, when all life came to me in your coming.' And then in a low voice that none may overhear—'Alas! I am greatly afraid that the more they cry against you the more I love you'.

There are two kinds of poetry, and they are commingled in all the greatest works. When the tide of life sinks low there are pictures, as in the *Ode on a Grecian Urn* and in Virgil at the plucking of the Golden Bough. The pictures make us sorrowful. We share the poet's separation from what he describes. It is life in the mirror, and our desire for it is as the desire of the lost souls for God; but when Lucifer stands among his friends, when Villon sings his dead ladies to so gallant a rhythm, when Timon makes his epitaph, we feel no sorrow, for life herself has made one of her eternal gestures, has called up into our hearts her energy that is eternal delight. In Ireland, where the tide of life is rising, we turn, not to picture-making, but to the imagination of personality—to drama, gesture.

The Irish Dramatic Movement

THE PLAY, THE PLAYER, AND THE SCENE

I HAVE been asked to put into this year's *Samhain* Miss Horniman's letter offering us the use of the Abbey Theatre. I have done this, but as Miss Horniman begins her letter by stating that she has made her offer out of 'great sympathy with the Irish National Theatre Company as publicly explained by Mr. Yeats on various occasions', she has asked me to go more into detail as to my own plans and hopes than I have done before. I think they are the plans and hopes of my fellow-dramatists, for we are all of one movement, and have influenced one another, and have in us the spirit of our time. I discussed them all very shortly in the last *Samhain*. And I know that it was that *Samhain*, and a certain speech I made in front of the curtain, that made Miss Horniman entrust us with her generous gift. But last *Samhain* is practically out of print, and my speech has gone even out of my own memory. I will repeat, therefore, much that I have said already, but adding a good deal to it.

First. Our plays must be literature or written in the spirit of literature. The modern theatre has died away to what it is because the writers have thought of their audiences instead of their subject. An old writer saw his hero, if it was a play of character, or some dominant passion, if it was a play of passion, like *Phèdre* or *Andromaque*, moving before him, living with a life he did not endeavour to control. The persons acted upon

164

one another as they were bound by their natures to act, and the play was dramatic, not because he had sought out dramatic situations for their own sake, but because will broke itself upon will and passion upon passion. Then the imagination began to cool, the writer began to be less alive, to seek external aids, remembered situations, tricks of the theatre, that had proved themselves again and again. His persons no longer will have a particular character, but he knows that he can rely upon the incidents, and he feels himself fortunate when there is nothing in his play that has not succeeded a thousand times before the curtain has risen. Perhaps he has even read a certain guide-book to the stage published in France, and called *The Thirty-six Situations of Drama*. The costumes will be magnificent, the actresses will be beautiful, the Castle in Spain will be painted by an artist upon the spot. We will come from his play excited if we are foolish, or can condescend to the folly of others, but knowing nothing new about ourselves, and seeing life with no new eyes and hearing it with no new ears. The whole movement of theatrical reform in our day has been a struggle to get rid of this kind of play, and the sincere play, the logical play, that we would have in its place, will always seem, when we hear it for the first time, undramatic, unexciting. It has to stir the heart in a long-disused way, it has to awaken the intellect to a pleasure that ennobles and wearies. I was at the first performance of an Ibsen play given in England. It was *A Doll's House*, and at the fall of the curtain I heard an old dramatic critic say, 'It is but a series of conversations terminated by an accident'. So far, we here in Dublin mean the same thing as do Mr. Max Beerbohm, Mr. Walkley, and Mr. Archer, who are seeking to restore sincerity to the English stage, but I am not certain that we mean the same thing all through. The utmost sincerity, the most unbroken logic, give me, at any rate, but an imperfect pleasure if there is not a vivid and beautiful language. Ibsen has sincerity and logic beyond any writer of our time, and we are all seeking to learn them at his hands; but is he not a good deal less than the greatest of all times, because he lacks beautiful and vivid language? 'Well, well, give me time and you shall hear all about it. If only I had Peter here now', is very like life, is entirely in its place where it comes, and when it is united to other sentences exactly like itself, one is moved, one knows not how, to pity and terror, and yet not moved as if the words themselves could sing and shine. Mr. Max Beerbohm wrote once that a play cannot have style because the people must talk as they talk in daily life. He was thinking, it is obvious, of a play made out of that typically modern life where there is no longer vivid speech. Blake says that a work of art must be minutely articulated by God or man, and man has too little help from that occasional *collaborateur* when he writes of people whose language has become abstract and dead. Falstaff gives one the sensation of reality, and when one remembers the abundant vocabulary of a time when all but everything present to the mind was present to the senses, one imagines that his words were but little magnified from the words of such a man in real life. Language was still alive then, alive as it is in Gaelic to-day, as it is in English-speaking Ireland where the schoolmaster or the newspaper has not corrupted it. I know that we are at the mere beginning, laboriously learning our craft, trying our hands in little plays for the most part, that we may not venture too boldly in our ignorance; but I never hear the vivid, picturesque, ever-varied language of Mr. Synge's persons without feeling that the great *collaborateur* has his finger in our business. May it not be that the only realistic play that will live as Shakespeare has lived, as Calderón has lived, as the Greeks have lived, will arise out of the common life, where language is as much alive as if it were new come out of Eden? After all, is not the greatest play not the play that gives the sensation of an external reality but the play in which there is the greatest abundance of life itself, of the reality that is in our minds? Is it possible to make a work of art, which needs every subtlety of expression if it is to reveal what hides itself continually, out of a dying, or at any rate a very ailing, language? and all language but that of the poets and of the poor is already bed-ridden. We have, indeed, persiflage, the only speech of educated men that expresses a deliberate enjoyment of words: but persiflage is not a true language. It is impersonal; it is not in the midst but on the edge of life; it covers more character than it discovers: and yet, such as it is, all our comedies are made out of it.

What the ever-moving, delicately moulded flesh is to human beauty, vivid musical words are to passion. Somebody has said that every nation begins with poetry and ends with algebra, and passion has always refused to express itself in algebraical terms.

Have we not been in error in demanding from our playwrights personages who do not transcend our common actions any more than our common speech? If we are in the right, all antiquity has been in error. The scholars of a few generations ago were fond of deciding that certain persons were unworthy of the dignity of art. They had, it may be, an over-abounding preference for kings and queens, but we are, it may be, very stupid in thinking that the average man is a fit subject at all for the finest art. Art delights in the exception, for it delights in the soul expressing itself according to its own laws and arranging the world about it in its own pattern, as sand strewn upon a drum will change itself into different patterns, according to the notes of music that are sung or played to it. But the average man is average because he has not attained to freedom. Habit, routine, fear of public opinion, fear of punishment here or hereafter, a myriad of things that are 'something other than human life', something less than flame, work their will upon his soul and trundle his body here and there. At the first performance of *Ghosts* I could not escape from an illusion unaccountable to me at the time. All the characters seemed to be less than life-size; the stage, though it was but the little Royalty stage, seemed larger than I had ever seen it. Little whimpering puppets moved here and there in the middle of that great abyss. Why did they not speak out with louder voices or move with freer gestures? What was it that weighed upon their souls perpetually? Certainly they were all in prison, and yet there was no prison. In India there are villages so obedient that all the gaoler has to do is to draw a circle upon the ground with his staff, and to tell his thief to stand there so many hours; but what law had these people broken that they had to wander round that narrow circle all their lives? May not such art, terrible, satirical, inhuman, be the medicine of great cities, where nobody is ever alone with his own strength? Nor is Maeterlinck very different, for his persons 'enquire after Jerusalem in the regions of the grave, with weak voices almost inarticulate, wearying repose'. Is it the mob that has robbed those angelic persons of the energy of their souls? Will not our next art be rather of the country, of great open spaces, of the soul rejoicing in itself? Will not the generations to come begin again to have an over-abounding faith in kings and queens, in masterful spirits, whatever names we call them by? I had Molière with me on my way to America, and as I read I seemed to be at home in Ireland listening to that conversation of the people which is so full of riches because so full of leisure, or to those old stories of the folk which were made by men who believed so much in the soul, and so little in anything else, that they were never entirely certain that the earth was solid under the foot-sole. What is there left for us, that have seen the newly discovered stability of things changed from an enthusiasm to a weariness, but to labour with a high heart, though it may be with weak hands, to rediscover an art of the theatre that shall be joyful, fantastic, extravagant, whimsical, beautiful, resonant, and altogether reckless? The arts are at their greatest when they

seek for a life growing always more scornful of everything that is not itself and passing into its own fullness,
as it were, ever more completely as all that is created
out of the passing mode of society slips from it; and
attaining that fullness, perfectly it may be—and from
this is tragic joy and the perfectness of tragedy—when
the world itself has slipped away in death. We, who
are believers, cannot see reality anywhere but in the
soul itself, and seeing it there we cannot do other than
rejoice in every energy, whether of gesture, or of action, or of speech, coming out of the personality, the
soul's image, even though the very laws of Nature seem
as unimportant in comparison as did the laws of Rome
to Coriolanus when his pride was upon him. Has not
the long decline of the arts been but the shadow of de-
clining faith in an unseen reality?

> If the sun and moon should doubt,
> They'd immediately go out.

Second. If we are to make a drama of energy, of extravagance, of fantasy, of musical and noble speech,
we shall need an appropriate stage-management. Up to
a generation or two ago, and to our own generation,
here and there, lingered a method of acting and of
stage-management, which had come down, losing much
of its beauty and meaning on the way, from the days of
Shakespeare. Long after England, under the influence
of Garrick, began the movement towards Naturalism,
this school had a great popularity in Ireland, where it
was established at the Restoration by an actor who probably remembered the Shakespearean players. France

has inherited from Racine and from Molière an equivalent art, and, whether it is applied to comedy or to tragedy, its object is to give importance to the words. It is not only Shakespeare whose finest thoughts are inaudible on the English stage. Congreve's *Way of the World* was acted in London last spring, and revived again a month ago, and the part of Lady Wishfort was taken by a very admirable actress, an actress of genius who has never had the recognition she deserves. There is a scene where Lady Wishfort turns away a servant with many words. She cries: 'Go, set up for yourself again, do; drive a trade, do, with your three-pennyworth of small ware, flaunting upon a packthread, under a brandy-seller's bulk, or against a dead wall by a ballad-monger; go, hang out an old frisoneer-gorget, with a yard of yellow colberteen again, do; an old gnawed mask, two rows of pins, and a child's fiddle; a glass necklace with the beads broken, and a quilted nightcap with one ear. Go, go, drive a trade.' The conversation of an older time, of Urquhart, the translator of Rabelais, let us say, awakes with a little of its old richness. The actress acted so much and so admirably that when she first played it—I heard her better a month ago, perhaps because I was nearer to the stage—I could not understand a word of a passage that required the most careful speech. Just as the modern musician, through the over-development of an art that seems exterior to the poet, writes so many notes for every word that the natural energy of speech is dissolved and broken and the words made inaudible, so did this actress, a perfect mistress of her own art, put into her voice so many different notes,

so run up and down the scale under an impulse of anger
and scorn that one had hardly been more affronted by a
musical setting. Everybody who has spoken to large
audiences knows that he must speak difficult passages,
in which there is some delicacy of sound or of thought,
upon one or two notes. The larger his audience, the
more he must get away, except in trivial passages, from
the methods of conversation. Where one requires the
full attention of the mind, one must not weary it with
any but the most needful changes of pitch and note, or
by an irrelevant or obtrusive gesture. As long as drama
was full of poetical beauty, full of description, full
of philosophy, as long as its words were the very
vesture of sorrow and laughter, the players understood
that their art was essentially conventional, artificial,
ceremonious.

The stage itself was differently shaped, being more
a platform than a stage, for they did not desire to picture
the surface of life, but to escape from it. But realism
came in, and every change towards realism coincided
with a decline in dramatic energy. The proscenium was
imported into England at the close of the seventeenth
century, appropriate costumes a generation later. The
audience were forbidden to sit upon the stage in the
time of Sheridan, the last English-speaking playwright
whose plays have lived. And the last remnant of the
platform, the part of the stage that still projected beyond the proscenium, dwindled in size till it disappeared
in our own day. The birth of science was at hand, the
birth-pangs of its mother had troubled the world for
centuries. But now that Gargantua is born at last, it may

be possible to remember that there are other giants.

We can never bring back old things precisely as they were, but must consider how much of them is necessary to us, accepting, even if it were only out of politeness, something of our own time. The necessities of a builder have torn from us, all unwilling as we were, the apron, as the portion of the platform that came in front of the proscenium used to be called, and we must submit to the picture-making of the modern stage. We would have preferred to be able to return occasionally to the old stage of statue-making, of gesture. On the other hand, one accepts, believing it to be a great improvement, some appropriateness of costume, but speech is essential to us. An Irish critic has told us to study the stage-management of Antoine, but that is like telling a good Catholic to take his theology from Luther. Antoine, who described poetry as a way of saying nothing, has perfected naturalistic acting and carried the spirit of science into the theatre. Were we to study his methods, we might, indeed, have a far more perfect art than our own, a far more mature art, but it is better to fumble our way like children. We may grow up, for we have as good hopes as any other sturdy ragamuffin.

An actor must so understand how to discriminate cadence from cadence, and so cherish the musical lineaments of verse or prose, that he delights the ear with a continually varied music. This one has to say over and over again, but one does not mean that his speaking should be a monotonous chant. Those who have heard Mr. Frank Fay speaking verse will understand me. That speech of his, so masculine and so musical, could only sound monotonous to an ear that was deaf to poetic rhythm, and no man should, as do London managers, stage a poetical drama according to the desire of those who are deaf to poetical rhythm. It is possible, barely so, but still possible, that some day we may write musical notes as did the Greeks, it seems, for a whole play, and make our actors speak upon them—not sing, but speak. Even now, when one wishes to make the voice immortal and passionless, as in the Angel's part in my *Hour-Glass*, one finds it desirable for the player to speak always upon pure musical notes, written out beforehand and carefully rehearsed. On the one occasion when I heard the Angel's part spoken in this way with entire success, the contrast between the crystalline quality of the pure notes and the more confused and passionate speaking of the Wise Man was a new dramatic effect of great value.

If a song is brought into a play it does not matter to what school the musician belongs if every word, if every cadence, is as audible and expressive as if it were spoken. It must be good speech, and we must not listen to the musician if he promise to add meaning to the words with his notes, for one does not add meaning to the word 'love' by putting four o's in the middle, or by subordinating it even slightly to a musical note. But where can we find a musician so mild, so quiet, so modest, unless he be a sailor from the forecastle or some ghost out of the twelfth century? One must ask him for music that shall mean nothing, or next to nothing, apart from the words, and after all he is a musician.

When I heard the Aeschylean Trilogy at Stratford-on-Avon last spring I could not hear a word of the chorus, except in a few lines here and there which were spoken without musical setting. The chorus was not without dramatic, or rather operatic effect; but why should those singers have taken so much trouble to learn by heart so much of the greatest lyric poetry of Greece? 'Twinkle, twinkle, little star', or any other memory of their childhood, would have served their turn. If it had been comic verse, the singing-master and the musician would have respected it, and the audience would have been able to hear. Mr. Dolmetsch and Miss Florence Farr have been working for some time to find out some way of setting serious poetry which will enable us to hear it, and the singer to sing sweetly and yet never to give a word, a cadence, or an accent that would not be given it in ordinary passionate speech. It is difficult, for they are trying to rediscover an art that is only remembered or half remembered in ships and in hovels and among wandering tribes of uncivilised men, and they have to make their experiment with singers who have been trained by a method of teaching that professes to change a human being into a musical instrument, a creation of science, 'something other than human life'. In old days the singer began to sing over the rocking cradle or among the wine-cups, and it was as though life itself caught fire of a sudden; but to-day the poet, fanatic that he is, watches the singer go up on to the platform, wondering and expecting every moment that he will punch himself as if he were a bag. It is certainly impossible to speak with perfect expression after you have been a bagpipes for many years, even though you have been making the most beautiful music all the time.

The success of the chorus in the performance of *Hippolytus* last spring—I did not see the more recent performance, but hear upon all hands that the chorus was too large—the expressiveness of the greater portion as mere speech, has, I believe, re-created the chorus as a dramatic method. The greater portion of the singing, as arranged by Miss Farr, even when four or five voices sang together, though never when ten sang together, was altogether admirable speech, and some of it was speech of extraordinary beauty. When one lost the meaning, even perhaps where the whole chorus sang together, it was not because of a defective method, but because it is the misfortune of every new artistic method that we can only judge of it through performers who must be for a long time unpractised and amateurish. This new art has a double difficulty, for the training of a modern singer makes articulate speech, as a poet understands it, nearly impossible, and those who are masters of speech very often, perhaps usually, are poor musicians. Fortunately, Miss Farr, who has some knowledge of music, has, it may be, the most beautiful voice on the English stage, and is, in her management of it, an exquisite artist.

That we may throw emphasis on the words in poetical drama, above all where the words are remote from real life as well as in themselves exacting and difficult, the actors must move, for the most part, slowly and quietly, and not very much, and there should be something in their movements decorative and rhythmical as

if they were paintings on a frieze. They must not draw
attention to themselves at wrong moments, for poetry
and indeed all picturesque writing is perpetually making
little pictures which draw the attention away for a
second or two from the player. The actress who played
Lady Wishfort should have permitted us to give a part
of our attention to that little shop or wayside booth.
Then, too, one must be content to have long quiet
moments, long grey spaces, long level reaches, as it
were—the leisure that is in all fine life: for what we
may call the business-will in a high state of activity is
not everything, although contemporary drama knows
of little else.

Third. We must have a new kind of scenic art. I have
been the advocate of the poetry as against the actor, but
I am the advocate of the actor as against the scenery.
Ever since the last remnant of the old platform disappeared, and the proscenium grew into the frame of a
picture, the actors have been turned into a picturesque
group in the foreground of a meretricious landscape-
painting. The background should be of as little importance as the background of a portrait-group, and it
should, when possible, be of one colour or of one tint,
that the persons on the stage, wherever they stand, may
harmonise with it or contrast with it and preoccupy our
attention. Their outline should be clear and not broken
up into the outline of windows and wainscoting, or
lost into the edges of colours. In a play which copies
the surface of life in its dialogue we may, with this
reservation, represent anything that can be represented
successfully—a room, for instance—but a landscape

painted in the ordinary way will always be meretricious and vulgar. It will always be an attempt to do something which cannot be done successfully except in easel painting, and the moment an actor stands near to your mountain, or your forest, one will perceive that he is standing against a flat surface. Illusion, therefore, is impossible, and should not be attempted. We should be content to suggest a scene upon a canvas, whose vertical flatness we accept and use, as the decorator of pottery accepts the roundness of a bowl or a jug. Having chosen the distance from naturalism which will keep one's composition from competing with the illusion created by the actor, who belongs to a world with depth as well as height and breadth, one must keep this distance without flinching. The distance will vary according to the distance the playwright has chosen, and especially in poetry, which is more remote and idealistic than prose, one will insist on schemes of colour and simplicity of form, for every sign of deliberate order gives remoteness and ideality. But, whatever the distance be, one's treatment will always be more or less decorative. We can only find out the right decoration for the different types of play by experiment, but it will probably range between, on the one hand, woodlands made out of recurring pattern, or painted like old religious pictures upon a gold background, and upon the other the comparative realism of a Japanese print. This decoration will not only give us a scenic art that will be a true art because peculiar to the stage, but it will give the imagination liberty, and without returning to the bareness of the Elizabethan stage. The poet cannot evoke a picture to the mind's eye if a second-rate painter has set his imagination of it before the bodily eye; but decoration and suggestion will accompany our moods, and turn our minds to meditation, and yet never become obtrusive or wearisome. The actor and the words put into his mouth are always the one thing that matters, and the scene should never be complete of itself, should never mean anything to the imagination until the actor is in front of it.

If we remember that the movement of the actor, and the graduation and the colour of the lighting, are the two elements that distinguish the stage picture from an easel painting, we may not find it difficult to create an art of the stage ranking as a true fine art. Mr. Gordon Craig has done wonderful things with the lighting, but he is not greatly interested in the actor, and his streams of coloured direct light, beautiful as they are, will always seem, apart from certain exceptional moments, a new externality. We should rather desire, for all but exceptional moments, an even, shadowless light, like that of noon, and it may be that a light reflected out of mirrors will give us what we need.

M. Appia and M. Fortuni are making experiments in the staging of Wagner for a private theatre in Paris, but I cannot understand what M. Appia is doing, from the little I have seen of his writing, excepting that the floor of the stage will be uneven like the ground, and that at moments the lights and shadows of green boughs will fall over the player that the stage may show a man wandering through a wood, and not a wood with a man in the middle of it. One agrees with all the destructive part of his criticism, but it looks as if he himself is seeking, not convention, but a more perfect realism. I cannot persuade myself that the movement of life is flowing that way, for life moves by a throbbing as of a pulse, by reaction and action. The hour of convention and decoration and ceremony is coming again.

The experiments of the Irish National Theatre Society will have of necessity to be for a long time few and timid, and we must often, having no money and not a great deal of leisure, accept for a while compromises, and much even that we know to be irredeemably bad. One can only perfect an art very gradually; and good play-writing, good speaking, and good acting are the first necessity.

Samhain : 1905

SAMHAIN: 1905

OUR first season at the Abbey Theatre has been tolerably successful. We drew small audiences, but quite as big as we had hoped for, and we end the year with a little money. On the whole, we have probably more than trebled our audiences of the Molesworth Hall. The same people come again and again, and others join them, and I do not think we lose any of them. We shall be under more expense in our new season, for we have decided to pay some of the company and send them into the provinces, but our annual expenses will not be as heavy as the weekly expenses of the most economical London manager. Mr. Philip Carr, whose revivals of Elizabethan plays and old comedies have been the finest things one could see in a London theatre, spent three hundred pounds and took twelve pounds during his last week; but here in Ireland enthusiasm can do half the work, and nobody is accustomed to get much money, and even Mr. Carr's inexpensive scenery costs more than our simple decorations. Our staging of *Kincora*, the work of Mr. Robert Gregory, was beautiful, with a high, grave dignity and that strangeness which Ben Jonson thought to be a part of all excellent beauty; and the expense of scenery, dresses, and all was hardly above thirty pounds. If we find a good scene we repeat it in other plays, and in course of time we shall be able to put on new plays without any expense for scenery at all. I do not think that even the most expensive decoration would increase in any way the pleasure of an audience that comes to us for the play and the acting.

We shall have abundance of plays, for Lady Gregory has written us a new comedy besides her *White Cockade*, which is in rehearsal; Mr. Boyle, a satirical comedy in three acts; Mr. Colum has made a new play out of his *Broken Soil*; and I have made almost a new one out of my *Shadowy Waters*; and Mr. Synge has practically finished a longer and more elaborate comedy than his last. Since our start last Christmas we have shown eleven plays created by our movement and very varied in substance and form, and six of these were new: *The Well of the Saints, Kincora, The Building Fund, The Land, On Baile's Strand,* and *Spreading the News.*

One of our plays, *The Well of the Saints,* has been accepted for immediate production by the Deutsches Theater of Berlin; and another, *The Shadow of the Glen,* is to be played during the season at the National Bohemian Theatre at Prague; and my own *Cathleen ni Houlihan* has been translated into Irish and been played at the Oireachtas, before an audience of some thousands. We have now several dramatists who have taken to drama as their most serious business, and we claim that a school of Irish drama exists, and that it is founded upon sincere observation and experience.

As is natural in a country where the Gaelic League has created a preoccupation with the countryman, the greatest number of our plays are founded on the comedy and tragedy of country life, and are written more or less in dialect. When the Norwegian National movement began, its writers chose for their maxim, 'To understand the saga by the peasant and the peasant by the saga'. Ireland in our day has rediscovered the old heroic literature of Ireland, and she has rediscovered the imagination of the folk. My own preoccupation is more with the heroic legend than with the folk, but Lady Gregory in her *Spreading the News*, Mr. Synge in his *Well of the Saints*, Mr. Colum in *The Land*, Mr. Boyle in *The Building Fund*, have been busy, much or little, with the folk and the folk-imagination. Mr. Synge alone has written of the peasant as he is to all the ages; of the folk-imagination as it has been shaped by centuries of life among fields or on fishing-grounds. His people talk a highly coloured musical language, and one never hears from them a thought that is of to-day and not of yesterday. Lady Gregory has written of the people of the markets and villages of the West, and their speech, though less full of peculiar idiom than that of Mr. Synge's people, is still always that vivid speech which has been shaped through some generations of English speaking by those who still think in Gaelic. Mr. Colum and Mr. Boyle, on the other hand, write of the countryman or villager of the East or centre of Ireland, who thinks in English, and the speech of their people shows the influence of the newspaper and the National Schools. The people they write of, too, are not the true folk. They are the peasant as he is being transformed by modern life, and for that very reason the man of the towns may find it easier to understand them. There is less surprise, less wonder in what he sees, but there is more of himself there, more of his vision of the world and of the problems that are troubling him.

It is not fitting for the showman to overpraise the show, but he is always permitted to tell you what is in his booths. Mr. Synge is the most obviously individual of our writers. He alone has discovered a new kind of sarcasm, and it is this sarcasm that keeps him, and may long keep him, from general popularity. Mr. Boyle satirises a miserly old woman, and he has made a very vivid person of her, but as yet his satire is such as all men accept; it brings no new thing to judgment. We have never doubted that what he assails is evil, and we are never afraid that it is ourselves. Lady Gregory alone writes out of a spirit of pure comedy, and laughs without bitterness and with no thought but to laugh. She has a perfect sympathy with her characters, even with the worst of them, and when the curtain goes down we are so far from the mood of judgment that we do not even know that we have condoned many sins. In Mr. Colum's *Land* there is a like comedy when Cornelius and Sally fill the scene, but then he is too young to be content with laughter. He is still interested in the reform of society, but that will pass, for at about thirty every writer, who is anything of an artist, comes to understand that all a work of art can do is to show us the reality that is within our minds, and the reality that our eyes look on. He is the youngest of us all by many years, and we are all proud to foresee his future.

I think that a race or a nation or a phase of life has but few dramatic themes, and that when these have

been once written well they must afterwards be written
less and less well until one gets at last but 'soulless self-
reflections of man's skill'. The first man writes what it
is natural to write, the second man what is left to him,
for the imagination cannot repeat itself. The hoydenish
young woman, the sentimental young woman, the
villain and the hero alike ever self-possessed, of contemporary drama, were once real discoveries, and one
can trace their history through the generations like a
joke or a folk-tale, but, unlike these, they grow always
less interesting as they get farther from their cradle.
Our opportunity in Ireland is not that our playwrights
have more talent—it is possible that they have less
than the workers in an old tradition—but that the
necessity of putting a life that has not hitherto been
dramatised into their plays excludes all these types
which have had their origin in a different social order.

An audience with National feeling is alive; at the
worst it is alive enough to quarrel with. One man came
up from the scene of Lady Gregory's *Kincora* at Killaloe
that he might see her play, and having applauded
loudly, and even cheered for the Dalcassians, became
silent and troubled when Brian took Gormleith for his
wife. 'It is a great pity', he said to the man next to him,
'that he didn't marry a quiet girl from his own district.'
Some have quarrelled with me because I did not take
some glorious moment of Cuchulain's life for my play,
and not the killing of his son, and all our playwrights
have been attacked for choosing bad characters instead
of good, and called slanderers of their country. In so
far as these attacks come from National feeling, that is

to say, out of an interest or an affection for the life of
this country now and in past times, as did the countryman's trouble about Gormleith, they are in the long
run the greatest help to a dramatist, for they give him
something to startle or to delight. Every writer has had
to face them where his work has aroused a genuine
interest. The Germans at the beginning of the nineteenth century preferred Schiller to Goethe, and thought
him the greater writer, because he put nobler characters
into his books; and when Chaucer encounters Eros in
the month of May, that testy god complains that though
he had 'sixty bookkes olde and newe', and all full of
stories of women and the life they led, and though for
every bad woman there are a hundred good, he has
chosen to write only of the bad ones. He complains
that Chaucer by his *Troilus* and his *Romaunt of the Rose*
has brought love and women to discredit. It is the same
in painting as in literature, for when a new painter
arises men cry out, even when he is a painter of the
beautiful like Rossetti, that he has chosen the exaggerated or the ugly or the unhealthy, forgetting that
it is the business of art and of letters to change the
values and to mint the coinage. Without this outcry
there is no movement of life in the arts, for it is the sign
of values not yet understood, of a coinage not yet
mastered. Sometimes the writer delights us, when we
grow to understand him, with new forms of virtue discovered in persons where one had not hitherto looked
for it, and sometimes—and this is more and more true
of modern art—he changes the values not by the
persons he sets before one, who may be mean enough,

Samhain : 1905

but by his way of looking at them, by the implications that come from his own mind, by the tune they dance to, as it were. Eros, into whose mouth Chaucer, one doubts not, puts arguments that he had heard from his readers and listeners, objected to Chaucer's art in the interests of pedantic mediaeval moralising; the contemporaries of Schiller commended him for reflecting vague romantic types from the sentimental literature of his predecessors; and those who object to the peasant as he is seen in the Abbey Theatre have their imaginations full of what is least observant and most sentimental in the Irish novelists. When I was a boy I spent many an afternoon with a village shoemaker who was a great reader. I asked him once what Irish novels he liked, and he told me there were none he could read. 'They sentimentalised the people', he said angrily; and it was against Kickham that he complained most. 'I want to see the people', he said, 'shown up in their naked hideousness.' That is the peasant mind as I know it, a mind that delights in strong sensations whether of beauty or of ugliness, in bare facts, and is quite without sentimentality. The sentimental mind is found among the middle classes, and it was this mind which came into Irish literature with Gerald Griffin and later on with Kickham.

It is the mind of the town, and it is a delight to those only who have seen life, and above all country life, with unobservant eyes, and most of all to the Irish tourist, to the patriotic young Irishman who goes to the country for a month's holiday with his head full of vague idealisms. It is not the art of Mr. Colum, born of the people, and when at his best looking at the town and not the country with strange eyes, nor the art of Mr. Synge, spending weeks and months in remote places talking Irish to fishers and islanders. I remember meeting, about twenty years ago, a lad who had a little yacht at Kingstown. Somebody was talking of the sea paintings of a great painter, Hook, I think, and this made him very angry. No yachtsman believed in them or thought them at all like the sea, he said. Indeed, he was always hearing people praise pictures that were not a bit like the sea, and thereupon he named certain of the greatest painters of water—men who more than all others had spent their lives in observing the effects of light upon cloud and wave. I met him again the other day, well on in middle life, and though he is not even an Irishman, indignant with Mr. Synge's and Mr. Boyle's peasants. He knew the people, he said, and neither he nor any other person that knew them could believe that they were properly represented in *The Well of the Saints* or *The Building Fund*. Twenty years ago his imagination was under the influence of popular pictures, but to-day it was overpowered by the conventional idealism writers like Kickham and Griffin substitute for the ever-varied life of the cottages, and by that conventional idealism that the contemporary English theatre substitutes for all life whatsoever. I saw *Caste*, the earliest play of the modern school, a few days ago, and found there more obviously than I expected, for I am not much of a theatre-goer, the English half of the mischief. Two of the minor persons had a certain amount of superficial characterisation, as if out of the halfpenny comic papers; but the central persons, the man and woman that created the dramatic excitement, such as it was, had not characters of any kind, being vague ideals, perfection as it is imagined by a commonplace mind. The audience could give them its sympathy without the labour that comes from awakening knowledge. If the dramatist had put into his play whatever man or woman of his acquaintance seemed to come closest to perfection, he would have had to make it a study, among other things, of the little petty faults and perverted desires that arise out of the nature of its surroundings. He would have troubled that admiring audience by making a self-indulgent sympathy more difficult. He might have even seemed, like Ibsen or the early Christians, an enemy of the human race. We have gone down to the roots, and we have made up our minds upon one thing quite definitely—that in no play that professes to picture life in its daily aspects shall we admit these white phantoms. We can do this, not because we have any special talent, but because we are dealing with a life which has for all practical purposes never been set upon the stage before. The conventional types of the novelists do not pervert our imagination, for they are built, as it were, into another form, and no man who has chosen for himself a sound method of drama, whether it be the drama of character or of crisis, can use them. The Gaelic League and *Cumann na n-Gaedheal* play does indeed show the influence of the novelists; but the typical Gaelic League play is essentially narrative and not dramatic. Every artist necessarily imitates those who have worked in the same form before him, and when the preoccupation has been with the same life he almost always, consciously or unconsciously, borrows more than the form, and it is this very borrowing—affecting thought, language, all the vehicles of expression—which brings about the most of what we call decadence.

After all, if our plays are slanders upon their country; if to represent upon the stage a hard old man like Cosgar, or a rapacious old man like Shan, or a faithless wife like Nora Burke, or to select from history treacherous Gormleith for a theme, is to represent this nation at something less than its full moral worth; if every play played in the Abbey Theatre now and in times to come be something of a slander, is anybody a penny the worse? Some ancient or mediaeval races did not think so. Jusserand describes the French conquerors of mediaeval England as already imagining themselves in their literature, as they have done to this day, as a great deal worse than they are, and the English imagining themselves a great deal better. The greater portion of the *Divine Comedy* is a catalogue of the sins of Italy, and Boccaccio became immortal because he exaggerated with an unceasing playful wit the vices of his countryside. The Greeks chose for the themes of their serious literature a few great crimes, and Corneille, in his article on the theory of the drama, shows why the greatness and notoriety of these crimes is necessary to tragic drama. The public life of Athens found its chief celebration in the monstrous caricature of Aristo-

phanes, and the Greek nation was so proud, so free
from morbid sensitiveness, that it invited the foreign
ambassadors to the spectacle. And I answer to those
who say that Ireland cannot afford this freedom because of her political circumstances, that if Ireland
cannot afford it, Ireland cannot have a literature.
Literature has never been the work of slaves, and
Ireland must learn to say:

> Stone walls do not a prison make,
> Nor iron bars a cage.

The misrepresentation of the average life of a
nation that follows of necessity from an imaginative
delight in energetic characters and extreme types, en-
larges the energy of a people by the spectacle of energy.
A nation is injured by the picking out of a single type
and setting that into print or upon the stage as a type
of the whole nation. Ireland suffered for a century from
that single whiskey-drinking, humorous type which
seemed for a time the accepted type of all. The Englishwoman is, no doubt, injured in the same way in the
minds of various Continental nations by a habit of
caricaturing all Englishwoman as having big teeth.
But neither nation can be injured by imaginative writers
selecting types that please their fancy. They will never
impose a general type on the public mind, for genius
differs from the newspapers in this, that the greater and
more confident it is, the more is its delight in varieties
and species. If Ireland were at this moment, through
a misunderstanding terror of the stage Irishman, to
deprive her writers of freedom, to make their imaginations timid, she would lower her dignity in her own

eyes and in the eyes of every intellectual nation. That old caricature did her very little harm in the long run, perhaps a few car-drivers have copied it in their lives, while the mind of the country remained untroubled; but the loss of imaginative freedom and daring would turn us into old women. In the long run, it is the great writer of a nation that becomes its image in the minds of posterity, and even though he represent no man of worth in his art, the worth of his own mind becomes the inheritance of his people. He takes nothing away that he does not give back in greater volume.

If Ireland had not lost the Gaelic she never would have had this sensitiveness as of a *parvenu* when presented at Court for the first time, or of a negro newspaper. When Ireland had the confidence of her own antiquity, her writers praised and blamed according to their fancy, and even, as throughout all mediaeval Europe, laughed when they had a mind to at the most respected persons, at the sanctities of Church and State. The story of *The Shadow of the Glen*, found by Mr. Synge in Gaelic-speaking Aran, and by Mr. Curtain in Munster; the song of *The Red-haired Man's Wife*, sung in all Gaelic Ireland; *The Midnight Court* of MacGiolla Meidhre; *The Vision of MacCoinglinne;* the old romancers, with their Bricriu and their Conan, laughed and sang as fearlessly as Chaucer or Villon or Cervantes. It seemed almost as if those old writers murmured to themselves: 'If we but keep our courage, let all the virtues perish, for we can make them over again; but if that be gone, all is gone'. I remember

Samhain : 1905

when I was an art student at the Metropolitan School of Art a good many years ago, saying to Mr. Hughes the sculptor, as we looked at the work of our fellow-students, 'Every student here that is doing better work than another is doing it because he has a more intrepid imagination; one has only to look at the line of a drawing to see that'; and he said that was his own thought also. All good art is extravagant, vehement, impetuous, shaking the dust of time from its feet, as it were, and beating against the walls of the world.

If a sincere religious artist were to arise in Ireland in our day, and were to paint the Holy Family, let us say, he would meet with the same opposition that sincere dramatists are meeting with to-day. The half-educated mind is never sincere in the arts, and one finds in Irish chapels, above all in Irish convents, the religious art that it understands. A Connacht convent a little time ago refused a fine design for stained glass, because of the personal life in the faces and in the attitudes, which seemed to them ugly, perhaps even impious. They sent to the designer an insipid German chromo-lithograph, full of faces without expression or dignity, and gestures without personal distinction, and the designer, too anxious for success to reject any order, has carried out this meaningless design in glass of beautiful colour and quality. Let us suppose that Meister Stefan were to paint in Ireland to-day that exquisite Madonna of his, with her lattice of roses; a great deal that is said of our plays would be said of that picture. Why select for his model a little girl selling newspapers in the streets, why slander with that miserable little body the Mother of God? He could only answer, as the imaginative artist always answers, 'That is the way I have seen her in my mind, and what I have made of her is very living'. All art is founded upon personal vision, and the greater the art the more surprising the vision; and all bad art is founded upon impersonal types and images, accepted by average men and women out of imaginative poverty and timidity, or the exhaustion that comes from labour.

Nobody can force a movement of any kind to take any prearranged pattern to any very great extent; one can, perhaps, modify it a little, and that is all. When one says that it is going to develop in a certain way, one means that one sees, or imagines that one sees, certain energies which left to themselves are bound to give it a certain form. Writing in *Samhain* some years ago, I said that our plays would be of two kinds, plays of peasant life and plays of a romantic and heroic life, such as one finds in the folk-tales. To-day I can see other forces, and can foretell, I think, the form of technique that will arise. About fifty years ago, perhaps not so many, the playwrights of every country in the world became persuaded that their plays must reflect the surface of life; and the author of *Caste*, for instance, made a reputation by putting what seemed to be average common life and average common speech for the first time upon the stage in England, and by substituting real loaves of bread and real cups of tea for imaginary ones. He was not a very clever nor a very well-educated man, and he made his revolution superficially; but in other countries men of intellect and knowledge created that intellectual drama of real life, of which Ibsen's later plays are the ripened fruit. This change coincided with the substitution of science for religion in the conduct of life, and is, I believe, as temporary, for the practice of twenty centuries will surely take the sway in the end. A rhetorician in that novel of Petronius which satirises, or perhaps one should say celebrates, Roman decadence, complains that the young people of his day are made blockheads by learning old romantic tales in the schools, instead of what belongs to common life. And yet is it not the romantic tale, the extravagant and ungovernable dream which comes out of youth; and is not that desire for what belongs to common life, whether it comes from Rome or Greece or England, the sign of fading fires, of ebbing imaginative desire? In the arts I am quite certain that it is a substitution of apparent for real truth. Mr. George Moore has a very vivid character; he is precisely one of those whose characters can be represented most easily upon the stage. Let us suppose that some dramatist had made even him the centre of a play in which the moderation of common life was carefully preserved, how very little he could give us of that headlong intrepid man, as we know him, whether through long personal knowledge or through his many books. The more carefully the play reflected the surface of life the more would the elements be limited to those that naturally display themselves during so many minutes of our ordinary affairs. It is only by extravagance, by an emphasis far greater than that of life as we observe it, that we can crowd into a few minutes the knowledge of years. Shakespeare or Sophocles can so quicken, as it were, the circles of the clock, so heighten the expression of life, that many years can unfold themselves in a few minutes, and it is always Shakespeare or Sophocles, and not Ibsen, that makes us say, 'How true, how often I have felt as that man feels'; or 'How intimately I have come to know those people on the stage'. There is a certain school of painters that has discovered that it is necessary in the representation of light to put little touches of pure colour side by side. When you went up close to that big picture of the Alps by Segantini, in Mr. Hugh Lane's Loan Exhibition a year ago, you found that the grass-seeds, which looked brown enough from the other side of the room, were full of pure scarlet colour. If you copy Nature's moderation of colour you do not imitate her, for you have only white paint and she has light. If you wish to represent character or passion upon the stage, as it is known to the friends, let us say, of your principal persons, you must be excessive, extravagant, fantastic even, in expression; and you must be this, more extravagantly, more excessively, more fantastically than ever, if you wish to show character and passion as they would be known to the principal person of your play in the depths of his own mind. The greatest art symbolises not those things that we have observed so much as those things that we have experienced, and when the imaginary saint or lover or hero moves us most deeply, it is the moment when he awakens within us for an instant our own heroism, our own sanctity, our own desire. We possess these things—the greatest of men not more than Seaghan the Fool—not at all moderately, but to an infinite extent, and though we control or ignore them, we know that the moralists speak true when they compare them to angels or to devils, or to beasts of prey. How can any dramatic art, moderate in expression, be a true image of Hell or Heaven or the wilderness, or do anything but create those faint histories that but touch our curiosity, those groups of persons that never follow us into our intimate life, where Odysseus and Don Quixote and Hamlet are with us always?

The scientific movement is ebbing a little everywhere, and here in Ireland it has never been in flood at all. And I am certain that everywhere literature will return once more to its old extravagant fantastical expression, for in literature, unlike science, there are no discoveries, and it is always the old that returns. Everything in Ireland urges us to this return, and it may be that we shall be the first to recover after the fifty years of mistake.

The antagonist of imaginative writing in Ireland is not a habit of scientific observation but our interest in matters of opinion. A misgoverned country seeking a remedy by agitation puts an especial value upon opinion, and even those who are not conscious of any interest in the country are influenced by the general habit. All fine literature is the disinterested contemplation or expression of life, but hardly any Irish writer can liberate his mind sufficiently from questions of practical reform for this contemplation. Art for art's sake, as he understands it, whether it be the art of the *Ode on a Grecian Urn* or of the imaginer of Falstaff, seems to him a neglect of public duty. It is as though the telegraph-boys botanised among the hedges with the undelivered envelopes in their pockets; a man must calculate the effect of his words before he writes them, whom they are to excite and to what end. We all write, if we follow the habit of the country, not for our own delight but for the improvement of our neighbours, and this is not only true of such obviously propagandist work as *The Spirit of the Nation* or a Gaelic League play, but of the work of writers who seemed to have escaped from every National influence like Mr. Bernard Shaw, Mr. George Moore, or even Mr. Oscar Wilde. They never keep their heads for very long out of the flood of opinion. Mr. Bernard Shaw, the one brilliant writer of comedy in England to-day, makes his comedies something less than life by never forgetting that he is a reformer, and Mr. Wilde could hardly finish an act of a play without denouncing the British public; and Mr. Moore—God bless the hearers! —has not for ten years now been able to keep himself from the praise or blame of the Church of his fathers. Goethe, whose mind was more busy with philosophy than any modern poet's, has said, 'The poet needs all philosophy, but he must keep it out of his work'. One remembers Dante, and wishes that Goethe had left some commentary upon that saying, some definition of philosophy perhaps; but one cannot be less than certain that the poet, though it may be well for him to have right opinions, above all if his country be at death's door, must keep all opinion that he holds to merely because he thinks it right, out of his poetry, if it is to be poetry at all. At the inquiry which preceded the granting of a patent to the Abbey Theatre I was asked if *Cathleen ni Houlihan* was not written to affect opinion. Certainly it was not. I had a dream one night which gave me a story, and I had certain emotions about this country, and I gave those emotions expression for my own pleasure. If I had written to convince others I would have asked myself, not 'Is that exactly what I think and feel?' but 'How would that strike so-and-so? How will they think and feel when they have read it?' And all would be oratorical and insincere. If we understand our own minds, and the things that are striving to utter themselves through our minds, we move others, not because we have understood or thought about those others, but because all life has the same root. Coventry Patmore has said, 'The end of art is peace', and the following of art is little different from the following of religion in the intense preoccupation that it demands. Somebody has said, 'God asks nothing of the highest soul except attention'; and so necessary is attention to mastery in any art, that there are moments when we think that nothing else is necessary, and nothing else so difficult. The religious life has created for itself monasteries and convents where men and women may forget in prayer and contemplation everything that seems necessary to the most useful and busy citizens of their towns and villages, and one imagines that even in the monastery and the convent there are passing things, the twitter of a sparrow in the window, the memory of some old quarrel, things lighter than air, that keep the soul from its joy. How many of those old religious sayings can one not apply to the life of art? 'The Holy Spirit', wrote Saint Thomas à Kempis, 'has liberated me from a multitude of opinions.' When one sets out to cast into some mould so much of life merely for life's sake, one is tempted at every moment to twist it from its eternal shape to help some friend or harm some enemy. Alas! all men, we in Ireland more than others, are fighters, and it is a hard law that compels us to cast away our swords when we enter the house of the Muses, as men cast them away at the doors of the banqueting-hall at Tara. A weekly paper, in reviewing last year's *Samhain*, convinced itself, or at any rate its readers—for that is the heart of the business in propaganda—that I only began to say these things a few months ago under I know not what alien influence; and yet I seem to have been saying them all my life. I took up an anthology of Irish verse that I edited some ten years ago, and I found them there, and I think they were a chief part of an old fight over the policy of the New Irish Library. Till they are accepted by writers and readers in this country it will never have a literature, it will never escape from the election rhyme and the pamphlet. So long as I have any control over the National Theatre Society it will be carried on in this spirit, call it art for art's sake if you will; and no plays will be produced at it which were written, not for the sake of a good story or fine verses or some revelation of character, but to please those friends of ours who are ever urging us to attack the priests or the English, or wanting us to put our imagination into handcuffs that we may be sure of never seeming to do one or the other.

I have had very little to say this year in *Samhain*, and I have said it badly. When I wrote *Ideas of Good and Evil* and *The Celtic Twilight*, I wrote everything very slowly and a great many times over. A few years ago, however, my eyesight got so bad that I had to dictate the first drafts of everything, and then rewrite these drafts several times. I did the last *Samhain* this way, dictating all the thoughts in a few days, and rewriting them in two or three weeks; but this time I am letting the first draft remain with all its carelessness of phrase and rhythm. I am busy with a practical project which needs the saying of many things from time to time, and it is better to say them carelessly and harshly than to take time from my poetry. One casts something away every year, and I shall, I think, have to cast away the hope of ever having a prose style that amounts to anything.

The Irish Dramatic Movement

LITERATURE AND THE LIVING VOICE [1]

I

ONE Sunday, in summer, a few years ago, I went to the little village of Killeenan, that is not many miles from Galway, to do honour to the memory of Raftery, a blind Gaelic poet who died a little before the famine. A headstone had been put over his grave in the half-ruined churchyard, and a priest had come to bless it, and many countrypeople to listen to his poems. After the shawled and frieze-coated people had knelt down and prayed for the repose of his soul, they gathered about a little wooden platform that had been put up in a field. I do not remember whether Raftery's poem about himself was one of those they listened to, but certainly it was in the thoughts of many, and it was the image reflected in that poem that had drawn some of them from distant villages.

> I am Raftery the poet,
> Full of hope and love;
> With eyes without light;
> With gentleness without misery.
>
> Going west on my journey
> With the light of my heart;

---

[1] This essay was written immediately after the opening of the Abbey Theatre, though it was not printed, through an accident, until the art of the Abbey had become an art of peasant comedy. It tells of things we have never had the time to begin. We still dream of them.—March 1908.

Samhain : 1906

Weak and tired
To the end of my road.

I am now,
And my face to a wall,
Playing music
To empty pockets.

Some few there remembered him, and one old man came out among the reciters to tell of the burying, where he himself, a young boy at the time, had carried a candle.

The verses of other Gaelic poets were sung or recited too, and, although certainly not often fine poetry, they had its spirit, its *naïveté*—that is to say, its way of looking at the world as if it were but an hour old—its seriousness even in laughter, its personal rhythm.

A few days after, I was in the town of Galway, and saw there, as I had often seen in other country towns, some young men marching down the middle of a street singing an already outworn London music-hall song, that filled the memory, long after they had gone by, with a rhythm as pronounced and as impersonal as the noise of a machine. In the shop-windows there were, I knew, the signs of a life very unlike that I had seen at Killeenan: halfpenny comic papers and story papers, sixpenny reprints of popular novels, and, with the exception of a dusty Dumas or Scott strayed thither, one knew not how, and one or two little books of Irish ballads, nothing that one calls literature, nothing that would interest the few thousands who alone out of many millions have what we call culture. A few miles had divided the sixteenth century, with its equality of culture, of good taste, from the twentieth, where if a man has fine taste he has either been born to leisure and opportunity or has in him an energy that is genius. One saw the difference in the clothes of the people of the town and of the village, for, as the Emerald Tablet says, outward and inner things answer to one another. The village men wore their bawneens, their white flannel jackets; they had clothes that had a little memory of clothes that had once been adapted to their calling by centuries of continual slight changes. They were sometimes well dressed, for they suggested nothing but themselves and wore little that had suited another better. But in the town nobody was well dressed; for in modern life, only a few people—some few thousands—set the fashion, and set it to please themselves and to fit their lives; and as for the rest, they must go shabby—the ploughman in clothes cut for a life of leisure, but made of shoddy, and the tramp in the ploughman's cast-off clothes, and the scarecrow in the tramp's battered coat and broken hat.

II

All that love the arts or love dignity in life have at one time or another noticed these things, and some have wondered why the world has for some three or four centuries sacrificed so much, and with what seems a growing recklessness, to create an intellectual aristocracy, a leisured class—to set apart, and above all others, a number of men and women who are not very well pleased with one another or the world they have to live in. It is some comparison, like this that I have made,

which has been the origin, as I think, of most attempts
to revive some old language in which the general business of the world is no longer transacted. The Provençal movement, the Welsh, the Czech, have all, I
think, been attempting, when we examine them to the
heart, to restore what is called a more picturesque way
of life—that is to say, a way of life in which the
common man has some share in imaginative art. That
this is the decisive element in the attempt to revive
and to preserve the Irish language I am very certain.
A language enthusiast does not put it that way to
himself; he says, rather, 'If I can make the people talk
Irish again they will be the less English'; but if you
talk to him till you have hunted the words into their
burrow you will find that the word 'Ireland' means to
him a form of life delightful to his imagination, and
that the word 'England' suggests to him a cold, joyless,
irreligious and ugly life. The life of the villages, with
its songs, its dances and its pious greetings, its conversations full of vivid images shaped hardly more by
life itself than by innumerable forgotten poets, all that
life of good-nature and improvisation grows more
noble as he meditates upon it, for it mingles with the
Middle Ages until he no longer can see it as it is, but
as it was when it ran, as it were, into a point of fire in
the courtliness of kings' houses. He hardly knows
whether what stirred him yesterday was that old
fiddler, playing an almost-forgotten music on a fiddle
mended with twine, or a sudden thought of some
king that was of the blood of that old man, some
O'Loughlin or O'Byrne, listening amid his soldiers, he

and they at the one table, they too, lucky, bright-eyed, while the minstrel sang of angry Cuchulain, or of him men called 'Golden salmon of the sea, clean hawk of the air'. It will not please him, however, if you tell him that he is fighting the modern world, which he calls 'England', as Mistral and his fellows called it Paris, and that he will need more than language if he is to make the monster turn up its white belly. And yet the difference between what the word England means and all that the word Gaelic suggests is greater than any that could have been before the imagination of Mistral. Ireland, her imagination at its noon before the birth of Chaucer, has created the most beautiful literature of a whole people that has been anywhere since Greece and Rome, while English literature, the greatest of all literatures but that of Greece, is yet the literature of a few. Nothing of it but a handful of ballads about Robin Hood has come from the folk or belongs to them rightly, for the good English writers, with a few exceptions that seem accidental, have written for a small cultivated class; and is not this the reason? Irish poetry and Irish stories were made to be spoken or sung, while English literature, alone of great literatures, because the newest of them all, has all but completely shaped itself in the printing-press. In Ireland to-day the old world that sang and listened is, it may be for the last time in Europe, face to face with the world that reads and writes, and their antagonism is always present under some name or other in Irish imagination and intellect. I myself cannot be convinced that the printing-press will be always victor, for change is inconceivably swift, and when it begins—well, as the proverb has it, everything comes in at the hole. The world soon tires of its toys, and our exaggerated love of print and paper seems to me to come out of passing conditions and to be no more a part of the final constitution of things than the craving of a woman in childbed for green apples. When a man takes a book into the corner, he surrenders so much life for his knowledge, so much, I mean, of that normal activity that gives him life and strength; he lays away his own handiwork and turns from his friend, and if the book is good he is at some pains to press all the little wanderings and tumults of the mind into silence and quiet. If the reader be poor, if he has worked all day at the plough or the desk, he will hardly have strength enough for any but a meretricious book; nor is it only when the book is on the knees that his own life must be given for it. For a good and sincere book needs the preparation of the peculiar studies and reveries that prepare for good taste, and make it easier for the mind to find pleasure in a new landscape; and all these reveries and studies have need of so much time and thought that it is almost certain a man cannot be a successful doctor, or engineer, or Cabinet Minister, and have a culture good enough to escape the mockery of the ragged art student who comes of an evening sometimes to borrow a half-sovereign. The old culture came to a man at his work; it was not at the expense of life, but an exaltation of life itself; it came in at the eyes as some civic ceremony sailed along the streets, or as we arrayed ourselves before the looking-glass; or it came in at the ears in a song as we bent over the plough or the anvil, or at that great table where rich and poor sat down together and heard the minstrel bidding them pass around the wine-cup and say a prayer for Gawain[1] dead. Certainly it came without a price; it did not take us from our friends and our handiwork; but it was like a good woman who gives all for love and is never jealous and is ready to do all the talking when we are tired.

How the old is to come again, how the other side of the penny is to come up, how the spit is to turn the other side of the meat to the fire, I do not know, but that the time will come I am certain. When one kind of desire has been satisfied for a long time it becomes sleepy, and other kinds, long quiet, after making a noise begin to order life. Of the many things, desires or powers or instruments, that are to change the world, the artist is fitted to understand but two or three, and the less he troubles himself about the complexity that is outside his craft, the more will he find it all within his craft, and the more dexterous will his hand and his thought become. I am trying to see nothing in the world but the arts, and nothing in this change —which I cannot prove but only foretell—but the share my art will have in it.

III

One thing is entirely certain. Wherever the old imaginative life lingers it must be stirred to more life,

[1] No, it was some other Knight of the Table.—1923.

or at the worst, kept alive, and in Ireland this is the work, it may be, of the Gaelic movement. But the nineteenth century, with its moral zeal, its insistence upon irrelevant interests, having passed over, the artist can admit that he cares about nothing that does not give him a new subject or a new technique. Propaganda would be for him a dissipation, but he may compare his art, if he has a mind to, with the arts that belonged to a whole people, and discover, not how to imitate the external form of an epic or a folk-song but how to express in some equivalent form whatever in the thoughts of his own age seems, as it were, to press into the future. The most obvious difference is that when literature belonged to a whole people, its three great forms, narrative, lyrical, and dramatic, found their way to men's minds without the mediation of print and paper. That narrative poetry may find its minstrels again, and lyrical poetry adequate singers, and dramatic poetry adequate players, he must spend much of his time with these three lost arts, and the more technical is his interest the better. When I first began working in Ireland at what some newspaper has called the Celtic Renaissance, I saw that we had still even in English a sufficient audience for song and speech. Certain of our young men and women, too restless and sociable to be readers, had amongst them an interest in Irish legend and history, and years of imaginative politics had kept them from forgetting, as most modern people have, how to listen to serious words. I always saw that some kind of theatre would be a natural centre for a tradition of feeling and thought, but that it must—and this was its chief opportunity—appeal to the interest appealed to by lively conversation or by oratory. In other words, that it must be made for young people who were sufficiently ignorant to refuse a pound of flesh even though the Nine Worthies offered their wisdom in return. They are not, perhaps, very numerous, for they do not include the thousands of conquered spirits who in Dublin, as elsewhere, go to see *The Girl from Kay's*, or when Mr. Tree is upon tour, *The Girl from Prospero's Island*; and the peasant in Ireland, as elsewhere, has not taken to the theatre, and can, I think, be moved through Gaelic only.

If one could get them, I thought, one could draw to oneself the apathetic people who are in every country, and people who don't know what they like till somebody tells them. Now, a friend has given me that theatre. It is not very big, but it is quite big enough to seat those few thousands and their friends in a seven days' run of a new play; and I have begun my real business. I have to find once again singers, minstrels, and players who love words more than any other thing under heaven, for without fine words there is no literature.

IV

I will say but a little of dramatic technique, as I would have it in this theatre of speech, of romance, of extravagance, for I have written of all that so many times. In every art, when we consider that it has need of a renewing of life, we go backward till we light upon a time when it was nearer to human life and instinct, before it had gathered about it so many mechanical specialisations and traditions. We examine that earlier condition and think out its principles of life that we may be able to separate accidental from vital things. William Morris, for instance, studied the earliest printing, the founts of type that were made when men saw their craft with eyes that were still new, and with leisure, and without the restraints of commerce and custom. And then he made a type that was really new, that had the quality of his own mind about it, though it reminds one of its ancestry, of its high breeding as it were. Coleridge and Wordsworth were influenced by the publication of Percy's *Reliques* to the making of a simplicity altogether unlike that of old ballad-writers. Rossetti went to early Italian painting, to Holy Families and choirs of angels, that he might learn how to express an emotion that had its roots in sexual desire and in the delight of his generation in fine clothes and in beautiful rooms. Nor is it otherwise with the reformers of Churches and of the social order, for reform must justify itself by a return in feeling to something that our fathers have told us in the old time.

So it is with us. Inspired by players who played before a figured curtain, we have made scenery, indeed, but scenery that is little more than a suggestion—a pattern with recurring boughs and leaves of gold for a wood, a great green curtain with a red stencil upon it to carry the eye upward for a palace, and so on. More important than these, we have looked for the centre of our art where the players of the time of Shakespeare and of Corneille found theirs—in speech, whether it be the perfect mimicry of the conversation of two countrymen of the roads, or that idealised speech poets have imagined for what we think but do not say. Before men read, the ear and the tongue were subtle, and delighted one another with the little tunes that were in words; every word would have its own tune, though but one main note may have been marked enough for us to name it. They loved language, and all literature was then, whether in the mouth of minstrels, players, or singers, but the perfection of an art that everybody practised, a flower out of the stem of life. And language continually renewed itself in that perfection, returning to daily life out of that finer leisure, strengthened and sweetened as from a retreat ordered by religion. The ordinary dramatic critic, when you tell him that a play, if it is to be of a great kind, must have beautiful words, will answer that you have misunderstood the nature of the stage and are asking of it what books should give. Sometimes when some excellent man, a playgoer certainly and sometimes a critic, has read me a passage out of some poet, I have been set wondering what books of poetry can mean to the greater number of men. If they are to read poetry at all, if they are to enjoy beautiful rhythm, if they are to get from poetry anything but what it has in common with prose, they must hear it spoken by men who have music in their voices and a learned understanding of its sound. There is no poem so great that a fine speaker cannot make it greater or that a bad ear cannot make it nothing. All the arts when young and happy are but the point of the spear whose handle is our daily life. When they grow old and unhappy they perfect themselves away from life, and life, seeing that they are sufficient to themselves, forgets them. The fruit of the tree that was in Eden grows out of a flower full of scent, rounds and ripens, until at last the little stem, that brought to it the sap out of the tree, dries up and breaks, and the fruit rots upon the ground.

The theatre grows more elaborate, developing the player at the expense of the poet, developing the scenery at the expense of the player, always increasing the importance of whatever has come to it out of the mere mechanism of a building or the interests of a class, specialising more and more, doing whatever is easiest rather than what is most noble, and shaping imaginations before the footlights as behind, that are stirred to excitements that belong to it and not to life; until at last life, which knows that a specialised energy is not itself, turns to other things, content to leave it to weaklings and triflers, to those in whose body there is the least quantity of itself.

v

But if we are to delight our three or four thousand young men and women with a delight that will follow them into their own houses, and if we are to add the countryman to their number, we shall need more than the play, we shall need those other spoken arts. The player rose into importance in the town, but the minstrel is of the country. We must have narrative as well as dramatic poetry, and we are making room for it in the theatre in the first instance, but in this also we must go to an earlier time. Modern recitation is not, like modern theatrical art, an over-elaboration of a true art, but an entire misunderstanding. It has no tradition at all. It is an endeavour to do what can only be done well by the player. It has no relation of its own to life. Some young man in evening clothes will recite to you *The Dream of Eugene Aram*, and it will be laughable, grotesque and a little vulgar. Tragic emotions that need scenic illusion, a long preparation, a gradual heightening of emotion, are thrust into the middle of our common affairs. That they may be as extravagant, as little tempered by anything ideal or distant as possible, he will break up the rhythm, regarding neither the length of the lines nor the natural music of the phrases, and distort the accent by every casual impulse. He will gesticulate wildly, adapting his movements to the drama as if Eugene Aram were in the room before us, and all the time we see a young man in evening dress who has become unaccountably insane. Nothing that he can do or say will make us forget that he is Mr. Robinson the bank clerk, and that the toes of his boots turn upward. We have nothing to learn here. We must go to the villages or we must go back hundreds of years to Wolfram of Eschenbach and the castles of Thuringia. In this, as in all other arts, one finds its law and its true purpose when one is near the source. The minstrel never dramatised anybody but himself. It was impossible, from the nature of the words the poet had put into his mouth, or that he had made for himself, that he should speak as another person. He will go no nearer to drama than we do in daily speech, and he will not allow you for any long time to forget himself. Our own Raftery will stop the tale to cry, 'This is what I, Raftery, wrote down in the book of the people'; or, 'I, myself, Raftery, went to bed without supper that night'. Or, if it is Wolfram, and the tale is of Gawain or Parzival, he will tell the listening ladies that he sings of happy love out of his own unhappy love, or he will interrupt the story of a siege and its hardships to remember his own house, where there is not enough food for the mice. He knows how to keep himself interesting that his words may have weight—so many lines of narrative, and then a phrase about himself and his emotions. The reciter cannot be a player, for that is a different art; but he must be a messenger, and he should be as interesting, as exciting, as are all that carry great news. He comes from far off, and he speaks of far-off things with his own peculiar animation, and instead of lessening the ideal and beautiful elements of speech he may, if he has a mind to, increase them. He may speak to actual notes as a singer does if they are so simple that he never loses the speaking voice, and if the poem is long he must do so, or his own voice will become weary and formless. His art is nearer to pattern than that of the player. It is always allusion, never illusion; for what he tells of, no matter how impassioned he may become, is always distant, and for this reason he may permit himself every kind of nobleness. In a short poem he may interrupt the narrative with a burden, which the audience will soon learn to sing, and this burden, because it is repeated and need not tell a story to a first hearing, can have a more elaborate musical notation, can go nearer to ordinary song. Gradually other devices will occur to him—effects of loudness and softness, of increasing and decreasing speed, certain rhythmic movements of his body, a score of forgotten things, for the art of speech is lost, and when we begin at it every day is a discovery. The reciter must be made exciting and wonderful in himself, apart from what he has to tell, and that is more difficult than it was in the Middle Ages. We are not mysterious to one another; we can come from far off and yet be no better than our neighbours. We are no longer like those Egyptian birds that flew out of Arabia, their claws full of spices; nor can we, like an ancient or mediaeval poet, throw into our verses the emotions and events of our lives, or even dramatise, as they could, the life of the minstrel into whose mouth we are to put our words. I can think of nothing better than to borrow from the tellers of old tales, who will often pretend to have been at the wedding of the princess or afterwards 'when they were throwing out children by the basketful', and to give the story-teller definite fictitious personality and find for him an appropriate costume. Many costumes and persons come into my imagination. I imagine an old countryman upon the stage of the theatre or in some little country court-house where a Gaelic society is meeting, and I can hear him say that he is Raftery or a brother, and that he has tramped through France and Spain and the whole world. He has seen everything, and he has all country love-tales at his finger-tips. I can imagine, too—and now the story-teller is more serious and more naked of country circumstance—a jester with black cockscomb and black clothes. He has been in the faery hills; perhaps he is the terrible *Amadán-na-Breena* himself; or he has been so long in the world that he can tell of ancient battles. It is not as good as what we have lost, but we cannot hope to see in our time, except by some rare accident, the minstrel who differs from his audience in nothing but the exaltation of his mood, and who is yet as exciting and as romantic in their eyes as were Raftery and Wolfram to their people.

It is perhaps nearly impossible to make recitation a living thing, for there is no existing taste we can appeal to; but it should not be hard here in Ireland to interest people in songs that are made for the word's sake and not for the music, or for that only in a secondary degree. They are interested in such songs already, only the songs have little subtlety of thought and of language. One does not find in them that richness of emotion which but seems modern because it has been brought so very lately out of the cellar. At their best they are the songs of children and of countrypeople, eternally young for all their centuries, and yet not even in old days, as one thinks, a vintage for kings' houses. We require a method of setting to music that will make it possible to sing or to speak to notes, a poem like Rossetti's translation of *The Ballad of Dead Ladies* in such a fashion that no word shall have an intonation or accentuation it could not have in passionate speech. It must be set for the speaking voice, like the songs that sailors make up or remember, and a man at the far end of the room must be able to take it down on a first hearing. An English musical paper said the other day, in commenting on something I had written, 'Owing to musical necessities, vowels must be lengthened in singing to an extent which in speech would be ludicrous if not absolutely impossible'. I have but one art, that of speech, and my feeling for music dissociated from speech is very slight, and listening as I do to the words with the better part of my attention, there is no modern song sung in the modern way that is not to my taste 'ludicrous' and 'impossible'. I hear with older ears than the musician, and the songs of countrypeople and of sailors delight me. I wonder why the musician is not content to set to music some arrangement of meaningless liquid vowels, and thereby to make his song like that of the birds; but I do not judge his art for any purpose but my own.[1] It is worthless for my purpose certainly, and it is one of the causes that are bringing about in modern countries a degradation of language. I have to find men with more music than I have, who will develop to a finer subtlety the singing of the cottage and the forecastle, and develop it more on the side of speech than that of music, until it has become intellectual and nervous enough to be the vehicle of a Shelley or a Keats. For some purposes it will be necessary to divine the lineaments of a still older art, and re-create the regulated declamations that died out when music fell into its

[1] I have heard musicians excuse themselves by claiming that they put the words there for the sake of the singer; but if that be so, why should not the singer sing something she may wish to have by rote? Nobody will hear the words; and the local time-table, or, so much suet and so many raisins, and so much spice and so much sugar, and whether it is to be put in a quick or a slow oven, would run very nicely with a little management.

earliest elaborations. Miss Farr has divined enough of
this older art, of which no fragment has come down to
us—for even the music of *Aucassin and Nicolette,* with
its definite tune, its recurring pattern of sound, is something more than declamation—to make the chorus of
Hippolytus and of *The Trojan Women,* at the Court
Theatre or the Lyric, intelligible speech, even when
several voices spoke together. She used very often definite melodies of a very simple kind, but always when
the thought became intricate and the measure grave and
slow, fell back upon declamation regulated by notes.
Her experiments have included almost every kind of
verse, and every possible elaboration of sound compatible with the supremacy of the words. I do not think
Homer is ever so moving as when she recites him to a
little tune played on a stringed instrument not very unlike a lyre. She began at my suggestion with songs in
plays, for it was clearly an absurd thing that words
necessary to one's understanding of the action, either
because they explained some character, or because they
carried some emotion to its highest intensity, should be
less intelligible than the bustling and ruder words of the
dialogue. We have tried our art, since we first tried it in
a theatre, upon many kinds of audiences, and have found
that ordinary men and women take pleasure in it and
sometimes say that they never understood poetry before. It is, however, more difficult to move those—
fortunately for our purpose but a few—whose ears are
accustomed to the abstract emotion and elaboration of
notes in modern music.

The Irish Dramatic Movement

If we accomplish this great work, if we make it possible again for the poet to express himself, not merely through words, but through the voices of singers, of minstrels, of players, we shall certainly have changed the substance and the manner of our poetry. Everyone who has to interest his audience through the voice discovers that his success depends upon the clear, simple and varied structure of his thought. I have written a good many plays in verse and prose, and almost all those plays I have rewritten after performance, sometimes again and again, and every rewriting that has succeeded upon the stage has been an addition to the masculine element, an increase of strength in the bony structure.

Modern literature, above all poetical literature, is monotonous in its structure and effeminate in its continual insistence upon certain moments of strained lyricism. William Morris, who did more than any modern to recover mediaeval art, did not in his *Earthly Paradise* copy from Chaucer—from whom he copied so much that was naïve and beautiful—what seems to me essential in Chaucer's art. He thought of himself as writing for the reader, who could return to him again and again when the chosen mood had come, and became monotonous, melancholy, too continuously lyrical in his understanding of emotion and of life. Had he accustomed himself to read out his poems upon those Sunday evenings that he gave to Socialist speeches, and to gather an audience of average men, precisely such an audience as I have often seen in his house, he would have been forced to Chaucer's variety, to his delight in the height and depth, and would have found expression for that humorous, many-sided nature of his. I owe to him many truths, but I would add to those truths the certainty that all the old writers, the masculine writers of the world, wrote to be spoken or to be sung, and in a later age to be read aloud for hearers who had to understand swiftly or not at all and who gave up nothing of life to listen, but sat, the day's work over, friend by friend, lover by lover.

The Irish Dramatic Movement

THE SEASON'S WORK

A CHARACTER of the winter's work will be the large number of romantic, poetic and historical plays— that is to say, of plays which require a convention for their performance; their speech, whether it be verse or prose, being so heightened as to transcend that of any form of real life. Our first two years of the Abbey Theatre have been expended mostly on the perfecting of the company in peasant comedy and tragedy. Every national dramatic movement or theatre in countries like Bohemia and Hungary, as in Elizabethan England, has arisen out of a study of the common people, who preserve national characteristics more than any other class, and out of an imaginative re-creation of national history or legend. The life of the drawing-room, the life represented in most plays of the ordinary theatre of to-day, differs but little all over the world, and has as little to do with the national spirit as the architecture of, let us say, Saint Stephen's Green, or Queen's Gate, or of the boulevards about the Arc de Triomphe.

As we wish our work to be full of the life of this country, our stage-manager has almost always to train our actors from the beginning, always so in the case of peasant plays, and this makes the building up of a theatre like ours the work of years. We are now fairly

---

[1] *The Arrow*, a briefer chronicle than *Samhain*, was distributed with the programme for a few months.

satisfied with the representation of peasant life, and we can afford to give the greater part of our attention to other expressions of our art and of our life. The romantic work and poetical work once reasonably good, we can, if but the dramatist arrive, take up the life of our drawing-rooms, and see if there is something characteristic there, something which our nationality may enable us to express better than others, and so create plays of that life and means to play them as truthful as a play of Hauptmann's or of Ibsen's upon the German or Scandinavian stage. I am not myself interested in this kind of work, and do not believe it to be as important as contemporary critics think it is, but a theatre such as we project should give a reasonably complete expression to the imaginative interests of its country. In any case it was easier, and therefore wiser, to begin where our art is most unlike that of others, with the representation of country life.

Is it possible to speak the universal truths of human nature whether the speakers be peasants or wealthy men, for—

> Love doth sing
> As sweetly in a beggar as a king?

So far as we have any model before us it is the national and municipal theatres in various Continental towns, and, like the best of these, we must have in our repertory masterpieces from every great school of dramatic literature, and play them confidently, even though the public be slow to like that old stern art, and perhaps a little proudly, remembering that no other English-speaking theatre can be so catholic. Certainly the weathercocks of our imagination will not turn those painted eyes of theirs too long to the quarter of the Scandinavian winds. If the wind blow long from the Mediterranean, the paint may peel before we pray for a change in the weather.

The Playboy of the Western World

THE CONTROVERSY OVER
THE PLAYBOY OF THE WESTERN WORLD

WE have claimed for our writers the freedom to find in their own land every expression of good and evil necessary to their art, for Irish life contains, like all vigorous life, the seeds of all good and evil, and a writer must be free here as elsewhere to watch where weed or flower ripens. No one who knows the work of our theatre as a whole can say we have neglected the flower; but the moment a writer is forbidden to take pleasure in the weed, his art loses energy and abundance. In the great days of English dramatic art the greatest English writer of comedy was free to create *The Alchemist* and *Volpone*, but a demand born of Puritan conviction and shopkeeping timidity and insincerity, for what many second-rate intellects thought to be noble and elevating events and characters, had already at the outset of the eighteenth century ended the English drama as a complete and serious art. Sheridan and Goldsmith, when they restored comedy after an epoch of sentimentalities, had to apologise for their satiric genius by scenes of conventional love-making and sentimental domesticity that have set them outside the company of all—whether their genius be great or little—whose work is pure and whole. The quarrel of our theatre to-day is the quarrel of the theatre in many lands; for the old Puritanism, the old dislike of power and reality have not changed, even when they are called by some Gaelic name.

The Irish Dramatic Movement

[On the second performance of *The Playboy of the Western World*, about forty men who sat in the middle of the pit succeeded in making the play entirely inaudible. Some of them brought tin trumpets, and the noise began immediately on the rise of the curtain. For days articles in the Press called for the withdrawal of the play, but we played for the seven nights we had announced; and before the week's end opinion had turned in our favour. There were, however, nightly disturbances and a good deal of rioting in the surrounding streets. On the last night of the play there were, I believe, five hundred police keeping order in the theatre and in its neighbourhood. Some days later our enemies, though beaten so far as the play was concerned, crowded into the cheaper seats for a debate on the freedom of the stage. They were very excited, and kept up the discussion until near twelve. The last paragraphs of my opening statement ran as follows.]

From Mr. Yeats's opening Speech in the Debate on February 4, 1907, at the Abbey Theatre.

The struggle of the last week has been long a necessity; various paragraphs in newspapers describing Irish attacks on theatres had made many worthy young men come to think that the silencing of a stage at their own pleasure, even if hundreds desired that it should not be silenced, might win them a little fame, and, perhaps, serve their country. Some of these attacks have been made on plays which are in themselves indefensible, vulgar and old-fashioned farces and comedies. But the attack, being an annihilation of civil rights, was never anything but an increase of Irish disorder. The last I heard of was in Liverpool, and there a stage was rushed, and a priest, who had set a play upon it, withdrew his play and apologised to the audience. We have not such pliant bones, and did not learn in the houses that bred us a so suppliant knee. But behind the excitement of example there is a more fundamental movement of opinion. Some seven or eight years ago the National movement was democratised and passed from the hands of a few leaders into those of large numbers of young men organised in clubs and societies. These young men made the mistake of the newly enfranchised everywhere: they fought for causes worthy in themselves with the unworthy instruments of tyranny and violence. Comic songs of a certain kind were to be driven from the stage; everyone was to wear Irish cloth; everyone was to learn Irish; everyone was to hold certain opinions; and these ends were sought by personal attacks, by virulent caricature and violent derision. It needs eloquence to persuade and knowledge to expound; but the coarser means come ready to every man's hand, as ready as a stone or a stick, and where these coarse means are all, there is nothing but mob, and the commonest idea most prospers and is most sought for.

Gentlemen of the little clubs and societies, do not mistake the meaning of our victory; it means something for us, but more for you. When the curtain of *The Playboy* fell on Saturday night in the midst of what *The Sunday Independent*—no friendly witness—described as 'thunders of applause', I am confident that I saw the rise in this country of a new thought, a new opinion, that we had long needed. It was not all approval of Mr. Synge's play that sent the receipts of the Abbey Theatre this last week to twice the height they had ever touched before. The generation of young men and girls who are now leaving schools or colleges are weary of the tyranny of clubs and leagues. They wish again for individual sincerity, the eternal quest of truth, all that has been given up for so long that all might crouch upon the one roost and quack or cry in the one flock. We are beginning once again to ask what a man is, and to be content to wait a little before we go on to that further question: What is a good Irishman? There are some who have not yet their degrees that will say to friend or neighbour, 'You have voted with the English, and that is bad'; or 'You have sent away your Irish servants, or thrown away your Irish clothes, or blacked your face for your singing. I despise what you have done, I keep you still my friend; but if you are terrorised out of doing any of these things, evil things though I know them to be, I will not have you for my friend any more.' Manhood is all, and the root of manhood is courage and courtesy.

On taking 'The Playboy' to London

1907

ON TAKING 'THE PLAYBOY' TO LONDON

THE failure of the audience to understand this powerful and strange work (*The Playboy of the Western World*) has been the one serious failure of our movement, and it could not have happened but that the greater number of those who came to shout down the play were no regular part of our audience at all, but members of parties and societies whose main interests are political. We have been denounced with even greater violence than on the first production of the play for announcing that we should carry it to London. We cannot see that an attack, which we believe to have been founded on a misunderstanding of the nature of literature, should prevent us from selecting, as our custom is, whatever of our best comes within the compass of our players at the time, to show in some English theatres. Nearly all strong and strange writing is attacked on its appearance, and those who press it upon the world may not cease from pressing it, for their justification is its ultimate acceptance. Ireland is passing through a crisis in the life of the mind greater than any she has known since the rise of the Young Ireland party, and based upon a principle which sets many in opposition to the habits of thought and feeling come down from that party, for the seasons change, and need and occupation with them. Many are beginning to recognise the right of the individual mind to see the world in its own way, to cherish the thoughts which separate men from one another, and that are the creators of distinguished life, instead of those thoughts that had made one man like another if they could, and have but succeeded in setting hysteria and insincerity in place of confidence and self-possession. To the Young Ireland writers, who have still the ear of Ireland, though not its distracted mind, truth was historical and external and not a self-consistent personal vision, and it is but according to ancient custom that the new truth should force its way amid riot and great anger.

Samhain: 1908

SAMHAIN: 1908

FIRST PRINCIPLES

SOME countrymen in Galway, whither we carried our plays in dialect a few weeks ago, said that it was no use going in to see them because they showed people that could be seen on the road every day; but these were but a few, and we had a great popular success, crowds being turned away every evening from the doors. Ireland is always Connacht to my imagination, for there more than elsewhere is the folk tradition that is the loftiest thing that has come down to us within the ring of Ireland. I knew an observant and cultivated French count, descendant of *émigrés*, who came for a few months in every summer to a property they had left him upon the Galway shore. He came from Paris or from Rome, but would not stay, if he could help it, even a few hours in Dublin, because Dublin was 'shabby England'. We find our most highly trained audiences of late in Dublin, but the majority of theatre-goers drift between what is Irish and what is English in confused uncertainty, and have not even begun the search for what is their own.

Somebody in *Un Grand Homme de province à Paris* says, with I know not what truth, that French actresses pay more for attacks than admiring criticism, for 'controversy is fame'. In Ireland this would be an unnecessary expense, and many of the attacks which have followed us from the beginning in such plenty have arisen out of conceptions of life which, unknown to the journalists who have made them, are essentially English, though of an England that has begun to change its clothes since Matthew Arnold and his contemporaries began a truer popular culture. Even at this moment the early Victorian thought is not so out of fashion that English newspapers would not revive it and talk of the duties of writers to preach and the like, all that old Utilitarianism, if the drama, let us say, were taken seriously enough for leading articles instead of being left to the criticism of a few writers who really know something of their business. Some fifteen years ago English critics themselves wrote of Ibsen very much as our more hysterical patriots write of us. These patriots, with an heretical preference for faith over works—for have not opinions and second- and third-hand conceptions of life, images of what we wish to be, a substance of things hoped for, come from the pawnshop of schismatical faith?—continually attack in the interest of some point of view popularised by Macaulay and his contemporaries, or of some reflection from English novelists and the like, Irish emotion and temperament discovered by some writer in himself after years of labour, for all reality comes to us as the reward of labour. Forms of emotion and thought which the future will recognise as peculiarly Irish, for no other country has had the like, are looked upon as un-Irish because of their novelty in a land that is so nearly conquered that it has all but nothing of its own. English provincialism shouts through the lips of Irish patriots who have no knowledge of other countries to give them a standard of comparison, and they, with the confidence of all who speak the opinions of others, labour to thwart everybody who would dig a well for Irish water to bubble in.

II

In 1892, when I started the National Literary Society, and began a movement that was intended to lead up to the establishment of an Irish Dramatic School, the songs and ballads of Young Ireland were used as examples to prove the personal, and therefore Irish, art of A. E., Lionel Johnson, Katharine Tynan, and myself (see Lionel Johnson's essay, *Poetry and Politics*), an un-Irish thing. And yet those songs and ballads, with the exception of a small number which are partly copied from Gaelic models, and a few, almost all by Mangan, that have a personal style, are imitations of the poetry of Burns and Macaulay and Scott. All literature in every country is derived from models, and as often as not these are foreign models, and it is the presence of a personal element alone that can give it nationality in a fine sense, the nationality of its maker. It is only before personality has been attained that a race struggling towards self-consciousness is the better for having, as in primitive times, nothing but native models, for before this has been attained it can neither assimilate nor reject. It was precisely at this passive moment, attainment approaching but not yet come, that the Irish heart and mind surrendered to England, or rather to what is most temporary in England; and Irish patriotism, content that the names and opinions should be Irish, was deceived and satisfied. It is always necessary to affirm and to reaffirm that nationality is in the things that escape analysis. We discover it, as we do the quality of saltness or sweetness, by the taste, and literature is a cultivation of taste.

III

The Irish novelists of the nineteenth century, who established themselves, like the Young Ireland poets, upon various English writers, without, except at rare moments—*Castle Rackrent* was, it may be, the most inspired of those moments—attaining to personality, have filled the popular mind with images of character, with forms of construction, with a criticism of life, which are all so many arguments to prove that some play that has arisen out of a fresh vision is unlike every Irish thing. A real or fancied French influence is pointed out at once and objected to, but the English influence which runs through the patriotic reading of the people is not noticed because it is everywhere. I say, with certainty, that *The Playboy of the Western World*, so rich in observation, so full of the temperament of a unique man, has more of Ireland in its characters, in its method of art, in its conception of morals, than all the novels of Kickham, Michael Banim (I have much respect for his brother John, perhaps because French influence in part annulled the influence of Mrs. Radcliffe, and so helped him to personality); Gerald Griffin, so full of amiable English sentiment; Carleton, in his longer tales, powerful spirit though he was; and, of course, much more in any page of it than in all those romances founded upon Walter Scott which are, or used to be, published in Irish newspapers to make boys and girls into patriots. Here and there, of course, one finds Irish elements. In Lever, for instance, even after one has put aside all that is second-hand, there is a rightful Irish gaiety, but one finds these elements only just in so far as the writers had come to know themselves in the Socratic sense. Of course, too, the tradition itself was not all English, but it is impossible to divide what is new, and therefore Irish, what is very old, and therefore Irish, from all that is foreign, from all that is an accident of imperfect culture, before we have had some revelation of Irish character, pure enough and varied enough to create a standard of comparison. I do not speak carelessly of the Irish novelists, for when I was in London during the first years of my literary life, I read them continually, seeking in them an image of Ireland that I might not forget what I meant to be the foundations of my art, trying always to winnow as I read. I only escaped from many misconceptions when, in 1897, I began an active Irish life, comparing what I saw about me with what I heard of in Galway cottages. Yet for all that, it was from the novelists and poets that I learned in part my symbols of expression. Somebody has said that all sound philosophy is but biography, and what I myself did, getting into an original relation to Irish life, creating in myself a new character, a new pose—in the French sense of the word—the literary mind of Ireland must do as a whole, always understanding that the result must be no bundle of formulas, not faggots but a fire. We never learn to know ourselves by thought, said Goethe, but by action only; and to a writer creation is action.

IV

A moment comes in every country when its character expresses itself through some group of writers, painters, or musicians, and it is this moment, the moment of Goethe in Germany, of the Elizabethan poets in England, of the Van Eycks in the Low Countries, of Corneille and Racine in France, of Ibsen and Björnson in Scandinavia, which fixes the finer elements of national character for generations. This moment is impossible until public opinion is ready to welcome in the mind of the artist a power, little affected by external things, being self-contained, self-created, self-sufficing, the seed of character. Generally up to that moment literature has tried to express everybody's thought, history being considered merely as a chronicle of facts, but now, at the instant of revelation, writers think the world is but their palette, and if history amuses them, it is but, as Goethe says, because they would do its personages the honour of naming after them their own thoughts.

In the same spirit they approach their contemporaries when they borrow for their own passions the images of living men, and, at times, external facts will be no more to them than the pewter pot gleaming in the sunlight that started Jacob Boehme into his seven days' trance. There are moments, indeed, when they will give

you more powerful and exact impressions of the outer
world than any other can, but these impressions are
always those which they have been the first to receive,
and more often than not, to make them the more vivid,
they will leave out everything that everybody can see
every day. The man of genius may be Signor Mancini
if he please, but never Mr. Lafayette.

Just as they use the life of their own times, they use
past literature—their own and that of other countries—
selecting here and there under what must always seem,
until their revelation is understood, an impulse of mere
caprice, and the more original, that is to say the more
pure, the revelation, the greater the caprice. It was a
moment of importance in Scandinavia when a certain
pamphlet announced that an historical play could not
find its justification in history alone, for it must
contain an idea, meaning by an idea thought flowing out of character, as opinions are thought arising
out of the necessities of organisation. We grow like
others through opinions, but through ideas discover
ourselves, for these are only true when images of our
own power.

v

In no country has this independence of mind, this
audacity I had almost said, been attained without controversy, for the men who affirm it seem the enemies
of all other interests. In Ireland, in addition to the
external art of our predecessors, full of the misunderstandings created by English influence, there is a preoccupation of a great part of the population with

opinions and a habit of deciding that a man is useful to his country, or otherwise, not by what he is in himself or by what he does in his whole life, but by the opinions he holds on one or two subjects. Balzac, in *Les Comédiens sans le Savoir*, describes a sculptor, a follower of the Socialist Fourier, who has made an allegorical figure of Harmony, and got into his statue the doctrine of his master by giving it six breasts and by putting under its feet an enormous Savoy cabbage. One of his friends promises that when everybody is converted to their doctrine he will be the foremost man of his craft, but another and a wiser says of him that 'while opinions cannot give talent they inevitably spoil it', and adds that an artist's opinion ought to be a faith in works, and that there is no way for him to succeed but by work, 'while nature gives the sacred fire'. In Paris, according to Balzac, it is ambition that makes artists and writers identify themselves with a cause that gives them the help of politicians, of journalists, or of society, as the case may be, but in Ireland, so far as I am able to see, they do it for sociability's sake, to have a crowd to shout with, and therefore by half-deliberate sophistry they persuade themselves that the old tale is not true, and that art is not ruined so. I do not mean that the artist should not as a man be a good citizen and hold opinions like another; Balzac was a Catholic and a Monarchist. We, too, in following his great example, have not put away in anything the strong opinions that we set out with, but in our art they have no place. Every trouble of our Theatre in its earlier years, every attack on us in any year, has come directly or indirectly either from those who prefer Mr. Lafayette to Signor Mancini, or from those who believe, from a defective education, that the writer who does not help some cause, who does not support some opinion, is but an idler, or if his air be too serious for that, the supporter of some hidden wickedness. A principal actor left us in our first year because he believed *The Hour-Glass* to be a problem play. This is all natural enough in a country where the majority have been denied University teaching. I found precisely the same prejudices among the self-educated working-men about William Morris, and among some few educated persons, generally women, who took their tune from the working-men. One woman used to repeat as often as possible that to paint pictures or to write poetry in this age was to fiddle while Rome was burning. The artist who permits opinion to master his work is always insincere, always what Balzac calls an unconscious comedian, a man playing to a public for an end, or a philanthropist who has made the most tragic and the most useless of sacrifices.

VI

Certain among the Nationalist attacks have been the work of ignorant men, untruthful, imputing unworthy motives, the kind of thing one cannot answer. But the Unionist hostility, though better-mannered, has been more injurious. Our Nationalist pit has grown to understand us, and night after night we have not been able to find room for all who came, but except at rare moments and under exceptional circumstances our stalls have been almost empty, though the people who keep away from us in Ireland flock to us in London, where there is culture enough to make us a fashion. I think that tide is turning, however, for we played before many Unionists at Galway matinées, *Cathleen ni Houlihan*, *The Gaol Gate*, and *The Rising of the Moon*, all plays that have been objected to at some time or other by some section or other of official Dublin, or that we have been warned against in friendlier moods. When *Cathleen ni Houlihan* was first played in the Abbey I was hissed by a group of young men at the door; and we were offered a good deal of support once towards the filling of our empty stalls if we would drop it from our list. I heard a while ago we had lost financial support through *The Rising of the Moon*, but returned to tranquillity when I found that it would have been a donation to the National Literary Society—God save the mark!—given under the belief that we and it were the same body.

VII

In most modern countries when the moment has arrived for a personal impulse, either for the first time or in some art hitherto external and conventional, the cry has been raised against the writer that he is preaching sexual immorality, for that is the subject upon which the newspapers, at any rate, most desire to see certain opinions always in force, and a view of the world as sexually unexciting as possible always displayed as if it were reality. Balzac in his preface to the *Comédie humaine* had to defend himself from this charge, but it is not the burning question with us at present, for politics are our national passion. We have to free our vision of reality from political prepossession, for entangled, as it were, with all that is exaggerated, lifeless, frozen, in the attitudes of party, there are true thoughts about all those things that Ireland is most interested in, a reverie over the emptiness and the fullness of Irish character which is not less a part of wisdom because politics, like art, have their exaggerations. We cannot renounce political subjects in renouncing mere opinions, for that pleasure in the finer culture of England, that displeasure in Irish disunions and disorders, which are the root of reasoned Unionism, are as certainly high and natural thoughts as the self-denying enthusiasm that leads Michael Gillane to probable death or exile, and Dervorgilla to her remorse, and Patrick Sarsfield of *The White Cockade* to his sense of what a king should be; and we cannot renounce them because politicians believe that one thought or another may help their opponents, any more than Balzac could have refused to write the *Comédie humaine* because somebody was afraid Madame l'Épicière might run away from her husband.

VIII

At the close of my speech at one of the performances we were asked to give to the British Association, I used these words: 'When I was coming up in the train the other day from Galway, I began thinking how unlike your work was to my work, and then suddenly it struck me that it was all the same. A picture arose before my mind's eye: I saw Adam numbering the creatures of Eden; soft and terrible, foul and fair, they all went before him. That, I thought, is the man of science, naming and numbering, for our understanding, everything in the world. But then, I thought, we writers, do we not also number and describe, though with a difference? You are busy with the exterior world, and we with the interior. Science understands that everything must be known in the world our eyes look at; there is nothing too obscure, too common, too vile, to be the subject of knowledge. When a man of science discovers a new species, or a new law, you do not ask the value of the law, or the value of the species, before you do him honour; you leave all that to the judgment of the generations. It is your pride that in you the human race contemplates all things with so pure, so disinterested, an eyesight that it forgets its own necessities and infirmities, all its hopes and fears, in the contemplation of truth for the sake of truth, reality for the sake of reality.

'We, on the other hand, are Adams of a different Eden, a more terrible Eden, perhaps, for we must name and number the passions and motives of men. There, too, everything must be known, everything understood, everything expressed; there, also, there is nothing common, nothing unclean; every motive must be followed through all the obscure mystery of its logic. Mankind must be seen and understood in every possible circumstance, in every conceivable situation. There is no laughter too bitter, no irony too harsh for utterance, no passion too terrible to be set before the minds of men. The Greeks knew that. Only in this way can mankind be understood, only when we have put ourselves in all the possible positions of life, from the most miserable to those that are so lofty that we can only speak of them in symbols and in mysteries, will entire wisdom be possible. All wise government depends upon this knowledge not less than upon that other knowledge which is your business rather than ours; and we and you alike rejoice in battle, finding the sweetest of all music to be the stroke of the sword.'

The Irish Dramatic Movement

A PEOPLE'S THEATRE[1]

A Letter to Lady Gregory

I

MY DEAR LADY GREGORY—Of recent years you have done all that is anxious and laborious in the supervision of the Abbey Theatre and left me free to follow my own thoughts. It is therefore right that I address to you this letter, wherein I shall explain, half for your ears, half for other ears, certain thoughts that have made me believe that the Abbey Theatre can never do all we had hoped. We set out to make a 'People's Theatre', and in that we have succeeded. But I did not know until very lately that there are certain things, dear to both our hearts, which no 'People's Theatre' can accomplish.

II

All exploitation of the life of the wealthy, for the eye and the ear of the poor and half-poor, in plays, in popular novels, in musical comedy, in fashion papers, at the cinema, in *Daily Mirror* photographs, is a travesty of the life of the rich; and if it were not would all but justify some Red Terror; and it impoverishes and vulgarises the imagination, seeming to hold up for envy and to commend a life where all is display and hurry, passion without emotion, emotion without in-

---

[1] I took the title from a book by Romain Rolland on some French theatrical experiments. 'A People's Theatre' is not quite the same thing as 'A Popular Theatre'. The essay was published in the *Irish Statesman* in the autumn of 1919.—1923.

tellect, and where there is nothing stern and solitary. The plays and novels are the least mischievous, for they still have the old-fashioned romanticism—their threepenny bit, if worn, is silver yet—but they are without intensity and intellect and cannot convey the charm of either as it may exist in those they would represent. All this exploitation is a rankness that has grown up recently among us and has come out of an historical necessity that has made the furniture and the clothes and the brains of all but the leisured and the lettered, copies and travesties.

Shakespeare set upon the stage kings and queens, great historical or legendary persons about whom there is nothing unreal except the circumstance of their lives which remain vague and summary, because he could only write his best—his mind and the mind of his audience being interested in emotion and intellect at their moment of union and at their greatest intensity— when he wrote of those who controlled the mechanism of life. Had they been controlled by it, intellect and emotion entangled by intricacy and detail could never have mounted to that union which, as Swedenborg said of the marriage of the angels, is a conflagration of the whole being. But since great crowds, changed by popular education with its eye always on some objective task, have begun to find reality in mechanism alone,[1] our popular commercial art has substituted for

[1] I have read somewhere statistics that showed how popular education has coincided with the lessening of Shakespeare's audience. In every chief town before it began, Shakespeare was constantly played.

Lear and Cordelia the real millionaire and the real peeress, and seeks to make them charming by insisting perpetually that they have all that wealth can buy, or rather all that average men and women would buy if they had wealth. Shakespeare's groundlings watched the stage in terrified sympathy, while the British working-man looks perhaps at the photographs of these lords and ladies, whom he admires beyond measure, with the pleasant feeling that they will all be robbed and murdered before he dies.

III

Then, too, that turning into ridicule of peasant and citizen and all lesser men could but increase our delight when the great personified spiritual power, but seems unnatural when the great are but the rich. During an illness lately I read two popular novels which I had borrowed from the servants. They were good stories and half consoled me for the sleep I could not get, but I was a long time before I saw clearly why everybody with less than a thousand a year was a theme of comedy and everybody with less than five hundred a theme of farce. Even Rosencrantz and Guildenstern, courtiers and doubtless great men in their world, could be but foils for Hamlet because Shakespeare had nothing to do with objective truth, but we who have nothing to do with anything else, in so far as we are of our epoch, must not allow a greater style to corrupt us.

An artisan or a small shopkeeper feels, I think, when he sees upon our Abbey stage men of his own trade, that they are represented as he himself would represent them if he had the gift of expression. I do not mean that he sees his own life expounded there without exaggeration, for exaggeration is selection and the more passionate the art the more marked is the selection, but he does not feel that he has strayed into some other man's seat. If it is comedy he will laugh at ridiculous people, people in whose character there is some contortion, but their station of life will not seem ridiculous. The best stories I have listened to outside the theatre have been told me by farmers or sailors when I was a boy, one or two by fellow-travellers in railway carriages, and most had some quality of romance, romance of a class and its particular capacity for adventure; and our theatre is a people's theatre in a sense which no mere educational theatre can be, because its plays are to some extent a part of that popular imagination. It is very seldom that a man or woman bred up among the propertied or professional classes knows any class but his own, and that a class which is much the same all over the world, and already written of by so many dramatists that it is nearly impossible to see its dramatic situations with our own eyes, and those dramatic situations are perhaps exhausted—as Nietzsche thought the whole universe would be some day—and nothing left but to repeat the same combinations over again.

When the Abbey Manager sends us a play for our opinion and it is my turn to read it, if the handwriting of the MS. or of the author's accompanying letter suggests a leisured life I start prejudiced. There will be no fresh observation of character, I think, no sense of dialogue, all will be literary second-hand, at best what Rossetti called the 'soulless self-reflections of man's skill'. On the other hand, until the Abbey plays began themselves to be copied, a handwriting learned in a National School always made me expect dialogue written out by some man who had admired good dialogue before he had seen it upon paper. The construction would probably be bad, for there the student of plays has the better luck, but plays made impossible by rambling and redundance have often contained some character or some dialogue that has stayed in my memory for years. At first there was often vulgarity, and there still is in those comic love scenes which we invariably reject, and there is often propaganda with all its distortion, but these weigh light when set against life seen as if newly created. At first, in face of your mockery, I used to recommend some reading of Ibsen or Galsworthy, but no one has benefited by that reading or by anything but the Abbey audience and our own rejection of all gross propaganda and gross imitation of the comic column in the newspapers. Our dramatists, and I am not speaking of your work or Synge's but of those to whom you and Synge and I gave an opportunity, have been excellent just in so far as they have become all eye and ear, their minds not smoking lamps, as at times they would have wished, but clear mirrors.

Our players, too, have been vivid and exciting because they have copied a life personally known to them, and of recent years, since our Manager has had to select from the ordinary stage-struck young men and women who have seen many players and perhaps no life but that of the professional class, it has been much harder, though players have matured more rapidly, to get the old, exciting, vivid playing. I have never recovered the good opinion of one recent Manager because I urged him to choose instead some young man or woman from some little shop who had never given his or her thoughts to the theatre. 'Put all the names into a hat', I think I said, 'and pick the first that comes.' One of our early players was exceedingly fine in the old woman in *Riders to the Sea*. 'She has never been to Aran, she knows nothing but Dublin, surely in that part she is not objective, surely she creates from imagination', I thought; but when I asked her she said, 'I copied from my old grandmother'. Certainly it is this objectivity, this making of all from sympathy, from observation, never from passion, from lonely dreaming, that has made our players, at their best, great comedians, for comedy is passionless.

We have been the first to create a true 'People's Theatre', and we have succeeded because it is not an exploitation of local colour, or of a limited form of drama possessing a temporary novelty, but the first doing of something for which the world is ripe, something that will be done all over the world and done more and more perfectly: the making articulate of all the dumb classes each with its own knowledge of the world, its own dignity, but all objective with the objectivity of the office and the workshop, of the newspaper and the street, of mechanism and of politics.

IV

Yet we did not set out to create this sort of theatre, and its success has been to me a discouragement and a defeat. Dante in that passage in the *Convito* which is, I think, the first passage of poignant autobiography in literary history, for there is nothing in Saint Augustine not formal and abstract beside it, in describing his poverty and his exile counts as his chief misfortune that he has had to show himself to all Italy and so publish his human frailties that men who honoured him unknown honour him no more. Lacking means, he had lacked seclusion, and he explains that men such as he should have but few and intimate friends. His study was unity of being, the subordination of all parts to the whole as in a perfectly proportioned human body—his own definition of beauty—and not, as with those I have described, the unity of things in the world; and like all subjectives he shrank, because of what he was, because of what others were, from contact with many men. Had he written plays he would have written from his own thought and passion, observing little and using little, if at all, the conversation of his time—and whether he wrote in verse or in prose his style would have been distant, musical, metaphorical, moulded by antiquity. We stand on the margin between wilderness and wilderness, that which we observe through our senses and that which we can experience only, and our art is always the description of one or the other. If our art is mainly from experience we have need of learned speech, of agreed symbols, because all those things whose names renew experience have accompanied that experience already many times. A personage in one of Turgenev's novels is reminded by the odour of, I think, heliotrope, of some sweetheart that had worn it, and poetry is any flower that brings a memory of emotion, while an unmemoried flower is prose, and a flower pressed and named and numbered science; but our poetical heliotrope need bring to mind no sweetheart of ours, for it suffices that it crowned the bride of Paris, or Peleus' bride. Neither poetry nor any subjective art can exist but for those who do in some measure share its traditional knowledge, a knowledge learned in leisure and contemplation. Even Burns, except in those popular verses which are as lacking in tradition, as modern, as topical, as Longfellow, was, as Henley said, not the founder but the last of a dynasty.

Once such men could draw the crowd because the circumstance of life changed slowly and there was little to disturb contemplation, and so men repeated old verses and old stories, and learned and simple had come to share in common much allusion and symbol. Where the simple were ignorant they were ready to learn and so became receptive, or perhaps even to pretend knowledge like the clowns in the mediaeval poem that describes the arrival of Chaucer's Pilgrims at Canterbury, who that they may seem gentlemen pretend to know the legends in the stained-glass windows. Shakespeare, more objective than Dante—for, alas, the world must move—was still predominantly subjective, and he wrote during the latest crisis of history that made possible a theatre of his kind. There were

still among the common people many traditional songs
and stories, while Court and University, which were
much more important to him, had an interest Chaucer
never shared in great dramatic persons, in those men
and women of Plutarch, who made their death a ritual of
passion; for what is passion but the straining of man's
being against some obstacle that obstructs its unity?

You and I and Synge, not understanding the clock,
set out to bring again the theatre of Shakespeare or
rather perhaps of Sophocles. I had told you how at
Young Ireland Societies and the like, young men when
I was twenty had read papers to one another about
Irish legend and history, and you yourself soon discovered the Gaelic League, then but a new weak thing,
and taught yourself Irish. At Spiddal or near it an inn-
keeper had sung us Gaelic songs, all new village work
that though not literature had *naïveté* and sincerity.
The writers, caring nothing for cleverness, had tried
to express emotion, tragic or humorous, and great
masterpieces, *The Grief of a Girl's Heart*, for instance,
had been written in the same speech and manner and
were still sung. We know that the songs of the Thames
boatmen, to name but these, in the age of Queen
Elizabeth had the same relation to great masterpieces.
These Gaelic songs were as unlike as those to the songs
of the music-hall with their clever ear-catching rhythm,
the work of some mind as objective as that of an
inventor or of a newspaper reporter. We thought we
could bring the old folk-life to Dublin, patriotic feeling to aid us, and with the folk-life all the life of the
heart, understanding heart, according to Dante's defini-

tion, as the most interior being; but the modern world is more powerful than any propaganda or even than any special circumstance, and our success has been that we have made a Theatre of the head, and persuaded Dublin playgoers to think about their own trade or profession or class and their life within it, so long as the stage curtain is up, in relation to Ireland as a whole. For certain hours of an evening they have objective modern eyes.

v

The objective nature and the subjective are mixed in different proportion as are the shadowed and the bright parts in the lunar phases. In Dante there was little shadow, in Shakespeare a larger portion, while you and Synge, it may be, resemble the moon when it has just passed its third quarter, for you have constant humour—and humour is of the shadowed part—much observation and a speech founded upon that of real life. You and he will always hold our audience, but both have used so constantly a measure of lunar light, have so elaborated style and emotion, an individual way of seeing, that neither will ever, till a classic and taught in school, find a perfect welcome.

The outcry against *The Playboy* was an outcry against its style, against its way of seeing; and when the audience called Synge 'decadent'—a favourite reproach from the objective everywhere—it was but troubled by the stench of its own burnt cakes. How could they that dreaded solitude love that which solitude had made? And never have I heard any that laugh the loudest at your comedies praise that musical and delicate style that makes them always a fit accompaniment for verse and sets them at times among the world's great comedies. Indeed, the louder they laugh the readier are they to rate them with the hundred ephemeral farces they have laughed at and forgotten. Synge they have at least hated. When you and Synge find such an uneasy footing, what shall I do there who have never observed anything, or listened with an attentive ear, but value all I have seen or heard because of the emotions they call up or because of something they remind me of that exists, as I believe, beyond the world? O yes, I am listened to—am I not a founder of the Theatre?—and here and there scattered solitaries delight in what I have made and return to hear it again; but some young Corkman, all eyes and ears, whose first rambling play we have just pulled together or half together, can do more than that. He will be played by players who have spoken dialogue like his every night for years, and sentences that it had been a bore to read will so delight the whole house that to keep my hands from clapping I shall have to remind myself that I gave my voice for the play's production and must not applaud my own judgment.

VI

I want to create for myself an unpopular theatre and an audience like a secret society where admission is by favour and never to many. Perhaps I shall never create it, for you and I and Synge have had to dig the stone

A People's Theatre

for our statue and I am aghast at the sight of a new quarry, and besides I want so much—an audience of fifty, a room worthy of it (some great dining-room or drawing-room), half a dozen young men and women who can dance and speak verse or play drum and flute and zither, and all the while, instead of a profession, I but offer them 'an accomplishment'. However, there are my *Four Plays for Dancers* as a beginning, some masks by Mr. Dulac, music by Mr. Dulac and by Mr. Rummell. In most towns one can find fifty people for whom one need not build all on observation and sympathy, because they read poetry for their pleasure and understand the traditional language of passion. I desire a mysterious art, always reminding and half-reminding those who understand it of dearly loved things, doing its work by suggestion, not by direct statement, a complexity of rhythm, colour, gesture, not space-pervading like the intellect, but a memory and a prophecy: a mode of drama Shelley and Keats could have used without ceasing to be themselves, and for which even Blake in the mood of *The Book of Thel* might not have been too obscure. Instead of advertisements in the Press I need a hostess, and even the most accomplished hostess must choose with more than usual care, for I have noticed that city-living cultivated people, those whose names would first occur to her, set great value on painting, which is a form of property, and on music, which is a part of the organisation of life, while the lovers of literature, those who read a book many times, are either young men with little means or live far away from big towns.

The Irish Dramatic Movement

What alarms me most is how a new art needing so elaborate a technique can make its first experiments before those who, as Molière said of the courtiers of his day, have seen so much. How shall our singers and dancers be welcomed by those who have heard Chaliapin in all his parts and who know all the dances of the Russians? Yet where can I find Mr. Dulac and Mr. Rummel or any to match them, but in London[1] or in Paris, and who but the leisured will welcome an elaborate art or pay for its first experiments? In one thing the luck might be upon our side. A man who loves verse and the visible arts has, in a work such as I imagined, the advantage of the professional player. The professional player becomes the amateur, the other has been preparing all his life, and certainly I shall not soon forget the rehearsal of *At the Hawk's Well*, when Mr. Ezra Pound, who had never acted on any stage, in the absence of our chief player rehearsed for half an hour. Even the forms of subjective acting that were natural to the professional stage have ceased. Where all now is sympathy and observation no Irving can carry himself with intellectual pride, nor any Salvini in half-animal nobility, both wrapped in solitude.

I know that you consider Ireland alone our business, and in that we do not differ, except that I care very little where a play of mine is first played so that it find some natural audience and good players. My rooks may sleep abroad in the fields for a while, but when the winter comes they will remember the way home to the

---

[1] I live in Dublin now, and indolence and hatred of travel will probably compel me to make my experiment there after all.—1923.

rookery trees. Indeed, I have Ireland especially in mind, for I want to make, or to help some man some day to make, a feeling of exclusiveness, a bond among chosen spirits, a mystery almost for leisured and lettered people. Ireland has suffered more than England from democracy, for since the Wild Geese fled who might have grown to be leaders in manners and in taste, she has had but political leaders. As a drawing is defined by its outline and taste by its rejections, I too must reject and draw an outline about the thing I seek; and say that I seek, not a theatre but the theatre's anti-self, an art that can appease all within us that becomes uneasy as the curtain falls and the house breaks into applause.

VII

Meanwhile the Popular Theatre should grow always more objective; more and more a reflection of the general mind; more and more a discovery of the simple emotions that make all men kin, clearing itself the while of sentimentality, the wreckage of an obsolete popular culture, seeking always not to feel and to imagine but to understand and to see. Let those who are all personality, who can only feel and imagine, leave it, before their presence become a corruption and turn it from its honesty. The rhetoric of D'Annunzio, the melodrama and spectacle of the later Maeterlinck, are the insincerities of subjectives, who being very able men have learned to hold an audience that is not their natural audience. To be intelligible they are compelled to harden, to externalise and deform. The popular play

left to itself may not lack vicissitude and development,
for it may pass, though more slowly than the novel
which need not carry with it so great a crowd, from
the physical objectivity of Fielding and Defoe to the
spiritual objectivity of Tolstoy and Dostoyevsky, for
beyond the whole we reach by unbiased intellect there
is another whole reached by resignation and the denial
of self.

VIII

The two great energies of the world that in Shakespeare's day penetrated each other have fallen apart as
speech and music fell apart at the Renaissance, and that
has brought each to greater freedom, and we have to
prepare a stage for the whole wealth of modern lyricism, for an art that is close to pure music, for those
energies that would free the arts from imitation, that
would ally acting to decoration and to the dance. We
are not yet conscious, for as yet we have no philosophy,
while the opposite energy is conscious. All visible history, the discoveries of science, the discussions of politics, are with it; but as I read the world, the sudden
changes, or rather the sudden revelations of future
changes, are not from visible history but from its anti-
self. Blake says somewhere in a 'Prophetic Book' that
things must complete themselves before they pass
away, and every new logical development of the objective energy intensifies in an exact correspondence a
counter-energy, or rather adds to an always deepening
unanalysable longing. That counter-longing, having
no visible past, can only become a conscious energy

suddenly, in those moments of revelation which are as a flash of lightning. Are we approaching a supreme moment of self-consciousness, the two halves of the soul separate and face to face? A certain friend of mine has written upon this subject a couple of intricate poems called *The Phases of the Moon* and *The Double Vision* respectively, which are my continual study, and I must refer the reader to these poems for the necessary mathematical calculations. Were it not for that other gyre turning inward in exact measure with the outward whirl of its fellow, we would fall in a generation or so under some tyranny that would cease at last to be a tyranny, so perfect our acquiescence.

> Constrained, arraigned, baffled, bent and unbent
> By these wire-jointed jaws and limbs of wood,
> Themselves obedient,
> Knowing not evil and good;
>
> Obedient to some hidden magical breath,
> They do not even feel, so abstract are they,
> So dead beyond our death,
> Triumph that we obey.

THE END

III
EXPLORATIONS II

IF I WERE FOUR-AND-TWENTY

I

ONE day when I was twenty-three or twenty-four this sentence seemed to form in my head, without my willing it, much as sentences form when we are half-asleep: 'Hammer your thoughts into unity'. For days I could think of nothing else, and for years I tested all I did by that sentence. I had three interests: interest in a form of literature, in a form of philosophy, and a belief in nationality. None of these seemed to have anything to do with the other, but gradually my love of literature and my belief in nationality came together. Then for years I said to myself that these two had nothing to do with my form of philosophy, but that I had only to be sincere and to keep from constraining one by the other and they would become one interest. Now all three are, I think, one, or rather all three are a discrete expression of a single conviction. I think that each has behind it my whole character and has gained thereby a certain newness—for is not every man's character peculiar to himself?—and that I have become a cultivated man. Certainly a cultivated man is not a man who can read difficult books or pass well at the Intermediate, but a man who brings to general converse, and business, character that informs varied interests. It is just the same with a nation—it is only a cultivated nation when it has related its main interests one to another. We are a religious nation. The priest of the ancient chapel of Saint Michel, on Mont Saint Michel where Montaigne's old woman offered a candle to the Dragon and a candle to the Saint, said to a certain friend of mine, 'What faith you Irish have!' on finding her early in the morning praying for the governing body of the National University. Yet is there any nation that has a more irreligious intellect, or that keeps its political thought so distinct from its religious thought? It is, indeed, this distinction that makes our priests and our politicians distrust one another.

II

I spent two summers of the war on the coast of Normandy, and a friend read out to me *Le Mystère de la charité de Jeanne d'Arc*, by Péguy, and certain poems of Jammes. Claudel I had already read myself. A school of literature, which owed something perhaps to Hauptmann's exposition of the symbolism of Chartres Cathedral, had begun to make Christianity French, and in Péguy's heroic patriotism had prepared young France for the struggle with Germany. These writers are full of history and of the scenery of France. The Eucharist in a continually repeated symbol makes them remember the wheat-fields and the vineyards of France; and, when Joan of Arc is told that the Apostles fled from Christ before the crucifixion, she, to that moment the docile shepherd girl, cries: 'The men of France would not have betrayed Him, the men of Lorraine would not have betrayed Him'. It is vain that the nun Gervaise tells her that these were the greatest of all saints and apostles, and that her words are wicked: she repeats, with half sullen obstinacy, 'The men of France would not have betrayed Him, the men of Lorraine would not have betrayed Him'. Péguy—a peasant born of peasants —can, for hundreds of pages, speak as the thirteenth century spoke, and use no thought that is of our time, yet it was amidst Socialist and Dreyfusard controversy that he discovered his belief, and it was so much a passion, so little an opinion, that somebody told me in Paris that he was always reminding himself to go to church and get married, or to go to church and get a child baptised, and always forgetting it.

Now, if I were four-and-twenty, I think I would write or persuade others to write such accounts as our young writers might read, of these men in whom an intellectual patriotism is not distinct from religion; and I would raise such a lively agitation that the Abbey or the Drama League would find an audience for Claudel's *L'Annonce faite à Marie* or his *L'Otage*. I do not think Claudel as pure a talent as Péguy, and do not like him with my whole heart, for he is prepense, deliberate—I am sure he never forgot his religious duties—oratorical, discursive, loving resounding words, vast sentiments, situations half melodrama and half religious ritual. He impresses me a little against my will, but then his intellect is powerful and it searches deep. Perhaps we would learn more at this moment of our history from Claudel than from Péguy. I would also, I think, read a paper to some little circle of poets on Jammes, and I would tell them that when he introduces a volume of **little lyrics with a preface repudiating beforehand any** heretical conclusions that may be deduced from it, and submits all to the Pope, he is certainly poking fun. I think, indeed, that the school—in its fine moments—has been compelled to speak all that it shares with religion and patriotism by a purely literary development. There has been a development in various forms of literature—in French *'unanisme'* for instance—towards the expression, through an intellectual difference, of an emotional agreement with some historical or local group or crowd: towards the celebration, for instance, not of oneself but of one's neighbours, of the countryside or the street where one lives. Many have grown weary of the individualism of the nineteenth century, which now seems less able in creation than in criticism. Intellectual agreements, propagandas, dogmas, we have always had, but emotional agreements, which are so much more lasting and put no constraint upon the soul, we have long lacked.

But if I were four-and-twenty, and without rheumatism, I should not, I think, be content with getting up performances of French plays and with reading papers. I think I would go—though certainly I am no Catholic and never shall be one—upon both of our great pilgrimages, to Croagh Patrick and to Lough Derg. Our churches have been unroofed or stripped; the stained glass of Saint Canice, once famous throughout Europe, was destroyed three centuries ago, and Christ Church looks as clean and unhistorical as a Methodist chapel, its sculptured tombs and tablets broken up or heaped one on t'other in the crypt; no congregation has climbed to the Rock of Cashel since the stout Church of Ireland bishop took the lead roof from the Gothic church to save his legs: but Europe has nothing older than our pilgrimages. In many little lyrics I would claim that stony mountain for all Christian and pagan faith in Ireland, believing, in the exultation of my youth, that in three generations I should have made it as vivid in the memory of all imaginative men among us as the sacred mountain of Japan is in that of the collectors of prints: and I would, being but four-and-twenty and a lover of lost causes, memorialise bishops to open once again that Lough Derg cave of vision once beset by an evil spirit in the form of a long-legged bird with no feathers on its wings.

A few years ago Bernard Shaw explained what he called 'the vulgarity and the savagery' of his writing by saying that he had sat once upon a time every Sunday morning in an Irish Protestant church. But mountain and lough have not grown raw and common; pillage and ravage could not abate their beauty; and the impulse that gathers these great companies in every year has outlasted armorial stone.

Then, too, I would associate that doctrine of purgatory, which Christianity has shared with Neo-Platonism, with the countryman's belief in the nearness of his dead 'working out their penance' in rath or at garden end: and I would find in the psychical research of our day detail to make the association convincing to intellect and emotion. I would try to create a type of man whose most moving religious experience, though it came to him in some distant country, and though his intellect wholly personal, would bring with

it imagery to connect it with an Irish multitude now
and in the past time.

III

We need also a logical unity. When I was a boy
William Morris came to Dublin to preach us into
Socialism. After an appeal from the chairman, on the
ground of national hospitality, an unwilling audience
heard him out, and after gave itself to mockery, till
somebody quenched the light. Now our young men
sing *The Red Flag*, for any bloody catastrophe seems
welcome that promises an Irish Republic. They condemned Morris's doctrine without examination. Now
for the most part they applaud it without examination;
but that will change, for the execution of Connolly has
given him many readers. I have already noticed Karl
Marx's *Kapital* in the same window with Mitchel's *Jail
Journal* and with *Speeches from the Dock*; and, being an
indolent man of four-and-fifty, with no settled habit
but the writing of verse, I did not remind the bookseller that he was a regular church-goer and suggest
that he display also Soloviev's *Justification of the Good*,
Distributive Justice, and some of those little works
edited by Father Plater of Oxford.

I admit that it is a spirited action to applaud the
economics of Lenin—in which I notice much that I
applauded as a boy when Morris was the speaker—
when we do it to affront our national enemy: but it
does not help one to express the character of the nation
through varied intellect. No man is less like an English-

man because he takes his opinion from the *Daily Herald* instead of the *Morning Post*; and it is likely that we shall take our opinion from one or the other till we have swung the hammer. 'Hammer your thoughts into unity'—but for my disabilities I think I would, in exposition of that sentence, persuade some of the Sinn Fein branches, which find it hard to fill up their evenings, to study the writers I have named and perhaps, if some local library would collect enough translations, I might set some exceptional young man, some writer perhaps of Abbey plays, to what once changed all my thought: the reading of the whole *Comédie humaine*.

IV

When I was a child I heard the names of men whose lives had been changed by Balzac, perhaps because he cleared them of Utopian vapours, then very prevalent; and I can remember someone saying to an old lion-painter: 'If you had to choose, would you give up Shakespeare or Balzac?' and his answering, 'I would keep the yellow-backs'. Balzac is the only modern mind which has made a synthesis comparable to that of Dante, and, though certain of his books are on the Index, his whole purpose was to expound the doctrine of his Church as it is displayed, not in decrees and manuals, but in the institutions of Christendom. Yet Nietzsche might have taken, and perhaps did take, his conception of the superman in history from his *Catherine de Medici*, and he has explained and proved, even more thoroughly than Darwin, the doctrine of the survival of the fittest species. Only, I think, when one has mastered his whole vast scheme can one understand clearly that his social order is the creation of two struggles, that of family with family, that of individual with individual, and that our politics depend upon which of the two struggles has most affected our imagination. If it has been most affected by the individual struggle we insist upon equality of opportunity, 'the career open to talent', and consider rank and wealth fortuitous and unjust; and if it is most affected by the struggles of families, we insist upon all that preserves what that struggle has earned, upon social privilege, upon the rights of property.

Throughout the *Comédie humaine* one finds—and in this Balzac was perhaps conscious of contradicting the cloudy Utopian genius of Hugo—that the more noble and stable qualities, those that are spread through the personality, and not isolated in a faculty, are the results of victory in the family struggle, while those qualities of logic and of will, all those qualities of toil rather than of power, belong most to the individual struggle. For a long time after closing the last novel one finds it hard to admire deeply any individual strength that has not family strength behind it.

He has shown us so many men of talent, to whom we have denied our sympathy because of their lack of breeding, and has refused to show us even Napoleon apart from his Corsican stock, as strong roots running backward to the Middle Ages.

For a while, at any rate, we must believe—and it is the doctrine of his Church—that we discover what is most lasting in ourselves in labouring for old men, for children, for the unborn, for those whom we have not even chosen. His beautiful ladies and their lovers, his old statesmen, and some occasional artist to whom he has given his heart, children of a double strength, all those who seek the perfection of some quality, love or unpersuadable justice, often have seemed to me like those great blossoming plants that rise through the gloom of some Cingalese forest to open their blossoms above the tops of the trees. He, too, so does he love all bitter things, cannot leave undescribed that gloom, that struggle, which had made them their own legislators, from the founder or renovator of their house, from some obscure toiler or notorious speculator, and often as not the beginning of it all has been some stroke of lawless rapacity. Perhaps he considers that the will is by its very nature an antagonist of the social order; if we can say 'he considers' of one in whom creation itself wrote and thought. I forget who has written of him: 'If I meet him at midday he is a very ignorant man, but at midnight, when he sits beside a cup of black coffee, he knows everything in the world'.

Here and there one meets among his two thousand characters certain men who do not interest him and whom he is perhaps too impatient to understand, the *Fouriéristes* and insurrectionists who would abate or abolish the struggle. I remember some artist of his who has made an absurd allegorical statue of regenerate mankind and who expects to be the most famous sculptor in the world, after the revolution; a figure of diluted emotion and a chiropodist noted for skill and delicacy of touch, who while cutting the corns of some famous man speaks of the coming abolition of all privilege: 'genius too is a privilege we shall abolish'.

In the world that Balzac has created it is the intensity of the struggle—an intensity beyond that of real life—which makes his common soldiers, his valets, his commercial travellers, all men of genius; and I doubt if law had for him any purpose but that of preserving the wine when the grapes had been trodden, and seeing to it that the treaders know their treads. 'The passionate-minded', says an Indian saying, 'love bitter food.'

v

When I close my eyes and pronounce the word 'Christianity' and await its unconscious suggestion, I do not see Christ crucified, or the Good Shepherd from the catacombs, but a father and mother and their children, a picture by Leonardo da Vinci most often. While Europe had still Christianity for its chief preoccupation men painted little but that scene. Yet what Christian economists said of the family seemed to me conventional and sentimental till I had met with Balzac. Now I understand them. Soloviev writes that every industrious man has a right to certain necessities and decencies of life; and I think he would not object to Aristotle's proposed limitation of fortunes, however much he might object to us, who are jealous and still lack philosophy, fixing the limit. But that the community should do more for a man than secure him these necessities and decencies, he denounces for devil's work. The desire of the father to see his child better off than himself, socially, financially, morally, according to his nature, is, he claims, the main cause of all social progress, of all improvements in civilisation. Yet all the while his attention is too much fixed upon the direct conscious effects—he sees the world as child, father, grandfather, and all virtues as derivable from our veneration for the past we inherit from, or our compassion for the future that inherits from us—and not enough upon its indirect unconscious effects, upon the creation of social species each bound together by its emotional quality.

Yesterday I came upon a little wayside well planted about with roses, a sight I had not seen before in Ireland, and it brought to mind all that planting of flowers, all that cleanness and neatness that the countryman's ownership of his farm has brought with it in Ireland, and also the curious doctrine of Soloviev, that no family has the full condition of perfection that cannot share in what he calls 'the spiritualisation of the soil'—a doctrine derivable, perhaps, from the truth that all emotional unities find their definition through the image, unlike those of the intellect, which are defined in the logical process. However, Soloviev is a dry ascetic half-man, and may see nothing beyond a round of the more obvious virtues approved by his Greek Church. I understand by 'soil' all the matter in which the soul works, the walls of our houses, the serving-up of our meals, and the chairs and tables of our rooms, and the instincts of our bodies; and by 'family' all institutions, classes, orders, nations, that arise out of the family and are held together, not by a logical process, but by historical association, and possess a personality for whose lack men are 'sheep without a shepherd when the snow shuts out the sun'.

Men who did not share their privileges have died for and lived for all these, and judged them little. Certainly no simple age has denied to monk or nun their leisure, nor thought that the monk's lamp and the nun's prayer, though from the first came truth and from the second denial of self, were not recompense enough, nor has any accomplished age begrudged the expensive leisure of women, knowing that they gave back more than they received in giving courtesy.

VI

If, as these writers affirm, the family is the unit of social life, and the origin of civilisation which but exists to preserve it, and almost the sole cause of progress, it seems more natural than it did before that its ecstatic moment, the sexual choice of man and woman, should be the greater part of all poetry. A single wrong choice may destroy a family, dissipating its tradition or its biological force, and the great sculptors, painters, and poets are there that instinct may find its lamp. When a young man imagines the woman of his hope, shaped for all the uses of life, mother and mistress and yet fitted to carry a bow in the wilderness, how little of it all is mere instinct, how much has come from chisel and brush. Educationalists and statesmen, servants of the logical process, do their worst, but they are not the matchmakers who bring together the fathers and mothers of the generations nor shall the type they plan survive.

VII

When we compare any modern writer, except Balzac, with the writers of an older world, with, let us say, Dante, Villon, Shakespeare, Cervantes, we are in the presence of something slight and shadowy. It is natural for a man who believes that man finds his happiness here on earth, or not at all, to make light of all obstacles to that happiness and to deny altogether the insuperable obstacles seen by religious philosophy. The strength and weight of Shakespeare, of Villon, of Dante, even of Cervantes, come from their preoccupation with evil. In Shelley, in Ruskin, in Wordsworth, who for all his formal belief was, as Blake saw, a descendant of Rousseau, there is a constant resolution to dwell upon good only; and from this comes their lack of the sense of character, which is defined always by its defects or its incapacity, and their lack of the dramatic sense; for them human nature has lost its antagonist. William Morris was and is my chief of men; but how would that strong, rich nature have grasped and held the world had he not denied all that forbade the millennium he longed for? He had to believe that men needed no spur of necessity and that men, not merely those who, in the language of Platonists, had attained to freedom and so become self-moving, but all men, would do all necessary work with no compulsion but a little argument. He was perhaps himself half aware of his lack, for in *News from Nowhere* he makes a crotchety old man complain that the novelists are not as powerful as before Socialism was established.

Bernard Shaw, compelled to believe, not as Morris did, that men will slaughter cattle and skin dead horses for a pastime, but that men can be found to force them to it, and yet neither bully, nor accept bribes, nor put the wrong man to the work, has invented a drama where ideas and not men are the combatants, and so dislikes whatever is harsh or incomprehensible that he complains of Shakespeare's 'ghosts and murders' and of Ibsen's 'morbid terror of death'. It has been the lot of both men, the one a great many-sided man, and the other a logician without rancour, and both lovers of the best, to delight the Garden City mind. To the Garden City mind the slightness and shadowiness may well seem that of the clouds at dawn; but how can it seem to us in Ireland who have faith—whether heathen or Christian—who have believed from our cradle in original sin, and that man lives under a curse, and so must earn his bread with the sweat of his face, but what comes from blotting out one half of life?

When I went every Sunday to the little lecture hall at the side of William Morris's house, Lionel Johnson said to me, his tongue unloosed by slight intoxication: 'I wish those who deny eternity of punishment could realise their unspeakable vulgarity'. I remember laughing when he said it, but for years I turned it over in my mind and it always made me uneasy. I do not think I believe in the eternity of punishment, and yet I am still drawn to a man that does—Swedenborg for instance—and rather repelled by those who have never thought it possible. I remember, too, old John O'Leary's contempt for a philanthropist, a contempt he could never explain. Is it that these men, who believe what they wish, can never be quite sincere and so live in a world of half-belief? But no man believes willingly in evil or in suffering. How much of the strength and weight of Dante and of Balzac comes from unwilling belief, from the lack of it how much of the rhetoric and vagueness of all Shelley that does not arise from personal feeling?

VIII

Logic is loose again, as once in Calvin and Knox, or in the hysterical rhetoric of Savonarola, or in Christianity itself in its first raw centuries, and because it must always draw its deductions from what every dolt can understand, the wild beast cannot but destroy mysterious life. We do not the less need, because it is an economic and not a theological process, those Christian writers whose roots are in permanent human nature. They, too, have their solution of the social question. To Balzac indeed it was but personal charity, the village providence of the eighteenth century, but Soloviev and the economists are more scientific, and have fostered a movement which, instead of attacking property, distributes it as widely as possible, and this movement has been in practice co-operation, and there Ireland is not Russia's pupil, but her teacher. Their design is always to guard and strengthen family ambition; content to be the midwife of Nature and not a juggling mechanist who would substitute an automaton for her living child.

A family is part of history and a part of the soil, and it seems to me a natural thing that co-operative Denmark should have invented the phrase: 'to understand the peasant by the saga and the saga by the peasant'. Socialism is as international as Capital or as Calvinism, and I have never met a Socialist who did not believe he could carry his oratory from London to Paris and from Paris to Jericho and there find himself at home.

If we could but unite our economics and our nationalism with our religion, that, too, would become philosophic—and the religion that does not become philosophic, as religion is in the East, will die out of modern Europe—and we, our three great interests made but one, would at last be face to face with the great riddle, and might, it may be, hit the answer. Yet no man can hit the answer till certain discoveries have had time to change the direction of speculation and research. To take but one straw from a haystack, I have known a dream to pass through a whole house—I can never blind myself to the implications of that fact—but what I do not know is whether it so passed because all were under one roof, or because all shared certain general interests, or because all had various degrees of affection for one another. Now all these writers of economics overrate the importance of work. Every man has a profound instinct that idleness is the true reward of work, even if it only come at the end of life, or if generations have to die before it comes at all, and literature and art are often little but its preparation that it may be an intensity. I have no doubt that the idleness, let us say, of a man devoted to his collection of Chinese paintings affects the mind even of men who do physical labour without spoken or written word, and all the more because physical labour increases mental pursuits.

I have studied the influence as it were in the laboratory, and I cannot exclude this fact, to which the world may not be converted for fifty years, from my judgment of the social system and its reformers; but I do not know if this influence would be strengthened if labourer and idler used churches, or furniture, or listened to or read stories, and wore clothes which had all, as let us say in Minoan or Egyptian civilisation, a common character. Albert de Rochas suspected something of the kind, and I do not know how large a portion of our day's thought—though I suspect the greater portion—has its direction or its intensity from such influence.

Did some perception of this create among primitive people the conviction that ordinary men had no immortality, but obtained it through a magical bond with some chief or king? Perhaps it may be possible in a few years to apportion the values of idleness by a science that traces the connections of thought and by a religion that judges the result. With Christianity came the realisation that a man must surrender his particular will to an implacable will, not his, though within his, and perhaps we are restless because we approach a realisation that our general will must surrender itself to another will within it, interpreted by certain men, at once economists, patriots, and inquisitors. As all realisation is through opposites, men coming to believe the subjective opposite of what they do and think, we may be about to accept the most implacable authority the world has known. Do I desire it or dread it, loving as I do the gaming-table of Nature where many are ruined but none is judged, and where all is fortuitous, unforeseen?

IX

When Dr. Hyde delivered in 1894 his lecture on the necessity of 'the de-anglicisation of Ireland', to a society that was a youthful indiscretion of my own I heard an enthusiastic hearer say: 'This lecture begins a new epoch in Ireland'. It did that, and if I were not four-and-fifty, with no settled habit but the writing of verse, rheumatic, indolent, discouraged, and about to move to the Far East, I would begin another epoch by recommending to the Nation a new doctrine, that of unity of being.

1919

'The Midnight Court'

'THE MIDNIGHT COURT'[1]

MONTHS ago Mr. Ussher asked me to introduce his translation of *The Midnight Court*. I had seen a few pages in an Irish magazine; praised its vitality; my words had been repeated; and because I could discover no reason for refusal that did not make me a little ashamed, I consented. Yet I could wish that a Gaelic scholar had been found, or failing that some man of known sobriety of manner and of mind —Professor Trench of Trinity College, let us say— to introduce to the Irish reading public this vital, extravagant, immoral, preposterous poem.

Brian Mac Giolla Meidhre—or to put it in English, Brian Merriman—wrote in Gaelic, one final and three internal rhymes in every line, pouring all his mediaeval abundance into that narrow neck. He was born early in the eighteenth century, somewhere in Clare, even now the most turbulent of counties, and the countrymen of Clare and of many parts of Munster have repeated his poem down to our own day. Yet this poem which is so characteristically Gaelic and mediaeval is founded upon *Cadenus and Vanessa*,[2] read

[1] *The Midnight Court*, translated from the Gaelic by Percy Arland Ussher (Jonathan Cape, London, 1926).

[2] Mr. Robin Flower pointed this out to me. *Cadenus and Vanessa*, which has the precision of fine prose, is the chief authority for the first meeting of Swift and Esther Vanhomrigh. I think it was Sir Walter Scott who first suggested 'a constitutional infirmity' to account for Swift's emotional entanglement, but this suggestion is not supported by Irish tradition. Some years ago a one-act play was submitted to the Abbey Theatre reading committee which showed Swift saved from English soldiers at the time of the *Drapier Letters*

perhaps in some country gentleman's library. The shepherds and nymphs of Jonathan Swift plead by counsel before Venus:

> Accusing the false creature man.
> The brief with weighty crimes was charged
> On which the pleader much enlarged,
> That Cupid now has lost his art,
> Or blunts the point of every dart.

Men have made marriage mercenary and love an intrigue; but the shepherds' counsel answers that the fault lies with women who have changed love for 'gross desire' and care but for 'fools, fops, and rakes'. Venus finds the matter so weighty that she calls the Muses and the Graces to her assistance and consults her books of law—Ovid, Virgil, Tibullus, Cowley, Waller—continually adjourns the court for sixteen years, and then after the failure of an experiment gives the case in favour of the women. The experiment is the creation of Vanessa, who instead of becoming all men's idol and reformer, all women's example, repels both by her learning and falls in love with her tutor Swift.

The Gaelic poet changed a dead to a living mythology, and called men and women to plead before

---

by a young harlot he was accustomed to visit. The author claimed that though the actual incident was his invention, his view of Swift was traditional, and enquiry proved him right. I had always known that stories of Swift and his serving-man were folk-lore all over Ireland and now I learned from country friends why the man was once dismissed. Swift sent him out to fetch a woman, and when Swift woke in the morning he found that she was a negress.

'The Midnight Court'

Eevell of Craglee, the chief of Munster spirits, and gave her court reality by seeing it as a vision upon a midsummer day under a Munster tree. No countryman of that time doubted, nor in all probability did the poet doubt, the existence of Eevell, a famous figure to every story-teller. The mediaeval convention of a dream or vision has served the turn of innumerable licentious rhymers in Gaelic and other languages, of Irish Jacobites who have substituted some personification of Ireland, some Dark Rosaleen, for a mortal mistress, of learned poets who call before our eyes an elaborate allegory of courtly love. I think of Chaucer's *Romaunt of the Rose*, his *Book of the Duchess*, and of two later poems that used to be called his, *Chaucer's Dream* and *The Complaint of the Black Knight*. But in all these the vision comes in May.

> That it was May, me thoughte tho,
> It is fyve yere or more ago;
> That it was May, thus dreamed me
> In tyme of love and jolitie
> That all things ginneth waxen gay.

One wonders if there is some Gaelic precedent for changing the spring festival for that of summer, the May-day singing of the birds to the silence of summer fields. Had Mac Giolla Meidhre before his mind the fires of Saint John's Night, for all through Munster men and women leaped the fires that they might be fruitful, and after scattered the ashes that the fields might be fruitful also? Certainly it is not possible to read his verses without being shocked and horrified as city onlookers were perhaps shocked and horrified at the free speech and buffoonery of some traditional country festival.

He wrote at a moment of national discouragement: the penal laws were still in force though weakening, the old order was a vivid memory, but, with the failure of the last Jacobite rising, hope of its return had vanished, and no new political dream had come. The state of Ireland is described: 'Her land purloined, her laws decayed . . . pastures with weeds o'ergrown, her ground untilled . . . hirelings holding the upper hand', and worst of all—and this the faery court has been summoned to investigate—'your lads and lasses have left off breeding'. Are the men or the women to blame? A woman speaks first, and it is Swift's argument but uttered with voluble country extravagance, and as she speaks one calls up a Munster hearth, farmers sitting round at the day's end, some old farmer famous through all the countryside for this long recitation, speaking or singing with dramatic gesture. If a man marries, the girl declares, he does not choose a young girl but some rich scold 'with a hairless crown and a snotty nose'. Then she describes her own beauty and asks if she is not more fit for marriage. She has gone everywhere 'bedizened from top to toe', but because she lacks money nobody will look at her and she is single still—

> After all I have spent upon readers of palms
> And tellers of tea-leaves and sellers of charms.

Then an old man replies, and heaps upon her and upon her poverty-stricken father and family all manner

of abuse: he is the champion of the men, and he will
show where the blame lies. He tells of his own marriage. He was a man of substance but has been ruined
by his wife who gave herself up to every sort of dissipation—Swift's argument again. A child was born,
but when he asked to see the child the women tried
to cover it up, and when he did see it, it was too fine,
too handsome and vigorous to be a child of his. And
now Swift is forgotten and dramatic propriety, the
poet speaks through the old man's mouth and asks
Eevell of Craglee to abolish marriage that such
children may be born in plenty.

> For why call a Priest in to bind and to bless
> Before candid nature can give one caress?
> Why lay the banquet and why pay the band
> To blow their bassoons and their cheeks to expand?
> Since Mary the Mother of God did conceive
> Without calling the clergy or begging their leave,
> The love-gotten children are famed as the flower
> Of man's procreation and nature's power;
> For love is a lustier sire than law
> And has made them sound without fault or flaw,
> And better and braver in heart and head
> Than the puny breed of the bridal bed.

The bastard's speech in *Lear* is floating through his
mind, mixed up doubtless with old stories of Diarmuid's and Cuchulain's loves, and old dialogues where
Oisin railed at Patrick; but there is something more,
an air of personal conviction that is of his age, something that makes his words—spoken to that audience
—more than the last song of Irish paganism. One remembers that Burns is about to write his beautiful

defiant *Welcome to his love-begotten daughter* and that Blake, who is defiant in thought alone, meditates perhaps his *Marriage of Heaven and Hell*. The girl replies to the old man that if he were not so old and crazed she would break his bones, and that if his wife is unfaithful what better could he expect seeing that she was starved into marrying him? However, she has her own solution. Let all the handsome young priests be compelled to marry. Then Eevell of Craglee gives her judgment, the priests are left to the Pope who will order them into marriage one of these days, but let all other young men marry or be stripped and beaten by her spirits, and let all old bachelors be tortured by the spinsters. The poem ends by the girl falling upon the poet and beating him because he is unmarried. He is ugly and humped, she says, but might look as well as another in the dark.

Standish Hayes O'Grady has described *The Midnight Court* as the best poem written in Gaelic, and as I read Mr. Ussher's translation I have felt, without sharing what seems to me an extravagant opinion, that Mac Giolla Meidhre, had political circumstances been different, might have founded a modern Gaelic literature. Mac Conmara, or Macnamara, though his poem is of historical importance, does not interest me so much. He knew Irish and Latin only, knew nothing of his own age, saw vividly but could not reflect upon what he saw, and so remained an amusing provincial figure.

1926

IV
PAGES FROM A DIARY WRITTEN IN
NINETEEN HUNDRED AND THIRTY
1944

Pages from a Diary in 1930

PORTOFINO VETTA. APRIL 7TH

I HAVE been ill for five months since I bled from the lung in London, four out of the five of Malta fever, and a couple of weeks ago the doctor told me it would be three months before I had recovered strength. But eight days ago we came from Rapallo to this hotel at Portofino Vetta some fifteen feet above the sea and I am almost well again. I work at the new version of *A Vision* every morning, then read Swift's Letters and only take to detective stories in the evening, and would be wholly well if my legs were stronger. Here I can slip in and out as I please, free from the stage fright I had at Rapallo whenever George brought me to the little café by the sea. After all there may be something in climate which I have always denied. Here no mountains shut us in; I think three weeks should make me well as ever.

II

I am reading Swift—his Letters, his essay on the end of Queen Anne's reign, and contrasting them with F. S. Oliver's *Endless Adventure*. Oliver, like all modern historians, sees history as a reasoned conflict of material interests intelligible to all. I think of Swift's account of Marlborough's demand to be made captain-general for life, of the Queen's fear that he had designs upon the throne, of Argyll's boast that he would fetch

289

him from the midst of his army dead or alive. These men sat next one another, suspected one another, and planned we do not know what. History seems to me a human drama, keeping the classical unities by the clear division of its epochs, turning one way or the other because this man hates or that man loves. Had any trade question at the opening of the eighteenth century as great an effect on subsequent history as Bolingbroke's impotence and Harley's slowness and secrecy? Was the French Revolution caused by the peasants' poverty or by that which used it? The peasant had been poor for centuries. Yet the drama has its plot, and this plot ordains character and passions and exists for their sake.

III

SUBJECT FOR A POEM. APRIL 30TH

Death of a friend. To describe how mixed with one's grief comes the thought that the witness of some foolish word or act of one's own is gone.

Describe Byzantium as it is in the system towards the end of the first Christian millennium. A walking mummy. Flames at the street corners where the soul is purified, birds of hammered gold singing in the golden trees, in the harbour, offering their backs to the wailing dead that they may carry them to Paradise.

These subjects have been in my head for some time, especially the last.

Pages from a Diary in 1930

IV

The heart well worn upon the sleeve may be the
best of sights,
But never, never dangling leave the liver and the
lights.

V

When my Instructors began their exposition of the
Great Year all the history I knew was what I remembered of English and Classical history from
school days, or had since learned from the plays of
Shakespeare or the novels of Dumas. When I had
the dates and diagrams I began to study it, but could
not so late in life, and with so much else to read, be a
deep student. So there is little in what follows but
what comes from the most obvious authorities. Sometimes I did indeed stray from them, and sometimes
the more vivid the fact the less do I remember my
authority. Where did I pick up that story of the
Byzantine bishop and the singer of Antioch, where
learn that to anoint your body with the fat of a lion
ensured the favour of a king?

VI

A DREAM

I dreamed that I was on shipboard, steerage on a
crowded steamer. A steward asked me for my ticket
but I had none. As the steamer had started he left me
without doing anything. Presently a small man I knew
to be a pickpocket said: 'I will protect you'. Then a

big man I knew to be a tramp called me over to the other side of the steamer and showed me a better seat than the one I was sitting on and said: 'I will protect you'. I saw a woman smiling and we fell into talk.

'I think you know who I am.'

'I know Sligo.'

'I am a stowaway, but a tramp and a pickpocket have promised to protect me.'

'There are people everybody protects.'

'Who?'

'Those who speak well of their wives.'

But another woman said: 'That is not true. Everybody protects those who praise everybody but there has to be wisdom in it.'

VII

Struck by this in Swift's *Discourse of the Contests and Dissensions between the Nobles and the Commons in Athens and Rome*. 'I think that the saying "Vox populi vox Dei" ought to be understood of the universal bent and current of a people, not of the bare majority of a few representatives, which is often procured by little art, and great industry and application; wherein those who engage in the pursuits of malice and revenge, are much more sedulous than such as would prevent them.' (Vol. II, page 408 of Sheridan's *Swift*.)

The whole essay leads up to Burke so clearly that one may claim that Anglo-Ireland re-created con-

servative thought as much in one as in the other.
Indeed the *Discourse* with its law of history might be
for us what Vico is to the Italians, had we a thinking
nation.

VIII

Burke is only tolerable in his impassioned moments,
but no matter what Swift talks of, one delights in his
animation and clarity. I think the reason is that Swift
always thought in English and is learned in that
tongue. The writers who seem most characteristic of
his time, Pope in his verse for instance, and the great
orators, think in French or in Latin. How much of my
reading is to discover the English and Irish originals
of my thought, its first language, and, where no such
originals exist, its relation to what original did. I seek
more than idioms, for thoughts become more vivid
when I find they were thought out in historical circumstances which affect those in which I live, or,
which is perhaps the same thing, were thought first by
men my ancestors may have known. Some of my
ancestors may have seen Swift, and probably my
Huguenot grandmother who asked burial near Bishop
King spoke both to Swift and Berkeley. I have before
me an ideal expression in which all that I have, clay
and spirit alike, assists; it is as though I most approxi-
mate towards that expression when I carry with me
the greatest possible amount of hereditary thought
and feeling, even national and family hatred and pride.

Our poetry and prose are often abstract and foreign.
I am a poor French scholar, yet in old days I felt my

sentences take a French form. Yet we must not put an artificial emphasis on what is English or Irish, for if we do we no longer find new richness. I think of that supreme ceremony wherein the Mormon offers his wisdom to his ancestors. But our language and thought are broken from the past by hurry, even when we do not think in any foreign tongue. I can hear Swift's voice in his letters speaking the sentences at whatever pace makes their sound and idiom expressive. He speaks and we listen at leisure.

Burke, whether he wrote a pamphlet or prepared a speech, wrote for men in an assembly, whereas Swift wrote for men sitting at table or fireside—from that come his animation and his naturalness. Upon the other hand the sense of an assembly, of an exceptional occasion, rouses Burke to his great moments of passion.

IX

Pound's conception of excellence, like that of all revolutionary schools, is of something so international that it is abstract and outside life. I do not ask myself whether what I find in Elizabethan English, or in that of the early eighteenth century, is better or worse than what I find in some other clime and time. I can only approach that more distant excellence through what I inherit, lest I find it and be stricken dumb. 'As ye came from Walsinghame' — *The Lamentation for Matthew Henderson*, 'For Matthew was a queer man' —that modern song of the man sailing from Mayo[1]—

1 F. R. Higgins, *The Ballad of O'Bruadir.*

show hereditary stamina and a great voice. A good poet must, as Henley said of Burns, be the last of a dynasty, and he must see to it that his Court expels the parvenu even though he gather all the riches of the world.

X

A poet whose free verse I have admired[1] rejects God and every kind of unity, calls the ultimate reality anarchy, means by that word something which for lack of metaphysical knowledge he cannot define. He thinks, however, that a baptismal and marriage service and some sort of ceremonial preparation for death are necessary, and that the Churches should stick to these and be content.

He now writes in the traditional forms because they satisfy a similar need. But why stop at the metrical forms? It has always seemed to me that all great literature at its greatest intensity displays the sage, the lover, or some image of despair, and that these are traditional attitudes. When I say the lover I mean all that heroic casuistry, all that assertion of the eternity of what Nature declares ephemeral; and when I speak of an image of despair I think of a passage in Sophocles, or many passages in Shakespeare and in the Old Testament; and when I say the sage I think of something Asiatic, and of something that belongs to modern Europe—the pedlar in *The Excursion*, an old hermit in *The Well at the World's End*, passages in Matthew Arnold.

[1] Basil Bunting, *Redimiculum Matellarum*. Milan, 1930.

Explorations II

All three have collapsed in our day because writers have grown weary of the old European philosophy and found no other. I think of the passage from Bacon quoted by Wordsworth as a motto to *The White Doe of Rylstone*—God puts divinity into a man as a man puts humanity into his dog. When the image of despair departed with poetical tragedy the others could not survive, for the lover and the sage cannot survive without that despair which is a form of joy and has certainly no place in the modern psychological study of suffering. Does not the soldier become the sage, or should I have granted him a different category, when some Elizabethan tragedy makes him reply to a threat of hanging: 'What has that to do with me?'

I asked, when a lad of seventeen or eighteen, a learned Brahmin how he taught philosophy to a man who denied the soul's immortality. 'I say to him', he said, '"What have you to do with that?"'—words which assert the soul's supremacy as do Hamlet's 'Absent thee from felicity awhile' and all of Shakespeare's other last words and closing scenes.

I find among some of the newer school of poets hatred of every monotheistic system.

XI

Protestant Ireland should ask permission to bring back the body of Grattan from Westminster Abbey to Saint Patrick's. He was buried in Westminster against the protests of his friends and followers—according to Sir Jonah Barrington, that there might be no place of pilgrimage—abandoned there without bust or monument. I would have him brought back through streets lined with soldiers that we might affirm that Saint Patrick's is more to us than Westminster; but, though Protestant Ireland should first move in this matter, I would have all descendants of Grattan's party, or of those who voted against the Union, lead the procession. When I was a young man the eighteenth century was all round me, O'Leary and J. F. Taylor praised it and seemed of it, and I had been to a school where Pope was the only poet since Shakespeare and, because I wanted romantic furniture, ignored it.

Then later on, because every political opponent used it to cry down Irish literature that sought audience or theme in Ireland, I hated it. But now I am like that woman in Balzac who, after a rich marriage and association with the rich, made in her old age the jokes of the concierge's lodge where she was born. I think constantly of some Irish lads I spoke to in California many years ago, and found as familiar with 'Young Ireland' as lads at home, because they gave me perhaps for the first time a sense of contact with a race scattered and yet one. My son who approaches his ninth year, when told that Italy excelled in painting, England in poetry, Germany in music, asked in what Ireland excelled, and was told that Ireland must not be judged like other nations because it had only just won back its freedom. I may suggest to him, if I live long enough, that the thought of Swift, enlarged and enriched by Burke, saddled and bitted reality, and that materialism was hamstrung by Berkeley, and

ancient wisdom brought back; that modern Europe
has known no men more powerful.

XII

I find this in Coleridge's *Fears in Solitude*:

> Meanwhile, at home,
> All individual dignity and power
> Engulfed in Courts, Committees, Institutions,
> Associations and Societies.

I think of some saying of Mussolini's that power is
the better for having a Christian name and address.
Balzac says that in France before the Revolution a man
gathered friends about his table, formed a mimic Court,
but since it he satisfies ambition by founding a society
and becoming its president or secretary. He seemed
to see in such societies and the causes they fostered,
personal ambition. Compare the rule of the 'many'
as described by Swift in his Greek and Roman essay.
Balzac and Swift saw predatory instinct where Coleridge
saw paralysis.

XIII

I find this in Coleridge's *Hexameters written during
a temporary Blindness*. He is talking of the eye of
a blind man:

> Even to him it exists, it stirs and moves in its
>   prison;
> Lives with a separate life, and 'Is it the Spirit?' he
>   murmurs:
> Sure it has thoughts of its own and to see is only its
>   language.

Pages from a Diary in 1930

These lines written in 1799 'during temporary blindness', must be taken as the sense in which he understood Berkeley, that given by Charpentier: Through the particular we approach the Divine Ideas—not, I think, the Berkeley of the *Commonplace Book*.

XIV

JUNE 6TH

Why does Coleridge delight me more as man than poet? Even if I believed, and I do not, the general assumption that he established nothing of value, it would not affect the matter. I think the reason is that from 1807 or so he seems to have some kind of illumination which was, as always, only in part communicable. The end attained in such a life is not a truth or even a symbol of truth, but a oneness with some spiritual being or beings. It is this that fixes our amazed attention on Oedipus when his death approaches, and upon some few historical men. It is because the modern philosopher has not sought this that he remains unknown to those multitudes who thought his predecessors sacred. Perhaps Coleridge needed opium to recover a state which, some centuries earlier, was accessible to the fixed attention of normal man.

JUNE 13TH

No, that is not the explanation, for I have remembered that I thought with like pleasure of Mallarmé's talk to his famous circle. I think the explanation must explain also why, during the most creative years of my artistic life, when Synge was writing plays and Lady Gregory translated early Irish poetry with an impulse that interpreted my own, I disliked the isolation of the work of art. I wished through the drama, through a commingling of verse and dance, through singing that was also speech, through what I called the applied arts of literature, to plunge it back into social life.

The use of dialect for the expression of the most subtle emotion—Synge's translation of Petrarch—verse where the syntax is that of common life, are but the complement of a philosophy spoken in the common idiom escaped from isolating method, gone back somehow from professor and pupil to Blind Tiresias.

XV

JUNE 19TH

The other day I came home from a call upon a friend very dissatisfied with my conversation. Presently I said to my wife: 'Now that my vitality grows less I should set up as sage'. She said: 'What do you mean by that?' and I said: 'Adapt my conversation to the company instead of the company to my conversation'. She said: 'It is too late to change'. Now I have been running over those words of mine and wonder with sudden excitement if they do not account for emotion in the presence of things so unlike as Swift's epitaph, Berkeley in his *Commonplace Book*, 'We Irish do not hold with this', Burke at certain famous moments,

Pages from a Diary in 1930

Coleridge at Highgate, Mallarmé on his Thursday evenings. They, as did Blind Tiresias, talked to the occasion, and seeing that they did not scorn our drama, lips as living as those in Fragonard's *Fountain of Life* drink of their stream. In that grim and wise account of the Thebaid, the *Lausiac History* of Palladius, men went on pilgrimage to Saint Anthony that they might learn about their spiritual states, what was about to happen and why it happened, and Saint Anthony would reply neither out of traditional casuistry nor common-sense but from supernatural power. When I think of Swift, of Burke, of Coleridge, or Mallarmé, I remember that they spoke as it were sword in hand, that they played their part in a unique drama, but played it, as a politician cannot though he stand in the same ranks, with the whole soul. Once or twice I have spoken words which came from nowhere, which I could not account for, which were even absurd, which have been fulfilled to the letter. I am trying to understand why certain metaphysicians whom I have spent years trying to master repel me, why those invisible beings I have learned to trust would turn me from all that is not conflict, that is not from sword in hand. Is it not like this? I cannot discover truth by logic unless that logic serve passion, and only then if the logic be ready to cut its own throat, tear out its own eyes—the cry of Hafiz, 'I made a bargain with that hair before the beginning of time', the cry of every lover. Those spiritual beings seem always as if they would turn me from every abstraction. I must not talk to myself about 'the truth' nor call myself 'teacher' nor another 'pupil'

—these things are abstract—but see myself set in a drama where I struggle to exalt and overcome concrete realities perceived not with mind only but as with the roots of my hair. The passionless reasoners are pariah dogs and devour the dead symbols. The clarified spirits own the truth, they have intellect; but we receive as agents, never as owners, in reward for victory.

XVI

Man can only love Unity of Being and that is why such conflicts are conflicts of the whole soul. Synge, for instance, must have felt compelled to his conflict with the pasteboard morality of political Dublin to make that world of his imagination more and more complete. If the man who sat behind me on the first night of *The Well of the Saints* and kept repeating 'Blasphemy—blasphemy—more blasphemy—' had attended to the stage he would have discovered in the strange miracle-worker, who comes and goes like cloud and rain, something, even, beyond the knowledge of its creator, a possibility of life not as yet in existence. All that our opponent expresses must be shown for a part of our greater expression, that he may become our thrall—be 'enthralled' as they say. Yet our whole is not his whole and he may break away and enthrall us in his turn, and there arise between us a struggle like that of the sexes. All life is such a struggle. When a plant draws from and feeds upon the soil, expression is its joy, but it is wisdom to be drawn forth and eaten.

Pages from a Diary in 1930

XVII

Even the most abstract thought has its conflict; Schoolman replies to Schoolman, but it is not of the whole nature. It is never as if we looked at the *Victory* of Samothrace and felt it in the soles of our feet.

XVIII

No matter how full the expression, the more it is of the whole man, the more does it require other expressions for its completion. As I watch *The Well of the Saints* upon the stage how can I help feeling that just as the actor's voice and form enlarge the written words, there are actions or thoughts, could I but find them, that would complete it all?

Certain abstract thinkers, whose measurements and classifications continually bring me back to concrete reality—the third book of *The World as Will and Idea*, Coleridge at Highgate. I think of the Tractarians, American transcendentalists at the first half of the nineteenth century and of the morbid profundity of French literature in its second half, though I do not know whether the influence of Schopenhauer or Flaubert and Baudelaire was direct or but in the air. An abstract thinker when he has this relation to concrete reality passes on both the thought and the passion; who has not remains in the classroom.

Explorations II

XIX

Berkeley thought that by showing that certain abstractions—the 'primary qualities'—did not exist he could create a philosophy so concrete that the common people could understand it. Had he founded his university in Bermuda we would certainly have seen an attempt to make it so intelligible, though perhaps not a successful attempt, for the whole world was sinking into abstraction. Sometimes when I think of him, what flitted before his eyes flits before mine also, I half perceive a world like that of a Zen priest in Japan or in China, but am hurried back into abstraction after but an instant.

XX

During the year and a half in which Coleridge wrote almost all his good poetry, the first part of *Christabel, The Ancient Mariner, Kubla Khan,* he was influenced by Berkeley—the influence of Burke came later. Berkeley's insistence on the particular and his hatred of abstraction possibly delivered Coleridge from rhymed opinions, though but for a time. Face to face with the seeming contradiction between the early Berkeley and the Berkeley of *Siris* he calls sight 'a language' . . . but if he means by this that through the particular we approach the divine ideas, which was perhaps the thought of Berkeley's later life though not that of the *Commonplace Book* (in *Siris* 'light' must be 'sight'), this, lacking some clear definition of those 'ideas', abstraction is once more upon us.

Pages from a Diary in 1930

I can call them spaceless, timeless beings that behold and determine each other, but what can they be to monotheistic Burke and Coleridge but God's abstract or separate thoughts?

XXI

I think that two conceptions, that of reality as a congeries of beings, that of reality as a single being, alternate in our emotion and in history, and must always remain something that human reason, because subject always to one or the other, cannot reconcile. I am always, in all I do, driven to a moment which is the realisation of myself as unique and free, or to a moment which is the surrender to God of all that I am. I think that there are historical cycles wherein one or the other predominates, and that a cycle approaches where all shall [be] as particular and concrete as human intensity permits. Again and again I have tried to sing that approach—*The Hosting of the Sidhe*, 'O sweet everlasting voices', and those lines about 'The lonely, majestical multitude'—and have almost understood my intention. Again and again with remorse, a sense of defeat, I have failed when I would write of God, written coldly and conventionally. Could those two impulses, one as much a part of truth as the other, be reconciled, or if one or the other could prevail, all life would cease.

XXII

When I was in my twenties I saw a drawing or etching by some French artist of an angel standing against a midnight sky. The angel was old, wingless, and armed like a knight, as impossibly tall as one of those figures at Chartres Cathedral, and its face was worn by time and by innumerable battles. I showed my father the drawing but he thought nothing of it because it was out of proportion, and I did not then know that an artist may exaggerate as he will for the sake of expression. Generally a judgment from my father would put me off anything, but this time that image remained and I imitated it in the old angels at at the end of *The Countess Cathleen*. I do not know whether it was before or after this that I made a certain girl see a vision of the Garden of Eden. She heard 'the music of Paradise coming from the Tree of Life', and, when I told her to put her ear against the bark, that she might hear the better, found that it was made by the continuous clashing of swords.

XXIII

If men are born many times, as I think, that must originate in the antinomy between human and divine freedom. Man incarnating, translating 'the divine ideas' into his language of the eye, to assert his own freedom, dying into the freedom of God and then coming to birth again. So too the assertions and surrender of sexual love, all that I have described elsewhere as antithetical and primary. My father once said to me that contemplative men had been for centuries in conspiracy to exalt their form of life, and I think I remember his denying that painter and poet were contemplative. I think I assert this when I assert that we hold down as it were on the sword's point what would, if undefeated, grow into the counter-truth, that when our whole being lives we create alike out of our love and hate.

XXIV

Plotinus calls well-nigh the most beautiful of Enneads *The Impassivity of the Disembodied*[1] but, as he was compelled to at his epoch, thought of man as re-absorbed into God's freedom as final reality. The ultimate reality must be all movement, all thought, all perception extinguished, two freedoms unthinkably, unimaginably absorbed in one another. Surely if either circuit, that which carries us into man or that which carries us into God, were reality, the generation had long since found its term.

XXV

The other day Gogarty wrote that John wanted to do a 'serious portrait'. I replied that 'I would think it a great honour'. And to-day I have been standing in front of the hotel mirror noticing certain lines about my mouth and chin marked strongly by shadows cast from a window on my right, and have wondered if John would not select those very lines and lay great emphasis upon them, and, if some friend complain that he has obliterated what good looks I have, insist that

[1] The Third Ennead, translated by Stephen MacKenna.

those lines show character, and perhaps that there are no good looks but character. In those lines I see the marks of recent illness, marks of time, growing irresolution, perhaps some faults that I have long dreaded; but then my character is so little myself that all my life it has thwarted me. It has affected my poems, my true self, no more than the character of a dancer affects the movement of the dance. When I was painted by John years ago, and saw for the first time the portrait (or rather the etching taken from it) now in a Birmingham gallery, I shuddered.

Always particular about my clothes, never dissipated, never unshaven except during illness, I saw myself there an unshaven, drunken bar-tender, and then I began to feel John had found something that he liked in me, something closer than character, and by that very transformation made it visible. He had found Anglo-Irish solitude, a solitude I have made for myself, an outlawed solitude.

XXVI

JUNE 23RD

Have we exhausted Deism, even that form which Blake denounced as pagan nature worship, which Wordsworth got from Coleridge? Certainly none of the writers who are most characteristic of our time turn it into poetry. Neither James Joyce, who is, someone tells me, a Thomist, nor T. S. Eliot, who is certainly Anglican. In so far as we believe that reality is a congeries we shall be uncertain of victory. We and those other souls to whom we are as it were bound and sworn, with whom we share a morality, may be defeated, and to those who believe in the final victory of Good there is greater heroism in our uncertainty. In morality itself there may be something arbitrary, as in the morals of Oedipus, as perhaps in all morality before the philosophy of Unity prevailed, as if it were the special discipline of a class, or a city, or a regiment. A young man[1] who was killed after he had been twice decorated said to me, 'I joined up out of friendship'. Yet there is always the other truth: 'Thou, Thou alone art everlasting, and the blessed spirits whom Thou includest as the sea its waves'.

XXVII

Spiritualism seems to announce such changes by its immense vogue; all that has to do with Christ, or angels, or Deism,—unlike the Swedenborgians who gave it doctrinal form—is sentimental make-believe, a pantomime stage where disembodied spirits re-create their human loves and hates.

XXVIII

If reality is timeless and spaceless this is a goal, an ultimate Good. But if I believe that it is also a congeries of autonomous selves I cannot believe in one ever-victorious Providence, though I may in Providences

[1] Robert Gregory.

that preside over a man, a class, a city, a nation, a world—Providences that may be defeated, the tutelary spirits of Plotinus.

XXIX

Two men of great ability, one rather famous, have said to me this winter, in repudiation of what they believed my thought, that the ultimate reality must be anarchy. I remember Madame Blavatsky, when alone with me and one other, talking of 'God-chaos, the which every man is seeking in his heart'. By the study of those impulses that shape themselves into words without context we find our thought, for we do not seek truth in argument or in books but clarification of what we already believe. It is for this reason that we hate those confident men and books who as it were trample in their top-boots or crack their whips between our cradles. Dissatisfaction with the old idea of God cannot but overthrow our sense of order, for the new conception of reality has not even begun to develop, it is still a phantom not a child.

XXX

RENVYLE. JULY 23RD

I have talked most of a long motor journey, talked even when I was hoarse. Why? Surely because I was timid, because I felt the other man was judging me, because I endowed his silence with all kinds of formidable qualities. Being on trial I must cajole my judge.

Pages from a Diary in 1930

XXXI

We approach influx. What is its form? A civilisation lasts two thousand years from nadir to nadir— Christ came at the Graeco-Roman meridian, physical maturity, spirit in celestial body, and was the first beginning of the One—all equal in the eyes of One. Our civilisation which began in A.D. 1000 approaches the meridian and once there must see the counter-birth. What social form will that birth take? It is multitudinous, the seat of the congeries of autonomous beings each seeing all within its own unity. I can only conceive of it as a society founded upon unequal rights and unequal duties which if fully achieved would include all nations in the European stream in one harmony, where each drew its nourishment from all though each drew different nourishment. But this ideal will be no more achieved than are the equal rights and duties before the One—God with the first Christians, Reason with Rousseau. There will be a weak unforeseen life moulding itself upon poor thought, war in all likelihood, discord till it become in its turn concord (spirit in celestial body), Olympus just as it breaks. It is founded by a Teacher not a Victim, and this Teacher is what he is because he creates and expresses the congeries, or concord of many, which must impose itself in the course of centuries. No, as Daimon of a dispensation he is that congeries, the family, the race, any group which is a kindred of any kind as distinct from an organised opinion. He will be preceded by opinion, but the

311

influx can only be kindred—the two daimons, the four daimons. He is not a being but a harmony of beings.

Spengler is right when he says all who preserve tradition will find their opportunity. Tradition is kindred. The abrogation of equality of rights and duties is because duties should depend on rights, rights on duties. If I till and dig my land I should have rights because of that duty done, and if I have much land, that, according to all ancient races, should bring me still more rights. But if I have much or little land and neglect it I should have few rights. This is the theory of Fascism and so far as land is concerned it has the history of the earth to guide it and that is permanent history. A day will come, however, when man's ever-increasing plasticity will make possible and compel a decision among the rights and duties which constitute refined society. Shall we grant the nun and the lady of fashion their leisure? Can we call their refinement duty and therefore the leisure essential to it a right? If so, what kind of lady, what kind of nun? We can no longer point to history, for we are plastic—as Flinders Petrie might say, we are no longer archaic, we control our material. The answer will not be given by man.

Can such a kindred once formed escape war? Will it not be war that must prove its strength? Its dead will return to it after death, for there can be no other fitting environment, and if it has religious ceremonies those ceremonies will remember this. I think of the Mormons, their baptisms for the dead, the ceremonies that offer their wisdom to the dead. Yet I must bear in mind that an antithetical revelation will be less miraculous (in the sense of signs and wonders), more psychological, than a primary which is from beyond man and mothered by the void. It is developed out of man and is man.

XXXII

Landed property gets its fascination from its inequality: divide it up into farms of equal size or fertility and it would still retain its inequality, no field or hedge like another.

When I was a young man I hated the solitary book, abstraction because its adepts sat in corners to pull out their solitary plums. The sight of Yvette Guilbert, a solitary, a performer to an alien crowd, filled me with distaste, for I would have seen her in some great house among her equals and her friends. I wanted a theatre where the greatest passions and all the permanent interests of men might be displayed that we might find them not alone over a book but, as I said again and again, lover by lover, friend by friend. All I wanted was impossible, and I wore out my youth in its pursuit, but now I know it is the mystery to come.

AUGUST 9TH. COOLE PARK

Swift's . . .[1] is more important to modern thought than Vico and certainly foreshadowed Flinders Petrie, Frobenius, Henry Adams, Spengler, and very exactly

---

[1] *A Discourse of the Contests and Dissensions between the Nobles and the Commons in Athens and Rome.*

and closely Gerald Heard. It needs interpretation, for it had to take the form of a pamphlet intelligible to the Whig nobility. He saw civilisations 'exploding'— to use Heard's term—just before the final state, and that final state as a tyranny, and he took from a Latin writer the conviction that every civilisation carries with it from the first what shall bring it to an end. Burke borrowed of him or re-discovered and Coleridge borrowed from Burke all but that inevitable end. Without the passion and style of either, Coleridge found through his very languor and hesitation time to approve the motives of acts that he hated. 'The victory of the Plebs' was 'explosive' but it originated in our civilisation from the misapplication of 'pure thought' which, rightly applied, is religion or philosophy. Though Luther was right to grant free judgment, Rousseau was not right, for though we have all the 'reason', 'pure thought' or conscience that judges motives, we have not all the 'understanding' or prudence to judge of acts and their consequences. There are children, even the French Revolution did not give them votes, lunatics, drunkards, dullards, persons too busy for thought or too dependent upon others to express it. All have 'reason' but not all have 'the means of exercising it and the materials, the facts and ideas upon which it is exercised', nor have all that have the means 'power of attention'. Historical society is founded upon these difficulties, but when we ignore them we create a government only possible among those that need no government. Swift thought that we set free a multitude of private interests to overbear all who by privilege of station, genius or training possessed the public mind, and thereby at last created a situation that had no issue but despotism. Roman history, as he saw it, was a struggle of classes, but Greek history, where the governing class was broken before history began, was the driving out or putting to death of all illustrious soldiers and statesmen. I think of Swift's own life, of the letter where he describes his love of this man and of that, and his hatred of all classes and professions. I remember his epitaph and understand that the liberty he served was that of intellect, not liberty for the masses but for those who could make it visible.

When Gulliver on the magical island is bid call up what ghosts he will, he calls up seven, all but one—Sir Thomas More—from Greece or Rome, seven exiled or murdered men to whom the world cannot add an eighth. Certainly when Swift describes the Houyhnhnms as 'the perfection of nature', he meant, like Rousseau, simplicity, but Swift's simplicity was the achievement of solitary men. Coleridge describes how social philosophers foretold that the French Revolution would be followed by despotism and were mocked at in the Press because, though such had happened from like cause in the past, it could not happen in the 'enlightened eighteenth century'; but when he would show the cause in action he lacks the lucidity of Berkeley and Swift. His description of France, all historical inequalities swept away, as a machine ready for Napoleon, reminds me that Kropotkin upon the one occasion when we talked—though I had often seen him—said that the Revolution by sweeping away old communal customs and institutions in the name of equal rights and duties left the French peasant at the mercy of the capitalist.

What has set me writing is Coleridge's proof, which seems to me conclusive, that civilisation is driven to its final phase not by the jealousy and egotism of the many, as Swift's too simple statement implies, but by 'pure thought', 'reason', what my System calls 'spirit' and 'celestial body', by that which makes all places and persons alike; that clay comes before the potter's thumb. I remember that my Instructors instance that understanding the 'faculties' wears thin at the end of an age, and begin to speculate about the plasticity that is the theme of Mr. Wyndham Lewis in *The Apes of God* and of Pirandello at all times.

Has 'pure thought' changed its ground, and so dissolved those historical forms and occupations wherefrom we have drawn our personalities, that we must take every chance suggestion, or deliberately create a personality and live henceforth as Homunculus in his bottle? Flinders Petrie shows where in the history of a civilisation sculpture, painting, mechanism, will put off what he calls archaism and gain control of their material, and, because vigour implies effort, begin their decline. Are those amusing people described by Mr. Wyndham Lewis not the first of a great multitude who, put in control and invited to create without a model, must make ready for the tyrant?

At the end of an epoch or civilisation I imagine a maturity, not of this or that science or art or condition, but, in so far as may be possible considering time and place, of the civilisation itself an instant before its dissolution or transformation, when it may, wherever it is most sensitive, submit not to this or that external tyrant but to a Being or an Olympus all can share.

AUGUST 10TH

'Pure thought', because it is concerned with universals, finds all alike, leaves all plastic, and its decisions, did it dwell equally in all men, would be a simultaneous decision, a world-wide general election, a last judgment, and for judge a terrible Christ like that in the apse at Cefalù.

But the understanding, because founded upon experience, upon many lives, let us say, cannot submit its decision to the vote of a moment.

Did Swift deliberately set 'pure thought' aside? He advised his clergy to preach the mysteries of religion once or twice a year and then speak no more of what none can or should understand. He thought missionaries in China should say nothing about Christ's divinity and said that the first Christians thought it 'too high' for general understanding and so kept silent about it. He prayed much, had the Communion Service by heart, but he received dogma and ritual from the State and condemned Huguenot and Dissenter alike. He was at one time the friend, the benefactor perhaps, of Berkeley, but never speaks of his philosophy.

Explorations II

Berkeley's essay on *Passive Obedience* asks a question that Berkeley, through the lack of the historical sense, cannot answer. Dreading, as Swift dreaded, a return of public disorder he forbids opposition to the State under all circumstances, though when such opposition has arisen, and the headship of the State is vacant or in doubt, a [man] may choose his party. No modern man can accept a conclusion that confounds red and white armies alike. Burke answered the question, and Swift, had he taken up again the thought of his essay on the Dissensions of the Greeks and Romans, could have answered it. Berkeley spoke his speech in the great drama of Anglo-Irish thought. The answer came when the curtain rose upon the second act. A State is organic and has its childhood and maturity and, as Swift saw and Burke did not, its decline. We owe allegiance to the government of our day in so far as it embodies that historical being.

SEPTEMBER 11TH

Last night a dream which I dream several times a year—a great house which I recognise as partly Coole and partly Sandymount Castle—though not by any exact physical resemblance. In all these dreams Sandymount gives the tragic element—in one which I remember vividly the house was built round a ruin and Sandymount was the ruin. This time all the house was castellated and about to pass into other hands, its pictures auctioned. I remember looking at a picture and thinking that it would now lose its value, for its value was that it had always hung in a particular place and had been put there by some past member of the family. Coole as a Gregory house is near its end, it will be before long an office and residence for foresters, a little cheap furniture in the great rooms, a few religious oleographs its only pictures, and yet when in my dream I had some such thought I stood in a Gothic door which I now recognise as the door at Sandymount. I never think of Sandymount Castle and would not have seen it except from the road had I not been shown over it by the headmaster of the school that had what remained—the garden disappeared long ago. The impression on my subconscious was made in childhood, when my uncle Corbet's bankruptcy and death was a recent tragedy, the book with Sandymount Castle printed on the cover open upon my knees. I vividly recall those photographs of ornamental waters, of a little rustic bridge, of the oak room where celebrated men had sat down to breakfast, of garden paths, of a great door suggesting not Abbotsford but Strawberry Hill—the door that my dream recalled.

Yet do I speak the truth when I say I never think of it? The other day at my Uncle Isaac's funeral I thought how little I had seen of him and that fear had kept me away. He was so much better bred than I— he had about him the sweetness of those gardens, so too have my old aunts who spent their childhood there. I have intellect, scornful, impatient, dissatisfied and always a little ashamed.

Berkeley in the *Commonplace Book* thought that 'we perceive' and are passive whereas God creates in perceiving. He creates what we perceive. I substitute for God the Thirteenth Cone, the Thirteenth Cone therefore creates our perceptions—all the visible world—as held in common by our wheel.

The chair in which I am sitting is covered in black silk with a pattern of pale pink roses with pale green leaves. This silk is from the dress worn by Lady Gregory when presented at Court. I think of my Japanese sword wrapped in a piece of silk from a Japanese lady's Court dress.

A LETTER TO MICHAEL'S SCHOOLMASTER

Dear Sir,

My son is now between nine and ten and should begin Greek at once and be taught by the Berlitz method that he may read as soon as possible that most exciting of all stories, the *Odyssey*, from that landing in Ithaca to the end. Grammar should come when the need comes. As he grows older he will read to me the great lyric poets and I will talk to him about

Pages from a Diary in 1930

Plato. Do not teach him one word of Latin. The Roman people were the classic decadence, their literature form without matter. They destroyed Milton, the French seventeenth and our own eighteenth century, and our schoolmasters even to-day read Greek with Latin eyes. Greece, could we but approach it with eyes as young as its own, might renew our youth. Teach him mathematics as thoroughly as his capacity permits. I know that Bertrand Russell must, seeing that he is such a featherhead, be wrong about everything, but as I have no mathematics I cannot prove it. I do not want my son to be as helpless. Do not teach him one word of geography. He has lived on the Alps, crossed a number of rivers and when he is fifteen I shall urge him to climb the Sugar Loaf. Do not teach him a word of history. I shall take him to Shakespeare's history plays, if a commercialised theatre permit, and give him all the historical novels of Dumas, and if he cannot pick up the rest he is a fool. Don't teach him one word of science, he can get all he wants in the newspapers and in any case it is no job for a gentleman. If you teach him Greek and mathematics and do not let him forget the French and German that he already knows you will do for him all that one man can do for another. If he wants to learn Irish after he is well founded in Greek, let him—it will clear his eyes of the Latin miasma. If you will not do what I say, whether the curriculum or your own will restrain, and my son comes from school a smatterer like his father, may your soul lie chained on the Red Sea bottom.

Explorations II

XXXIV

SEPTEMBER 13TH

I met at Miss Grigsby's two months ago a New York clairvoyant—a woman—I forget her name or never knew it. Knew I had been ill: said, 'You are through with illness, should have ten wonderful years. It is unfortunate that spiritual change is impossible without illness.' Spoke of my philosophic work, saw it do something I would hate—found 'a cult'. She spoke of notes written for my own eye and said that their publication would be very successful, seemed to think more of them than of the more serious work. Before I finished them I would, however, do something quite simple at the suggestion of a woman, 'about a beggar, no, not exactly a beggar'. Is this my Swift play? My wife who urged me to do it added the detail about the medium refusing money and then looking to see what each gave.

XXXV

SEPTEMBER 15TH

Reading Hone's unpublished life of Berkeley[1] I get that sense of unreality before the historical figure that I had before the portrait in the Fellows' Room in Trinity College, Dublin. That philanthropic serene Bishop, that pasteboard man, never wrote the *Com-*

---

[1] *Bishop Berkeley*, by J. M. Hone and M. M. Rossi, with an introduction by W. B. Yeats, 1931.

monplace Book. Attracted beyond expression by Berkeley's thought I have been repelled by the man as we have received him from tradition, a saint and sage who takes to tar water, who turns from the most overwhelming philosophic generalisations since Plato to convert negroes, and who in *Siris* writes as if he had forgotten it. But now that I reject the saint and sage I find Berkeley lovable. The Berkeley of the *Commonplace Book* wore an alien mask, the mask of preposterous benevolence that prevailed in sculpture and painting down to the middle of the nineteenth century —the monument to the Prince Consort on Leinster Lawn—to hide his clamorous, childlike, naïve, mischievous curiosity. The mischief of a man is malicious; when he pulls the skeleton out of the cupboard he calculates the whole effect, but Berkeley knew nothing of men and women. He loved discourse for its own sake as a child does, and said out of the contented solitude of a child the most embarrassing things. What did he really say in those three sermons to undergraduates that got him into such a political mess?— not quite, I think, what he says in that irrational essay on *Passive Obedience* written to save his face. Was the Bermuda project more than a justification for curiosity and discourse? Was not that curiosity already half satisfied when he drew the plans of his learned city— a steeple in the centre and markets in the corners?

He left behind those three earnest Fellows of College who might have liked converting negroes—even to-day there is a T.C.D. mission to savage parts— and took to America a portrait painter and a couple of pleasant young men of fortune, and when he got there associated with fox-hunters and American 'Immaterialist' disciples. When Walpole refused the money he came home without apparent regret—and, as I think, with relief. His curiosity was satisfied. Had an American disciple turned Boswell and had the genius for the task, we would have had another *Commonplace Book*, the old theme with vivid new illustrations drawn from the passing show. He returned to Ireland, the eighteenth-century mask—itself one of those abstractions he denounced—clapped firmly on his face. There is a famine in Ireland; a Bishop must be benevolent, besides a child has never thought of being anything else, but his curiosity is even more powerful. Had he not been told in America of Indians that cured all kinds of things with a concoction of tar? He had already put the mathematicians and philosophers by the ears, why not the doctors? And the tar water, and the cures it worked, what a subject for discourse! Could he not lead his reader—especially if that reader drank tar water every morning—from tar to light? Newton, made ignorant by his very knowledge, his contact with other men, his lack of childish solitude, had postulated an Ether, an abstraction, a something that did not exist because unperceived. If this is a foundation stuff it has visibility, light—mind and light the Siamese twins that constitute the whole of reality. But he is also the burned child so he writes as if he had never heard of Immaterialism, he becomes a materialist stoic philosopher, playing with some harmless symbol. The American Samuel Johnson and his Irish disciples will understand that this light, this intellectual Fire, is that continuity which holds together 'the perceptions', that it is a substitute for the old symbol God. Is it to adjust his mask more carefully, to pose himself as it were against remote antiquity, or a need for symbol that makes him talk of the Neo-platonic Trinity?

When I think of him, I think of my father, and of others born into the Anglo-Irish solitude, of their curiosity, their discourse, their spontaneity, their ir-responsibility, their innocence, their sense of mystery as they grow old, their readiness to dress up at the suggestion of others though never quite certain what dress they wear.

Berkeley the Bishop was a humbug. His wife, that charming daughter who played the viol, Queen Caroline, Ministers of State, imposed it upon him; but he was meant for a Greek tub or an Indian palm tree. Only once in his life was he free, when, still an under-graduate, he filled the *Commonplace Book* with snorts of defiance.

Descartes, Locke, and Newton took away the world and gave us its excrement instead. Berkeley restored the world. I think of the Nirvana Song of the Japanese monk: 'I sit on the mountain side and look up at the little farm—I say to the old farmer: "How many times have you mortgaged your land and paid off the mortgagee?" I take pleasure in the sound of the reeds'.

Berkeley has brought back to us the world that only exists because it shines and sounds. A child, smothering its laughter because the elders are standing round, has opened once more the great box of toys.

Explorations II

XXXVI

SEPTEMBER 20TH

Toyohiko Kagawa like Gandhi seems to rely on a subtlety of moral understanding no popular leader can rely upon in Europe. It is the Divine Man as an organising force. America and Russia have founded labour politics or 'mutual aid', but how can there be mutual aid between 'a labour group' and the sick, the old, 'the foundling picked up at the street corner' or any other person 'who cannot earn a living'? We should give without seeking a return. Kagawa interprets Genesis as the creation of the human soul. God created Eden for the unborn souls of Adam and Eve. A love for others must in the same way include their lives, their lives which are as yet unknown and unlived. We re-make the world for the sake of those lives. Karl Marx puts too much emphasis upon this re-made world and not enough upon the living; only when we contemplate those living can we re-make the world. The re-creation is from love of the perfect and mercy for the imperfect. Kagawa insists that love is always creative—'The husband expresses himself to his wife'. 'Love is creation raised to a higher degree.' He talks much of love in connection with evolution. 'In desire there is no selection—selection is love.' This love when it forgives is God's love, for then mercy is added. 'When God's creative power, which formed heaven and earth, comes into me there is born in my heart the love that forgives the sinner.'

Pages from a Diary in 1930

He says, 'There lies buried in the Cosmos a love which does not rise to the level of human consciousness but is like the root buried underneath the stem'. It elaborated the placenta of the higher animals. He thinks that the command 'Love your enemies' may come from this root.

He quotes a certain Kuriyagawa Hakuso as saying, 'A love surpassing sexual desire comes into being— it may be called passionate love', is mutual and in all its forms creates physical love. Passionate love is a form of psychic love; psychic love forms a group of two or more, it selects those who are akin to us. It does not tolerate any who are outside the kindred. The kindred or group persecutes all those who are too slow or too fast. The final love is conscientious love. A single sinner makes all the Universe suffer— it suffers as we do from a wound in a finger and as all our blood might flow out in the small wound so might the life of the Universe flow out. This suffering is the suffering of God which we share in 'conscientious love'. 'The sufferings of every individual become the defects and agonies of the whole world.' 'If we wish to live complete human lives we must atone for the sins of others. God to perfect his own life upon the earth saves beings who are imperfect.'

The fish in 'the miracle of the fishes', finding themselves excluded from the kindred, may have called Christ's love 'psychic'. A Japan which had completely accepted the Christianity of Kagawa might be attacked; it would still need oil, metals, tillage and pasture, still have hungry neighbours, still need soldiers and their psychic love, be still caught in the whirl. Yet how shall we arouse the multitude if we admit that our truths are partial?

He speaks of the love the Samurai gave to his Lord in 'return for his ration of rice' as 'physical love'. But this is to confuse the love with its occasion. It may have come from a deeper consciousness than that of those poverty-stricken Finlanders he praises because they sent money to the sufferers from the earthquake in Tokyo. When we come to balance the two forms of noble feeling one against the other we feel most confident in that given to a known living man.

I write this paragraph to protect myself against the fascination of Toyohiko Kagawa and his heroic life.

XXXVII

SEPTEMBER 26TH

In *The Times Literary Supplement* for September 18, 1930, a reviewer, apparently writing from personal knowledge, says: 'Mr. Sassoon was relied upon especially for actions of a markedly dangerous sort (no doubt he was summed up as a "fire-eater")'. I have read in some newspaper a letter from a private soldier speaking of the men's admiration and trust and a statement that when ordered to more comfortable and safe work in Egypt he petitioned the authorities to be sent back to France.

> Do thou not grieve nor blush to be
> As all th' inspired and tuneful men

Pages from a Diary in 1930

And all thy great forefathers were
From Homer down to Ben.
                    Cowley, from the Essay 'Myself'.

XXXVIII

Kagawa thus describes future parliaments: 'Parliaments of the present represent blind lotteries. In the new genuine society the representatives of the people will not be elected in this ridiculous fashion. All groups bound together industrially or psychically will as a rule have their representatives fixed; the representatives will express the will of their groups and make laws by mutual concession and inter-dependence and they will be free from hatred and slander.' 'Those who govern will be experts in social science, and the law-making bodies will be councils possessing affinities of conscience and representing all the elements which compose society.'

XXXIX

When I was a young man I used to discuss mystical experience with Cabbalists in a little restaurant near the British Museum long passed away; we spoke of nothing more often than of those 'pictures in the astral light' which had been until very lately 'a secret of the mystical societies'. Some man, whose name I forget, insisted that the mind in such a picture when it came into relation with our own could still create, though always within the limits of the picture. In such discussions the speaker would often describe some experience, and to-day I constantly find myself confirming with some philosophic argument what that man learned from tradition and experience. I too have had such experience and others 'spiritualistic' in type which I shall publish when ready—to adapt a metaphor from Erasmus—to make myself a post for dogs and journalists to defile. The pictures seem of two kinds. There are those described in the last verse of *The Sensitive Plant*:

> For love, and beauty, and delight
> There is no death nor change; their might
> Exceeds our organs, which endure
> No light, being themselves obscure.

To the second kind belongs that of the shade of Heracles in the *Odyssey* drawing its bow as though still in the passion of battle, while the true spirit of Heracles is on Olympus with his wife Hebe. To it belong also those apparitions of the murderer still dragging his victim, of the miser still counting his money, of the suicide still hanging from his rafter.

We become aware of those of the first kind when some symbol, shaped by the experience itself, has descended to us, and when we ourselves have passed, through a shifting of the threshold consciousness, into a similar state.

The second kind, because it has no universal virtue, because it is altogether particular, is related only to the soul whose creation it is, though we can sometimes perceive it through association of place or of some object. It was the opinion of those Cabbalist friends that the actions of life remained so pictured but that the intensity of the light depended upon the intensity of the passion that had gone to their creation. This is to assume, perhaps correctly, that the greater the passion the more clear the perception, for the light is perception. 'Light', said Grosseteste, 'is corporeality itself or that of which corporeality is made', whereas Bonaventura calls taste and smell forms of light. The 'pictures' appear to be self-luminous because the past sunlight or candle-light, suddenly made apparent, is as it were broken off from whatever light surrounds it at the moment. Passion is conflict, consciousness is conflict.

Blake did not use the word 'picture' but spoke of the bright sculptures of Los's Halls from which all love stories renew themselves, and that remain on, one does not see the picture as it appeared to the living actor but the action itself, and that we feel as if we could walk round it as if there was no fixed point of view. Whose perception then do we share? I put this point once to my Instructors. They replied that the 'picture' had nothing to do with memory—it was not a remembered perception—and left me to find the explanation. I have to face Berkeley's greatest difficulty: to account for the continuity of perception, but my problem is limited to the continuity of the perception that constitutes, in my own and other eyes, my body and its acts. That continuity is in the Passionate Body of the permanent self or daimon. Should I see the ghost of murderer and victim I should do so because my Spirit has from those other Passionate

Explorations II

Bodies fabricated light, or perception. That fabrication is not enforced by the Passionate Body, is an act of attention on my Spirit's part; but for the act the murderer's own Spirit must be present, for as the Passionate Body is not in space and can only be found through its Spirit or daimon which is only present during its moments of retrocession or sleep, I should have said not that the living mind of Keats or Shakespeare but their daimon is present and the Passionate Bodies that constituted its moment, for images in the mind acquire their identity also from the Passionate Body. The daimon of Shakespeare or Keats has, however, entered into a sleepless universality.

OCTOBER 17TH

Light then—colour, light and shade—fabricated by the intellect and changed with its forms is perception, that which gives a visible unity to the multiple Passionate Body.

The 'perception' may be considered as a circle or space of light encircling each man, and it is the Husk. The dead past thrown off by the living present.

XL

THREE ESSENTIALS

I would found literature on the three things which Kant thought we must postulate to make life livable— Freedom, God, Immortality. The fading of these three before 'Bacon, Newton, Locke' has made literature decadent. Because Freedom is gone we have Stendhal's 'mirror dawdling down a lane'; because God has gone we have realism, the accidental, because Immortality is gone we can no longer write those tragedies which have always seemed to me alone legitimate—those that are a joy to the man who dies. Recent Irish literature has only delighted me in so far as it implies one or the other, in so far as it has been a defiance of all else, in so far as it has created those extravagant characters and emotions which have always arisen spontaneously from the human mind when it sees itself exempt from death and decay, responsible to its source alone.

James Joyce differs from Arnold Bennett and Galsworthy, let us say, because he can isolate the human mind and its vices as if in eternity. So could Synge, so could O'Casey till he caught the London contagion in *The Silver Tassie* and changed his mountain into a mouse. The movement began with A. E.'s first little verses made out of the Upanishads, and my *Celtic Twilight*, a bit of ornamental trivial needlework sewn on a prophetic fury got by Blake and Boehme. James Stephens has read the *Tain* in the light of the *Veda* but the time is against him and he is silent.

Between Berkeley's account of his exploration of certain Kilkenny laws which speak of the 'natives' came that intellectual crisis which led up to the sentence in the *Commonplace Book*: 'We Irish do not hold with this'. That was the birth of the national intellect and it caused the defeat in Berkeley's philosophical secret society of English materialism, the Irish Salamis.

The capture of a Spanish treasure ship in the time of Elizabeth made England a capitalist nation. A nation of country gentlemen, who were paid more in kind than in money and had traditional uses for their money, were to find themselves in control of free power over labour, a power that could be used anywhere and for anything.

The first nation that can affirm the three convictions affirmed by Kant as free powers—*i.e.* without associations of language, dogma, and ritual—will be able to control the moral energies of the soul.

OCTOBER 19TH

It is, I think, because those convictions must return as free power that I feel, that so many feel, an unreality in French neo-Thomist movements, in T. S. Eliot's revival of seventeenth-century divines.

In the time of Swift, of Burke, and of Coleridge the habitual symbols seemed necessary to the order; Swift, who almost certainly hated sex, looked upon himself, he says somewhere, as appointed to guard a position; and tradition could claim the still unquestioned authority of the Bible. But to-day the man who finds belief in God, in the soul, in immortality, growing and clarifying, is blasphemous and paradoxical. He must above all things free his energies from all prepossessions not imposed by those beliefs themselves.

Pages from a Diary in 1930

The Fascist, the Bolshevist, seeks to turn the idea of the State into free power, and both have reached (though the idea of the State as it is in the mind of the Bolshevist is dry and lean) some shadow of that intense energy which shall come to those of whom I speak.

When I speak of the three convictions and of the idea of the State I do not mean any metaphysical or economic theory. That belief which I call free power is free because we cannot distinguish between the things believed in and the belief; it is something forced upon us bit by bit; as it liberates our energies we sink in on truth.

An idea of the State which is not a preparation for those three convictions, a State founded on economics alone, would be a prison house. A State must be made like a Chartres Cathedral for the glory of God and the soul. It exists for the sake of the virtues and must pay their price. The uneconomic leisure of scholars, monks, and women gave us truth, sanctity, and manners. Free power is not the denial of that past but such a conflagration or integration of that past that it can be grasped in a single thought.

Now that we think of the Gospels as evidence, not of an historical event, but of the mind of the early Church, we discover that mind not so much like our own as like what it will be when the clock has run down, when the dissolution of tradition is complete. I notice already men who suggest the Greek in his tub, the Fakir under his tree. I even connect with that coming State our emotion at the thought of crowds that seem beloved history, Synge's work, James Stephens's strange exciting figures. Is not the Bolshevist's passion for the machine, his creation in the theatre and the schools of mass emotion, a parody of what we feel? We are casting off crown and mitre that we may lay our heads on Mother Earth.

But I am no believer in Millenniums. I but foresee another moment of plasticity and disquiet like that which was at and before the commencement of our era, re-shaped by the moral impulse preserved in the Gospels, and that other present, according to Mr. Mackail, in Virgil. At the moment it seems more important that I should try the lots in Virgil than in the Gospels. What idea of the State, what substitute for that of the toga'd race that ruled the world, will serve our immediate purpose here in Ireland?

History is necessity until it takes fire in someone's head and becomes freedom or virtue. Berkeley's Salamis was such a conflagration, another is about us now.

When I try to make a practical rule I come once more to a truism—serve nothing from the heart that is not its own evidence, what Blake called 'naked beauty displayed', recognise that the rest is machinery and should [be] used as such. The great men of the eighteenth century were that beauty; Parnell had something of it, O'Leary something, but what have O'Connell and all his seed, breed, and generation but a roaring machine? Is the Gaelic revival, if the school-books are full, as a saintly old nun said to me, of pothouse literature, anything but a machine? Let us become homeless, helpless, obscure, that we may live by handiwork alone. One day thirty years ago, walking with Douglas Hyde I heard haymakers sing what he recognised as his own words and I begged him to give up all coarse oratory that he might sing such words. The factories will never run short of hands, and yet

> We built Nineveh with our sighing,
> And Babel itself with our mirth.

Preserve that which is living and help the two Irelands, Gaelic Ireland and Anglo-Ireland, so to unite that neither shall shed its pride. Study the great problems of the world, as they have been lived in our scenery, the re-birth of European spirituality in the mind of Berkeley, the restoration of European order in the mind of Burke. Every nation is the whole world in a mirror, and our mirror has twice been very bright and clear. Do not be afraid to boast so long as the boast lays burdens on the boaster. Study the educational system of Italy, the creation of the philosopher Gentile, where even religion is studied not in the abstract but in the minds and lives of Italian saints and thinkers; it becomes at once part of Italian history.

As for the rest we wait till the world changes and its reflection changes in our mirror and an hieratical society returns, power descending from the few to the many, from the subtle to the gross, not because some man's policy has decreed it but because what is so overwhelming cannot be restrained. A new beginning, a new turn of the wheel.

Explorations II

We have not an Irish Nation until all classes grant its right to take life according to the law and until it is certain that the threat of invasion, made by no matter who, would rouse all classes to arms. When Grattan's volunteers were formed such an Ireland seemed all but born. The refusal or postponement of Catholic Emancipation by the Irish Parliament brought disorder and the Act of Union. We have something like the same situation to-day with the actors reversed. One of the actors, however, has changed his habits. Anglo-Ireland attends church but has no dogmas, even less theology is read in Ireland than in other Protestant countries. There is hardly one of all those who sing hymns and say prayers perhaps even twice upon a Sunday who could see the absurdity of the theology in *Blanco Posnet* or think that it mattered if he did. This Anglo-Ireland which accepts many Catholics has accepted the Free State after much hesitation. It would not spring to arms in its defence. Will the devout Catholicism and enthusiastic Gaeldom commit the error committed at the close of the eighteenth century by dogmatic Protestantism? Much of the emotional energy in our civil war came from the indignant denial of the right of the State, as at present established, to take life in its own defence, whether by arms or by process of law, and that right is still denounced by a powerful minority. Only when all permit the State to demand the voluntary or involuntary sacrifice of its citizens' lives will Ireland possess that moral unity to which England, according to Coleridge, owes so large a part of its greatness. All I can see clearly, bound as I am within my own limited art, is that our moral unity is brought nearer by every play, poem or novel that is characteristically Irish.

XLI

When the directors of the Abbey Theatre rejected *The Silver Tassie* they did so because they thought it a bad play and a play which would mar the fame and popularity of its writer. It would seem from its failure in London that we were right; upon the other hand Mr. Shaw's and Mr. Augustus John's admiration suggests that it was at least better than we thought it, and yet I am certain that if any of our other dramatists sent us a similar play we would reject it. We were biased, we are biased, by the Irish Salamis. The war, as O'Casey has conceived it, is an equivalent for those primary qualities brought down by Berkeley's secret society, it stands outside the characters, it is not part of their expression, it is that very attempt denounced by Mallarmé to build as if with brick and mortar within the pages of a book. The English critics feel differently, to them a theme that 'bulks largely in the news' gives dignity to human nature, even raises it to international importance. We on the other hand are certain that nothing can give dignity to human nature but the character and energy of its expression. We do

not even ask that it shall have dignity so long as it can
burn away all that is not itself.

NOVEMBER 18TH

Science, separated from philosophy, is the opium
of the suburbs.

THE END

V
FROM 'WHEELS AND BUTTERFLIES'
1934

INTRODUCTION TO
'THE WORDS UPON THE WINDOW-PANE'

I

SOMEBODY said the other night that Dublin was full of clubs—he himself knew four—that met in Cellars and Garrets and had for their object our general improvement. He was scornful, said that they had all begun by drawing up a programme and passing a resolution against the censorship and would never do anything else. When I began my public life Dublin was full of such clubs that passed resolutions and drew up programmes, and though the majority did nothing else some helped to find an audience for a school of writers. The fall of Parnell had freed imagination from practical politics, from agrarian grievance and political enmity, and turned it to imaginative nationalism, to Gaelic, to the ancient stories, and at last to lyrical poetry and to drama. Political failure and political success have had the same result except that to-day imagination is turning full of uncertainty to something it thinks European, and whether that something will be 'arty' and provincial, or a form of life, is as yet undiscoverable. Hitherto we have walked the road, but now we have shut the door and turned up the lamp. What shall occupy our imagination? We must, I think, decide among these three ideas of national life: that of Swift; that of a great Italian of his day; that of modern England. If the Garrets and the Cellars listen I may throw light upon the matter, and I hope if all the time I seem thinking of something else I shall be forgiven. I must speak of things that come out of the common consciousness, where every thought is like a bell with many echoes.

My little play *The Words upon the Window-pane* came to me amidst considerations such as these, as a reward, as a moment of excitement. John O'Leary read, during an illness, the poems of Thomas Davis, and though he never thought them good poetry they shaped his future life, gave him the moral simplicity that made him so attractive to young men in his old age, but we can no longer permit life to be shaped by a personified ideal, we must serve with all our faculties some actual thing. The old service was moral, at times lyrical; we discussed perpetually the character of public men and never asked were they able and well-informed, but what would they sacrifice? How many times did I hear on the lips of J. F. Taylor these words: 'Holy, delicate white hands'? His patriotism was a religion, never a philosophy. More extreme in such things than Taylor and O'Leary, who often seemed to live in the eighteenth century, to acknowledge its canons alone in literature and in the arts, I turned from Goldsmith and from Burke because they had come to seem a part of the English system, from Swift because I acknowledged, being a romantic, no verse between Cowley and Smart's *Song to David*, no prose between Sir Thomas Browne and the *Conversations* of Landor. But now I read Swift for months together, Burke and Berkeley less often but always with excitement, and Goldsmith lures and waits. I collect materials for my thought and work, for some identification of my beliefs with the nation itself, I seek an image of the modern mind's discovery of itself, of its own permanent form, in that one Irish century that escaped from darkness and confusion. I would that our fifteenth, sixteenth, or even our seventeenth century had been the clear mirror, but fate decided against us.

Swift haunts me; he is always just round the next corner. Sometimes it is a thought of my great-great-grandmother, a friend of that Archbishop King who sent him to England about the 'First Fruits', sometimes it is Saint Patrick's, where I have gone to wander and meditate, that brings him to mind, sometimes I remember something hard or harsh in O'Leary or in Taylor, or in the public speech of our statesmen, that reminds me by its style of his verse or prose. Did he not speak, perhaps, with just such an intonation? This instinct for what is near and yet hidden is in reality a return to the sources of our power, and therefore a claim made upon the future. Thought seems more true, emotion more deep, spoken by someone who touches my pride, who seems to claim me of his kindred, who seems to make me a part of some national mythology, nor is mythology mere ostentation, mere vanity if it draws me onward to the unknown; another turn of the gyre and myth is wisdom, pride, discipline. I remember the shudder in my spine when Mrs. Patrick Campbell said, speaking words Hofmannsthal put into the mouth of Electra, 'I too am of that ancient race':

> Swift has sailed into his rest:
> Savage indignation there
> Cannot lacerate his breast.

From 'Wheels and Butterflies'

Imitate him if you dare,
World-besotted traveller; he
Served human liberty.

'In Swift's day men of intellect reached the height
of their power, the greatest position they ever attained
in society and the State. . . . His ideal order was the
Roman Senate, his ideal men Brutus and Cato; such
an order and such men had seemed possible once more.'
The Cambridge undergraduate into whose mouth I
have put these words may have read similar words in
F. S. Oliver, 'the last brilliant addition to English
historians', for young men such as he read the newest
authorities; probably Oliver and he thought of the
influence at Court and in public life of Swift and of
Leibniz, of the spread of science and of scholarship over
Europe, its examination of documents, its destruction
of fables, a science and a scholarship modern for the
first time, of certain great minds that were mediaeval
in their scope but modern in their freedom. I must,
however, add certain thoughts of my own that affected
me as I wrote. I thought about a passage in the Gram-
mont *Memoirs* where some great man is commended
for his noble manner, as we commend a woman for her
beauty or her charm; a famous passage in the *Appeal
from the New to the Old Whigs* commending the old
Whig aristocracy for their intellect and power and
because their doors stood open to like-minded men;
the palace of Blenheim, its pride of domination that
expected a thousand years, something Asiatic in its
carved intricacy of stone.

'Everything great in Ireland and in our character,

in what remains of our architecture, comes from that day . . . we have kept its seal longer than England.' The overstatement of an enthusiastic Cambridge student, and yet with its measure of truth. The battle of the Boyne overwhelmed a civilisation full of religion and myth, and brought in its place intelligible laws planned out upon a great blackboard, a capacity for horizontal lines, for rigid shapes, for buildings, for attitudes of mind that could be multiplied like an expanding book-case: the modern world, and something that appeared and perished in its dawn, an instinct for Roman rhetoric, Roman elegance. It established a Protestant aristocracy, some of whom neither called themselves English[1] nor looked with contempt or dread upon conquered Ireland. Indeed the battle was scarcely over when Molyneux, speaking in their name, affirmed the sovereignty of the Irish Parliament.[2] No one had the

---

[1] Nor were they English: the newest arrivals soon inter-married with an older stock, and that older stock had inter-married again and again with Gaelic Ireland. All my childhood the Coopers of Markree, County Sligo, represented such rank and fashion as the County knew, and I had it from my friend the late Bryan Cooper that his supposed Cromwellian ancestor being childless adopted an O'Brien; while local tradition thinks that an O'Brien, promised the return of her confiscated estate if she married a Cromwellian soldier, married a Cooper and murdered him three days after. Not, how-ever, before he had founded a family. The family of Yeats, never more than small gentry, arrived, if I can trust the only man among us who may have seen the family tree before it was burnt by Canadian Indians, 'about the time of Henry VII'. Ireland, divided in religion and politics, is as much one race as any modern country.

[2] 'Until 1691 Roman Catholics were admitted by law into both Houses of Legislature in Ireland' (MacNeill's *Constitutional and Parliamentary History of Ireland*, p. 10).

347

right to make our laws but the King, Lords and Commons of Ireland; the battle had been fought to change not an English but an Irish Crown; and our Parliament was almost as ancient as that of England. It was this doctrine[1] that Swift uttered in the fourth *Drapier Letter* with such astringent eloquence that it passed from the talk of study and parlour to that of road and market, and created the political nationality of Ireland. Swift found his nationality through the *Drapier Letters*, his convictions came from action and passion, but Berkeley, a much younger man, could find it through contemplation. He and his fellow-students but knew the war through the talk of the older men. As a boy of eighteen or nineteen he called the Irish people 'natives' as though he were in some foreign land, but two or three years later, perhaps while still an undergraduate, defined the English materialism of his day in three profound sentences, and wrote after each that 'we Irish' think otherwise—'I publish ... to know whether other men have the same ideas as we Irishmen' —and before he was twenty-five had fought the Salamis of the Irish intellect. The Irish landed aristocracy, who knew more of the siege of Derry and the battle of the

---

[1] A few weeks ago the hierarchy of the Irish Church addressed without any mandate from Protestant Ireland, not the Irish people as they had every right to, even in the defence of folly, but the Imperial Conference, and begged that the Irish Courts might remain subservient to the Privy Council. Terrified into intrigue where none threatened, they turned from Swift and Molyneux. I remind them that when the barons of the Irish Court of Exchequer obeyed the English Privy Council in 1719 our ancestors clapped them into gaol. (1931).

Boyne delineated on vast tapestries for their House of
Lords by Dublin Huguenots than of philosophy, found
themselves masters of a country demoralised by generations of war and famine and shared in its demoralisa-
tion. In 1730 Swift said from the pulpit that their
houses were in ruins and no new building anywhere,
that the houses of their rack-ridden tenants were no
better than English pigsties, that the bulk of the people
trod barefoot and in rags. He exaggerated, for already
the Speaker, Connolly, had built that great house at
Celbridge where slate, stone, and furniture were Irish,
even the silver from Irish mines; the new Parliament
House had perhaps been planned; and there was a
general stir of life. The old age of Berkeley passed amid
art and music, and men had begun to boast that in these
no country had made such progress; and some dozen
years after Berkeley's death Arthur Young found everywhere in stately Georgian houses scientific agricultural-
ists, benefactors of their countryside, though for the
half-educated, drunken, fire-eating, impoverished lesser
men he had nothing but detestation. Goldsmith might
have found likeable qualities, a capacity for mimicry[1]
perhaps, among these lesser men, and Sir Jonah Barrington made them his theme, but, detestable or not,
they were out of fashion. Miss Edgeworth described
her *Castle Rackrent* upon the title-page of its first
edition as 'the habits of the Irish squirearchy before
1782'. A few years more and the country people would
have forgotten that the Irish aristocracy was founded

---

[1] He wrote that he had never laughed so much at Garrick's acting
as at somebody in an Irish tavern mimicking a Quaker sermon.

like all aristocracies upon conquest, or rather, would
have remembered, and boasted in the words of a
mediaeval Gaelic poet, 'We are a sword people and we
go with the sword'. Unhappily the lesson first taught
by Molyneux and Swift had been but half learnt when
the test came—country gentlemen are poor politicians
—and Ireland's 'dark insipid period' began. During
the entire eighteenth century the greatest land-owning
family in the neighbourhood I best knew in childhood
sent not a single man into the English army and navy,
but during the nineteenth century one or more in every
generation; a new absenteeism, foreseen by Miss Edgeworth, began; those that lived upon their estates
bought no more fine editions of the classics; separated
from public life and ambition they sank, as I have
heard Lecky complain, 'into grass farmers'. Yet their
genius did not die out; they sent everywhere adminis-
trators and military leaders, and now that their ruin
has come—what resolute nation permits a strong alien
class within its borders?—I would, remembering obscure ancestors that preached in their churches or fought
beside their younger sons over half the world, and
despite a famous passage of O'Grady's, gladly sing
their song.

'He foresaw the ruin to come, Democracy, Rousseau, the French Revolution; that is why he hated the
common run of men—,"I hate lawyers, I hate doctors",
he said, "though I love Dr. So-and-so and Judge So-
and-so",—that is why he wrote *Gulliver*, that is why
he wore out his brain, that is why he felt *saeva indig-
natio*, that is why he sleeps under the greatest epitaph

in history.' The *Discourse of the Contests and Dissensions between the Nobles and the Commons in Athens and Rome*, published in 1703 to warn the Tory Opposition of the day against the impeachment of Ministers, is Swift's one philosophical work. All States depend for their health upon a right balance between the One, the Few, and the Many. The One is the executive, which may in fact be more than one—the Roman republic had two Consuls—but must for the sake of rapid decision be as few as possible; the Few are those who through the possession of hereditary wealth, or great personal gifts, have come to identify their lives with the life of the State, whereas the lives and ambitions of the Many are private. The Many do their day's work well, and so far from copying even the wisest of their neighbours, affect 'a singularity' in action and in thought; but set them to the work of the State and every man Jack is 'listed in a party', becomes the fanatical follower of men of whose characters he knows next to nothing, and from that day on puts nothing into his mouth that some other man has not already chewed and digested. And furthermore, from the moment of enlistment thinks himself above other men and struggles for power until all is in confusion. I divine an Irish hatred of abstraction likewise expressed by that fable of Gulliver among the inventors and men of science, by Berkeley in his *Commonplace Book*, by Goldsmith in the satire of *The Good-Natured Man*, in the picturesque, minute observation of *The Deserted Village*, and by Burke in his attack upon mathematical democracy. Swift enforced his moral by proving that

Rome and Greece were destroyed by the war of the Many upon the Few; in Rome, where the Few had kept their class organisation, it was a war of classes, in Greece, where they had not, war upon character and genius. Miltiades, Aristides, Themistocles, Pericles, Alcibiades, Phocion, 'impeached for high crimes and misdemeanours . . . were honoured and lamented by their country as the preservers of it, and have had the veneration of all ages since paid justly to their memories'. In Rome parties so developed that men born and bred among the Few were compelled to join one party or the other and to flatter and bribe. All civilisations must end in some such way, for the Many obsessed by emotion create a multitude of religious sects but give themselves at last to some one master of bribes and flatteries and sink into the ignoble tranquillity of servitude. He defines a tyranny as the predominance of the One, the Few, or the Many, but thinks that of the Many the immediate threat. All States at their outset possess a ruling power seated in the whole body as that of the soul in the human body, a perfect balance of the three estates, the king some sort of chief magistrate, and then comes 'a tyranny: first either of the Few or the Many; but at last infallibly of a single person'. He thinks the English balance most perfect in the time of Queen Elizabeth, but that in the next age a tyranny of the Many produced that of Cromwell, and that, though recovery followed, 'all forms of government must be mortal like their authors', and he quotes from Polybius, 'those abuses and corruptions, which in time destroy a government, are sown along

with the very seeds of it' and destroy it 'as rust eats
away iron, and worms devour wood'. Whether the
final tyranny is created by the Many—in his eyes all
Caesars were tyrants—or imposed by foreign power,
the result is the same. At the fall of liberty came 'a dark
insipid period through all Greece'—had he Ireland in
his mind also?—and the people became, in the words
of Polybius, 'great reverencers of crowned heads'.

Twenty-two years later Giambattista Vico published that *Scienza nuova* which Mr. James Joyce is
expounding or symbolising in the strange fragments
of his *Work in Progress*. He was the opposite of Swift
in everything, an humble, peaceful man, son of a Nea-
politan bookseller and without political opinions; he
wrote panegyrics upon men of rank, seemed to admire
all that they did, took their gratuities and yet kept his
dignity. He thought civilisation passed through the
phases Swift has described, but that it was harsh and
terrible until the Many prevailed, and its joints cracked
and loosened, happiest when some one man, surrounded
by able subordinates, dismissed the Many to their
private business, that its happiness lasted some generations until, sense of the common welfare lost, it grew
malicious and treacherous, fell into 'the barbarism of
reflection', and after that into an honest, plain barbarism
accepted with relief by all, and started upon its round
again. Rome had conquered surrounding nations because those nations were nearer than it to humanity
and happiness; was not Carthage already almost a
democratic state when destruction came? Swift seemed
to shape his narrative upon some clairvoyant vision of

his own life, for he saw civilisation pass from comparative happiness and youthful vigour to an old age of
violence and self-contempt, whereas Vico saw it begin
in penury like himself and end as he himself would end
in a long inactive peace. But there was a greater difference: Swift, a practical politician in everything he
wrote, ascribed its rise and fall to virtues and vices all
could understand, whereas the philosophical Vico
ascribed them to 'the rhythm of the elemental forms of
the mind', a new idea that would dominate philosophy.
Outside Anglo-Saxon nations where progress, im-
pelled by moral enthusiasm and the Patent Office, seems
a perpetual straight line, this 'circular movement', as
Swift's master, Polybius, called it, has long been the
friend and enemy of public order. Both Sorel and
Marx, their eyes more Swift's than Vico's, have preached
a return to a primeval state, a beating of all down into
a single class that a new civilisation may arise with its
Few, its Many, and its One. Students of contemporary
Italy, where Vico's thought is current through its
influence upon Croce and Gentile, think it created, or
in part created, the present government of one man
surrounded by just such able assistants as Vico foresaw. Some philosopher has added this further thought:
the classes rise out of the matrix, create all mental and
bodily riches, sink back, as Vico saw civilisation rise
and sink, and government is there to keep the ring and
see to it that combat never ends. These thoughts in the
next few generations, as elaborated by Oswald Spengler, who has followed Vico without essential change,
by Flinders Petrie, by the German traveller Frobenius,

'The Words upon the Window-pane'

by Henry Adams, and perhaps by my friend Gerald Heard, may affect the masses. They have already deepened our sense of tragedy and somewhat checked the naïver among those creeds and parties who push their way to power by flattering our moral hopes. Pascal thought there was evidence for and against the existence of God, but that if a man kept his mind in suspense about it he could not live a rich and active life, and I suggest to the Cellars and Garrets that though history is too short to change either the idea of progress or the eternal circuit into scientific fact, the eternal circuit may best suit our preoccupation with the soul's salvation, our individualism, our solitude. Besides we love antiquity, and that other idea—progress—the sole religious myth of modern man, is only two hundred years old.

Swift's pamphlet had little effect in its day; it did not prevent the impeachment and banishment a few years later of his own friends; and although he was in all probability the first—if there was another 'my small reading cannot trace it'—to describe in terms of modern politics the discord of parties that compelled revolutionary France, as it has compelled half a dozen nations since the war, to accept the 'tyranny' of a 'single person', it was soon forgotten; but for the understanding of Swift it is essential. It shows that the defence of liberty boasted upon his tombstone did not come from political disappointment (when he wrote it he had suffered none), and what he meant by liberty. Gulliver, in those travels written twenty years later, calls up from the dead 'a sextumvirate to which all the

ages of the world cannot add a seventh': Epaminondas
and Socrates, who suffered at the hands of the Many;
Brutus, Junius Brutus, Cato the Younger, Thomas
More, who fought the tyranny of the One; Brutus with
Caesar still his inseparable friend, for a man may be a
tyrant without personal guilt.

Liberty depended upon a balance within the State,
like that of the 'humours' in a human body, or like
that 'unity of being' Dante compared to a perfectly
proportioned human body, and for its sake Swift was
prepared to sacrifice what seems to the modern man
liberty itself. The odds were a hundred to one, he
wrote, that 'violent zeal for the truth' came out of
'petulancy, ambition, or pride'. He himself might
prefer a republic to a monarchy, but did he open his
mouth upon the subject would be deservedly hanged.
Had he religious doubts he was not to blame so long as
he kept them to himself, for God had given him reason.
It was the attitude of many a modern Catholic who
thinks, though upon different grounds, that our civilisation may sink into a decadence like that of Rome. But
sometimes belief itself must be hidden. He was devout;
had the Communion Service by heart; read the Fathers
and prayed much, yet would not press the mysteries of
his faith upon any unwilling man. Had not the early
Christians kept silent about the divinity of Christ;
should not the missionaries to China 'soften' it? He
preached as law commanded; a man could save his soul
doubtless in any religion which taught submission to
the Will of God, but only one State could protect his
body; and how could it protect his body if rent apart

by those cranks and sectaries mocked in his *Tale of a Tub*? Had not French Huguenots and English Dissenters alike sinned against the State? Except at those moments of great public disturbance, when a man must choose his creed or his king, let him think his own thoughts in silence.

What was this liberty bought with so much silence, and served through all his life with so much eloquence? 'I should think', he wrote in the *Discourse*, 'that the saying, *vox populi, vox dei* ought to be understood of the universal bent and current of a people, not of the bare majority of a few representatives, which is often procured by little art, and great industry and application; wherein those who engage in the pursuits of malice and revenge are much more sedulous than such as would prevent them.' That *vox populi* or 'bent and current', or what we even more vaguely call national spirit, was the sole theme of his *Drapier Letters*; its right to express itself as it would through such men as had won or inherited general consent. I doubt if a mind so contemptuous of average men thought, as Vico did, that it found expression also through all individual lives, or asked more for those lives than protection from the most obvious evils. I remember J. F. Taylor, a great student of Swift, saying 'Individual liberty is of no importance, what matters is national liberty'.

The will of the State, whether it build a cage for a dead bird or remain in the bird itself, must always, whether interpreted by Burke or Marx, find expression through some governing class or company identified with that 'bent and current', with those 'elemental forms', whether by interest or training. The men of Swift's day would have added that class or company must be placed by wealth above fear and toil, though Swift thought every properly conducted State must limit the amount of wealth the individual could possess. But the old saying that there is no wisdom without leisure has somewhat lost its truth. When the physical world became rigid; when curiosity inherited from the Renaissance, and the soul's anxiety inherited from the Middle Ages, passed, man ceased to think; his work thought in him. Spinoza, Leibniz, Swift, Berkeley, Goethe, the last typical figure of the epoch, recognised no compulsion but the 'bent and current' of their lives; the Speaker, Connolly, could still call out a posse of gentlemen to design the façade of his house, and though Berkeley thought their number too great, that work is still admired; Swift called himself a poor scholar in comparison with Lord Treasurer Harley. Unity of being was still possible though somewhat over-rationalised and abstract, more diagram than body; whereas the best modern philosophers are professors, their pupils compile notebooks that they may be professors some day; politicians stick to their last or leave it to plague us with platitudes; we poets and artists may be called, so small our share in life, 'separated spirits', words applied by the old philosophers to the dead. When Swift sank into imbecility or madness his epoch had finished in the British Isles, those 'elemental forms' had passed beyond him; more than the 'great Ministers' had gone. I can see in a sort of nightmare vision the 'primary qualities' torn from the side of Locke, Johnson's ponderous body bent above the letter to Lord Chesterfield, some obscure person somewhere inventing the spinning-jenny, upon his face that look of benevolence kept by painters and engravers, from the middle of the eighteenth century to the time of the Prince Consort, for such as he, or, to simplify the tale—

> Locke sank into a swoon;
> The Garden died;
> God took the spinning-jenny
> Out of his side.

'That arrogant intellect free at last from superstition': the young man's overstatement full of the unexamined suppositions of common speech. I saw Asia in the carved stones of Blenheim, not in the pride of great abstract masses, but in that humility of flowerlike intricacy—the particular blades of the grass; nor can chance have thrown into contiguous generations Spinoza and Swift, an absorption of the whole intellect in God, a fakir-like contempt for all human desire; 'take from her', Swift prayed for Stella in sickness, 'all violent desire whether of life or death'; the elaboration and spread of Masonic symbolism, its God made in the image of a Christopher Wren; Berkeley's declaration, modified later, that physical pleasure is the *Summum Bonum*, Heaven's sole reality, his counter-truth to that of Spinoza.

In judging any moment of past time we should leave out what has since happened; we should not call the Swift of the *Drapier Letters* nearer truth because of their influence upon history than the Swift who attacked in *Gulliver* the inventors and logicians; we should see certain men and women as if at the edge of a cliff, time broken away from their feet. Spinoza and the Masons, Berkeley and Swift, speculative and practical intellect, stood there free at last from all prepossessions and touched the extremes of thought; the Gymnosophists of Strabo close at hand, could they but ignore what was harsh and logical in themselves, or the China of the Dutch cabinet-makers, of the *Citizen of the World*: the long-settled rule of powerful men, no great dogmatic structure, few great crowded streets, scattered unprogressive communities, much handiwork, wisdom wound into the roots of the grass.

'I have something in my blood that no child must inherit.' There have been several theories to account for Swift's celibacy. Sir Walter Scott suggested a 'physical defect', but that seems incredible. A man so outspoken would have told Vanessa the truth and stopped a tragic persecution, a man so charitable have given Stella the protection of his name. The refusal to see Stella when there was no third person present suggests a man that dreaded temptation; nor is it compatible with those stories still current among our country people of Swift sending his servant out to fetch a woman, and dismissing that servant when he woke to find a black woman at his side. Lecky suggested dread of madness—the theory of my play—of madness already present in constant eccentricity; though, with a vagueness born from distaste of the theme, he saw nothing incompatible between Scott's theory and his own. Had Swift dreaded transmitting madness he might well have been driven to consorting with the nameless barren women of the streets. Somebody else suggests syphilis contracted doubtless between 1699 when he was engaged to Varina and some date soon after Stella's arrival in Ireland. Mr. Shane Leslie thinks that Swift's relation to Vanessa was not platonic,[1] and that whenever his letters speak of a cup of coffee they mean the sexual act; whether the letters seem to bear him out I do not know, for those letters bore me; but whether they seem to or not he must, if he is to get a hearing, account for Swift's relation to Stella. It seems certain that Swift loved her though he called it by some other name, and she him, and that it was platonic love.

> Thou, Stella, wert no longer young,
> When first for thee my harp was strung,
> Without one word of Cupid's darts,
> Of killing eyes or bleeding hearts;
> With friendship and esteem possest,
> I ne'er admitted Love a guest.
> In all the habitudes of life,
> The friend, the mistress, and the wife,
> Variety we still pursue,
> In pleasure seek for something new;
> Or else comparing with the rest,
> Take comfort that our own is best;
> The best we value by the worst,
> As tradesmen show their trash at first;
> But his pursuits are at an end,
> Whom Stella chooses for a friend.

---

[1] Rossi and Hone take the same view, though uncertain about the coffee. When I wrote, their book had not appeared.

From 'Wheels and Butterflies'

If the relation between Swift and Vanessa was not platonic there must have been some bar that affected Stella as well as Swift. Dr. Delaney is said to have believed that Swift married Stella in 1716 and found in some exchange of confidences that they were brother and sister, but Sir William Temple was not in Ireland during the year that preceded Swift's birth, and so far as we know Swift's mother was not in England.

There is no satisfactory solution. Swift, though he lived in great publicity, and wrote and received many letters, hid two things which constituted perhaps all that he had of private life: his loves and his religious beliefs.

'Was Swift mad? Or was it the intellect itself that was mad?' The other day a scholar in whose imagination Swift has a pre-eminence scarcely possible outside Ireland said: 'I sometimes feel that there is a black cloud about to overwhelm me, and then comes a great jet of life; Swift had that black cloud and no jet. He was terrified.' I said, 'Terrified perhaps of everything but death', and reminded him of a story of Dr. Johnson's.[1] There was a reward of £500 for the identification of the author of the *Drapier Letters*. Swift's butler, who had carried the manuscript to the printer, stayed away from work. When he returned Swift said, 'I know that my life is in your hands, but I will not bear, out of fear, either your insolence or negligence'. He dismissed the butler, and when the danger had passed he restored him to his post, rewarded him, and said to

[1] Sheridan has a different version, but as I have used it merely to illustrate an argument I leave it as Dr. Johnson told it.

the other servants, 'No more Barclay, henceforth Mr. Barclay'. 'Yes,' said my friend, 'he was not afraid of death but of life, of what might happen next; that is what made him so defiant in public and in private and demand for the State the obedience a Connacht priest demands for the Church.' I have put a cognate thought into the mind of John Corbet. He imagines, though but for a moment, that the intellect of Swift's age, persuaded that the mechanicians mocked by Gulliver would prevail, that its moment of freedom could not last, so dreaded the historic process that it became in the half-mad mind of Swift a dread of parentage: 'Am I to add another to the healthy rascaldom and knavery of the world?' Did not Rousseau within five years of the death of Swift publish his *Discourse upon Arts and Sciences* and discover instinctive harmony not in heroic effort, not in Cato and Brutus, not among impossible animals—I think of that noble horse Blake drew for Hayley—but among savages, and thereby beget the *sans-culottes* of Marat? After the arrogance of power the humility of a servant.

II

When I went into the theatre café after the performance a woman asked a question and I replied with some spiritualistic anecdote. 'Did that happen with the medium we have seen to-night?' she said: and yet May Craig who played the part had never seen a séance. I had, however, assisted her by self-denial. No character upon the stage spoke my thoughts. All were people I had met or might have met in just such a séance. Taken as a whole, the man who expected to find whippet-racing beyond the grave, not less than the old man who was half a Swedenborgian, expresses an attitude of mind of millions who have substituted the séance-room for the church. At most séances there is somebody who finds symbol where his neighbour finds fact, but the average man or woman thinks that the dead have houses, that they eat and sleep, hear lectures, or occasionally talk with Christ as though He were a living man; and certainly the voices are at times so natural, the forms so solid, that the plain man can scarce think otherwise.

If I had not denied myself, if I had allowed some character to speak my thoughts, what would he have said? It seems to me that after reading many books and meeting many phenomena, some in my own house, some when alone in my room, I can see clearly at last. I consider it certain that every voice that speaks, every form that appears, whether to the medium's eyes and ears alone or to some one or two others or to all present, whether it remains a sight or sound or affects the sense of touch, whether it is confined to the room or can make itself apparent at some distant place, whether it can or cannot alter the position of material objects, is first of all a secondary personality or dramatisation created by, in, or through the medium. Perhaps May Craig, when alone in her room after the play, went, without knowing what she was doing, through some detail of her performance. I once saw an Abbey actor going up the stairs to his dressing-room after playing the part of a lame man and saw that he was still limping. I see no difference except one of degree between such unconscious movements and the strange powerful grotesque faces imprinted by the controls of Eusapia Palladino upon paraffin wax. The Polish psychologist Ochorowicz, vexed by the mischievous character of his medium's habitual control, created by suggestion a docile and patient substitute that left a photograph of its hand and arm upon an unopened coil of film in a sealed bottle. But at most séances the suggestions come from sub-conscious or unspoken thought. I found the preacher who wanted Moody's help at a séance where the mind of an old doting general turned all into delirium. We sat in the dark and voices came about us in the air; crowned head after crowned head spoke until Cromwell intervened and was abused by one of the sitters for cutting off the head of 'Charles the Second', while the preacher kept repeating, 'He is monopolising the séance, I want Mr. Moody, it is most important I should get Mr. Moody'. Then came a voice, 'King George is here'. I asked which of the Georges, and the sitter who hated Cromwell said, 'King George, our George; we should all stand up', but the general thought it would be enough if we sang 'God save the King'. We sang, and then there was silence, and in the silence from somewhere close to the ceiling the clear song of a bird. Because mediumship is dramatisation, even honest mediums cheat at times either deliberately or because some part of the body has freed itself from the control of the waking will, and almost always truth and lies are mixed together. But what shall we say of their knowledge of events, their assumption of forms and names beyond the medium's knowledge or ours? What of the arm photographed in the bottle?

The Indian ascetic passing into his death-like trance knows that if his mind is not pure, if there is anything there but the symbol of his God, some passion, ambition, desire, or phantasy will confer upon him its shape or purpose, for he is entering upon a state where thought and existence are the same. One remembers those witches described by Glanvil who course the field in the likeness of hares while their bodies lie at home, and certain mediumistic phenomena. The ascetic would say, did we question him, that the unpurified dead are subject to transformations that would be similar were it not that in their case no physical body remains in cave or bed or chair, all is transformed. They examine their past if undisturbed by our importunity, tracing events to their source, and as they take the form their thought suggests, seem to live backward through time; or if incapable of such examination, creatures not of thought but of feeling, renew as shades certain detached events of their past lives, taking the greater excitements first. When Achilles came to the edge of the blood-pool (an ancient substitute for the medium) he was such a shade. Tradition affirms that, deprived of the living present by death, they can create nothing, or, in the Indian phrase, can originate no new Karma. Their aim, like that of the ascetic in meditation, is to enter at last into their own archetype, or into all being: into that which is there always. They are not, however, the personalities which haunt the séance-room: these when they speak from, or imply, supernormal knowledge, when they are more than transformations of the medium, are, as it were, new beings begotten by spirit upon medium to live short but veritable lives, whereas the secondary personalities resemble those eggs brought forth without the assistance of the male bird. They, within their narrow limits, create; they speak truth when they repeat some message suggested by the past lives of the spirit, remembered like some prenatal memory, or when, though such instances must be few, begotten by some spirit obedient to its source, or, as we might say, blessed; but when they neither repeat such message nor were so begotten they may justify passages in Swedenborg that denounce them as the newspapers denounce cheating mediums, seeing that they find but little check in their fragmentary knowledge or vague conscience.

Let images of basalt, black, immovable,
Chiselled in Egypt, or ovoids of bright steel
Hammered and polished by Brancusi's hand,
Represent spirits. If spirits seem to stand
Before the bodily eyes, speak into the bodily ears,
They are not present but their messengers.
Of double nature these, one nature is
Compounded of accidental phantasies.
We question; it but answers what we would
Or as phantasy directs—because they have drunk the blood.

I have not heard of spirits in a European séance-room re-enacting their past lives; our séances take their characteristics from the desire of those present to speak to, or perhaps obtain the counsel of, their dead; yet under the conditions described in my play such re-enacting might occur, indeed most hauntings are of that nature. Here, however, is a French traveller's account of a séance in Madagascar, quoted by César de Vesme:

> . . . One, Taimandebakaka, of the Bara race, and renowned in the valley of the Menamaty as a great sorcerer, evoked one day in my presence in his village the souls of Captain Flayelle and of Lieutenant Montagnole, both killed at Vohingheso in a fight with the Baras four years before. Those present—myself and some privileged natives—saw nothing when Taimandebakaka claimed to see the two persons in question; but we could hear the voices of officers issuing orders to their soldiers, and these voices were European voices which could not be imitated by natives. Similarly, at a distance we could hear the echoes of firing and the cries of the wounded and the lowing of frightened cattle—oxen of the Fahavalos.

III

It is fitting that Plotinus should have been the first philosopher to meet his daimon face to face, though the boy attendant out of jealousy or in convulsive terror strangled the doves, for he was the first to establish as sole source the timeless individuality or daimon instead of the Platonic Idea, to prefer Socrates to his thought. This timeless individuality contains archetypes of all possible existences whether of man or brute, and as it traverses its circle of allotted lives, now one, now another, prevails. We may fail to express an archetype or alter it by reason, but all done from nature is its unfolding into time. Some other existence may take the place of Socrates, yet Socrates can never cease to exist. Once a friend of mine was digging in a long-neglected garden and suddenly out of the air came a voice thanking her, an old owner of the garden, she was told later, long since reborn, yet still in the garden. Plotinus said that we should not 'baulk at this limit-lessness of the intellectual; it is an infinitude having nothing to do with number or part' (*Ennead V.* 7. I.); yet it seems that it can at will re-enter number and part and thereby make itself apparent to our minds. If we accept this idea many strange or beautiful things become credible. The Indian pilgrim has not deceived us; he did hear the bed where the sage of his devotion slept a thousand years ago creak as though someone turned over in it, and he did see—he himself and the old shrine-keeper—the blankets all tossed about at dawn as if someone had just risen; the Irish country-woman did see the ruined castle lit up, the bridge across the river dropping; those two Oxford ladies did find themselves in the garden of the Petit Trianon with Marie Antoinette and her courtiers, see that garden as those saw it; the gamekeeper did hear those footsteps the other night that sounded like the footsteps of a stag where stag has not passed these hundred years. All about us there seems to start up a precise inexplic-able teeming life, and the earth becomes once more, not in rhetorical metaphor, but in reality, sacred.

1931

From 'Wheels and Butterflies'

'FIGHTING THE WAVES'

INTRODUCTION

I

I WROTE *The Only Jealousy of Emer* for performance in a private house or studio, considering it, for reasons which I have explained, unsuited to a public stage. Then somebody put it on a public stage in Holland and Hildo van Krop made his powerful masks. Because the dramatist who can collaborate with a great sculptor is lucky, I rewrote the play not only to fit it for such a stage but to free it from abstraction and confusion. I have retold the story in prose which I have tried to make very simple, and left imaginative suggestion to dancers, singers, musicians. I have left the words of the opening and closing lyrics unchanged, for sung to modern music in the modern way they suggest strange patterns to the ear without obtruding upon it their difficult, irrelevant words. The masks get much of their power from enclosing the whole head; this makes the head out of proportion to the body, and I found some difference of opinion as to whether this was a disadvantage or not in an art so distant from reality; that it was not a disadvantage in the case of the Woman of the Sidhe all were agreed. She was a strange, noble, unforgettable figure.

I do not say that it is always necessary when one writes for a general audience to make the words of the dialogue so simple and so matter-of-fact; but it is necessary where the appeal is mainly to the eye and to

370

the ear through songs and music. *Fighting the Waves* is in itself nothing, a mere occasion for sculptor and dancer, for the exciting dramatic music of George Antheil.

II

'It is that famous man Cuchulain. . . .' In the eighties of the last century Standish O'Grady, his mind full of Homer, retold the story of Cuchulain that he might bring back an heroic ideal. His work, which founded modern Irish literature, was hasty and ill-constructed, his style marred by imitation of Carlyle; twenty years later Lady Gregory translated the whole body of Irish heroic legend into the dialect of the cottages in those great books *Cuchulain of Muirthemne* and *Gods and Fighting Men*, her eye too upon life. In later years she often quoted the saying of Aristotle: 'To think like a wise man, but express oneself like the common people', and always her wise man was heroic man. Synge wrote his *Deirdre of the Sorrows* in peasant dialect, but died before he had put the final touches to anything but the last act, the most poignant and noble in Irish drama. I wrote in blank verse, which I tried to bring as close to common speech as the subject permitted, a number of connected plays—*Deirdre, At the Hawk's Well, The Green Helmet, On Baile's Strand, The Only Jealousy of Emer*. I would have attempted the Battle of the Ford and the Death of Cuchulain, had not the mood of Ireland changed.

From 'Wheels and Butterflies'

When Parnell was dragged down, his shattered party gave itself up to nine years' vituperation, and Irish imagination fled the sordid scene. A. E.'s *Homeward: Songs by the Way*; Padraic Colum's little songs of peasant life; my own early poems; Lady Gregory's comedies, where, though the dramatic tension is always sufficient, the worst people are no wickeder than children; Synge's *Well of the Saints* and *Playboy of the Western World*, where the worst people are the best company, were as typical of that time as Lady Gregory's translations. Repelled by what had seemed the sole reality, we had turned to romantic dreaming, to the nobility of tradition.

About 1909 the first of the satirists appeared, 'The Cork Realists', we called them, men that had come to maturity amidst spite and bitterness. Instead of turning their backs upon the actual Ireland of their day, they attacked everything that had made it possible, and in Ireland and among the Irish in England made more friends than enemies by their attacks. James Joyce, the son of a small Parnellite organiser, had begun to write, but remained unpublished.

> An age is the reversal of an age;
> When strangers murdered Emmet, Fitzgerald, Tone,
> We lived like men that watch a painted stage.
> What matter for the scene, the scene once gone!
> It had not touched our lives; but popular rage,
> *Hysterica passio*, dragged this quarry down.
> None shared our guilt; nor did we play a part
> Upon a painted stage when we devoured his heart.

'Fighting the Waves'

But even if there had been no such cause of bitterness, of self-contempt, we could not, considering that every man everywhere is more of his time than of his nation, have long kept the attention of our small public, no, not with the whole support, and that we never had, of the Garrets and Cellars. Only a change in European thought could have made that possible. When Stendhal described a masterpiece as a 'mirror dawdling down a lane' he expressed the mechanical philosophy of the French eighteenth century. Gradually literature conformed to his ideal; Balzac became old-fashioned; romanticism grew theatrical in its strain to hold the public; till, by the end of the nineteenth century, the principal characters in the most famous books were the passive analysts of events, or had been brutalised into the likeness of mechanical objects. But Europe is changing its philosophy. Some four years ago the Russian Government silenced the mechanists because social dialectic is impossible if matter is trundled about by some limited force. Certain typical books—*Ulysses*, Virginia Woolf's *The Waves*, Mr. Ezra Pound's *Draft of XXX Cantos*—suggest a philosophy like that of the *Samkara* school of ancient India, mental and physical objects alike material, a deluge of experience breaking over us and within us, melting limits whether of line or tint; man no hard bright mirror dawdling by the dry sticks of a hedge, but a swimmer, or rather the waves themselves. In this new literature announced with much else by Balzac in *Le Chef-d'œuvre inconnu*, as in that which it superseded, man in himself is nothing.

From 'Wheels and Butterflies'

IV

I once heard Sir William Crookes tell half a dozen people that he had seen a flower carried in broad daylight slowly across the room by what seemed an invisible hand. His chemical research led to the discovery of radiant matter, but the science that shapes opinion has ignored his other research that seems to those who study it the slow preparation for the greatest, perhaps the most dangerous, revolution in thought Europe has seen since the Renaissance, a revolution that may, perhaps, establish the scientific complement of certain philosophies that in all ancient countries sustained heroic art. We may meet again, not the old simple celebration of life tuned to the highest pitch, neither Homer nor the Greek dramatists, something more deliberate than that, more systematised, more external, more self-conscious, as must be at a second coming, Plato's Republic, not the Siege of Troy.

I shall remind the Garrets and Cellars of certain signs, that they may, as a Chinese philosopher has advised, shape things at their beginning, when it is easy, not at the end, when it is difficult. I first name Mr. Sacheverell Sitwell's lovely 'Pastoral'; point out that he has celebrated those Minoan shepherds, those tamers of the wild bulls, their waists enclosed from childhood in wide belts of bronze, that they might attain wasp-like elegance; that he prefers them to the natural easy Sicilian shepherds, preferring as it were cowboys to those that 'watched their flocks by night'; then Dr. Gogarty's praise of 'the Submarine Men trained through a lifetime'; and remind them of their own satisfaction in that praise. Then they might, after considering the demand of the black, brown, green, and blue shirts, 'Power to the most disciplined', ask themselves whether D'Annunzio and his terrible drill at Fiume may not prove as symbolic as Shelley, whose art and life became so completely identified with romantic contemplation that young men in their late teens, when I was at that age, identified him with poetry itself.

Here in Ireland we have come to think of self-sacrifice, when worthy of public honour, as the act of some man at the moment when he is least himself, most completely the crowd. The heroic act, as it descends through tradition, is an act done because a man is himself, because, being himself, he can ask nothing of other men but room amid remembered tragedies; a sacrifice of himself to himself, almost, so little may he bargain, of the moment to the moment. I think of some Elizabethan play where, when mutineers threaten to hang the ship's captain, he replies: 'What has that to do with me?' So lonely is that ancient act, so great the pathos of its joy, that I have never been able to read without tears a passage in *Sigurd the Volsung* describing how the new-born child lay in the bed and looked 'straight on the sun'; how the serving-women washed him, bore him back to his mother, wife of the dead Sigmund; how 'they shrank in their rejoicing before the eyes of the child'; 'the best sprung from the best'; how though 'the spring morn smiled . . . the hour seemed awful to them'.

From 'Wheels and Butterflies'

But Hiordis looked on the Volsung,
    on her grief and her fond desire.
And the hope of her heart was quickened,
    and her heart was a living fire;
And she said: 'Now one of the earthly
    on the eyes of my child hath gazed
Nor shrunk before their glory,
    nor stayed her love amazed:
I behold thee as Sigmund beholdeth,—
    and I was the home of thine heart—
Woe's me for the day when thou wert not,
    and the hour when we shall part!'

How could one fail to be moved in the presence of the central mystery of the faith of poets, painters, and athletes? I am carried forty years back and hear a famous old athlete wind up a speech to country lads— 'The holy people have above them the communion of saints; we the communion of the *Tuatha de Danaan* of Erin'.

Science has driven out the legends, stories, superstitions that protected the immature and the ignorant with symbol, and now that the flower has crossed our rooms, science must take their place and demonstrate as philosophy has in all ages, that States are justified, not by multiplying or, as it would seem, comforting those that are inherently miserable, but because sustained by those for whom the hour seems 'awful', and by those born out of themselves, the best born of the best.

Since my twentieth year, these thoughts have been in my mind, and now that I am old I sing them to the Garrets and the Cellars:

'Fighting the Waves'

Move upon Newton's town,
The town of Hobbes and of Locke,
Pine, spruce, come down
Cliff, ravine, rock:
What can disturb the corn?
What makes it shudder and bend?
The rose brings her thorn,
The Absolute walks behind.

V

Yet it may be that our science, our modern philosophy, keep a subconscious knowledge that their raft, roped together at the end of the seventeenth century, must, if they so much as glance at that slow-moving flower, part and abandon us to the storm, or it may be, as Professor Richet suggests at the end of his long survey of psychical research from the first experiments of Sir William Crookes to the present moment, that all it can do is, after a steady scrutiny, to prove the poverty of the human intellect, that we are lost amid alien intellects, near but incomprehensible, more incomprehensible than the most distant stars. We may, whether it scrutinise or not, lacking its convenient happy explanations, plunge as Rome did in the fourth century according to some philosopher of that day into 'a fabulous, formless darkness'.

Should H. G. Wells afflict you,
Put whitewash in a pail;
Paint: 'Science—opium of the suburbs'
On some waste wall.

From 'Wheels and Butterflies'

VI

'First I must cover up his face, I must hide him from the sea.' I am deeply grateful for a mask with the silver glitter of a fish, for a dance with an eddy like that of water, for music that suggested, not the vagueness, but the rhythm of the sea. A Dublin journalist showed his scorn for 'the new paganism' by writing: 'Mr. Yeats' play is not really original, for something of the kind doubtless existed in Ancient Babylon', but a German psycho-analyst has traced the 'mother complex' back to our mother the sea—after all, Babylon was a modern inland city—to the loneliness of the first crab or crayfish that climbed ashore and turned lizard; while Gemistus Plethon not only substituted the sea for Adam and Eve, but, according to a friend learned in the Renaissance, made it symbolise the garden's ground or first original, 'that concrete universal which all philosophy is seeking'.

VII

'Everything he loves must fly', everything he desires; Emer too must renounce desire, but there is another love, that which is like the man-at-arms in the Anglo-Saxon poem, 'doom eager'. Young, we discover an opposite through our love; old, we discover our love through some opposite neither hate nor despair can destroy, because it is another self, a self that we have fled in vain.

———

'Fighting the Waves'

Three Musicians   Cuchulain
The Ghost of Cuchulain   Emer
Eithne Inguba   The Figure of Cuchulain
        The Woman of the Sidhe

PROLOGUE

Musicians and speaker off stage. There is a curtain with a wave pattern. A man wearing the Cuchulain mask enters from one side with sword and shield. He dances a dance which represents a man fighting the waves. The waves may be represented by other dancers: in his frenzy he supposes the waves to be his enemies: gradually he sinks down as if overcome, then fixes his eyes with a cataleptic stare upon some imaginary distant object. The stage becomes dark, and when the light returns it is empty. The Musicians enter. Two stand, one on either side of the curtain, singing.

FIRST MUSICIAN

A woman's beauty is like a white
Frail bird, like a white sea-bird alone
At daybreak after stormy night
Between two furrows upon the ploughed land:
A sudden storm and it was thrown
Between dark furrows upon the ploughed land.
How many centuries spent
The sedentary soul
In toil of measurement
Beyond eagle or mole,

379

From 'Wheels and Butterflies'

Beyond hearing or seeing,
Or Archimedes' guess,
To raise into being
That loveliness?

A strange, unserviceable thing,
A fragile, exquisite, pale shell,
That the vast troubled waters bring
To the loud sands before day has broken.
The storm arose and suddenly fell
Amid the dark before day had broken.
What death? What discipline?
What bonds no man could unbind,
Being imagined within
The labyrinth of the mind,
What pursuing or fleeing,
What wounds, what bloody press
Dragged into being
This loveliness?

[*When the curtain is drawn the Musicians take their
place against the wall. One sees a bed with curtains:
the man lying on the bed is Cuchulain; the part is
taken, however, by a different actor, who has a mask
similar to that of the dancer—the Cuchulain mask.
Emer stands beside the bed. The Ghost of Cuchulain
crouches near the foot of the bed.*]

FIRST MUSICIAN [*speaking*]. I call before your eyes
some poor fisherman's house dark with smoke, nets
hanging from the rafters, here and there an oar perhaps,
and in the midst upon a bed a man dead or swooning.

'Fighting the Waves'

It is that famous man Cuchulain, the best man with every sort of weapon, the best man to gain the love of a woman; his wife Queen Emer is at his side; there is no one with her, for she has sent everyone away, but yonder at the door someone stands and hesitates, wishes to come into the room and is afraid to do so; it is young Eithne Inguba, Cuchulain's mistress. Beyond her, through the open door, the stormy sea. Beyond the foot of the bed, dressed in grave-clothes, the ghost of Cuchulain is kneeling.

FIRST MUSICIAN [*singing*]

White shell, white wing!
I will not choose for my friend
A frail, unserviceable thing
That drifts and dreams, and but knows
That waters are without end
And that wind blows.

EMER. Come hither, come sit beside the bed; do not be afraid, it was I that sent for you.

EITHNE INGUBA. No, madam, I have wronged you too deeply to sit there.

EMER. We two alone of all the people in the world have the right to watch together here, because we have loved him best.

EITHNE INGUBA [*coming nearer*]. Is he dead?

EMER. The fishermen think him dead, it was they that put the grave-clothes upon him.

EITHNE INGUBA [*feeling the body*]. He is cold. There is no breath upon his lips.

From 'Wheels and Butterflies'

EMER. Those who win the terrible friendship of the gods sometimes lie a long time as if dead.

EITHNE INGUBA. I have heard of such things; the very heart stops and yet they live after. What happened?

EMER. He fought and killed an unknown man, and found after that it was his own son that he had killed.

EITHNE INGUBA. A son of yours and his?

EMER. So that is your first thought! His son and mine. [*She laughs.*] Did you think that he belonged to you and me alone? He loved women before he heard our names, and he will love women after he has forgotten us both. The man he killed was the son of some woman he loved long ago, and I think he loved her better than he has loved you or me.

EITHNE INGUBA. That is natural, he must have been young in those days and loved as you and I love.

EMER. I think he loved her as no man ever loved, for when he heard the name of the man he had killed, and the name of that man's mother, he went out of his senses utterly. He ran into the sea, and with shield before him and sword in hand he fought the deathless sea. Of all the many men who had stood there to look at the fight not one dared stop him or even call his name; they stood in a kind of stupor, collected together in a bunch like cattle in a storm, until, fixing his eyes as it seemed upon some new enemy, he waded out further still and the waves swept over him.

EITHNE INGUBA. He is dead indeed, and he has been drowned in the sea.

EMER. He is not dead.

'Fighting the Waves'

EITHNE INGUBA. He is dead, and you have not kissed his lips nor laid your head upon his breast.

EMER. That is some changeling they have put there, some image of somebody or something bewitched in his likeness, a sea-washed log, it may be, or some old spirit. I would throw it into the fire, but I dare not. They have Cuchulain for a hostage.

EITHNE INGUBA. I have heard of such changelings.

EMER. Before you came I called his name again and again. I told him that Queen Maeve and all her Connacht men are marching north and east, and that there is none but he to make a stand against them, but he would not hear me. I am but his wife, and a man grows tired of a wife. But if you call upon him with that sweet voice, that voice that is so dear to him, he cannot help but listen.

EITHNE INGUBA. I am but his newest love, and in the end he will turn to the woman who has loved him longest, who has kept the house for him no matter where he strayed or to whom.

EMER. I have indeed that hope, the hope that some day he and I will sit together at the fire as when we were first married.

EITHNE INGUBA. Women like me awake a violent love for a while, and when the time is over are flung into some corner like an old eggshell. Cuchulain, listen!

EMER. No, not yet; for first I must cover up his face, I must hide him from the sea. I must throw new logs upon the fire and stir the half-burnt logs into a flame. The sea is full of enchantment, whatever lies on that bed is from the sea, but all enchantments dread the hearth-fire.

[*She pulls the curtains of the bed so as to hide the sick man's face, that the actor may change his mask unseen. She goes to one side of the stage and moves her hand as though putting logs on a fire and stirring it into a blaze. While she makes these movements the Musicians play, marking the movements with drum and flute perhaps. Having finished, she stands beside the imaginary fire at a distance from Cuchulain and Eithne Inguba.*

Call on Cuchulain now.

EITHNE INGUBA. Can you hear my voice, Cuchulain?

EMER. Bend over whatever thing lies there, call out dear secrets and speak to it as though it were his very self.

EITHNE INGUBA. Cuchulain, listen!

EMER. Those are timid words. To be afraid because his wife is standing by when there is so great need but proves that he chose badly. Remember who you are and who he is, that we are two women struggling with the sea.

EITHNE INGUBA. O my beloved! Pardon me, pardon me that I could be ashamed when you were in such need. Never did I send a message, never did I call your name, scarce had I a longing for your company but that you have known and come. Remember that never up to this hour have you been silent when I would have you speak, remember that I have always made you talkative. If you are not lying there, if that is some stranger or someone or something bewitched into your likeness, drive it away, remember that for someone to take your likeness from you is a great insult. If you are lying there, stretch out your arms and speak, open your mouth and speak. [*She turns to Emer.*] He does not hear me, no sound reaches him, or it reaches him and he cannot speak.

EMER. Then kiss that image; these things are a great mystery, and maybe his mouth will feel the pressure of your mouth upon that image. Is it not so that we approach the gods?

EITHNE INGUBA [*starting back*]. I felt it was some evil, devilish thing!

EMER. No, his body stirs, the pressure of your mouth has called him. He has thrown the changeling out.

EITHNE INGUBA [*going further off*]. Look at that hand! That hand is withered to the bone.

EMER [*going up to the bed*] What are you, what do you come for, and from where?

FIGURE OF CUCHULAIN. I am one of the spirits from the sea.

EMER. What spirit from the sea dares lie upon Cuchulain's bed and take his image?

FIGURE OF CUCHULAIN. I am called Bricriu, I am the maker of discord.

EMER. Come for what purpose?

[*Exit Eithne Inguba.*

FIGURE OF CUCHULAIN. I show my face and everything he loves must fly.

EMER. I have not fled your face.

From 'Wheels and Butterflies'

FIGURE OF CUCHULAIN. You are not loved.

EMER. And therefore have no dread to meet your eyes and to demand my husband.

FIGURE OF CUCHULAIN. He is here, your lamentations and that woman's lamentations have brought him in a sort of dream, but you can never win him without my help. Come to my left hand and I will touch your eyes and give you sight.

EMER [seeing the Ghost of Cuchulain]. Husband! Husband!

FIGURE OF CUCHULAIN. He seems near, and yet is as much out of reach as though there were a world between. I have made him visible to you. I cannot make you visible to him.

EMER. Cuchulain! Cuchulain!

FIGURE OF CUCHULAIN. Be silent, woman! He can neither see nor hear. But I can give him to you at a price. [Clashing of cymbals, etc.] Listen to that. Listen to the horses of the sea trampling! Fand, daughter of Manannan, has come. She is reining in her chariot, that is why the horses trample so. She is come to take Cuchulain from you, to take him away for ever, but I am her enemy, and I can show you how to thwart her.

EMER. Fand, daughter of Manannan!

FIGURE OF CUCHULAIN. While he is still here you can keep him if you pay the price. Once back in Manannan's house he is lost to you for ever. Those who love the daughters of the sea do not grow weary, nor do the daughters of the sea release their lovers.

EMER. There is no price I will not pay.

FIGURE OF CUCHULAIN. You spoke but now of a hope

that some day his love may return to you, that some day you may sit by the fire as when first married.

EMER. That is the one hope I have, the one thing that keeps me alive.

FIGURE OF CUCHULAIN. Renounce it, and he shall live again.

EMER. Never, never!

FIGURE OF CUCHULAIN. What else have you to offer?

EMER. Why should the gods demand such a sacrifice?

FIGURE OF CUCHULAIN. The gods must serve those who living become like the dead.

EMER. I will get him in despite of all the gods, but I will not renounce his love.

[*Fand, the Woman of the Sidhe, enters. Emer draws a dagger and moves as if to strike her.*

FIGURE OF CUCHULAIN [*laughing*]. You think to wound her with a knife! She has an airy body, an invulnerable body. Remember that though your lamentations have dragged him hither, once he has left this shore, once he has passed the bitter sea, once he lands in Manannan's house, he will be as the gods who remember nothing.

[*The Woman of the Sidhe, Fand, moves round the crouching Ghost of Cuchulain at front of stage in a dance that grows gradually quicker as he awakes. At moments she may drop her hair upon his head, but she does not kiss him. She is accompanied by string and flute and drum. Her mask and clothes must suggest gold or bronze or brass and silver, so that she seems more an idol than a human being.*

From 'Wheels and Butterflies'

This suggestion may be repeated in her movements. Her hair, too, must keep the metallic suggestion. The object of the dance is that having awakened Cuchulain he will follow Fand out; probably he will seek a kiss and the kiss will be withheld.

FIGURE OF CUCHULAIN. Cry out that you renounce his love, cry that you renounce his love for ever.

[*Fand and Cuchulain go out.*

EMER. No, no, never will I give that cry.

FIGURE OF CUCHULAIN. Fool, fool! I am Fand's enemy. I come to tell you how to thwart her and you do nothing. There is yet time. Listen to the horses of the chariot, they are trampling the shore. They are wild and trampling. She has mounted into her chariot. Cuchulain is not yet beside her. Will you leave him to such as she? Renounce his love, and all her power over him comes to an end.

EMER. I renounce Cuchulain's love. I renounce it for ever.

[*Figure of Cuchulain falls back upon the bed, drawing or partly drawing its curtain that he may change his mask.*

Eithne Inguba enters.

EITHNE INGUBA. Cuchulain, Cuchulain! Remember our last meeting. We lay all night among the sand-hills; dawn came; we heard the crying of the birds upon the shore. Come to me, beloved. [*The curtain of the bed moves.*] Look, look! He has come back, he is there in the bed, he has his own rightful form again. It is I who have won him. It is my love that has brought him back to life!

'Fighting the Waves'

[*The figure in the bed pulls back the curtain. He wears the mask of Cuchulain.*

EMER. Cuchulain wakes!

CUCHULAIN. Your arms, your arms! O Eithne Inguba, I have been in some strange place and am afraid.

EPILOGUE

[*The Musicians, singing as follows, draw the wave-curtain until it masks the bed, Cuchulain, Eithne Inguba, and Emer.*

FIRST MUSICIAN

Why does your heart beat thus?
Plain to be understood,
I have met in a man's house
A statue of solitude,
Moving there and walking,
Its strange heart beating fast
For all our talking;
O still that heart at last.

O bitter reward
Of many a tragic tomb!
And we though astonished are dumb
And give but a sigh and a word,
A passing word.

From 'Wheels and Butterflies'

Although the door be shut
And all seem well enough,
Although wide world hold not
A man but will give you his love
The moment he has looked at you,
He that has loved the best
May turn from a statue
His too human breast.

O bitter reward
Of many a tragic tomb!
And we though astonished are dumb
And give but a sigh and a word,
A passing word.

What makes your heart so beat?
Is there no man at your side?
When beauty is complete
Your own thought will have died
And danger not be diminished;
Dimmed at three-quarter light,
When moon's round is finished
The stars are out of sight.

O bitter reward
Of many a tragic tomb!
And we though astonished are dumb
And give but a sigh and a word,
A passing word.

'Fighting the Waves'

[*The Musicians return to their places, Fand, the Woman of the Sidhe, enters and dances a dance which expresses her despair for the loss of Cuchulain. As before, there may be other dancers who represent the waves. It is called, in order to balance the first dance, 'Fand mourns among the waves'. It is essentially a dance which symbolises, like water in the fortune-telling books, bitterness. As she takes her final pose of despair the Curtain falls.*

From 'Wheels and Butterflies'

INTRODUCTION TO 'THE RESURRECTION'

I

THIS play, or the first sketch of it, more dialogue than play, was intended for my drawing-room, where my *Hawk's Well* had just been played.

For years I have been preoccupied with a certain myth that was itself a reply to a myth. I do not mean a fiction, but one of those statements our nature is compelled to make and employ as a truth though there cannot be sufficient evidence. When I was a boy everybody talked about progress, and rebellion against my elders took the form of aversion to that myth. I took satisfaction in certain public disasters, felt a sort of ecstasy at the contemplation of ruin, and then I came upon the story of Oisin in Tir nà nOg and reshaped it into my *Wanderings of Oisin*. He rides across the sea with a spirit, he passes phantoms, a boy following a girl, a hound chasing a hare, emblematical of eternal pursuit, he comes to an island of choral dancing, leaves that after many years, passes the phantoms once again, comes to an island of endless battle for an object never achieved, leaves that after many years, passes the phantoms once again, comes to an island of sleep, leaves that and comes to Ireland, to Saint Patrick and old age. I did not pick these images because of any theory, but because I found them impressive, yet all the while abstractions haunted me. I remember rejecting, because it spoilt the simplicity, an elaborate metaphor of a breaking wave intended to prove that all life rose and fell as in my poem. How hard it was to refrain from pointing out that Oisin after old age, its illumination half accepted, half rejected, would pass in death over another sea to another island. Presently Oisin and his islands faded and the sort of images that come into *Rosa Alchemica* and *The Adoration of the Magi* took their place. Our civilisation was about to reverse itself, or some new civilisation about to be born from all that our age had rejected, from all that my stories symbolised as a harlot, and take after its mother; because we had worshipped a single god it would worship many or receive from Joachim de Flora's Holy Spirit a multitudinous influx. A passage in *La Peau de chagrin* may have started me, but because I knew no ally but Balzac, I kept silent about all I could not get into fantastic romance. So did the abstract ideas persecute me that *On Baile's Strand*, founded upon a dream, was only finished when, after a struggle of two years, I had made the Fool and Blind Man, Cuchulain and Conchubar whose shadows they are, all image, and now I can no longer remember what they meant except that they meant in some sense those combatants who turn the wheel of life. Had I begun *On Baile's Strand* or not when I began to imagine, as always at my left side just out of the range of the sight, a brazen winged beast[1] that I associated with laughing, ecstatic destruction? Then I wrote, spurred by an external necessity, *Where there is Nothing*, a crude play with some dramatic force, since changed with Lady Gregory's help into

[1] Afterwards described in my poem 'The Second Coming'.

From 'Wheels and Butterflies'

The Unicorn from the Stars. A neighbourhood inflamed with drink, a country house burnt down, a spiritual anarchy preached! Then after some years came the thought that a man always tried to become his opposite, to become what he would abhor if he did not desire it, and I wasted some three summers and some part of each winter before I had banished the ghost and turned what I had meant for tragedy into a farce: *The Player Queen.* Then unexpectedly and under circumstances described in *A Packet to Ezra Pound* came a symbolic system displaying the conflict in all its forms:

> Where got I that truth?
> Out of a medium's mouth,
> Out of nothing it came,
> Out of the forest loam,
> Out of dark night where lay
> The crowns of Nineveh.

II

> And then did all the Muses sing
> Of Magnus Annus at the spring.

In 1894 Gorky and Lunacharsky tried to correct the philosophy of Marxian socialism by the best German philosophy of their time, founding schools at Capri and Bologna for the purpose, but Lenin founded a rival school at Paris and brought Marxian socialism back to orthodoxy: 'we remain materialist, anything else would lead to religion'. Four or five years later Pius X saw a Commission of Catholic scholars considering the text of the Bible and its attribution to certain authors and dissolved the Commission: 'Moses and the Four Evangelists wrote the Books that are called by their names; any other conclusion would lead to scepticism'. In this way did two great men[1] prepare two great movements, purified of modernism, for a crisis when, in the words of Archbishop Downey, they must dispute the mastery of the world.

So far I have the sympathy of the Garrets and Cellars, for they are, I am told, without exception Catholic, Communist, or both! Yet there is a third myth or philosophy that has made an equal stir in the world. Ptolemy thought the precession of the equinoxes moved at the rate of a degree every hundred years, and that somewhere about the time of Christ and Caesar the equinoctial sun had returned to its original place in the constellations, completing and recommencing the thirty-six thousand years, or three hundred and sixty incarnations of a hundred years apiece, of Plato's Man of Ur. Hitherto almost every philosopher had some different measure for the Greatest Year, but this Platonic Year, as it was called, soon displaced all others; it was a Christian heresy in the twelfth century, and in the East, multiplied by twelve as if it were but a month of a still greater year, it became the Manvantra[2] of 432,000 years, until animated by the Indian jungle

---

[1] It is not true, according to Prince Mirsky, that Marxian socialism denies the existence of great men. 'Great men are the embodiment of great social movements, and it is natural that the greater the movement the greater the "great man" produced by it.'

[2] This explanation of the Manvantra comes from an Arab who visited India at the beginning of the tenth century. He is quoted in Pierre Duhem, *Système du monde*, vol. i. pp. 67 and 68.

it generated new noughts and multiplied itself into Kalpas.

It was perhaps obvious, when Plotinus substituted the archetypes of individual men in all their possible incarnations for a limited number of Platonic Ideas, that a Greatest Year for whale and gudgeon alike must exhaust the multiplication table. Whatever its length, it divided, and so did every unit whose multiple it was, into waxing and waning, day and night, or summer and winter. There was everywhere a conflict like that of my play between two principles or 'elemental forms of the mind', each 'living the other's life, dying the other's death'. I have a Chinese painting of three old sages sitting together, one with a deer at his side, one with a scroll open at the symbol of *yen* and *yin*, those two forms that whirl perpetually, creating and re-creating all things. But because of our modern discovery that the equinox shifts its ground more rapidly than Ptolemy believed, one must, somebody says, invent a new symbolic scheme. No, a thousand times no; I insist that the equinox does shift a degree in a hundred years; anything else would lead to confusion.

All ancient nations believed in the re-birth of the soul and had probably empirical evidence like that Lafcadio Hearn found among the Japanese. In our time Schopenhauer believed it, and McTaggart thinks Hegel did, though lack of interest in the individual soul had kept him silent. It is the foundation of McTaggart's own philosophical system. Cardinal Mercier saw no evidence for it, but did not think it heretical; and its rejection compelled the sincere and noble Von

Introduction to 'The Resurrection'

Hügel to say that children dead too young to have earned Heaven suffered no wrong, never having heard of a better place than Limbo. Even though we think temporal existence illusionary it cannot be capricious; it is what Plotinus called the characteristic act of the soul and must reflect the soul's coherence. All our thought seems to lead by antithesis to some new affirmation of the supernatural. In a few years, perhaps, we may have much empirical evidence, the only evidence that moves the mass of men to-day, that man has lived many times; there is some not yet perfectly examined—I think of that Professor's daughter in Palermo. This belief held by Plato and Plotinus, and supported by weighty argument, resembles the mathematical doctrines of Einstein before the experimental proof of the curvature of light.

We may come to think that nothing exists but a stream of souls, that all knowledge is biography, and with Plotinus that every soul is unique; that these souls, these eternal archetypes, combine into greater units as days and nights into months, months into years, and at last into the final unit that differs in nothing from that which they were at the beginning: everywhere that antinomy of the One and the Many that Plato thought in his *Parmenides* insoluble, though Blake thought it soluble 'at the bottom of the graves'. Such belief may arise from Communism by antithesis, declaring at last even to the common ear that all things have value according to the clarity of their expression of themselves, and not as functions of changing economic conditions or as a preparation for some Utopia.

From 'Wheels and Butterflies'

There is perhaps no final happy state except in so far as men may gradually grow better; escape may be for individuals alone who know how to exhaust their possible lives, to set, as it were, the hands of the clock racing. Perhaps we shall learn to accept even innumerable lives with happy humility ('I have been always an insect in the roots of the grass') and, putting aside calculating scruples, be ever ready to wager all upon the dice.

Even our best histories treat men as function. Why must I think the victorious cause the better? Why should Mommsen think the less of Cicero because Caesar beat him? I am satisfied, the Platonic Year in my head, to find but drama. I prefer that the defeated cause should be more vividly described than that which has the advertisement of victory. No battle has been finally won or lost; 'to Garret or Cellar a wheel I send'.

III

'What if there is always something that lies outside knowledge, outside order? . . . What if the irrational return? What if the circle begin again?' Years ago I read Sir William Crookes' *Studies in Psychical Research*. After excluding every possibility of fraud, he touched a materialised form and found the heart beating. I felt, though my intellect rejected what I read, the terror of the supernatural described by Job. Just before the war a much respected man of science entering a room in his own house found there two girl visitors—I have questioned all three—one lying asleep on the table, the

398

other sitting on the end of the table screaming, the table floating in the air, and 'immediately vomited'. I took from the beating heart, from my momentary terror, from the shock of a man of science, the central situation of my play: the young man touching the heart of the phantom and screaming. It has seemed to me of late that the sense of spiritual reality comes whether to the individual or to crowds from some violent shock, and that idea has the support of tradition.

From 'Wheels and Butterflies'

INTRODUCTION TO
'THE CAT AND THE MOON'

I

THESE plays, which substitute speech and music for painted scenery, should suit Cellars and Garrets, though I do not recommend *The Resurrection* to the more pious Communist or Republican Cellars; it may not be as orthodox as I think; I recommend *The Cat and the Moon*, for no audience could discover its dark, mythical secrets. Myth is not, as Vico perhaps thought, a rudimentary form superseded by reflection. Belief is the spring of all action; we assent to the conclusions of reflection but believe what myth presents; belief is love, and the concrete alone is loved; nor is it true that myth has no purpose but to bring round some discovery of a principle or a fact. The saint may touch through myth the utmost reach of human faculty and pass not to reflection but to unity with the source of his being.

The Japanese labour leader and Christian saint Kagawa,[1] perhaps influenced by Vico though his millennium-haunted mind breaks Vico's circle, speaks of that early phase of every civilisation where a man must follow his father's occupation, where everything is prescribed, as buried under dream and myth. It was because the Irish country people kept something of

---

[1] 'What is so wonderful about our Saviour', he writes, 'is that though He lived surrounded by women here was never any scandal.'

that early period (had they not lived in Asia until the battle of the Boyne?) that I wrote my *Celtic Twilight*, that Lady Gregory wrote her much richer *Poets and Dreamers*, that she wrote and I annotated those *Visions and Beliefs* in whose collection I had some share. Though Lady Gregory's work is careful and accurate we had little scientific curiosity, but sought wisdom, peace, and a communion with the people. Perhaps a similar emotion made my brother paint country fairs and little streets and the remembered faces of pilots seen at Rosses in his childhood, and Synge create *The Well of the Saints*. I feel at the entrance of the saint in the last act of the play what Lady Gregory must have felt when at the sight of an old man in a wood she said to me, 'That old man may know the secret of the ages'. Dr. Hyde and his League were different; they sought the peasant, and it is the peasant perhaps who prevails wherever Gaelic is taught, but we sought the peasant's imagination which presses beyond himself as if to the next age. 'Twenty years have I spent upon the battle-fields of the world', said the pensioner in my brother's picture. The choral song, a life lived in common, a futile battle, then thought for its own sake, the last island, Vico's circle and mine, and then the circle joined.

> Decline of day,
> A leaf drifts down;
> O dark leaf clay
> On Nineveh's crown!

From 'Wheels and Butterflies'

II

A couple of miles as the crow flies from my Galway house is a blessed well. Some thirty years ago the Gaelic League organised some kind of procession or 'pattern' there, somebody else put a roof over it, somebody else was cured of a lame leg or a blind eye or the falling sickness. There are many offerings at the well-side left by sufferers; I seem to remember bits of cloth torn perhaps from a dress, hair-pins, and little pious pictures. The tradition is that centuries ago a blind man and a lame man dreamed that somewhere in Ireland a well would cure them and set out to find it, the lame man on the blind man's back. I wanted to give the Gaelic League, or some like body, a model for little plays, commemorations of known places and events, and wanted some light entertainment to join a couple of dance plays or *The Resurrection* and a dance play, and chose for theme the lame man, the blind man, and the well. It seemed that I could be true to the associations of such places if I kept in mind, while only putting the vaguest suggestion of it into the play, that the blind man was the body, the lame man was the soul. When I had finished I found them in some mediaeval Irish sermon as a simile of soul and body, and then that they had some like meaning in a Buddhist Sutra. But as the populace might well alter out of all recognition, deprive of all apparent meaning, some philosophical thought or verse, I wrote a little poem where a cat is disturbed by the moon, and in the

changing pupils of its eyes seems to repeat the movement of the moon's changes, and allowed myself as I
wrote to think of the cat as the normal man and of the
moon as the opposite he seeks perpetually, or as having
any meaning I have conferred upon the moon elsewhere. Doubtless, too, when the lame man takes the
saint upon his back, the normal man has become one
with that opposite, but I had to bear in mind that I was
among dreams and proverbs, that though I might discover what had been and might be again an abstract
idea, no abstract idea must be present. The spectator
should come away thinking the meaning as much his
own manufacture as that of the blind man and the lame
man had seemed mine. Perhaps some early Christian
—Bardaisan had speculations about the sun and moon
nobody seems to have investigated—thought as I do,
saw in the changes of the moon all the cycles : the soul
realising its separate being in the full moon, then, as the
moon seems to approach the sun and dwindle away, all
but realising its absorption in God, only to whirl away
once more: the mind of a man, separating itself from
the common matrix, through childish imaginations,
through struggle—Vico's heroic age—to roundness,
completeness, and then externalising, intellectualising,
systematising, until at last it lies dead, a spider
smothered in its own web: the choice offered by the
sages, either with the soul from the myth to union with
the source of all, the breaking of the circle, or from the
myth to reflection and the circle renewed for better or
worse. For better or worse according to one's life, but
never progress as we understand it, never the straight

line, always a necessity to break away and destroy, or to sink in and forget.

III

When Lady Gregory's *Visions and Beliefs* had all been collected I began, that I might write my notes, to study spiritualism, of which I had hitherto known nothing. I went from medium to medium, choosing by preference mediums in poor districts where the questioners were small shopkeepers, workmen, and workmen's wives, and found there almost all that Lady Gregory had recorded, though without some of its beauty. It seemed at first that all was taken literally, but I soon found that the medium and some of the questioners knew that something from beyond time was expressing itself in whatever crude symbols they could best understand. I remembered a Sligo visionary who could neither read nor write and said her faeries were big or little according to something in her mind. I began taking notes, piecing together a philosophy resembling that of the villages and of certain passages in the *Spiritual Diary* and *Heaven and Hell* of Swedenborg, and to study natures that seemed upon the edge of the myth-haunted semi-somnambulism of Kagawa's first period. Perhaps now that the abstract intellect has split the mind into categories, the body into cubes, we may be about to turn back towards the unconscious, the whole, the miraculous; according to a Chinese sage darkness begins at midday. Perhaps in my search, as in that first search with Lady Gregory among the cottages, I but showed a first effect of that slight darkening.

VI
FROM 'ON THE BOILER'
1939

THE NAME

WHEN I was a child and wandering about the Sligo Quays I saw a printed, or was it a painted notice? On such-and-such a day 'the great McCoy will speak on the old boiler'. I knew the old boiler, very big, very high, the top far out of reach, and all red rust. I wanted to go and hear him for the boiler's sake, but nobody encouraged me. I was told then or later that he was a mad ship's carpenter, very good at his trade if he would stick to it, but he went to bed from autumn to spring and during his working months broke off from time to time to read the Scriptures and denounce his neighbours. Then I saw him at a Rosses Point regatta alone in a boat; sculling it in whenever he saw a crowd, then, bow to seaward, denouncing the general wickedness, then sculling it out amid a shower of stones.

> Why should not old men be mad?
> Some have known a likely lad
> That had a sound fly-fisher's wrist
> Turn to a drunken journalist;
> A girl that knew all Dante once
> Live to bear children to a dunce;
> A Helen of social welfare dream,
> Climb on a wagonette to scream.
> Some think it a matter of course that chance
> Should starve good men and bad advance,
> That if their neighbours figured plain,
> As though upon a lighted screen,
> No single story would they find
> Of an unbroken happy mind,

From 'On the Boiler'

A finish worthy of the start.
Young men know nothing of this sort;
Observant old men know it well;
And when they know what old books tell,
And that no better can be had,
Know why an old man should be mad.

Preliminaries

PRELIMINARIES

I

LAST year the Lord Mayor sent out an intelligent Christmas card, an eighteenth-century print of some Dublin street; but this year his card had a drawing of the Mansion House as it is to-day. It is clear that architecture interests him. Let him threaten to resign if the Corporation will not tell the City Architect to scrape off the stucco, pull down the cast-iron porch, lift out the plate glass, and get the Mansion House into its eighteenth-century state. It would only cost a few hundred pounds, for the side walls and their windows are as they should be, and Dublin would have one more dignified ancestral building. All Catholic Ireland, as it was before the National University and a victory in the field had swept the penal laws out of its bones, swells out in that pretentious front. Old historic bricks and window-panes obliterated or destroyed, its porch invented when England was elaborating the architecture and interior decoration of the gin-palace, its sole fitting inhabitant that cringing firbolg Tom Moore cast by some ironmonger—bronze costs money—now standing on the other side of Trinity College near the urinal.

This has not occurred to the Lord Mayor, a good, amiable, clever man, I am told, because he thinks, like English royalty, that his duty is to make himself popular among the common people, and architectural taste is at present articulate only in the few. His time is taken up opening crèches, talking everything but politics, presiding at dinners, going sober to bed. The whole State should be so constructed that the people should think it their duty to grow popular with King and Lord Mayor instead of King and Lord Mayor growing popular with them; yet, as it is even, I have known some two or three men and women who never, apart from the day's natural kindness, gave the people a thought, or who despised them with that old Shakespearean contempt and were worshipped after their death or even while they lived. Try to be popular and you think another man's thought, sink into that slow, slothful, inanimate, semi-hypocritical thinking Dante symbolised by hoods and cloaks of lead.

II

I read in the *Irish Times* of October 20, 1937, that the Galway Library Committee is indignant and has written to a firm of publishers to protest. John Eglinton said in his memoir of A. E. that a mob had broken into a public library, taken out the books of certain eminent authors and burnt them in the street. The Committee did not require, it seems, the dictation of a mob to do their duty. They had some years ago discussed whether 'the works of Mr. Bernard Shaw were works which should be kept in a public library, and on a division it was decided that the books of Shaw be not kept. It was suggested at the time that any book which was offensive should be burned. There was no other way of getting rid of them.' I do not mention this incident because of its importance—there have been similar burnings elsewhere in Ireland—but that I may stand between these men and their critics. They are probably clever, far-seeing men when ploughing their fields, selling porter, or, if they make their living by teaching class, when they have shut the school doors behind them; but show them a book and they buzz like a bee in a bottle. I know nothing of them except those few printed words, but it seems probable that many men in Irish public life should not have been taught to read and write, and would not have been in any country before the middle of the nineteenth century. Some of the Galway Committee may have a family tradition of some grandfather, or grandfather's cousin or nephew, who set out to seek learning supported by the contributions of relations and friends, and found at the journey's end, if he had reasonable luck, not a government-appointed dunce, but a man who loved his book and taught something of great people and great literature. Thackeray heard two ragged boys leaning over the Liffey parapet discussing 'wan of the Ptolemies'. Forcing reading and writing on those who wanted neither was the worst part of the violence which for two centuries has been creating that hell wherein we suffer, unless indeed the spoilt priest in *John Bull's Other Island* was right and the world itself is Hell. I once travelled up from Limerick with an old priest and a girl of thirteen or fourteen. He had written an essay on Gladstone and it lay upon his knees. He began talking to the girl about it. 'Who was Gladstone?' 'I don't know, Father.' 'Was he at the Siege of Limerick?'

[margin handwritten note: Anti-democratic—But we can see why.]

From 'On the Boiler'

'Yes, Father', this with a sudden brightening. When he asked about Parnell and the Land Bill and found that she had heard of neither he turned to me with 'Sir, if you ever meet anyone of importance please tell them that this kind of ignorance is spreading everywhere from the schools'.

Perhaps now they learn these names by rote, but I see nowhere evidence that ignorance has abated. Our representative system has given Ireland to the incompetent. There are no districts in County Galway of any size without a Catholic curate, a young shop-keeper, a land-owner, a sawyer, with enough general knowledge to make a good library committee. I remember the volunteers who policed the country, dealt out justice, and had all men's respect.

III

When I was first a member of the Irish Senate I discovered to my surprise that one learned in three months more about every Senator's character and capacity than could have been learned from years of ordinary life. I came to know the Ministers more slowly, for each attended only when his own department was concerned. The thirty men nominated by President Cosgrave were plainly the most able and the most educated. I attached myself to a small group led by an old friend of my father's, Andrew Jameson, for I knew that he would leave me free to speak my mind. The few able men among the elected Senators had been nominated for election by Ministers. As the nominated element began to die out—almost all were old men—the Senate declined in ability and prestige. In its early days some old banker or lawyer would dominate the House, leaning upon the back of the chair in front, always speaking with undisturbed self-possession as at some table in a board-room. My imagination sets up against him some typical elected man, emotional as a youthful chimpanzee, hot and vague, always disturbed, always hating something or other.

The Ministers had not been elected. They had destroyed a system of election and established another, made terrible decisions, the ablest had signed the death-warrant of his dearest friend. They seemed men of skill and mother-wit, men who had survived hatred. But their minds knew no play that my mind could play at; I felt that I could never know them. One of the most notable said he had long wanted to meet me. We met, but my conversation shocked and embarrassed him. No, neither Gogarty nor I, with our habit of outrageous conversation, could get near those men. Yet their descendants, if they grow rich enough for the travel and leisure that make a finished man, will constitute our ruling class, and date their origin from the Post Office as American families date theirs from the *May-flower*. They have already intermarried, able stocks have begun to appear, and recent statistics have shown that men of talent everywhere are much linked through marriage and descent. The Far East has dynasties of painters, dancers, politicians, merchants, but with us the dancer may be the politician's mother, though I cannot think of any example; the painter his rebellious son.

[handwritten marginalia: "Irish Revolution — Easter Rebellion"]

[handwritten marginalia: "Purgatory"]

413

From 'On the Boiler'

I was six years in the Irish Senate; I am not ignorant of politics elsewhere, and on other grounds I have some right to speak. I say to those that shall rule here: 'If ever Ireland again seems molten wax, reverse the process of revolution. Do not try to pour Ireland into any political system. Think first how many able men with public minds the country has, how many it can hope to have in the near future, and mould your system upon those men. It does not matter how you get them, but get them. Republics, Kingdoms, Soviets, Corporate States, Parliaments, are trash, as Hugo said of something else, "not worth one blade of grass that God gives for the nest of the linnet". These men, whether six or six thousand, are the core of Ireland, are Ireland itself.'

IV

As I write these words the Abbey Players are finishing a successful American tour. These tours, and Irish songs and novels, when they come from a deeper life than their nineteenth-century predecessors, are taking the place of political speakers, political organisations, in holding together the twenty scattered millions conscious of their Irish blood. The attitude towards life of Irish writers and dramatists at this moment will have historical importance. The success of the Abbey Theatre has grown out of a single conviction of its founders: I was the spokesman because I was born arrogant and had learnt an artist's arrogance —'Not what you want but what we want'—and we were the first modern theatre that said it. I did not

414

speak for John Synge, Augusta Gregory, and myself alone, but for all the dramatists of the theatre. Again and again somebody speaking for our audience, for an influential newspaper or political organisation, has demanded more of this kind of play, or less or none of that. They have not understood that we cannot, and if we could would not comply; the moment any dramatist has some dramatic sense and applies it to our Irish theme he is played. We may help him with his technique or to clear his mind of the second-hand or the second-rate in their cruder forms, but beyond that we can do nothing. He must find himself and mould his dramatic form to his nature after his own fashion, and that is why we have produced some of the best plays of modern times, and a far greater number of the worst. And what I have said of the dramatists is true of the actors, though there the bad comedians do not reach our principal company. I have seen English producers turn their players into mimics; but all our producers do for theirs, or so it was in my day and I suppose it is still the same, is to help them to understand the play and their own natures.

Yet the theatre has not, apart from this one quality, gone my way or in any way I wanted it to go, and often, looking back, I have wondered if I did right in giving so much of my life to the expression of other men's genius. According to the Indians a man may do much good yet lose his own soul. Then I say to myself, I have had greater luck than any other modern English-speaking dramatist; I have aimed at tragic ecstasy, and here and there in my own work and in the

415

work of my friends I have seen it greatly played. What does it matter that it belongs to a dead art and to a time when a man spoke out of an experience and a culture that were not of his time alone, but held his time, as it were, at arm's length, that he might be a spectator of the ages? I am haunted by certain moments: Miss O'Neill in the last act of Synge's *Deirdre*, 'Draw a little back with the squabbling of fools'; Kerrigan and Miss O'Neill playing in a private house that scene in Augusta Gregory's *Full Moon* where the young mad people in their helpless joy sing *The Boys of Queen Anne*; Frank Fay's entrance in the last act of *The Well of the Saints*; William Fay at the end of *On Baile's Strand*; Mrs. Patrick Campbell in my *Deirdre*, passionate and solitary; and in later years that great artist Ninette de Valois in *Fighting the Waves*. These things will, it may be, haunt me on my death-bed; what matter if the people prefer another art, I have had my fill.

To-morrow's Revolution

TO-MORROW'S REVOLUTION

I

WHEN I was in my 'teens I admired my father above all men; from him I learnt to admire Balzac and to set certain passages in Shakespeare above all else in literature, but when I was twenty-three or twenty-four I read Ruskin's *Unto This Last*, of which I do not remember a word, and we began to quarrel, for he was John Stuart Mill's disciple. Once he threw me against a picture with such violence that I broke the glass with the back of my head. But it was not only with my father that I quarrelled, nor were economics the only theme. There was no dominant opinion I could accept. Then finding out that I (having no clear case—my opponent's case had been clarifying itself for centuries) had become both boor and bore, I invented a patter, allowing myself an easy man's insincerity, and for honesty's sake a little malice, and now it seems that I can talk nothing else. But I think I have succeeded, and that none of my friends know that I am a fanatic. My reader may say that it was all natural, that every generation is against its predecessor, but that conflict is superficial, an exaltation of the individual life that had little importance before modern journalism; that other war, where opposites die each other's life, live each other's death, is a slow-moving thing. We who are the opposites of our times should for the most part work at our art and for good manners' sake be silent. What matter if our art or science lack hearty acquiescence, seem narrow and traditional? Horne built the smallest church in London, went to Italy and became the foremost authority upon Botticelli. Ricketts made pictures that suggest Delacroix by their colour and remind us by their theatrical composition that Talma once invoked the thunderbolt; Synge fled to the Aran Islands to escape 'the squalor of the poor and the nullity of the rich', and found among forgotten people a mirror for his bitterness. I gave certain years to writing plays in Shakespearean blank verse about Irish kings for whom nobody cared a farthing. After all, Asiatic conquerors before battle invoked their ancestors, and a few years ago a Japanese admiral thanked his for guiding the torpedoes.

"*Purgatory*"

II

But now I must, if I can, put away my patter, speak to the young men before the ox treads on my tongue. Here is my text; I take it from the *Anatomy of Melancholy*.

'So many different ways are we plagued and punished for our fathers' defaults: insomuch that, as Fernelius truly saith, "it is the greatest part of our felicity to be well born, and it were happy for human kind, if only such parents as are sound of body and mind should be suffered to marry." An husbandman will sow none but the best and choicest seed upon his land; he will not rear a bull or an horse except he be right shapen in all parts, or permit him to cover a mare, except he be well assured of his breed; we make choice of the best rams for our sheep, rear the neatest kine, and keep the best dogs, *quanto id diligentius in procreandis liberis observandum!* (And how careful then should we be in begetting our children!) In former times some countries have been so chary in this behalf, so stern, that, if a child were crooked or deformed in body or mind, they made him away; so did the Indians of old by the relation of Curtius, and many other well-governed commonwealths, according to the discipline of those times. Heretofore in Scotland, saith Hect. Boethius, "if any were visited with the falling sickness, madness, gout, leprosy, or any such dangerous disease, which was likely to be propagated from the father to the son, he was instantly gelded: a woman kept from all company of men; and if by chance, having some such disease, she were found to be with child, she with her brood were buried alive": and this was done for the common good, lest the whole nation should be injured or corrupted. A severe doom, you will say, and not to be used among Christians, yet more to be looked into than it is. For now by our too much facility in this kind, in giving way for all to marry that will, too much liberty and indulgence in tolerating all sorts, there is a vast confusion of hereditary diseases, no family secure, no man almost free from some grievous infirmity or other. When no choice is had, but still the eldest must marry, as so many stallions of the race; or if rich, be they fools or dizzards, lame or maimed, inable, intemperate, dissolute, exhaust through riot, as he said, *jure haereditario sapere jubentur* (they must be wise and able by inheritance); it comes to pass that our generation is corrupt, we have many weak persons, both in body and mind, many feral diseases raging amongst us, crazed families, *parentes peremptores*; our fathers bad, and we are like to be worse.'[1]

III

Though well-known specialists are convinced that the principal European nations are degenerating in body and in mind, their evidence remains almost unknown because a politician and newspaper that gave it adequate exposition would lose, the one his constituency, the other its circulation. That upon which success in life in the main depends may be called co-ordination or a capacity for sustained purpose,[2] and this capacity, this innate intelligence or mother-wit, can be measured, in children especially, with great accuracy. The curious and elaborate tests are unlike school examinations because they eliminate, or almost eliminate, the child's acquired knowledge. This mother-wit is not everything and may have been the same in Bluebeard and Saint Augustine; Gray's 'Milton' re-

[1] *The Anatomy of Melancholy*, by Robert Burton, edited by the Rev. A. R. Shilleto, M.A., published by G. Bell & Sons, London, 1912. Part. I, Sect. 2, Mem. I, Subs. vi.

[2] I have deduced this rough definition of intelligence from the general nature of the 'intelligence tests' and from *The Measurement of Intelligence* by Lewis M. Terman (pages 44-47). I am indebted to the Secretary of the Eugenics Society for a long typed extract from this book. I am, indeed, indebted to his patience and courtesy for much of my information.

mained for lack of acquired knowledge 'mute, in-glorious'; but it outweighs everything else by, let us say, six to one, and is hereditary like the speed of a dog or a horse. Take a pair of twins and educate one in wealth, the other in poverty, test from time to time; their mother-wit will be the same. Pick a group of slum children, examine for mother-wit, move half the children to some other neighbourhood where they have better food, light and air, and after several months or years re-examine. Except for the increase which comes with age—it increases until we are seventeen and declines after thirty-five—there will be little or no difference.[1] Furthermore, if you arrange an ascending scale from the unemployed to skilled labour, from skilled labour to shopkeepers and clerks, from shop-keepers and clerks to professional men,[2] there is not

[1] A test of this kind with three hundred Glasgow children was summarised by Shephard Dawson in an address to the British Association in 1934. On re-examination eighteen months after re-moval to better surroundings they did show 'a just appreciable improvement'. Cattell considers this seeming 'improvement' the result of tests which did not sufficiently exclude acquired knowledge. Shephard Dawson, a cautious man, while considering it encouraging to philanthropists, says that it was so small that those who initiate 'social welfare schemes may have to rely on the formation of habits that have to be learned, rather than on any improvement in intelli-gence'. Cattell, with later and fuller information from his own exhaustive investigations in Devonshire and in the town of Leicester, would say not 'may' but 'must'.

[2] A well-known authority writes in answer to a question of mine: 'We have no statistics for the leisured classes, owing to the difficulty of getting them into groups for examination'. It is a pity, for I want to know what happens to the plant when it gets from under the stone.

only an increase of mother-wit but of the size of the body and its freedom from constitutional defects.[1] Intelligence and bodily vigour are not in themselves connected, but those who in their mating have sought intelligence have sought vigour also. As intelligence and freedom from bodily defect increase, wealth increases in exact measure until enough for the necessities of life is reached—fixed by Cattell at £140 a year —and after that, with many exceptions, for men have other goals. There are exceptions throughout: clever men are born among dunces, dunces among clever men, and here and there a dunce earns much money, but in every country the statistics work out the same average.

But this ascending scale has another character which may, or must, turn all politics upside down: the families grow smaller as we ascend; among the unemployed they average between four and five, among the professional classes between two and three; among the unemployed there are still families of twelve and thirteen, but when we reach skilled labour, families of six have come to an end, and this is true of all Western

---

[1] The physical degeneration is the most easy to measure. In England since 1873 the average stature has declined about two inches, chest measurement about two inches and weight about twenty pounds. In almost all European countries, especially those where Catholicism encourages large families among the poor, there has been an equal or greater decline. Military standards have been lowered almost everywhere; Spain has lowered hers four times in the last forty years. Holland seems the one exception, and there, presumably because the poor have reduced the size of their families, the average stature has risen with astonishing rapidity. I summarise from Cattell's *Psychology and Social Progress*, pp. 102 and 112.

To-morrow's Revolution

Europe, Catholic and Protestant alike. Since about 1900 the better stocks have not been replacing their numbers, while the stupider and less healthy have been more than replacing theirs. Unless there is a change in the public mind every rank above the lowest must degenerate, and, as inferior men push up into its gaps, degenerate more and more quickly. The results are already visible in the degeneration of literature, newspapers, amusements (there was once a stock company playing Shakespeare in every considerable town), and, I am convinced, in benefactions like that of Lord Nuffield, a self-made man, to Oxford, which must gradually substitute applied science for ancient wisdom. Not that it will matter much what they teach. Mr. Bernard Shaw, contemplating the impressive English school system, has remarked that his old nurse was right when she said that you couldn't make a silk purse out of a sow's ear.[1] Then, too, think of the growing cohesiveness, the growing frenzy, everybody thinking like everybody else, preoccupation of all sorts with 'the youthful chimpanzee'. Any notable eighteenth-century orator contrasts with Lloyd George, as an orator of the great period in Greece and Rome with the Emperor Julian among his troops in Gaul.

[1] I recommend to my readers Cattell's *Fight for the National Intelligence*, a book recommended by Lord Horder and Leonard Darwin. I have taken most of the facts in this section, and some of the arguments and metaphors that follow, from this book.

From 'On the Boiler'

The United States organised their troops sent to
Europe in the Great War by tests of mother-wit,
'intelligence tests', and yet differ little from other democratic nations in their daily practice, and the new-
formed democratic parliaments of India will doubtless
destroy, if they can, the caste system that has saved
Indian intellect. The Fascist countries know that
civilisation has reached a crisis, and found their
eloquence upon that knowledge, but from dread of
attack or because they must feed their uneducatable
masses, put quantity before quality; any hale man can
dig or march. They offer bounties for the seventh,
eighth, or ninth baby, and accelerate degeneration. In
Russia, where the most intelligent families restrict
their numbers as elsewhere, the stupidest man can
earn a bounty by going to bed. Government there has
the necessary authority, but as it thinks the social
problem economic and not eugenic and ethnic—what
was Karl Marx but Macaulay with his heels in the air?
—it is the least likely to act. One nation has solved the
problem in its chief city: in Stockholm all families are
small; but the greater the intelligence the larger the
family. Plato's Republic with machines instead of
slaves may dawn there, but like the other Scandinavian
countries Sweden has spent on education far more than
the great nations can afford with their imperial responsibilities and ambitions, their always increasing
social services and public works. That increase, too,
can be calculated mathematically. But even if all

Europe becomes sufficiently educated to follow the Swedish example, can it, or can Sweden itself, escape violence? If some financial reorganisation such as Major Douglas plans, and that better organisation of agriculture and industry which many economists expect, enable everybody without effort to procure all necessities of life and so remove the last check upon the multiplication of the uneducatable masses, it will become the duty of the educated classes to seize and control one or more of those necessities. The drilled and docile masses may submit, but a prolonged civil war seems more likely, with the victory of the skilful, riding their machines as did the feudal knights their armoured horses. During the Great War Germany had four hundred submarine commanders, and sixty per cent of the damage done was the work of twenty-four men. The danger is that there will be no war, that the skilled will attempt nothing, that the European civilisation, like those older civilisations that saw the triumph of their gangrel stocks, will accept decay. When I was writing *A Vision* I had constantly the word 'terror' impressed upon me, and once the old Stoic prophecy of earthquake, fire, and flood at the end of an age, but this I did not take literally. It was because of that indefinable impression that I made Michael Robartes say in *A Vision*: 'Dear predatory birds, prepare for war, prepare your children and all that you can reach. . . . Test art, morality, custom, thought, by Thermopylae, make rich and poor act so to one another that they can stand together there. Love war because of its horror, **that belief may be changed, civilisation renewed. We** desire belief and lack it. Belief comes from shock and is not desired.'

v

The American intelligence tests put the Irish immigrant lowest in the scale, the English, the German, and the Swede highest. Skilled men leave the industrial countries attracted by higher wages; what Irish go there are unskilled men driven by necessity, those that succeed are the few who, as a successful Irish-American lawyer said to me, escape from toil before it has killed them. These immigrants are our unemployed, and balance those that go to posts all over the British Empire as doctors, lawyers, soldiers, civil servants, or drift away drawn to the lights of London. In the opinion of most sociologists the level of mother-wit in all West-European countries is still much the same. But we are threatened as they are; already we have almost twice as many madmen as England for every hundred thousand. Sooner or later we must limit the families of the unintelligent classes, and if our Government cannot send them doctor and clinic it must, till it gets tired of it, send monk and confession-box. We cannot go back as some dreamers would have us, to the old way of big families everywhere, even if the intelligent classes would consent, because that old way worked through lack of science and consequent great mortality among the children of those least fitted for modern civilisation.

Some of the inferiority of our emigrants in the United States and in Scotland may depend upon differ-

ence of historical phase. The tests usually employed
are appropriate to a civilisation dominated by towns,
by their objectivity and curiosity. Some of the tests are
rectilinear mazes of increasing difficulty. The child
marks with a pointer the way in, the way out at the
other side, avoiding if he can turnings that lead nowhere. Probably he thinks of neighbouring streets
where every turn is a right angle; an Achill child
having no such image would probably fail through lack
of attention. Other tests consist of fitting certain objects
into pictures, but pictures are almost or wholly unknown in our remote districts. A Canadian artist told
me that she once lodged with French-Canadian
farmers and, noticing the thought they gave in planting
a tree to the composition of the landscape, she gave the
farmer's wife a picture. When she returned a year later
the farmer's wife said, 'I made this apron out of that
bit of canvas, but it took hours of scrubbing to get the
dirt off.'[1] Then, we Irish are nearer than the English
to the Mythic Age. Once, coming up from Cork, I
got into talk with a fellow-traveller and learned that
he lived in County Cork, and as there was nothing
noticeable about his accent I assumed that he was a
Cork man. Presently he said, 'We have passed through
three climates since we started; first our breath
congealed on the glass, and then it ceased to do so, and

[1] Since I wrote this passage a friend has described to me Mayo
boys and girls looking at a film or magazine page for the first time.
It takes some little time before they understand that black and
white splashes or black lines can represent natural objects. If it is
a magazine page, some one will presently say 'That is a horse',
or, 'That is a man'.

427

now it congeals again'. I said, 'You are English?' He said, 'Yes, but how did you find out?' I said, 'No Irishman would have made that observation'. I forget what more I said, but it may have been that we are not disinterested observers, being much taken up with our own thoughts and emotions. The English are an objective people; they have no longer a sense of tragedy in their theatre; pity, which is fed by observation instead of experience, has taken its place; their poets are psychological, looking at their own minds from without. Ninette de Valois, herself an Irish woman, protested the other day because somebody had called the theatre the province of the Jews and the Irish. 'The Irish', she said, 'are adaptable immigrants, the bigger and emptier a country the better it pleases them. When England fills up, they will disappear; they will lunch in bed instead of merely breakfasting there, they will be scared off by the Matriculation papers.'

Private Thoughts

(*Should be skipped by Politicians and Journalists*)

I

I AM philosophical, not scientific, which means that observed facts do not mean much until I can make them part of my experience. Now that I am old and live in the past I often think of those ancestors of whom I have some detailed information. Such-and-such a diner-out and a charming man never did anything; such-and-such lost the never very great family fortune in some wild-cat scheme; such-and-such, perhaps deliberately, for he was a strange, deep man, married into a family known for harsh dominating strength of character. Then, as my mood deepens, I discover all these men in my single mind, think that I myself have gone through the same vicissitudes, that I am going through them all at this very moment, and wonder if the balance has come right; then I go beyond those minds and my single mind and discover that I have been describing everybody's struggle, and the gyres turn in my thoughts. Vico was the first modern philosopher to discover in his own mind, and in the European past, all human destiny. 'We can know nothing', he said, 'that we have not made.' Swift, too, Vico's contemporary, in his first political essay saw history as a personal experience, so too did Hegel in his *Philosophy of History*;[1] Balzac in his letter to the

[1] Hegel's historical dialectic is, I am persuaded, false, and its falsehood has led to the rancid ill-temper of the typical Communist

From 'On the Boiler'

Duchess de Castries, and here and there in *La Peau de chagrin* and *Catherine de Medici*.

When I allow my meditation to expand until the mind of my family merges into everybody's mind, I discover there, not only what Vico and Balzac found, but my own particular amusements and interests. First, no man can do the same thing twice if he has to put much mind into it, as every painter knows. Just when some school of painting has become popular, reproductions in every print-shop window, millionaires outbidding one another, everybody's affection stirred, painters wear out their nerves establishing something else, and this something else must be the other side of the penny—for Heraclitus was in the right. Opposites are everywhere face to face, dying each other's life, living each other's death. When a man loves a girl it should be because her face and character offer what he lacks; the more profound his nature the more should he realise his lack and the greater be the difference. It is as though he wanted to take his own death into his arms and beget a stronger life upon that death. We should count men and women who pick, as it were, the dam or sire of a Derby winner from between the shafts of a cab, among persons of genius, for this genius makes all other kinds possible.

---

and his incitements or condonations of murder. When the spring vegetables are over they have not been refuted, nor have they suffered in honour or reputation. Hegel in his more popular writings seems to misrepresent his own thought. Mind cannot be the ultimate reality, seeing that in his *Logic* both mind and matter have their ground in spirit. To Hegel, as to the ancient Indian Sages, spirit is that which has value in itself.

Private Thoughts

Our present civilisation began about the first Crusade, reached its mid-point in the Italian Renaissance; just when that point was passing Castiglione recorded in his *Courtier* what was said in the Court of Urbino somewhere about the first decade of the sixteenth century. These admirable conversationalists knew that the old spontaneous life had gone, and what a man must do to retain unity of being, mother-wit expressed in its perfection; he must know so many foreign tongues, know how to dance and sing, talk well, walk well, and be always in love. Elsewhere Titian was painting great figures of the old, simple generations; a little later came Vandyke and his sensitive fashionable faces where the impulse of life was fading. Somebody has written, 'There can be no wisdom without leisure', and those rich men of leisure still kept war and government for perquisites, and all else was done under their patronage. A City Father of a defeated Spanish town said that he could not understand it because their commander was not less well born than his opponent. They were at times great architects, they travelled everywhere, read the classic authorities and designed buildings that still stir our admiration. When Bishop Berkeley was asked to help to design the façade of Speaker Connolly's fine house at Celbridge, he refused because too many country gentlemen were already at the task. Meanwhile a famous event happened with much notoriety; Sir William Temple and certain of his distinguished friends had affirmed the genuineness of the letters of Phalaris, and the coarse, arrogant Bentley had proved them in

the wrong; culture, unity of being, no longer sufficed,
and the specialists were already there. Swift, when little
more than a boy, satirised what *Gulliver* would satirise:

But what does our proud ignorance Learning call?
　　We oddly Plato's paradox make good,
Our knowledge is but mere remembrance all;
　　Remembrance is our treasure and our food;
Nature's fair table-book, our tender souls,
We scrawl all o'er with old and empty rules,
　　Stale memorandums of the schools:
　　For Learning's mighty treasures look
　　　In that deep grave a book;
　　Think that she there does all her treasures hide,
And that her troubled ghost still haunts there since she dy'd.
Confine her walks to colleges and schools;
　　Her priest, her train, and followers show
　　As if they all were spectres too!
　　They purchase knowledge at th' expense
　　Of common breeding, common sense,
　　And grow at once scholars and fools;
　　Affect ill-manner'd pedantry,
Rudeness, ill-nature, incivility,
　　And, sick with dregs of knowledge grown,
　　Which greedily they swallow down,
Still cast it up, and nauseate company.

II

The leisured men had still a characteristic work to
do. During the eighteenth century they bred cattle
instead of men, turning the fence-jumping, climbing,
muscular cow and sheep of antiquity into fat and slothful butcher's meat. And now, their great task done, as

it seems, they live the life of pleasure, taking what comes, marrying what's there, but now and again married by some reigning beauty, daughter of a bar-maid man-picker who had doubled her own mettle with that of a man whose name she had forgotten or never known.

The specialist's job is anybody's job, seeing that for the most part he is made, not born. My best-informed relative says: 'Because Ireland is a backward country everybody is unique and knows that if he tumbles down somebody will pick him up. But an Englishman must be terrified, for there is a man exactly like him at every street corner.' A poet in an old Irish poem, travelling from great house to great house on his poet's business, meets a woman poet and asks for a child because a child of theirs would be a great poet. Parted, they died of love. The hero Finn, wishing for a son not less strong of body, stood on the top of a hill and said he would marry the first woman that reached him. According to the tale, two thousand started level; but why should Jones of Twickenham bother? [1]

We cannot do the same thing twice, and the new thing must employ a new set of nerves or muscles. When a civilisation ends, task having led to task until everybody was bored, the whole turns bottom up-wards, Nietzsche's 'transvaluation of all values'. As

---

[1] In a fragment from some early version of *The Courting of Emer*, Emer is chosen for the strength and volume of her bladder. This strength and volume were certainly considered signs of vigour. A woman of divine origin was murdered by jealous rivals because she made the deepest hole in the snow with her urine.

we approach the phoenix' nest the old classes, with their power of co-ordinating events, evaporate, the mere multitude is everywhere with its empty photographic eyes. Yet we who have hated the age are joyous and happy. The new discipline wherever enforced or thought will recall forgotten beautiful faces. Whenever we or our forefathers have been most Christian—not the Christ of Byzantine mosaic but the soft, domesticated Christ of the painter's brush—perhaps even when we have felt ourselves abounding and yielding like the too friendly man who blabs all his secrets, we have been haunted by those faces dark with mystery, cast up by that other power that has ever more and more wrestled with ours, each living the other's death, dying the other's life. A woman's face, though she be lost or childless, may foretell a transformation of the people, be a more dire or beneficent omen than those trumpets heard by Etruscan seers in middle air.

III

But if I would escape from patter I must touch upon things too deep for my intellect and my knowledge, and besides I want to make my readers understand that explanations of the world lie one inside another, each complete in itself, like those perforated Chinese ivory balls. The mathematician Poincaré, according to Henry Adams, described space as the creation of our ancestors, meaning, I conclude, that mind split itself into mind and space. Space was to antiquity mind's inseparable 'other', coincident with objects, the table not the place it occupies. During the seventeenth century it was separated from mind and objects alike, and thought of as a nothing yet a reality, the place not the table, with material objects separated from taste, smell, sound, from all the mathematician could not measure, for its sole inhabitants, and this new matter and space, men were told, had preceded mind and would live after. Nature or reality as known to poets and tramps has no moment, no impression, no perception like another, everything is unique, and nothing unique is measurable.

A line, whether made with rule and plummet or with a compass, must start somewhere. How convenient if men were but those dots, all exactly alike, all pushable, arrangeable, or, as Blake said, all intermeasurable by one another. Two and two must make four, though no two things are alike. A time has come when man must have certainty, and man knows what he has made. Man has made mathematics, but God reality. Instead of hierarchical society, where all men are different, came democracy; instead of a science which had re-discovered *Anima Mundi*, its experiments and observations confirming the speculations of Henry More, came materialism: all that Whiggish world Swift stared on till he became a raging man. The ancient foundations had scarcely dispersed when Swift's young acquaintance Berkeley destroyed the new for all that would listen, created modern philosophy and established for ever the subjectivity of space.[1] No educated

[1] For a modern re-statement, see Boyce Gibbons' translation from Husserl's *Ideas*, pp. 128, 129, and elsewhere.

435

man to-day accepts the objective matter and space of popular science, and yet deductions made by those who believed in both dominate the world, make possible the stimulation and condonation of revolutionary massacre and the multiplication of murderous weapons by substituting for the old humanity with its unique irreplaceable individuals something that can be chopped and measured like a piece of cheese; compel denial of the immortality of the soul by hiding from the mass of the people that the grave-diggers have no place to bury us but in the human mind.

When I began to grow old I could no longer spend all my time amid masterpieces and in trying to make the like. I gave part of every day to mere entertainment, and it seemed when I was ill that great genius was 'mad as the mist and snow'. Already in mid-Renaissance the world was weary of wisdom, science began to appear in the elaborate perspectives of its painters, in their sense of weight and tangibility; man was looking for some block where he could lay his head. But better than that, with Jacob's dream threatening, get rid of man himself. Civilisation slept in the masses, wisdom in science. Is it criminal to sleep? I do not know; I do not say it.

IV

Among those our civilisation must reject, or leave unrewarded at some level below that co-ordination that modern civilisation finds essential, exist precious faculties. When I was seven or eight I used to run about with a little negro girl, the only person at Rosses Point who could find a plover's nest, and I have noticed that clairvoyance, prevision, and allied gifts, rare among the educated classes, are common among peasants. Among those peasants there is much of Asia, where Hegel has said every civilisation begins. Yet we must hold to what we have that the next civilisation may be born, not from a virgin's womb, nor a tomb without a body, not from a void, but of our own rich experience. These gifts must return, not in the mediumistic sleep, dreaming or dreamless, but when we are wide awake. Eugenical and psychical research are the revolutionary movements with that element of novelty and sensation which sooner or later stir men to action. It may be, or it must be, that the best bred from the best shall claim again their ancient omens. And the serving-women 'shrank in their rejoicing before the eyes of the child', and 'the hour seemed awful to them' as they brought the child to its mother:

And she said: 'Now one of the earthly on the eyes of my
    child has gazed,
Nor shrunk before their glory, nor stayed her love amazed:
I behold thee as Sigmund beholdeth—and I was the home of
    thine heart—
Woe's me for the day when thou wert not, and the hour when
    we shall part'.

From 'On the Boiler'

IRELAND AFTER THE REVOLUTION

I

I ASSUME that some tragic crisis shall so alter Europe and all opinion that the Irish Government will teach the great majority of its school-children nothing but ploughing, harrowing, sowing, curry-combing, bicycle-cleaning, drill-driving, parcel-making, bale-pushing, tin-can-soldering, door-knob-polishing, threshold-whitening, coat-cleaning, trouser-patching, and playing upon the squiffer, all things that serve human dignity, unless indeed it decide that these things are better taught at home, in which case it can leave the poor children at peace.

Having settled that matter I return to more important things. Teach nothing but Greek, Gaelic, mathematics, and perhaps one modern language. I reject Latin because it was a language of the Graeco-Roman decadence, all imitation and manner and other feminine tricks; the much or little Latin necessary for a priest, doctor, or lawyer should be part of professional training and come later. D'Arbois de Jubainville worked on old Irish for thirty years because it brought him back to the civilisation immediately behind that of Homer, and when I prepared *Oedipus at Colonus* for the Abbey stage I saw that the wood of the Furies in the opening scene was any Irish haunted wood. No passing beggar or fiddler or benighted countryman has ever trembled or been awe-struck by nymph-haunted or Fury-haunted wood described in Roman poetry. Roman poetry is founded upon documents, not upon belief.

Translate into modern Irish all that is most beautiful in old and middle Irish, what Frank O'Connor and Augusta Gregory, let us say, have translated into English; let every schoolmaster point out where in his neighbourhood this or that thing happened, or is said to have happened, but teach Irish and Greek together, make the pupil translate Greek into Irish, Irish into Greek. The old Irish poets lay in a formless matrix; the Greek poets kept the richness of those dreams and yet were completely awake. Sleep has no bottom, waking no top. Irish can give our children love of the soil underfoot; but only Greek, co-ordination or intensity.

When I was a very young man, fresh from my first study of Elizabethan drama, I began to puzzle my elders with the question: 'Why has the audience deteriorated?' I would go on to explain that the modern theatre audience was as inferior to the Elizabethan as that was to the Greek; I spoke of the difficult transition from topic to topic in Shakespearean dialogue, of the still more difficult in those long speeches of Chapman; we could not give that close attention to-day. And then I would compare the Elizabethan plot broken up into farce and spectacle with the elaborate unity of Greek drama; no Elizabethan had the Greek intensity. No one could answer my question, nor could I myself, for I still half-believed in progress. But I can answer it now: civilisation rose to its high-tide mark in Greece, fell, rose again in the Renaissance but not to the same level. But we may, if we choose, not now or soon but at the next turn of the wheel, push ourselves up, being ourselves the tide, beyond that first mark. But no, these things are fated; we may be pushed up.

Mathematics should be taught because being certainty without reality it is the modern key to power, but not till the child is thirteen or fourteen years old and has begun to reason. Children before that age are the only born mimics, and they learn all through mimicry and should be taught languages and nothing else, though not so many that they will lose intensity of expression in their own, and these languages should be taught by word of mouth. Greek and Irish they should speak as fluently as they now speak English. If Irish is to become the national tongue the change must come slowly, almost imperceptibly; a sudden or forced change of language may be the ruin of the soul. England has forced English upon the schools and colleges of India, and now after generations of teaching no Indian can write or speak animated English and his mother tongue is despised and corrupted. Catholic Ireland is but slowly recovering from its change of language in the eighteenth century. Irishmen learn English at their mother's knee, English is now their mother-tongue, and a sudden change would bring a long barren epoch.

Let schools teach what is too difficult for grown men but is easy to the imitation or docility of childhood; English, history, and geography and those pleasant easy things which are the most important of all should be taught by father and mother, ancestral tradition, **and the child's own reading, and if the child lack this** teaching let father, mother, and child be ashamed, as they are if it lack breeding and manners. I would restore the responsibilities of the family.

II

Armament comes next to education. The country must take over the entire defence of its shores.[1] The formation of military families should be encouraged. I know enough of my countrymen to know that, once democratic plausibility has gone, their small army will be efficient and self-reliant, highly trained though not highly disciplined. Armed with modern weapons, officered by men from such schools as I have described, it could throw back from our shores the disciplined uneducated masses of the commercial nations.

If human violence is not embodied in our institutions the young will not give them their affection, nor the young and old their loyalty. A government is legitimate because some instinct has compelled us to give it the right to take life in defence of its laws and its shores.

Desire some just war, that big house and hovel, college and public-house, civil servant—his Gaelic certificate in his pocket—and international bridge-playing woman, may know that they belong to one nation.

I write with two certainties in mind: first that a hundred men, their creative power wrought to the highest pitch, their will trained but not broken, can do

[1] This was written before De Valera's London agreement.

more for the welfare of a people, whether in war or peace, than a million of any lesser sort no matter how expensive their education, and that although the Irish masses are vague and excitable because they have not yet been moulded and cast, we have as good blood as there is in Europe. Berkeley, Swift, Burke, Grattan, Parnell, Augusta Gregory, Synge, Kevin O'Higgins, are the true Irish people, and there is nothing too hard for such as these. If the Catholic names are few history will soon fill the gap. My imagination goes back to those Catholic exiled gentlemen of whom Swift said that their bravery exceeded that of all nations.

III

The recognition of the Crown should be the minimum the law requires, there must be no royal visits; a royal opening of the Dail might be too great a price to pay for the Unity of Ireland. The English royal family must always embody an English ideal. I have been told that King George V asked that the Russian royal family should be brought to England. The English Prime Minister refused, fearing the effect upon the English working classes. That story may be no more true than other stories spoken by word of mouth, but it will serve for an example. The average Englishman would think King George's submission, his abandonment of his relations to a fate already foreseen, if proved, a necessary, even a noble sacrifice. It was indeed his submission, his correctness as a constitutional sovereign that made his popularity so unbounded that he became a part of the English educational system. Some thousands of examination papers were distributed to school-children in a Northern industrial district with the question, 'Who was the best man who ever lived?' The vast majority answered, 'King George the Fifth'. Christ was runner-up.

We, upon the other hand, would think that he showed lack of personality, of manhood even, because he did not abdicate. No propaganda must be permitted which might recommend a sovereign who cannot boast in the words of a Sophoclean chorus:

... I would be praised as a man,
That in my words and my deeds I have kept those laws in
    mind
Olympian Zeus, and that high, clear Empyrean,
Fashioned, and not some man or people of mankind,
Even those sacred laws nor age nor sleep can blind.

Indeed I beg our governments to exclude all alien appeal to mass instinct. The Irish mind has still, in country rapscallion or in Bernard Shaw, an ancient, cold, explosive, detonating impartiality. The English mind, excited by its newspaper proprietors and its schoolmasters, has turned into a bed-hot harlot.

From 'On the Boiler'

OTHER MATTERS

I

As there is no Dublin criticism I propose to criticise plays produced by the Abbey, books published or written by members of my family or by my friends, Cuala embroidery, or whatever else I have a mind to. The reader can make allowances for my bias, and certainly I am a biased man.

II

Some years ago I voted for the production by the Abbey Theatre of a play that I disliked because I thought the author had won the right to decide upon the merits of his own work. A few weeks ago I saw that play upon the stage for the first time, and certainly if I had understood how performance would solidify its demerits I would, despite all theory to the contrary, have voted and spoken against it. It displayed a series of base actions without anything to show that its author disapproved or expected us to do so. I left before the finish, feeling that neither I nor anyone else in that audience could help transferring to the author himself the horror inspired by his characters. Yet that was unreasonable, for his other plays are charming and amusing and there all are judged as we would have them judged. The wicked should be punished, the innocent rewarded, marriage bells sound for no evil man, unless an author calls his characters before a more private tribunal and has so much intellect and culture that we respect it as though it were our own. Shakespeare and the ballads judge as we would have them judge. In Jonson's *Volpone*, one of the greatest satiric comedies, Volpone goes to his doom, but innocence is not rewarded, the young people who have gone through so much suffering together leave in the end for their fathers' houses with no hint of marriage, and this excites us because it makes us share in Jonson's cold implacability. His tribunal is private, that of Shakespeare public.

I have learnt much of Ireland as a reader for the Abbey Theatre, perhaps as much as a priest learns in the confessional. During our first years we sometimes rejected plays because they were incoherent or commonplace imitations of Boucicault or of old Queen's Theatre melodrama. There was little vulgarity, tradition was still unshaken, the sixpence had worn thin but it was still silver. But of recent years a form of jocularity incompatible with personal fastidiousness has begun to replace or degrade characterisation, and I was glad when infirmity permitted me to leave to others the search for some quality that could be separated from what seemed the comic paragraphs of some base penny newspaper or the inscriptions on the walls of a Corporation urinal. I once drew the attention of some member of the Executive Council to this disappearance from great spaces of the public mind of the old idealistic tradition, and as political revolution and thirty years of Gaelic grammar had been in vain, I asked for such drastic thought as that of the Abbey Theatre at its best.

From 'On the Boiler'

Two or three recent plays have gone to the other extreme. The persons sit around in a circle and talk—and, that unreality as of a glass chandelier which lifts certain plays of Shaw into philosophic dialogue altogether lacking—turn some question over and over. The pit stays at home, but those who educate themselves through the circulating libraries are delighted; they congratulate the Abbey Board upon its belated discovery that thought is more important than action. But thought is not more important than action; masterpieces, whether of the stage or study, excel in their action, their visibility—who can forget Odysseus, Don Quixote, Hamlet, Lear, Faust, all figures in a peepshow?— and we are not coherent to ourselves through thought but because our visible image changes slowly. English producers slur over that scene where Hamlet changes the letters and sends Rosencrantz and Guildenstern to their death, because they define him through his thought and think that scene but old folk material incompatible with Shakespeare's Hamlet. Yet no imaginative man has ever complained, and Shakespeare, when he made Hamlet kill the father of Fortinbras in single combat, showed that he meant it. Hamlet's hesitations are hesitations of thought, and are concerned with certain persons on whom his attention is fixed; outside that he is a mediaeval man of action. Take some seemingly average man or woman, touch some psychological gadget and they turn to angel or devil. Our bodies are nearer to our coherence because nearer to the 'unconscious' than our thought. Sargent once said to me: 'All people are exactly what they look. I have just painted a woman who thinks herself completely serious; here is her portrait, I show her as she looks and is, completely frivolous.' This new art, this art of the circulating libraries, has no interest in anything that cannot be understood through opinion: unlike ancient art, it is urban, it belongs not to the small ancient town serrated by its green gardens but to the great modern town where meditation is impossible, where action is a mechanical routine, where the chest narrows and the stature sinks, where 'individuality' or intellectual coherence is the sole distinction left.

IV

Our Abbey Theatre some years ago took over from the English repertory theatre a play which failed with our audience and is bound to fail with every audience which has not been educated out of its instincts. Flecker's *Santorin* is almost the most moving and romantic of modern lyrics, but in *Hassan* I can discover nothing but the perversity and petulance of the disease from which its author was already fading. I find it even more horrible than the vulgar jocularity of certain ignorant Irish dramatists. With them tradition is dying because neither the old folk-feeling nor the superficial ideality of Young Ireland can resist a contagion from English and American slums. But this play was written during those ten years before the war when the English urban mind was turning against culture as Arnold defined it, the knowledge of the best that is said and thought in the world, and seeking to substitute contemporary thought merely because contemporary. It began with a distaste for romantic subject-matter. Presently would come a desire for a contemporary urban style. In Flecker subject-matter and style were unchanged, but in his illness he seems to have suddenly accepted everything else in the point of view of his critics. In *Hassan* he assumed that at least one masterpiece was already forgotten. We know Harun ar Rashid through the *Arabian Nights* alone, and there he is the greatest of all traditional images of generosity and magnanimity. In one beautiful story he finds that a young girl of his harem loves a certain young man, and though he himself loves that girl he sets her free and arranges her marriage; and there are other stories of like import. Considered as history, *Hassan* is a forgery, as literature an impertinence, for it makes him put two such lovers to death with every horror of cruelty. One feels that its nightmare-ridden author longed to make Galahad lecherous, Lancelot a coward, and Adam impotent; to employ against them, because they are still in some sense reigning sovereigns, all the revolutionist's baser tricks. But even if we could condone its false history we must condemn it as a work of art, for there is nothing there but wanton, morbid cruelty.

The arts are all the bridal chambers of joy. No tragedy is legitimate unless it leads some great character to his final joy. Polonius may go out wretchedly, but I can hear the dance music in 'Absent thee from felicity awhile', or in Hamlet's speech over the dead Ophelia, and what of Cleopatra's last farewells, Lear's rage under the lightning, Oedipus sinking down at the story's end into an earth 'riven' by love? Some French-man has said that farce is the struggle against a ridicu-lous object, comedy against a movable object, tragedy against an immovable; and because the will, or energy, is greatest in tragedy, tragedy is the more noble; but I add that 'will or energy is eternal delight', and when its limit is reached it may become a pure, aimless joy, though the man, the shade, still mourns his lost object. It has, as it were, thrust up its arms towards those angels who have, as Villiers de L'Isle-Adam quotes from Saint Thomas Aquinas, returned into themselves in an eternal moment.

v

I have described in some diary pages, and later in an essay on Berkeley, a dream or nightmare that went through my sisters' house. My sisters and their maid dreamt different events complementary to one another. Another such dream affected my wife, my daughter and her nurse. My wife dreamt of a cat, daughter and nurse had a rat and a mouse between them. Events in time come upon us head-on like waves, each wave in some main character the opposite of its predecessor. But there are other events that lie side by side in space, complements one of another. Of late I have tried to understand in its practical details the falsehood that is in all knowledge, science more false than philosophy, but that too false. Yet, unless we cling to knowledge, until we have examined its main joints, it comes at us with staring eyes. Should we drive it away at last, we must enter the Buddhist monastery in Auden's play and for the reason there given. And now comes my brother's extreme book, *The Charmed Life*. He does not care that few will read it, still fewer recognise its genius; it is his book, his *Faust*, his pursuit of all that through its unpredictable, unarrangeable reality least resembles knowledge. His style fits his purpose, for every sentence has its own taste, tint, and smell.

VI

I undertook to find designers for my sister's needle, but found nothing altogether suitable until a friend brought me Diana Murphy. I put her to making designs from my own poetry; four are made or in making, *Innisfree*, *The Happy Townland*, *The Land of Youth* from my early poetry and prose, and either *Sailing to Byzantium* or *Byzantium*. My sister will have put the first three into needlework before this paragraph is published. Sold or unsold, they will lodge somewhere to keep the name of the designer and the Yeats name in memory.

I delight in Diana Murphy's work with one reservation. Of recent years artists, to clear their minds of what Rossetti called 'the soulless self-reflections of man's skill' depicted in commercial posters and on the covers of magazines, have exaggerated anatomical details. Miss Murphy's forms are deliberately thick and heavy, and I urge upon her the exclusion of all exaggerations, a return to the elegance of Puvis de Chavannes. There are moments when I am certain that art must once again accept those Greek proportions which carry into plastic art the Pythagorean numbers, those faces which are divine because all there is empty and measured. Europe was not born when Greek galleys defeated the Persian hordes at Salamis; but when the Doric studios sent out those broad-backed marble statues against the multiform, vague, expressive Asiatic sea, they gave to the sexual instinct of Europe its goal, its fixed type. In the warm sea of the French and Italian Riviera I can still see it. I recall a Swedish actress standing upon some boat's edge between Portofino and Rapallo, or riding the foam upon a plank towed behind a speed-boat, but one finds it wherever the lucky or the well-born uncover their sunburnt bodies. There, too, are doubtless flesh-tints that Greek painters loved as have all the greatest since; nowhere upon any beautiful body, whether of man or woman, those red patches whereby our democratic painters prove that they have really studied from the life.

VII

In my savage youth I was accustomed to say that no man should be permitted to open his mouth in Parliament until he had sung or written his *Utopia*, for lacking that we could not know where he was taking us, and I still think that artists of all kinds should once again praise or represent great or happy people.

From 'On the Boiler'

Here in Monte Carlo, where I am writing, somebody talked of a man with a monkey and some sort of stringed instrument, and it has pleased me to imagine him a great politician. I will make him sing to the sort of tune that goes well with my early sentimental poems.

I lived among great houses,
Riches drove out rank,
Base drove out the better blood,
And mind and body shrank.
No Oscar ruled the table,
But I'd a troop of friends
That knowing better talk had gone
Talked of odds and ends.
Some knew what ailed the world
But never said a thing,
So I have picked a better trade
And night and morning sing:
Tall dames go walking in grass-green Avalon.

Am I a great Lord Chancellor
That slept upon the Sack?
Commanding officer that tore
The khaki from his back?
Or am I De Valéra,
Or the King of Greece,
Or the man that made the motors?
Ach, call me what you please!
Here's a Montenegrin lute,
And its old sole string
Makes me sweet music
And I delight to sing:
Tall dames go walking in grass-green Avalon.

Other Matters

With boys and girls about him,
With any sort of clothes,
With a hat out of fashion,
With old patched shoes,
With a ragged bandit cloak,
With an eye like a hawk,
With a stiff straight back,
With a strutting turkey walk,
With a bag full of pennies,
With a monkey on a chain,
With a great cock's feather,
With an old foul tune.
Tall dames go walking in grass-green Avalon.